THREE SINS

JAZLYN SPARROW

ISBN: 979-8303145221

CONTENT WARNINGS

This book is a dark romance and is intended for mature audiences only. It contains themes which may be distressing to some readers.

Subject matter includes rape, murder, violence, trauma, dub-con, horror, drugs, branding, burning, emotional and physical abuse and smutty sex scenes.

Your mental health matters; please consider these triggers before reading this book.

THE PRESENT – 2023

There are only THREE SINS we will not commit.

1

LAZARO

The low hum of conversation from the main dining area barely penetrates the insulated silence of our secluded corner. I lean back against the worn leather of the booth, eyes scanning the room, but my mind is on my brother, Romeo. His eyes never quite meet mine, and I catch the flicker of something—tension, unease—just before he buries it. That's not like him.

Before I can pull myself from the thought, the sound of heavy footsteps draws my attention. Vincenzo Bianchi, my loyal shadow, appears at my side.

"Lazaro," he growls, his voice low, meant only for me. "We've got trouble."

The words hit like a punch to the gut. Trouble, I know, is Vince's wet dream. It's what he lives for. It finds us even when we're at our sharpest, our most prepared.

"What's going on?" I ask, keeping my voice steady, a sharp edge to it. A leader doesn't flinch in a storm. He commands it.

"Someone's set up shop on one of our corners." His eyes lock onto mine, sharp as knives. It's more than just a business move. Someone's stepping on our turf.

"Drugs?" The word tastes bitter, like a venom in my mouth. We deal in a lot of things—guns, protection, favors—but narcotics? That's a line we've never crossed. A promise I made to myself, to the family.

Vince's jaw tightens, and he gives a single, clipped nod. "Drugs." His voice is cold, the news colder.

A surge of anger hits me like a flash of fire. This isn't just business. It's personal. A slap to the Riccardi name, a violation of everything we've fought for. The code we live by.

"And how do you know this?" I ask, keeping my tone measured, though inside, I'm burning.

Vince's lips tighten. "We've already had an overdose. Fourteen-year-old kid... didn't make it."

A rush of air leaves me. My chest tightens, my fists clenching involuntarily.

"Romeo!" I snap, motioning for my brother. His eyes snap to mine, catching the cold fury in my voice as he crosses the room.

Romeo leans in close, his gaze hardening, every inch of his youthful face suddenly transformed. I whisper the details to him, each word sharp and calculated. He nods once, then stands to his full height, his body radiating a dangerous calm. His fists are clenched, ready to tear through the problem with surgical precision.

Romeo may be the youngest, but his quiet fury makes him the most dangerous. Beneath it is a cold, ruthless determination. A warrior who will burn the world to the ground to protect what's his. Sometimes, it scares the hell out of me.

"Strategic and precise," he mutters, his voice steady, unwavering. "I'll gut each and every one of the motherfuckers."

Vince's lips twitch with something like amusement, his eyes flickering between us. Watching Romeo is always a spectacle, a reminder of just how far he's come from the boy he used to be. How far he's willing to go to defend what we've built.

"I want eyes on them," I tell Vince, my voice low but carrying. "Find out who they are, where they came from. Take no action until we know everything."

Vince doesn't hesitate. "Understood," he says, as he turns to leave.

I call after him, my voice sharper than steel. "And make sure everyone gets the message: The Riccardi brothers do *not* deal in drugs."

The air shifts as Vince disappears into the shadows, his figure swallowed up by the dark. For a moment, it's just Romeo and me. The weight of what's coming presses down like a storm on the horizon.

"This could escalate fast," Romeo says, his voice flat, unbothered. His words aren't a warning. They're a request for permission. A request to set the city on fire.

I look him in the eyes, my mind racing. Everything we've built—everything our father bled for—is teetering on the edge. We don't have the luxury of hesitation.

"Let it burn," I say, my voice cold, unshaken. "We didn't choose this life, but we sure as hell aren't going to let anyone take it from us."

DETECTIVE HANDLER, that vulture in a rumpled suit, darkens our doorstep with his presence. He slinks into my office like he owns the place, his eyes darting around the room, always searching, always sniffing for weakness. But there's nothing here for him to find. Not today. Not ever.

I feel my spine stiffen, the air in the room tightening with every step he takes. His presence is like a dark cloud, hovering just over the horizon, waiting to burst. That smug grin on his face, the one he wears like armor, is a direct challenge. One I'm not willing to back down from.

"Lazaro Riccardi," he sneers, dragging my name through his teeth. "Or should I say, Saint Lazaro? Still pretending to keep your hands clean?"

My fists clench, rage simmering beneath the surface, but I keep it in check. There's a game being played here, and I'm not about to let him know he's already lost.

"Detective," I reply coldly, letting the venom drip into my voice. "To what do we owe this displeasure on a Friday night?"

He doesn't take the bait. Instead, his eyes flicker to the empty chair beside me, scanning the room like he's looking for something more than just answers.

"Cut the crap," he says, his voice low and dangerous. "There's a new stash of poison being peddled on your turf. I'm not blind, Riccardi. And I'm not here for small talk."

The words hit me like a sucker punch. Drugs. The one thing we don't touch, the one thing we've never allowed on our streets. The thought alone twists my gut. I lean back in my chair, feigning indifference, but inside, the rage is rising like a tide.

"And here I thought the city paid you to solve such problems, not to chat about them over drinks."

Handler steps closer, his face darkening as he lowers his voice to a dangerous whisper. "Maybe you need a reminder, Lazaro," he says, inching closer and lowering his voice to a dangerous whisper. ""Your reluctance to play ball could make things... difficult for your family."

The word "family" lingers in the air between us like a promise. My teeth grind together as the urge to break his neck simmers under my skin. I want to beat him, show him exactly how unholy this family can be. But I can't. Not yet. Not unless I want to paint a target on our backs, and that's a line I won't cross. Not over this. Not over him.

"Threats, Handler?" I let out a dry, humorless laugh. "You should know better than to try and shake down a Riccardi."

His grin widens, as if he's already won. "Let's just say I'll be keeping a close eye on things," he murmurs.

"Watch all you want," I shoot back, "but you won't find dirt where there isn't any. But I'm more than happy to donate a shovel to your cause."

He turns on his heel, that insufferable grin still plastered on his face as he leaves the room. His words float in the air like poison, but I don't flinch. He's a dog with no bite. And I'll let him bark until he's nothing more than a nuisance.

The door slams shut behind him, and I let the silence settle like dust. My mind whirs, thoughts shifting to the empty seat across from me. Sandro's chair. Vacant. Untouched.

Romeo walks in, his heavy boots striking the floor with purpose. His eyes flick to me, then the space where our brother used to sit.

"Was that Detective Handler I saw leaving?" he asks, his voice low, sharp.

"In the flesh."

"What the hell does that parasite want?"

I let out a slow breath, swallowing my anger as I look up at him. "He's sniffing around for the new stash on the corner. Trying to remind us he still has a dick to swing around."

Romeo's lips curl into a grimace. "Damn fool's gonna get himself killed one of these days."

The words come out like a dark prophecy. I know the type. Handler's the kind of cop who'll cross the wrong line, piss off the wrong people, and end up with a bullet in his head. It's inevitable. But it can't be us who puts him down. Not yet. We don't need the heat. Not right now.

I catch Romeo's eye, the silent warning unspoken but clear. His cocky grin flickers, then fades. I know what that look means. He's on the edge. He's about to make another decision that could turn every-thing to ash. And I can't let that happen. Not again.

He tries to smile, but it doesn't reach his eyes. It never does anymore.

Sandro's death has changed us both in ways we can't ignore. The warmth in the room has vanished. The tension is thicker now. Cold, suffocating. It's been two years, but his ghost is still here, hanging over us like a shadow. Every time I look at Romeo, I see the same cold emptiness in his eyes that I feel in mine.

Romeo's gaze flicks to the empty chair again, and his voice drops to a whisper. "He filled that chair like nobody else could. Arguing with you... pushing you... reminding us what it means to be part of something."

I feel the lump in my throat. A heavy weight settles on my chest. The ache is still raw, a jagged wound that never fully heals. I fight the urge to bury it, but it comes anyway—like a storm that rises out of nowhere, tearing through the walls I've spent years building.

"Living in our world comes at a price," I remind him, my voice rough, eyes hard as I turn away. "And we paid it."

Romeo meets my eyes again, his gaze unwavering, almost... desperate. "Sometimes," he says quietly, "I wonder what life would've been like if we were just... ordinary."

I stand, the weight of the question settling deep in my bones. My hand rests on the back of the chair, the cool wood beneath my fingers grounding me. "Ordinary was never an option for us, brother," I say, my voice quiet but final. "There's no room for what-ifs in our world."

I straighten my jacket, looking at him one last time. The fantasy of a different life—one where we aren't hunted by our past, one where we aren't forced to carry the weight of every decision—is a fleeting thought. And I let it die before it can take root.

There's no room for it. Not here. Not in our blood.

2

BAYLIN

The hospital corridors blur into a chaotic whirl of noise and motion. The harsh overhead lights flicker as I glide through the crowd, my sneakers squeaking on the smooth, sterile floors. Nurses rush by, their white coats billowing like ghosts in the frenzied dance of the hospital, while patients shuffle by in paper-thin gowns.

I move with purpose, my eyes darting from one chart to the next, my mind ticking through numbers and dosages, a thousand things to check, a hundred lives to touch. There's a rhythm to this place, an unspoken cadence that feels as much a part of me as the blood running through my veins. My clipboard is an extension of myself, guiding me as I navigate the maze of bodies and white walls, each step a careful calculation, each breath a quiet prayer.

A voice calls my name, distant yet sharp, but I don't stop. Here, my name is one of many—just another whisper swallowed by the hospital's endless hum.

"Baylin, room 204," the voice calls again, more insistent. "They're waiting."

"Got it," I reply without missing a beat, moving with precision as my fingers flip through charts, prepping syringes with practiced ease.

A glance at the monitors, a soft word to the patient, a quick touch to reassure them. Every action deliberate, every moment spent with them an unspoken promise to do my best before I move on.

"Easy now," I murmur to a toddler as I carefully administer the injection. His tiny face scrunches up, a sharp, sweet cry escaping him, but the tears stop almost as quickly as they came when I offer him a sticker. His little hand reaches up, small and trusting, and his gap-toothed grin pulls at something deep inside me. It's only a moment, but it's enough to remind me why I do this. To make the pain go away, even if just for a minute.

Stepping back into the hallway, I feel something shift in the air. It's not the usual hum of the hospital, not the whirring machines or the rustling of paperwork—it's the feeling of eyes on me, sharp and unwavering.

I turn, and there he is. My nephew, Luca, sitting on the bench by the jungle animal mural. His legs dangle above the floor, kicking rhythmically as his eyes flick from the clock on the wall to his fidgeting fingers. He's waiting.

My heart tugs in a way it's become too familiar with. His blue eyes mirror his father's, too wise for his ten years, too old for the grief he carries.

I want to go to him, to smooth the worry from his brow and tell him everything will be okay. But duty pulls at me, sharp and unyielding. I can't. Not yet.

"Baylin!" A nurse's voice snaps me back to the present, urgent.

"Two minutes," I mouth to Luca, holding up two fingers.

He nods, understanding the unspoken promise. I know he's counting, just like I am—heartbeats, respirations, time slipping away between us, pulling us in opposite directions.

Five years ago, when Luca's parents were taken from us by a drunk driver, everything changed. My sister Magdalene—his mother —and her husband Daniel, my closest friend, were ripped away from this world. And I've been left to pick up the pieces, to carry a burden I never asked for. My mother and I do our best to care for Luca, but I can feel the weight of it, feel the aching gap where they should be. It never feels like enough.

I slip back into the rhythm of the ward, floating from one patient to the next, pretending that I can outrun the ache in my chest.

When I return to Luca, his eyes follow me, a silent question in them.

"Hey there, champ," I say softly, resting my hand on his shoulder. The warmth of his small body is a sharp contrast to the cold, clinical waiting room. I try to smile, to reassure him, but I can see the shadow of fear lingering in the lines of his face.

"Hey," he replies, his voice a whisper. He doesn't need to say more. I can feel his uncertainty, his worry, hanging thick between us.

"Talk to me, Luca," I say, crouching to meet his gaze, my heart tightening.

He pulls at the hem of his shirt, his fingers twisting nervously. "It's just... this place," he says, pausing, the words heavy with meaning. He swallows hard. "It reminds me of—"

"Them," I finish for him, my voice soft, but the ache behind it undeniable. Magdalene was my sister. Daniel was my brother. Their loss is as much a part of me as anything else. It cuts deeper than any wound.

Luca nods, his eyes too old, too tired. "What if something happens to you too, Aunt Bay? You're always here, helping sick people..."

The guilt hits me like a wave. I throw myself into my work, trying to outrun my own grief, trying to outrun the fear that one day, I won't come back. That one day, I'll be gone, and he'll be left alone, just like I was.

I clear my throat, pushing back the lump that has formed. "Luca, look at me." I crouch to his level, my hands cupping his face gently. His eyes lock on mine, wide and desperate.

"As long as I'm breathing, I'm not going anywhere. I'll always be here for you."

A small smile flickers across his face, fragile but real. It's enough to break me. I pull him into a hug, holding him close, trying to convey everything my words cannot. Love. Protection. A promise.

"Let's get some fresh air," I suggest, my voice thick with emotion as I stand and take his hand.

Together, we walk down the corridor. His little hand in mine feels like a lifeline, a tether to something solid in this world of uncertainty.

"Feeling better?" I ask, squeezing his hand gently.

He nods, his blue eyes catching the last slivers of light from the setting sun. The moment is quiet. Peaceful. For a brief second, it feels like everything could be okay.

Then, my pager beeps—loud, urgent, and cutting through the fragile calm between us. I glance down, my heart skipping a beat as I read the code flashing across the screen.

"Luca," I say, already turning back toward the ward. "I need to go. It's an emergency."

His grip tightens, and he looks at me with wide, fearful eyes.

I kneel in front of him, lifting his chin with my hand so that I can look him in the eye. "You're my brave little boy," I whisper. "I'll be back before you know it."

I press a kiss to his forehead, feeling the weight of the promise settle in my chest.

"Be careful," he murmurs, his voice small but full of concern.

"Always am," I reply, though I know the lie is as bitter as it is necessary.

I stand, giving him one last, lingering look before rushing back down the hallway. My feet pound the linoleum as I navigate through the late-afternoon crowd, each step a beat in the rhythm of a life constantly balanced on the edge of life and death.

"Reyes, we need you!" A voice calls from ahead, snapping me from my thoughts.

I push through the double doors into the critical care unit, my mind already shifting into autopilot. "Here," I call, slipping into my role as easily as I breathe. "What do we have?"

"Overdose," my colleague responds, pointing toward the stretcher.

A young boy. Not much older than Luca.

The world feels like it's closing in as I take in the scene. Despite my training, bile rises in my throat, but I swallow it down, steeling myself.

I nod, grabbing gloves and prepping for the work ahead. "Let's save a life," I whisper, as I dive into the chaos, letting the adrenaline wash over me.

For now, Luca fades to the background. But the fire in my chest, the promise to him, keeps me moving.

EXHAUSTION WRAPS around me like a suffocating shroud, pulling at my bones, but it doesn't matter. Not now. Not when there's one person still waiting for me. One promise I can't break.

As I round the corner into the waiting area, time seems to stretch and bend, tugging at my heart like it's trying to pull me back into the chaos I just left behind.

Luca sits there, almost swallowed by the oversized hospital chair, his legs dangling over the edge. The harsh fluorescent lights cast long shadows, but his eyes—those piercing blue eyes—glow with a quiet hope as he spots me.

"Hey," I breathe, the weight of the day shifting, even if just for a moment. I close the distance between us, moving slowly, deliberately, because I know how much he's been counting on me. I need him to know I haven't forgotten, that I'm here, even if it feels like the world is falling apart around us.

"Thought you got lost," he says, his attempt at casual falling flat. The quiver in his voice betrays the worry he's been hiding behind those bright eyes.

"Never," I reply, sinking down beside him. Our shoulders brush— just a small thing, but the kind of touch that says everything. "I'm here, Luca. Always."

I take his tiny hand in mine, and I feel his grip tighten, like he's afraid I might slip away again. His eyes lock onto mine, full of so many things I can't name—relief, gratitude, but also that fragile thread of uncertainty that hangs between us.

"Promise?" he asks, his voice small but heavy with the weight of everything he's been through.

"I promise," I echo, my voice steady even as everything inside me aches. My body is a mess of fatigue, my mind a blur, but this moment —this tiny, perfect moment—is the balm that soothes me. It's the only thing that feels right.

"Let's go home, kiddo."

As we walk down the sterile hospital hallway, Luca's chatter fills the silence, a soft, sweet distraction from the world outside. He talks about school, his friends, and the rocket ship he drew in class. His words are like lifelines, pulling me out of my head and back into the present.

"Hey, Aunt Bay," he says suddenly, tugging at my sleeve, his voice filled with that boundless curiosity that only children can have. "Do you think there are nurses in space?"

I smile, the first real smile of the day. The kind that reaches my eyes and pushes away the weight of everything else.

"Absolutely," I answer, squeezing his hand a little tighter. "There's always someone to save, no matter where you are."

He grins, his face lighting up like the sun, and for a moment, the hospital, the pain, the weight of everything else—it all disappears. It's just me and him, and the promise I'll always keep.

3

ROMEO

Everyone knows the rules. No drugs. No women. No shitting where you eat. I know the night's going to get messy even before I've stepped out of the back exit of the family restaurant. It does well, the restaurant, even though everyone knows it's a front for other things. Not that anyone will ever be able to prove anything; we live and die by a code of morals that ensures everyone's too fond of their tongue to have it etched out of their mouth.

My Ermenegildo Zegna black leather boots slap against the pavement as I walk through the alley, flanked by half a dozen of our men. I take the cigarette out of my mouth and flick it to the ground, sniff the crisp night air.

"When did you start smoking again?" Vincenzo huffs. He has to walk twice as fast as I do to keep up to my long strides.

"I haven't," I tell him. The cigarette is a prelude to things to come. I shoot him a lop-sided grin. A grin he knows all too well. A grin that means there'll be bloodshed tonight and I'll be swimming in the scent of death and destruction. A pastime that helps me drown out my own pain. Helps me forget my own sorrow and torment. Anything to numb the pain.

"Romeo, this can't get messy," Vince warns, putting a hand on my arm. We stop walking, and our men pause a few yards away, waiting for direction. Vince's jaw is set in that stubborn line I know all too well. "The Feds are already hungry, and Detective Handler has a real hard-on for you boys."

"You boys?" I lift a pointed eyebrow. "You understand that you're one of said boys," I remind him.

"You know I'll always have your back, Romeo. But they're watching us twenty-four seven. We can't afford to lose any more good men."

"We don't tolerate drugs," I remind him. "If we let this go, we're opening the door for others. We won't lose our sons, our brothers, to this poison."

Vince shakes his head slightly, regards me with a look that tells me he understands there'll be no changing the outcome of what happens tonight.

"Don't you at least want to get changed first?"

His eyes sweep down my frame, taking in my attire. Black turtleneck, black dress pants, and a camel sports jacket. I won't lie and say I'm not fond of my outfit, but the business of culling and eliminating the garbage cannot wait.

I take off my camel jacket and fold it neatly over his arm for safekeeping.

"There we go," I say, patting his arm. "Blood washes out of black okay. Let's go."

WE'VE TRACED the drugs back to a local gang of youths called the Southside Legends. They may like to think of themselves as legends, but by the time I'm through with them, they'll be nothing more than a myth. Vincenzo tries to reason with me, these are kids and should be taught a lesson; I remind him that there's no room for mercy in our world.

We move through the city like a pack of thieves, the air thick with the scent of retribution. The image of Detective Handler meeting with my brother taunts me, his smug expression a constant reminder of our ongoing war against both rival gangs and corrupt law enforcement. My blood boils at the thought of cleaning up their mess yet again. And when Lazaro gave me a menacing warning with just a flicker of his eyes, I had to repress the urge to rip off Detective Handler' skin as a prelude to our night of mayhem.

The car pulls up to the dilapidated warehouse, the silence inside it stretching taut like a wire before snapping under the weight of what's to come. The air is thick with tension and adrenaline as I kick open the car door and step out with the coiled energy of a predator. Vincenzo follows suit and I take one last breath of clean air before leading my men to the door.

The warehouse, identified as a refuge for the drug peddlers, is our target for the night. We've done our homework; we know who the main players are in this dirty dance trying to edge into our territory and deal in illicit drugs. Now it's just a matter of severing the head of the snake as we shut this operation down.

"Make it quick," I instruct them, the familiar rush of adrenaline sharpening my focus as we pour out from the shadows like avenging ghosts.

The oppressive quiet of the night is shattered by the echo of heavy boots and the sharp squeal of the door as we kick it open. We burst into the warehouse, our heavy presence piercing the quiet.

The first burst of gunfire is like a cannon blast, lighting up the warehouse with flashes of bright muzzle fire. The men in the warehouse scatter for cover, what may have once been casual confidence replaced by a frantic scramble for safety. The sharp crack of automatic rifles mingles with the thud of bullets hitting steel and concrete.

My men, trained and disciplined, move in coordinated patterns. We duck behind crates, our weapons blazing in short, controlled bursts. Each shot is precise, aimed to incapacitate rather than kill. We're methodical when we have a mission to accomplish.

The so-called Southside Legends, disorganized and panicked, fire wildly and indiscriminately. Their shots ricochet off metal beams, and the air is filled with the smell of gunpowder and the harsh clatter of spent shells hitting the floor.

We have the advantage of surprise and preparation; it's obvious they didn't see us coming. We use flashbang grenades to disorient our enemies, the bright, deafening explosions adding to the confusion. The grenades are followed by a storm of bullets, our targets barely visible through the smoke and haze.

We maintain our discipline, even as a few of their men try to flee. I watch on as two men go down, capped in the knees. My intention is to maim, not kill. Not yet anyway.

As the last echoes of gunfire fade, the warehouse falls into a tense silence. My men emerge from their cover, clearly more experienced, more capable, more everything, to go up against. We survey the scene —the warehouse littered with debris, spent shells and blood. The gang members lay scattered, some dead, others wounded on the cement of the unforgiving floor.

I walk through the carnage, satisfied that we'd done well as I turn wounded men onto their backs with my rifle and kick their weapons away from their bodies. There are maybe eight men in the ware-house, and I can see they were probably in the middle of a poker game from the overturned table and cards scattered across the ground. When I get to a man writhing in pain as he holds his shat-tered knee up to his chest, I lower myself until I'm crouching beside him.

I smile.

I know my smile is disarming. It's never let me down.

"So...Southside Legends, huh?" I scoff. "What's so legendary about you?"

The man's eyes narrow as he hisses in pain, sucking in a deep breath, but he says nothing.

"Let me make this clear to you all."

I rise, addressing the wounded. Some are just passing out from delirium.

"Only one of you will walk out of here alive. One. That's all I'll allow. First man to tell me where you got the drugs lives."

I'd like to say there is silence all around me, but there isn't. A cacophony of groans and moans, then cursing, rises like smoke from the injured on the ground. It's irritating as fuck. I point my rifle at one of the men and shoot him. In the head.

The deafening silence is followed by screams. Pain, curses, then everyone suddenly wants to talk.

"I need a name," I say, my stony mask slipping into place. "No babbling. Give me a name."

Three men scream the same name all at once, as though in competition to get to the finish line.

"Jacob Arens!"

The warehouse becomes a silent monument to the audacity of those who dare cross us. With methodical precision, my crew goes to work, dousing the structure in fuel. The match strikes against rough skin, almost deafening in the hush that has befallen the place.

"Fire cleanses," I murmur, watching as the building erupts into an inferno that claws at the night sky. It's a declaration that the Riccardi family will not tolerate any threats to our dominion.

Before the fire department can even dream of quelling the blaze, we are miles away, hunting down the next mark — Jacob Arens. We've heard of him, vaguely. A small-time hood who's in the business of planning heists and robberies. As long as he's robbing the government, we don't give a fuck. It's kept him off our radar, but now the ambitious little fuck has to answer to us.

4

BAYLIN

I scroll through the list my mother sent me as I push through the automatic doors of the supermarket. The scent of fresh produce mingles with the faint aroma of coffee from the café counter. The familiar sounds of carts rolling and faint chatter surround me, creating a sense of normalcy after a long day at the hospital. I glance at my watch, mentally calculating how long it'll take to grab what my mother needs.

"Just a few things," I mutter to myself, foregoing a trolley for a basket. I navigate the aisles with practiced ease; the routine is comforting, a small escape from the stress of my job.

After going through the checkout, I juggle my phone while trying to hold the one paper bag as I make my way out of the supermarket, shooting off a text to my mother about my ETA. The sun has begun its descent, casting a warm glow over the pavement, and I breathe in the fresh air, ready to put the day behind me. It's not that I don't love my job; it's just that it sucks the energy right out of me.

The tranquility of the early evening night is shattered as I step off the pavement and into the parking lot. For a moment, I think I imagine the rat-tat-tat of gunfire, but then I'm sure as a second burst of gunfire comes out of no-where. I'm rooted to the spot as I drop the bag, fear wrapping around me like a noose around my neck. The sharp cracks echo through the parking lot, jolting my heart into a frantic race. I watch as just a few feet away, two bodies drop, then a third.

"Get down!" someone shouts, but I barely register the words. Time slows as I watch, paralyzed, the chaos unfolding before me.

The shooter fires again, and another man collapses, hitting the ground hard. My stomach twists as I see the blood pooling beneath him. The shooter's car screeches then speeds away, and I watch as it exits the carpark, before my eyes move back toward those laying injured on the ground. Time snaps back into focus, and adrenaline surges through my veins. I'm a nurse—trained to save lives—and that instinct kicks in.

I shout for an ambulance as I rush forward, kneeling beside an injured man. He looks to be in his 40's, dressed in work boots and overalls, and the only thing I can think is that he was heading home from work for the day. He's bleeding heavily from his side, the crimson spreading out like a dark halo. "You're going to be okay." My voice is steadier than I feel.

He looks up at me, his eyes wide with pain and fear. "He..." he gasps, and I can see the realization of his injuries dawning on him.

"Hold on." I tear off a piece of my shirt, wrapping it around his wound to apply pressure. The sight of his blood makes my stomach churn, but I push the nausea down. This is no time to falter. This is what I've been trained for. What my life's work has been all about.

But what nobody tells you is that you could be a superstar at helping save lives in the operating room. You could be a hero in the emergency room; someone's savior for a moment in time, a day, a lifetime. But when it comes to repairing someone after you witness the trauma, a shutter slides down, blinding you, stripping you of all your training and your courage and the rhythms you've kept for the past years. Suddenly, you are no-one and nothing, and you are no longer in control of your own hands. I look down at my blood-stained fingers as they shake uncontrollably, and he must see the fear in my eyes.

"Please…" he murmurs, his breath shallow, and I can see the life fading from his eyes.

"Focus on my voice," I instruct, forcing myself to maintain eye contact. "Help is on the way." I dig my phone out of my pocket, my hands trembling as I dial 911, my eyes never leaving him. I put the phone on speaker and lay it on the ground as I cradle the man's head in my arms. My eyes scan the parking lot, taking in the other injured bodies strewn on the ground.

"911, what's your emergency?" a calm voice answers.

I rattle off the address, inform the operator there's been a shooting and multiple wounded. My heart races as I look at the man in front of me, bleeding heavily.

"Stay on the line," the operator insists, but I can't afford to wait. I hang up and return my focus to the man, who is trying to shift but clearly in pain.

"Stay still!" I command, applying more pressure to the wound. "You need to keep your breathing steady. Just breathe with me." I demonstrate, taking slow, deep breaths, hoping he'll follow.

He nods, but panic flickers in his eyes as he coughs, blood seeping from the corner of his mouth. "I can't—"

"Yes, you can!" I insist, leaning closer to him.

I glance around, scanning the area for help. There's nothing like a drive by shooting to kill a person's Friday night. Most people have fled, hiding behind their cars or dashing into the store. A knot forms in my stomach. This man could die right here, right now, and I'm on my own. With other bodies to tend to.

"I need to check on the others," I tell the man, but he grabs my hand, won't let go.

The sound of sirens is faint, but I know they're on the way. The realization that I am a witness to this horrific carnage sinks in, making my heart race even faster.

"Please," he whispers again, his voice barely audible. "Don't…"

"I'm right here. The ambulance is just around the corner." I don't know this for sure, but I guess any hope is better than none at all.

Finally, the distant sound of sirens grows louder, and relief washes over me, but I know it's not enough. "Stay with me!" I urge, wiping sweat from my brow, my heart heavy with dread. The seconds feel like hours, and the pressure in my chest tightens as I watch him.

When the ambulance arrives, paramedics leap into action, and I reluctantly relinquish my hold. "He's losing a lot of blood!" I shout, my voice rising over the chaos. "He needs immediate attention!"

The paramedics nod, working quickly, but I can't just stand by. I assist them as best I can, relaying what I know about what happened, the pressure points I tried to stabilize.

They load him onto a stretcher, and as he's whisked away, I can't shake the strange feeling of relief that overcomes me after the sense of helplessness that I couldn't do more.

An officer approaches me next, notebook in hand, and I feel the weight of his gaze. "Ma'am, can you tell us what happened?"

My heart races as I stare at the officer, the enormity of being a witness feeling like a stone in my chest. "I—it happened so quick," I stammer, my voice trembling as I recount the event, each detail feeling heavier than the last. "I didn't see anything."

I shake my head. I take a shaky breath, realizing the trauma of witnessing such violence will leave its mark. The officer takes notes, and I watch the scene around me with a sort of detachment that leaves me breathless.

"But you were first on the scene? You got here pretty quick."

"I was standing at the supermarket entry."

He shakes his head, like something's not sitting right for him. I feel like I'm being interrogated as he addresses me with words that are all too obviously laced with suspicion.

"Then you must've seen something," he urges.

"I saw nothing."

"Yet you were still the first on sight, you called the ambulance. All on your own..." his words hang heavy between us, full of insinuation.

"I'm a registered nurse," I tell him. "It's my job to assist."

"Still...you kept your wits about you enough to do all that, yet you can't identify the shooters?"

"Are we done here?" I ask, folding my arms across my chest. I don't like his tone, and as though I'm not already traumatized enough, he insists on throwing accusations at me.

Later, as I stand in the parking lot, the air still heavy with tension, I feel the adrenaline begin to fade, leaving me trembling. When I finally walk to my car, after hours waiting to repeat the same story to multiple officers, I've all but forgotten my groceries. The darkness has enveloped the last remnants of the day as I realize that this day will forever change me—not just as a nurse, but as a person grappling with the fragility of life in a world that can turn dark in an instant.

5

BAYLIN

The detective leading the investigation into the shooting calls me into the precinct the next day. More questions, he says. My feet are heavy with reluctance – I don't want to be talking about the thing that kept me up all night, playing like a loop in my head. When I finally fell asleep, I woke screaming, in a sweat as the scene committed to my memory replayed itself again. Reluctantly, I head out to meet him, when I'd rather be anywhere else than in the company of the pushy detective who won't stop calling me.

The precinct is stark and cold, every corner lit by harsh fluorescent lights. My steps feel leaden as I'm led towards the interview room.

And then my step falters. I pass a man in the corridor as I'm being led to detective Handler' office—his presence is imposing, and our eyes meet briefly. Denim blue eyes pierce through my soul; a sense of familiarity flashes through me, sending a shiver down my spine. He looks familiar, but I can't place him; I'm gripped with fear, yet my curiosity has me wondering who he is as I brush past him through the corridor.

Detective Handler is waiting in a nearby doorway, his eyes darting between me and the man who just walked by. Did he plan this? Did he time it so I'd run into this man here? His hawkish little eyes tell me he did.

"Ms. Reyes," Handler's voice slices through the tension. "You know that man?"

"No," I stammer, my heart racing. "Should I know him?"

Handler' eyes narrow. "That was quite a reaction for two strangers passing by each other in a hallway."

"I have no idea what you're talking about," I lie, trying to calm my nerves. "I have an appointment I can't cancel," I tell him, looking at my watch.

Handler raises an eyebrow, surprised by my attitude. "Let's continue this inside," he says, motioning to the interview room.

I step inside, my anxiety a tight knot in my chest. I know I'm dealing with dangerous people; the death of four men in one shooting says so. Yet I don't know where the real threat lies—whether it's with the shooters from last night or with Handler.

The interview room feels suffocatingly small as Detective Handler slides photo after photo across the table. Each picture makes my anxiety spike, but none of the faces trigger any recognition.

"Take your time," Handler says, but his tone is tight, like a taut spring about to snap.

I shuffle through the photos again, tracing edges worn by previous hands. None of these people match the fear that grips me when I think about last night.

"Nothing," I whisper, pushing the stack back towards him. "I don't know these people."

Handler leans forward, his eyes locking onto mine, trying to unearth secrets I'm not even sure I have. We're locked in this stand-off, neither willing to be the first to look away, to admit defeat. He doesn't flinch, doesn't back down.

"What about these photos?" he asks. He slides a folder across the desk towards me. I make no move to open it; instead, I sit glaring at it, suspicion rising. "Go on, open it," he prompts.

I don't move for the longest time. This must be a trap. Otherwise, why would he just hand me a closed file? I suddenly know why; he wants the element of surprise. He wants to gauge my reaction to whatever is in that file. Which means he doesn't trust me anymore than I trust myself.

I steel myself, mentally count backwards from ten, then poise to open the file. I'm committed to switching off my emotions. I do that so well. Portraying a blank face, my best poker face, when I don't want someone to know what I'm thinking. It's a trick of the trade, the mask I have to don as a nurse when trying to keep a straight face with families begging for information on their loved ones.

Detective Handler is watching me so closely, I don't think he's blinked more than twice in the past three minutes.

As I open the file and spread the photos out in front of me, I try to remain as neutral as Switzerland. I don't know what he's hoping to find. I cross my eyes and look through the images instead of directly at them. It helps me stay detached from the content, especially when my mind is so scattered and I'd rather be anywhere else but here.

The pictures are blurry, taken from a distance, and it's not hard to see that they're surveillance photos. Whoever these men are in the pictures either didn't know or didn't care that they were being photographed, although most of them are so grainy, it's hard to make out anything definitive. But I can't ignore the glimpse of black hair that immediately catches my attention. My eyes are drawn to it despite my attempts to remain objective. There must be around twenty or so pictures, with four of them featuring what could possibly be the man I saw in the corridor earlier. The photos are taken from a distance, but I would bet my last dollar it's him and Detective Handler orchestrated our meeting in the corridor earlier.

My heart catches in my throat as my eyes move to the next photo. Quickly, I move past the picture and concentrate on another, taking my time with each and every one so I won't ever have to come back here.

"I don't recognize any of these men," I say finally, settling back into the chair.

"Take a good look, Ms. Reyes."

"What do you want, Detective Handler?" It feels like he's interrogating me.

"I'm asking for your co-operation to put these killers where they belong."

"How do you expect me to cooperate if I didn't see anything?" I ask, my voice tight with barely suppressed anger.

Handler collects the photos then slams them back onto the table.

"The Riccardi crime family shot six men last night," he tells me. "Four of whom are dead. Just say so in court."

I stare past the photographs, my heart pounding. Regardless of whether or not I saw anything, it becomes absolutely clear that I need to keep my mouth shut. Everyone knows not to mess with crime lords, and I may be many things, but suicidal is not in my DNA.

"I've told you before, I didn't see anything," I insist, pushing the photos back.

Handler's face darkens. "You're playing a dangerous game, Ms. Reyes."

He doesn't care about the truth. His words are a venomous promise, sending a shiver down my spine. But he'll need more than fear to make me a pawn in his game.

"Remember these names, Ms. Reyes! They killed those men, and they will probably kill you next!" He points at one of the pictures, and my eyes follow his finger as it moves from one picture to another. "Lazaro Riccardi! Enzo Fiore! Vincenzo Malla! Hugo Riccardi! Ro…"

A pain throbs in his neck as his voice rises. I hold up my hand, cut him off.

"I was hundreds of yards away when they were shot!" I hiss. "I. Saw. Nothing!"

"Let's try this another way, shall we? Your nephew, Luca, he's a good kid, right?" Handler starts, his eyes searching mine. I say nothing. "It'd be a real shame to see him get caught up in… unfortunate circumstances where he could be thrown in juvie. Or taken away from you…you're his legal guardian, right?"

The threat is clear, unspoken but heavy as a sledgehammer. I clench my jaw, fighting the urge to lash out. He must have gone to some lengths to dig up this information about me.

"Are you threatening me?"

He shrugs and watches me carefully. "I will ask you one last time...do you know any of these men?"

"No. I fold the photos and put them in the folder, then close it shut.

"You're lying, Ms. Reyes."

My skin crawls under his scrutiny, the insinuation igniting something within me. Anger bubbles up, hot and fierce. Especially now that he's threatened Luca.

"You're baiting me!"

"I asked you if you know any of the men in the photos."

"Exactly! You asked me if I know them, which I don't!"

In an instant, I'm on my feet, chair scraping against the floor with a screech that matches the tumult inside me.

"One way or another, Ms. Reyes, I'm going to close this case and put these criminals in prison. It's up to you which side of the fence you're sitting on, but don't say I didn't warn you."

"Enough," I say, voice quaking. "I'm done here."

I don't wait for his response, don't look back to see if he's following. My heart thumps a reckless rhythm as I storm out, leaving behind the photos, the accusations, and the heavy weight of Handler's disbelief.

He's up to something, I know he is. He tried too hard to dig into my pause by the man in the corridor. And when he showed me a photograph of that same man, I wasn't lying when I said I didn't know him. I don't know him. He may seem familiar, but I don't know him! Why is Detective Handler trying to turn this investigation into something it isn't?

Outside, the air hits me like a slap—cool and bracing. It does little to calm the fire in my veins. I answer a phone call from my mother, my words comforting her in a way I can't even comfort myself, then I start walking, fast and aimless, just needing to put distance between myself and that room, between myself and all the questions rising in my head.

6

LAZARO

I wouldn't trust detective Handler as far as I could throw him. The man's had a hard-on for us ever since we moved here and refused to play ball with his corrupt ass. I, Lazaro Riccardi, duly refuse to be shaken down by a member of law enforcement. He can kiss my ass and shove it under his pillow at night. Then start all over again.

I watch as the girl emerges from the precinct, looking flustered. She raises a hand and wipes it across her face before she lifts her phone to her ear and answers a call. She has one hand on her hip as she walks around in circles, her eyes turned toward the sky in exasperation. When she lowers the phone, her head falls to her chest in resignation, before she starts to walk quickly down the street.

There's a reason why she was at the precinct, I just know it. Handler, the cocky bastard, called me in and kept going round in circles, chasing his tail as he asked different variations of the same question. And then he got that call and suddenly seemed in a hurry to usher me out of the office. Perfect timing for us to pass each other in the corridor. All this after he told me – definitively – that there was an eyewitness able to place me at the scene of last night's shooting. Which is bullshit through and through – I know this without a doubt because I know I wasn't there. So his thing is to either have her see me and plant that seed in her head, or to have me retaliate and kill her so then he could really get me on a murder rap. Yeah, I wouldn't put it past the bastard.

"Follow her," I tell Salvatore, and he merges into the traffic, which mercifully is crawling along at a steady pace, just enough for us to keep up with her.

The girl settles into a local coffee shop and takes a window seat by herself, where she sits for an hour lost in her thoughts as her coffee grows tepid.

I watch her through the window simultaneously as I attend to my work via phone, before I realize she could sit here all day, and I don't have that privilege. I call Vincenzo and wait until he rolls to a stop beside our car.

"Keep following her," I tell Salvatore. "Find out everything there is to know." I gather my things and exchange one car for another, before we drive away.

~

"Lazaro?" Salvatore's familiar voice slices through my chaotic thoughts. Normally, his presence is a balm, but tonight, it barely quiets the restless tapping of my fingers against the desk.

"Tell me about the girl," I demand, my grip tightening on the armrest as I try to keep my voice steady.

Salvatore nods, pulling out a file from the leather satchel slung over his shoulder.

She's a nurse at Mercy," Salvatore says, pulling out documents filled with hospital rosters and photos of a modest home. "Lives with her mother and her nephew—the boy's been with her since his parents' car crash five years back."

I let out a slow exhale, feeling the air get caught in my chest. He hands me the file and I open it, finding Baylin Reyes' profile inside. The nurse who happens to be the only witness to our encounter with Jacob Arens. Her unassuming photo stares back at me; her dark hair is pulled back in a simple ponytail. She wears minimal makeup, with a touch of gloss on her lips. Her expression is neutral, giving away nothing about her thoughts or emotions. She wears a plain white nurse's uniform, her posture straight and confident. Her dark eyes hold secrets and determination, just like the woman I saw at the police station. My mind keeps going back to our meeting at the precinct; I'm almost certain that Detective Handler planned for her to show up while I was leaving his office. Did he want her to identify me as the shooter? I know he has been trying to indict me for years, but this seems like a stretch, especially since I wasn't even present that night.

I scan the pages, her life unfolding before me; the tragedies that have helped shape her, the battles she has fought alone. She is like us in ways she probably doesn't even realize. Carved from the same stone of loss and defiance. But still, she's a liability. One I can't afford to risk.

She's the only witness to the murders.

"Keep an eye on her," I instruct, handing back the file. "But keep it discreet. Handler is already circling her like a vulture. We don't need to arouse more suspicion."

"Detective Handler?" Salvatore raises an eyebrow. His face hardens and his hand twitches towards his concealed weapon. He's never liked the man, been hankering to put a bullet in him for close to a year. But rules are rules, and where possible, we want to keep our hands clean when it comes to removing law enforcement.

"He won't stop talking about the evidence he has against us. But he's only fixated on one person - that girl. He thinks she holds all the secrets to our downfall." I let out a humorless laugh. "As if one girl could bring down the entire empire we've built."

THE OFFICE FEELS SUFFOCATING. The walls are closing in, the weight of everything—everything that's slipping through my fingers—pressing down on me like the thick fog outside. I glance at the door, then back at the file in my hands, the words blurring as my mind races in circles. Despite what I told Salvatore, I'm not going to lie to myself or fool myself into believing that this girl couldn't cause us serious harm. And yet...there's the rule. *That rule...*

Romeo steps into the room, his boots thudding heavy against the floor. The usual smirk is absent from his face. His expression is unreadable, the tension in his posture tighter than I've seen in a while. He can sense it, too—the storm that's about to hit.

"It must be serious if you've brought out the Macallan," he says, nodding toward my drink.

I don't need to ask if he knows. Of course, he does. He's been in the loop from the start. But there's something about saying it out loud, about acknowledging the threat, that makes it feel more real. More dangerous.

"You're here about the girl?" I say, my voice a low rasp, like it's dragging itself out of my chest with difficulty.

Romeo leans against the desk, crossing his arms. "I've heard. Mercy nurse. Baylin Reyes. The one who claims to have seen the drive-by. You think she's our problem?"

I don't answer right away. Instead, I flick open the file again, letting the picture of her stare back at me. She's just a woman. Just a nurse, a mother, a niece. Someone who's fought her own battles, but nothing that should have brought her into our world. Nothing that should make her a threat.

But she's not just a witness. She's the witness. The only one who could tie us to that night. And in this game, the only thing more dangerous than an enemy with too much information is one who doesn't realize how much power they hold.

"I think Handler is our problem," I finally say, my voice flat. "He's more dangerous than we thought."

Romeo narrows his eyes. "You think she'll talk?"

I shake my head. "No. Not in the way you're thinking. But she's the key. If Handler gets to her, if he convinces her to talk, we're screwed. At the moment, she's adamant that she saw nothing. But Handler's being one obnoxious pain in the ass."

He pushes off the desk, pacing a few steps before turning to face me, his jaw tight. "What do you need me to do?"

I exhale, dragging a hand through my hair. The thought is there, lingering at the edge of my mind, but I'm not ready to go that far—yet. Not yet.

"Leave it for now," I say. "If the time comes, we just need to make her quiet. We don't need to make her disappear."

Romeo raises an eyebrow, clearly not buying my restraint. "How do we even know she's not already talking to Handler?"

I don't answer right away. The truth is, I don't know. I don't know if she's already talking, if Handler has made his move yet. All I know is she was at the precinct and Handler is pinning his hopes on her.

Romeo's face hardens. "She's a liability, Lazaro. If Handler plays his cards right, she could destroy everything we've built."

I run a hand over my face, clearly thinking, weighing the options. Romeo has always been the one who pushes the limits, who finds the most direct route to getting what we want. But this? This is different. The stakes are higher than I've ever seen them. One wrong move and we both end up six feet under.

Romeo leans back against the wall, his expression darkening as he waits for my response. "You want me to keep eyes on her? Make sure she stays in line?"

I'm silent for a moment, before I nod slowly. "Keep an eye on her. But I don't want you hurting her. She can't be tied back to us, Romeo."

Romeo doesn't speak right away, but I can feel the weight of his agreement, even without words. It's always been like that with him. No need to say much when we both know what's at stake.

"I'll handle it," he says at last.

I nod, a cold shiver crawling up my spine as the gravity of the situation sinks in. Baylin Reyes holds the fate of everything we've built in her hands—whether she realizes it or not. And I'll be damned if I let her be the one to bring this whole empire crashing down.

7

BAYLIN

The feeling of being watched lingers as I walk through the foggy streets, my thoughts scattered. The city is quiet now, the usual noise softened by the thick mist hanging over everything. I pull my arms around myself, trying to hold on to something familiar in a world that feels off-kilter. The cold dampness seeps into my skin, sending a chill through me. Memories of Maggie rush in—her laughter once filling these streets as we wandered, imagining the lives of the people in the houses we passed.

But she's gone now, and these walks only remind me of the emptiness. I try to avoid them, but sometimes the urge to walk these familiar paths is too strong.

Last week's shooting has ripped open old wounds. Grief and trauma have a way of finding me, especially in my darkest moments when memories of losing my sister and her husband to a drunk driver come flooding back. It's exhausting, both mentally and physically. The constant calls from the detective assigned to the case only add to the exhaustion, his persistence almost crossing over into harassment. But he's determined to find answers, even from a mere witness who didn't actually witness anything.

As weariness overtakes me, I know it's time to head back home and seek solace in the comfort of my bed. Maybe tomorrow will bring some peace and clarity amidst the chaos.

A sleek, jet black car with tinted windows sits idling by the curb, its powerful engine purring softly like a contented feline. My stomach tightens with unease as I approach my own car parked a few spaces down. Perhaps it's just paranoia from lack of sleep, but a nagging feeling settles in the pit of my stomach. Detective Handler is not one to be taken lightly, and I wouldn't put it past him to have me followed. The last thing I want or need right now is another run-in with him.

As I draw nearer to my car, the idling car's engine revs up slightly, causing my heart to race. A smooth, unfamiliar voice calls out, "Baylin Reyes?"

My body tenses and I keep my distance, wary of this unexpected encounter. "Who wants to know?" I respond cautiously.

"Let's not make this any harder than it needs to be," the man replies as the passenger door slides open with a sharp metallic click.

Before I can react, strong arms wrap around me from behind, lifting me off my feet. Panic sets in and I thrash and scream, but it's no use against the unknown assailant's iron grip. Before I know it, a cloth is pressed against my mouth and everything starts to spin and blur into obscurity. The last thing I hear before darkness overtakes me is the sound of the car door slamming shut, its deafening echo reverberating through my fading consciousness like a death knell.

WHEN I COME TO, my head is pounding and my body feels heavy, as if weighed down by bricks. Opening my eyes, I find myself in a dimly lit space with narrow walls that seem to close in on me. It's not long before I realize I'm in the boot of a car. Panic surges through me as I try to sit up, only to realize that my hands are bound behind my back with rough rope cutting into my skin.

The world outside is a cacophony of muffled noises, each bump and turn a jarring assault on my senses. Hours pass—or maybe it is minutes; time loses meaning in the cramped darkness. When the vehicle finally grinds to a halt and the boot pops open, the last remnants of daylight stab at my eyes like a physical force.

"Out," a man's voice commands, as curt as the cold air that rushes in.

I stumble out, legs unsteady, squinting against the late afternoon light. The scent of pine and earth fills my lungs, a sharp contrast to the sour tang of fear that has settled on my tongue.

I crane my neck, desperate to catch a glimpse of the man behind the hard plastic mask that clings to his face like a second skin. Its smooth, white surface reflects the dim light in the fading afternoon, and his jet-black hair is slicked back neatly beneath it. I should be afraid, but for some unfathomable reason, I'm not. I'm curious...and I'm awestruck by the features of the mask, the intricate details of every feature that so closely resemble a man's features. Handsome features. The sort of features that remind me of old Hollywood actors.

His grip on my arm is firm as he leads me to a cabin. He allows me to use the bathroom before pushing me into a chair. A plate with a sandwich, cut into four perfect triangles, slides across the table towards me. The thought of eating makes my stomach turn, but I force myself to take a few bites, if only to maintain my strength. That, and I haven't eaten since breakfast. He watches me with little interest, straddling the chair, his hulking frame too large for the seat. One hand casually rests over the top of the chair, the picture of nonchalance.

"What do you want?" I ask him, when I have had enough of him watching me like I'm a circus freakshow. I don't point out that he's the one in the mask.

The man says nothing. He watches me with a cool disposition, his eyes taking in every one of my movements as I bite into my sandwich, chew, then swallow down my food.

"Tell me, Baylin," he says after a while, his husky tone thick yet casual, almost bored. Two hard, beady pools of blue look out at me from beneath the mask. "Tell me why detective Handler is so interested in you?"

I almost choke on the sandwich.

"That's what this is about? Detective fucking Handler?" I reply, meeting his icy gaze head-on. There is power in silence, in withholding the words he expects to spill from my lips. For now, it's the only thing I can control, so I'll use it to my advantage any way I can. "Did he organize this?" Again, I wouldn't put it past him.

I imagine I see his smile stretch beneath the plastic; I could be wrong, but the undeniable flicker of something shifting is there for a second and gone in a heartbeat. He doesn't answer my questions. Instead, he commends me on my anger. "Good girl," he murmurs, almost approvingly. "Keep your secrets. They're safer with you, anyway."

Confusion wars with relief inside me. He couldn't have brought me all the way out here just to talk to me about Detective Handler. No, that could easily have been done within the city limits. He wants more.

"Why am I here?"

"Why am I here? What do you want? Let me go...always the same old lines."

He shakes his head in disgust, almost sarcastic in his response, taunting me. He's not big on giving out information, I see, but I just sit and wait, biding my time. And I refuse to back down from his glare; if anything, I give as good as I get.

"You must hear them often if you've made a life out of kidnapping innocents off the street."

He scoffs, angles his head and regards me thoughtfully. One thing becomes obviously clear to me; he doesn't intend to kill me – otherwise, why is he wearing the mask? If he were going to kill me, he wouldn't care about revealing his identity, and he'd show me his face. He wouldn't feed me; there's that small mercy.

"You'd better watch that mouth of yours, Reyes," he muses.

"I'm sorry, but I think I missed the memo about how to act after being kidnapped." My snarky attitude has him chuckling quietly, before he leans forward in his chair and stares me down with the stern mask.

A phone rings, and I watch as he takes out his phone, walks a little distance away and answers. I note every mannerism, every breath, even his height as I watch him speaking into the phone, his back turned to me. He's impeccably dressed for a man undertaking a kidnapping. He's wearing fancy black shoes with dress pants and a navy blazer. He could so easily have just stepped out of a prep school magazine. This is no ordinary kidnapper.

"So, which one are you?" I ask, as he puts his phone away and turns back to me. I may be a little slow to catch on, but process of elimination; it's never once let me down. If Detective Handler didn't orchestrate this, there's only one other option. I knew that his bullshit would put me on someone's radar.

"Which what?"

"Which Riccardi?"

He's silent for the longest time, but he doesn't miss a beat. His eyes are venomous as they twitch, assessing me. Perhaps I'm not as clueless as he thinks I am, after all.

"Romeo."

"Ah. Romeo, oh Romeo. But there's nothing in the least bit romantic about you, is there Romeo Riccardi?" I say, in a rare show of bravery.

He doesn't like that. I can tell in the way he stands facing me, his legs spread military style, arms folded across his chest, fixing me with malicious eyes. His body hums with untold aggression. I can see that my blasé attitude is aggravating the hell out of him.

"Better watch your mouth, Reyes," he repeats, "or it might land you somewhere you don't want to be."

"I'm already somewhere I don't want to be."

He shakes his head slowly, tutting as he moves slowly toward me. His very movements are lethal in the way they taunt me. I try to hide the lump in my throat by attempting to swallow past it, but his eyes are fixed on me, taking in every micro spasm, every angle.

The strangeness of my captor belies a puzzle my mind can't help but return to. The Riccardi name is a shadow that looms over the city, yet here he is, flesh and blood, hiding his identity from me. It's confounding.

There is something about him, an aura that commands attention. The way he moves, all coiled energy and latent threat, belies the calm facade he presents. And though disgust curdles in my gut at the thought of finding anything about my captor intriguing, I can't deny the pull of his enigmatic presence. The quiet, reserved way he holds himself hints at depths unexplored, a mystery wrapped in danger. It's intoxicating and terrifying in equal measure.

I'm exhausted. Exhausted from hours in the locked boot of a car as we made our way up to the middle of nowhere. Exhausted because I'm sick and tired of the spiral that is me losing control of my life. Exhausted because the culmination of the past two weeks is almost more than I've been through in the totality of my years.

"Man up and show me your face," I challenge him, trying to keep the tremor from my voice as I lift my chin in defiance. Asking such a thing could push him over the edge; his anger could devour me from the inside out. If he reveals himself to me, he'll have to kill me; even I'm not stupid enough to believe otherwise.

He tips his head toward the bed when the shadows grow long and I still sit rigid, afraid to let down my guard even for a moment. I'm exhausted but I'm too afraid to sleep. Too afraid to close my eyes and let my guard down. Instead, I stare at my captor, a predator in his element, unable to shake the feeling that there is more to this man than the violence that clings to his name.

8

BAYLIN

At some point, I must nod off, because it feels like a new day when I open my eyes. I lift my face from the table and crack my stiff neck, shaking my head as my muscles scream in agony.

The cabin door creaks open, and the daylight strikes me like a physical force, momentarily blinding. Romeo, standing in the doorway, gestures to the outdoors with a tilt of his head. "Fresh air," he grunts, his voice a low rumble beneath the thick mask.

I stand and he lets me use the bedroom, where I relieve myself then splash cold water on my face, if only to wake my senses from this nightmare. I edge past him, hyper-aware of the space he occupies, of the sidearm that hangs at his hip—no doubt for my benefit. He doesn't have a hair out of order, his mask firmly in place and his clothes still pristine, not a single sign of fatigue on him.

The steady thump of my heart sounds foreign in the sprawling silence of the woods. The air is crisp, carrying with it the scent of pine and earth, a stark contrast to the stale confinement of the cabin.

I pace a few steps away, gazing out at the dense forest surrounding us without another human in sight. Thoughts of escape clutter my mind as I take in my surroundings. How far could

I run before he catches me? My outfit certainly wouldn't hinder me - jeans, a long-sleeved shirt, and an oversized cardigan that constantly falls off my shoulders. I also have on combat boots, which have always made me agile on my feet. Certainly more agile than Romeo Riccardi in his fancy leather boots. He could easily shoot me in the back while I'm running away. Maybe it's worth taking my chances; either way, he's probably going to kill me sooner or later. After all, he didn't bring me here for a casual chat over cookies and tea.

The trees whisper secrets to one another, their sounds brushing against my arms like a soft caress. It's almost peaceful, a cruel illusion given the circumstances.

"Feels good, doesn't it?" Romeo's voice shatters the moment. He leans against the cabin wall, arms folded, watching me with those unsettling blue eyes beneath the stony white mask. There is an intensity to his gaze that sets my nerves on edge.

"Freedom, even just a taste," he continues, his tone mocking, as though he can read my thoughts. Like he knows exactly what I'm thinking. "Do you feel like running, little bird? How far do you think you could get before I drag you back here by the hair? How far could you go before my bullet grazes your spine?"

The thought causes a shaky shiver to curl up my spine, and I sway as though being taunted by a breeze. My heart hammers against my ribs, and I clench my fists, trying to quell the rising panic. This man —the way he speaks to me, taunting, prodding—as though he's daring me to run just so he has a reason to shoot me in the back for target practice. I can see that he'd like nothing better, but something must be holding him back. I swallow, tasting fear and resolve mixed together like a bitter cocktail.

"Maybe I'd surprise you," I say, my voice steady despite the storm inside me. My mind reels, considering, discarding options. I'm a nurse by trade; I've never been one to accept helplessness, and I can't allow myself to be another victim. If I don't make it back home, Luca will be devastated. It will kill him. And I refuse to break my promise to him. The least I can do is try to escape him. I could try...and die doing so, but at least I would have died trying. I wouldn't have just handed over my soul to the devil.

The wild terrain calls to something primal within me.

"You're going to kill me." It's more a statement than a question. I know that's his end game, but he's probably psychotic enough to torture me first.

"Maybe," he says, the mask stretching across his lower face. He must be smiling, although I can't imagine it would be anything other than a cruel slash across his face. "Maybe not."

I take a deep breath, filling my lungs with cold air. My life, ever since my sister Magdalene's death... has been a series of calculated risks and desperate gambles. Maggie's death was just another roll of the dice. And now, there is only one thing left to do.

"Maybe you should find out," I whisper to myself. Then, without another thought, I turn on my heels and bolt into the woods. I would take my chances on a bullet in the back now than one in the head after he destroys me.

I don't hear him behind me. I'm deep into the woods, leaves crunching beneath my boots as I surge further and further into unfamiliar territory.

The forest floor is uneven, treacherous, but I don't care. Branches claw at my skin, roots threaten to trip me, but I push forward, fueled by adrenaline and the fierce desire to die on my own terms. Behind me, I hear a high-pitched laugh, hear the crunch of underbrush as my captor gives chase.

"Baylin!" His call is a growl, a predator's warning. But I am beyond hearing, beyond fear. I am flying, every muscle straining toward freedom.

I run.

∽

MY LEGS CARRY me as fast as they can, and in my mind, I can't help but think about Luca. He must be wondering why I didn't come home last night. Another broken promise to add to the list. The first was that he would always be safely cocooned in the arms of his parents, but now they're gone. Is it possible that I will also disappear, another person to disappear from his life? My thoughts then turn to my mother, who is probably beside herself with worry since I've not returned home and she hasn't been able to reach me by phone. Would she be toying with the possibility of burying yet another daughter? I know I have to stop these thoughts as I run; my focus needs to be on getting out of the woods and reaching safety.

The dense thicket of trees seems to close in around me as I push forward, my heart pounding in my chest. A sense of desperation drives me on, each step feeling heavier than the last. I can hear twigs snapping under my feet, the sound echoing through the stillness of the forest.

As I dart between the looming trees, a flicker of movement catches my eye to the left. I skid to a halt, my breath catching in my throat. A figure stands among the shadows, his silhouette obscured by the dim light filtering through the branches above. My pulse quickens, a surge of fear coursing through me.

"Who's there?" I call out, my voice trembling slightly. The figure doesn't move, doesn't make a sound. Panic claws at the edges of my mind, threatening to consume me. Is it him? Is it Romeo? Or is there someone else lurking in the darkness of the forest?

I have to make a decision – whether to confront this unknown presence or turn and flee deeper into the woods. But something holds me rooted to the spot, a strange curiosity mingling with my fear. As I stare at the figure, trying to make out any discernible features, a voice speaks from the shadows.

"Running won't help you now, Baylin." The voice is low and raspy, sending a shiver down my spine. It's too far to see, but I'm sure it's my captor, although I don't know how he would've caught up to me so quickly.

Taking a tentative step forward, I squint, trying to get a better look at the mysterious figure. And then, as if a switch has been flipped, recognition floods through me like a tidal wave. It couldn't be... could it?

I stutter over my own disbelief. The figure steps forward, right into a beam of dappled sunlight that illuminates his face. I'd all but forgotten about that night more than five years ago. How could I forget that night? It was the night my life ended. The night we lost Magdalene. As soon as I see him step out into my line of vision, his mask removed, I understand so many things I didn't before.

Tears well up in my eyes as I see his familiar features, his once bright eyes now hard stones that could cut through glass, their icy depths impenetrable.

"You!"

THEN - 2017

The only difference between a sinner and a saint is the timing of their mistakes.

9

BAYLIN

Jess gives me a tight-lipped smile and asks, "Why do men always swarm around the one woman who clearly doesn't want to be here?"

I shrug, but she cuts me off before I can answer.

"I know, I know. You didn't want to come. But I begged you to join me."

She sniffs and shoots me a sideways glance with a little pout. She's not angry, just puzzled. She never quite understands why I prefer staying in our dorm room, cozy on the couch with a good book. She just doesn't get it. She never will.

"Come on, you made it this far," she whines. "Indulge me and dance with me."

"No, Jess, please," I beg as she grabs my arm and drags me onto the dance floor. I am not a dancer; I don't even like parties. I'm just...me. All I want is to graduate, find a good job, and move on with my life.

But that's exactly why I let her persuade me to come out tonight; supposedly, to celebrate finishing university and starting the rest of our lives. On opposite sides of the world. Jess will be heading back to her native Australia next week and who knows when I'll see her again. I'll be heading back home, degree in hand, my family cheering me on from the sidelines.

I reluctantly let Jess pull me into the huddle of swaying bodies on the dance floor. The music is loud, the lights are dim, and the air smells of sweat and alcohol. I close my eyes and try to block out the chaos around me, focusing on the rhythm pulsing through my veins. Jess is twirling and laughing, lost in the euphoria of the moment as she dances a little way away from me, swept up in some random stranger's arms.

Just as I start to relax and let myself be carried away by the music, I feel a presence hovering too close for comfort. Opening my eyes, I see him - my ex-boyfriend, Alex, sidling up to me with a smile that makes my skin crawl. His eyes flicker with mischief as he leans in too close, invading my personal space. Rich, arrogant, entitled prick.

He places a possessive hand on my waist, ignoring my obvious discomfort. He stands at least two heads taller than me and fixes me with his signature smirk. His green eyes - what initially attracted me to him - are two brilliant emeralds that still sparkle with the same mischief he always flaunted.

"Well, well, well, if it isn't my favorite girlfriend," he drawls, his breath reeking of booze and arrogance. "You look even more stunning than I remember."

"Ex," I remind him. "Ex-girlfriend."

I take a step back, but he follows slowly, like a shadow refusing to be shaken off.

"Technicality, baby girl."

I plaster on a fake smile, masking the discomfort and apprehension brewing inside me. Alex is trouble, and I know it all too well. His reputation as a smooth talker and a heartbreaker precedes him, and I have no intention of becoming part of his games once again.

"Hi, Alex. Bye, Alex." I reply coolly, trying to edge away subtly, hoping the confrontation doesn't escalate as it usually does whenever we find ourselves in the same room. But he moves with me effortlessly, mirroring my steps with an infuriating smirk playing on his lips.

"Even more beautiful, if that's possible," he comments, his gaze lingering on me in a way that sends shivers down my spine. I should be flattered, but instead my skin starts to crawl as though it's home to an eight-legged friend. "Care for a dance?"

Never, I want to scream.

I shake my head firmly, steeling myself against his persistent advances. "No, thank you. I'm done here."

His chuckle, deviously hollow as it is, stabs at my heart and makes me feel faint. "Aw, don't be like that, Baylin. One dance won't hurt, will it?"

Before I can protest further, Jess appears at my side, a protective glint in her eyes that only seems to fuel Alex on. She slides her arm around mine, effectively cutting off any chance of further interaction between Alex and me.

"Sorry, she's taken," Jess interjects with a sweet smile that doesn't quite reach her eyes as she shoos him away with her hand. "Why don't you run along and go find someone else to bother?"

Alex raises an eyebrow, unaccustomed to being dismissed so easily. His smirk fades as he studies Jess, the air crackling with tension between them. He turns his attention back to me, a challenging glint in his eyes.

"Is that so?" he muses, crossing his arms defiantly. "She seems pretty possessive for just a friend." His voice is laced with skepticism, daring me to contradict him. Jess tightens her grip on my arm, a silent warning against engaging further with Alex. But something in me rebels against the idea of backing down.

I meet Alex's gaze with a steady look, refusing to be intimidated. There's a stubborn fire burning within me, pushing me to stand my ground. I can feel Jess tensing beside me, her silent plea for me to let it go echoing in the air.

"You're right," I respond coolly, a small smile playing on my lips. "She is pretty possessive, probably because she really, *truly* likes my man."

Alex's expression falters for a moment before a cocky grin spreads across his face. He extends his arms, encompassing the space around us. "Well, I don't see a man hanging off your arm, baby."

Before I can respond, Jess takes a step forward, her eyes flashing with warning. "I suggest you take a step back, turn around, and leave," she says sharply.

Alex's smirk wavers slightly at Jess's steely tone, a flicker of uncertainty crossing his face. But just as quickly as it appears, it is replaced by a challenging glint. "Or what?" he taunts, taking a step closer to us, invading our personal space. I can feel Jess bristling beside me, her protective instincts on high alert.

Before I can stop myself, a surge of anger rises within me at Alex's arrogance. "Fuck off, Alex," I retort, my voice surprisingly steady despite the adrenaline coursing through me. It's time for me to step up and rip this band-aid off, once and for all.

Alex's eyes narrow at my defiance, the air crackling with tension between us. For a moment, it feels like the world around us holds its breath, waiting to see what will happen next. The music, still thumping around us, seems to fade into the far distance at the silent standoff, even as a small crowd starts to congregate around us.

Jess's grip tightens on my arm, her eyes narrowing. I can feel the tension radiating off her, a silent warning to Alex that he's treading on dangerous ground. But Alex seems unfazed, standing his ground with a stubborn set to his jaw.

Suddenly, a voice cuts through the charged atmosphere like a knife.

"Is there a problem here?"

The man's voice echoes through the stand-off as he steps into our inner circle. His words drip with authority and danger, his presence like a sudden storm rolling in, casting a shadow over the tense group. I feel his arm as it tightens around my waist, and he pulls me into his side protectively. His mouth lands on the top of my head in a quick kiss that's not so quick because it feels like he lingers there, taking in the scent of my shampoo. "You okay, baby?"

I steal a surprised glance at him, but I don't move away when I see the cold determination in his eyes as he stares down Alex.

Alex meets the man's gaze head-on, his demeanor defiant and unyielding. The silence stretches between them, thick with unspoken threats and challenges. Jess shifts beside me, her fingers digging into my arm as if to ground her.

The mystery man takes a step forward, a man on either side of him flanking him like loyal soldiers ready for battle. He's wearing a suit with the jacket discarded, his shirt unbuttoned. The club seems to hold its breath, the music fading into a distant hum as all eyes turn towards the confrontation.

"What's going on here?" The man's voice is low but carries an authoritative weight that commands power and respect. I can feel the tension coiling in the air, a palpable force that threatens to suffocate everyone in its grasp. Alex squares his shoulders, a glint of defiance flashing in his eyes as he meets the stranger's unwavering gaze.

"There's no problem here, man," Alex replies, his voice steady despite the undercurrent of tension crackling between them. "Just talking to my girl."

The man's lips quirk into a dangerous smile, a predator scenting its prey. "Seems like there's one major problem from where I'm standing," he remarks, his tone deceptively calm. "That being, this is *my girl*." He claims me with a hiss, literally baring his teeth at Alex, daring him to challenge him.

I can feel the weight of the impending storm pressing down on me, a sense of dread knotting in my stomach.

"Come on, man," one of Alex's friends tugs at his arm, trying to pull him away. "She's not worth it," he hisses, but Alex stays firmly planted to the ground, unmoving.

"Oh, she's worth it, alright," the stranger says, undressing me with his eyes. He pulls away from me and starts to slowly, methodically roll up his sleeves. One, then the other, his eyes concentrated on folding the fabric over to perfection. "She's just not worth it to you." He lifts his head slowly and fixes his hard, glacial blue eyes on Alex. "If I ever see you near her again, I'll show you just how much she's worth."

"Man! Fuck! Move, Alex!" the friend yells at Alex, dragging him away from us by force. I watch as they straggle away, hear his friend as he hisses, "You know who the fuck that was, man? Are you suicidal?"

I turn to the stranger standing beside me, mesmerized by his icy blue eyes as he stares at me. An arrogant smirk plays at the corner of his lips.

"What was that?" I whisper.

Jess elbows me, urging me to shut up.

"You're welcome," the stranger says, combing a hand through his waves of dark brown hair.

"What the..."

He doesn't wait for me to finish my sentence. He turns to walk away without a backward glance, the men accompanying him falling into line behind him as they head to the bar.

"What was that?" I ask Jess.

"Girl, just shut the fuck up."

10

ROMEO

The girl glares at me from her table, trying to intimidate me. The insolence on her. I can't help but laugh at her feeble attempt. She scowls and turns away when I raise my glass in her direction. Whispering something to her friend, she crosses her arms over her chest.

"What a feisty little thing," my brother Sandro remarks as he notices the interaction.

He takes a sip of his drink and turns to face the bar.

"All these entitled college kids coming in here, causing trouble," I grumble.

"Good thing you stepped in," Sandro points out.

We've had our fair share of testosterone-fueled fights and damages to our property. It's becoming tiresome. And it's starting to piss me off.

That's why I intervened and helped the girl - just another way to prevent a tantrum and more damage to my establishment.

"She's popular with the boys," Sandro chucks his chin in her direction. He's taken to referring to the frat boys just as they are-frat boys.

I look over at the table again and groan. Her table is swarming with – yes, boys – vying for her attention. I'm not in the mood for any trouble tonight, and I'm seriously considering throwing her out on her ass.

"And there," he points out with a tip of his head. I follow his gaze to a darkened corner of the club, where the ex stands, working his jaw back and forth as he watches the commotion around her table. Obviously, he didn't fall for my little charade any more than anyone else did.

"Fuck me. Why can't I get one night off from the Rich Kids of Hanley Hall?"

Sandro scoffs "You've fucked through enough of them. What's a few more?"

Sandro's the dreamer amongst us. He's the charmer, the romantic. We're three brothers, each one different, but Sandro is the standout. In character as well as in the physical sense. He wears his dark brown hair with the tips highlighted a pale blonde, his blue eyes mesmerizing against his cherubic face. He's built like me, his well-defined muscles stretching his shirt against his wide quarterback's shoulders.

"I don't touch that shit anymore," I remind him. "Little girls parading as women."

"Not even if it's good shit?" He smirks, raises his brows in question and looks over at my fake girlfriend where she stands with a hand on her cocked hip, pointing the boys in the opposite direction.

"Not even if it's lined in gold, brother."

AT SOME POINT, the club is packed to capacity, bodies squeezing against each other like sardines. The bar's so busy, I slide behind it and help the bartenders out, expertly weaving from customer to customer to make sure everyone is taken care of.

Sandro points out that my fake girlfriend has been joined by even more friends, not that I'm keeping tabs. "Busiest we've been in months," he tells me.

"Busiest we've been – ever. Want to make yourself useful? Get behind the bar."

He gives me a sharp look but eventually makes his way over to our side. He's not as adept at handling drinks as I am - this environment is not his forte. Sandro's specialty lies in real estate. He has a talent for flipping properties quicker than the ink can dry on paperwork; it's something he's always been good at. I suppose, when I think about it, we all deal with property in some capacity. I oversee the running of the clubs. Our eldest brother Lazaro manages the hotels, and he does it exceptionally well. And Sandro, well...he just buys and buys and buys. He has a knack for spending our money, then doubling it.

The crowd at the bar dwindles and I take a step back, viewing the open space. The little table at the other end is almost empty, the newcomers succumbing to the beat of the music and making use of the dance floor. My fake girlfriend sits demurely at the table, fiddling with her phone, trying desperately to blend into the background as she begs off more dancing and more wandering hands.

"Mitch." I catch my head bartender's attention and motion toward the table. "Send that table some margaritas on the house," I tell him, before I turn to leave.

"Hey, what about me?" Sandro throws his arms up.

"You stay here," I tell him. "Mitch needs you."

I return to my office, turn on the wall-to-wall monitors and the overhead lamp at my desk, then grab the stack of paperwork demanding my attention. This is my nightly routine: a few hours on the club floor, followed by paperwork, a bit of quiet time, and then I head home. Tonight is no different.

I sift through the numerous documents needing signatures or review, then lean back in my chair, hands behind my neck, cracking the knots in my shoulders. I'm startled to see how much time has passed since I arrived. Glancing at the monitors, I notice that the crowd has thinned as the night stretches past midnight. I find myself focusing on the table where my fake girlfriend had been earlier; it's now empty. I don't even realize I'm doing it until the moment has passed, and I let out a relieved sigh as I shift my attention to another camera. Then another, until my gaze finally settles on the alleyway behind the club.

And it's there that I find my fake girlfriend, pinned up against a wall, her ex-boyfriend's hand wrapped around her throat.

HE LETS HER GO, dropping her like a ragdoll, and my fake girlfriend falls clumsily on her feet, almost toppling over. She coughs, then takes a huge gulp of air. Her breathing is labored, and she reaches up to rub at her throat, soothing away her pain. I watch from a dark corner of the alley, hidden in the shadows, waiting to see how this plays out. I'm almost amused at his stupidity.

"There's a special place in hell for people like you," my fake girlfriend hisses. I watch her shape in the glow of the dim alley lamp as she slowly rises.

The ex steps forward, grits his teeth and takes her throat again. She struggles against him, and when it looks like she's going to pass out, he drops her, and this time, she falls to her knees.

"I won't deprive you of pain, babe," he says, looking down at her. He grabs her shoulders and lifts her again until her back is pressed against the wall. I take in the jeans that are too tight against her skin, the green silk top that cuts low in the front, where his eyes now roam. He holds one hand against her throat while the other ghosts against her chest. She whimpers, tries to disappear into the wall to avoid his touch. It would be almost touching if it wasn't revolting.

He kicks her legs open, lifts a knee and plants it at the apex of her thighs, grinding into her. She turns her face away as his breath skates across her skin.

"I will return all the pain you put me through when you left me." Psychopath.

"You. Hurt. Me," she whispers.

Interesting.

"Nowhere near as much as you hurt me, baby girl. I still haven't lived down the humiliation of being dumped by Hanley's hottest co-ed. We have a score to settle, babe."

Her eyes go wide as he loosens his hand and moves the other to his pants, fumbling with the zipper.

"Don't," she pleads. "You hurt me. You... I told you..."

"Shut up, bitch!" he hisses, his hold on her tight again as he drops his pants, making his intention very clear.

I step out of the dark and take the few steps towards them, my boots tapping ominously against the concrete.

"I wouldn't do that if I were you," I tell him, nodding at his pants once his eyes meet mine. He stumbles back, confused, dropping the girl in the process. She falls to the ground with a thump, and I ignore her as I move toward her ex. He's fumbling with his pants, trying to do them up as he backs away from me.

"What did you think was going to happen, hmmm?" I ask, tilting my head in his direction curiously. "Did you think you'd just rape her and kill her and discard her out in this alley, and no-one would ever know? Your parents pay for your Ivy League education, but it looks like the only education you're getting is the one where you're being a dumbass."

"You're one to talk," he hisses. "What are you doing stalking girls in the middle of the night? I could have your head for this, you know. I know who you are, what you do."

"Is that so?"

"I have friends, you know. You won't get away with this."

"With what? Saving a girl from your limp dick and enormous ego?"

I smirk and shake my head slowly at his stupidity.

"They'll make sure you pay," he threatens.

"Well, they can certainly try."

11

BAYLIN

"Are you going to hurt him?"

He scoffs, lets out an incredulous laugh, as if my morals are unbelievable and my anxieties misplaced.

"The animal was going to rape you, probably kill you and leave your body in an alley to be found by some hapless kid with a ball, and you're worried if I'm going to hurt him?"

When he puts it into context, I can see where my savior is coming from. After he knocked him out with one punch, he hurried me to a parked car and told me he'd drop me off at the campus. Which is where I am now – in his car, that is. A car that, even in my limited knowledge of such things, I can see probably cost several years of one person's wage.

I sit in stunned silence, looking ahead, trying to ignore the waves of angry energy seeping off him. Instead of driving straight to campus, he makes a detour and we're in a drive-through ordering food.

"What'll you have?" he asks.

"No, thank you."

His brow creases as he regards me, then places an order; enough food to feed four people. He parks the car in the lot and rolls down the window, sniffing the night air.

"Can you just drop me off?" I ask.

"First, we eat. In all the excitement tonight, I've forgotten to have my dinner. Eat."

"Thank you, for saving me once again."

"Thank me by eating," he says, around a mouthful of food. He unwraps a burger and holds it up to my mouth. "You look like a girl who likes chicken." He presses it to my lips. The aroma of fried chicken, lettuce and mayo assaults my senses, and I open my mouth, taking a bite. He moves the burger toward him, takes a bite himself, then hands the burger back to me. I sit dumbfounded, looking down at the burger. "I hope you don't mind," he gives me a boyish grin. "I've never tried the chicken here."

I look up at him. His smile is disarming; he has a boyish charm about him, but I can see what's lurking beneath that façade. If it was potent enough to scare off Alex, it can only be some dark sort of evil to rival my ex-boyfriend's.

"Are you too revolted to eat that after I bit into it?"

I give him an odd look. The woman who's too revolted to eat the same burger he's bitten into should get her head examined. Then operated on. There's not a revolting thing about him, and this is never more evident than by the thrum of energy that tingles between my legs.

I lift the burger to my mouth, bite exactly where he did, and something sparks in his eyes. His brilliant blue eyes, a metallic ice shade, turn almost denim in their color, and I'm entranced by them as he sits watching my throat slowly move with every bite.

"I thought you said you were hungry," I remind him.

"I am."

I swallow. Two words, heavily laden with innuendo. The silence stretches between us, and my throat works to keep up with my breathing as we watch one another. In the silence that looms between us, a quiet understanding is reached.

My heart races as his intense stare penetrates me, sending a shiver down my spine. The tension between us is palpable, and I can't resist the magnetic pull drawing me closer to him. Despite the warning bells in my head, I lean in, unable to resist the allure of this mysterious stranger.

A surge of energy flows through me as our lips meet, igniting a fire that has been dormant for too long. My skin is alive, heat washing over it, sweeping me as though I'm floating against a tide.

His touch is warm, electric against my skin, sparking a hunger inside me that I never knew existed. We create our own world together, where nothing else matters except for the two of us. The outside world fades away as we lose ourselves in each other's movements, as if an unseen force conspired to throw us together.

In his arms, I feel free from my past and future worries. There is only this present moment, this unexplainable connection between us.

He grins, and something tugs inside me before he asks the most important question.

"Your place or mine?"

MY FAKE BOYFRIEND lives in a high rise. A fancy multi-level residential building in the heart of the city. I wonder who he is, but I don't stop to overthink things as he tosses his keys in a dish on an entry table and pulls me down a hall into what looks like a living room. Wall to wall windows extend into the night, the bright lights of the city winking in the dark. The city is magnificent from this height, breathtakingly so.

My eyes skirt around the room, take in the dark furniture, all chrome and black wood, very masculine. What little light there is in the room comes from lights that have been dimmed to cast a soft halo across the room, creating an almost romantic atmosphere. I take in the shadowy outline of his sharp jaw as he angles his head my way. In this moment, he is all the light I need.

He pulls me towards him, his grip on my belt secure as he draws me closer until there's barely an inch of space between us. His eyes search mine for any sign of hesitation.

"This is your last chance to back out, little one," he whispers huskily. Despite the condescending tone, I can't help but be drawn in by his intense gaze and the electricity between us. He may call me "little one" but he couldn't be much older than twenty-five himself.

"Why would I want to do that?" I reply breathlessly, the proximity of his body making it hard to form coherent thoughts.

"Because if you don't, I won't be held responsible for what happens next." His words send a shiver of anticipation down my spine. I should be scared; this stranger and his ominous warnings should terrify me. But instead, they only heighten my desire for him.

"That sounds like a warning," I say with a slight smirk.

"You have no idea," he responds, before nipping at my lip and pulling back slightly to look at me through half-closed eyes. I watch transfixed as his tongue darts out to wet his bottom lip before rolling it slowly between his teeth. It's enough to make me melt on the spot.

"What are we doing?" I'm suddenly breathy as I ask.

He lifts his lips in a smirk. "Anything you want to do."

I laugh. It seems my fake boyfriend likes to play games. So, I play along. "What do *you* want to do?"

He laughs playfully then shakes his head, and before I realize what's happening, he grabs me and guides me over to the glass wall. I gasp as my front is pressed against the cool glass and my arms are lifted above my head and locked in place by one of his hands. My body reacts instinctively to his touch, and I let out a small moan at the unexpected impact.

His hot breath skates across my skin as he leans in close and whispers in my ear, "Do you trust me?" Unable to speak, I shake my head ever so slightly, feeling the side of my face press against the glass.

"Good, because I'm not a man to be trusted," he admits with brutal honesty. "Especially not when it comes to women. I can't promise I won't hurt you, but I can promise you the ride of your life."

His words send an electric shock through my body; my senses are suddenly on high alert as his tongue trails sensually along the length of my ear. I let out a moan and my body goes limp in his arms. His hand is the only thing keeping me from sliding to the floor in a pool of desire. Any doubts I had about spending the night with him are quickly erased as I surrender myself completely to his touch and the collision course I've found myself on.

I feel his body press up against mine, all firm muscle and hard ridges; there's nothing soft about this man who rescued me not once but twice tonight. I wonder if he's in the habit of rescuing damsels in distress. I shake off the thought and come back to the moment as he tells me to keep my hands above my head and moves his hands to my waist. He wraps them around my front and works the front of my jeans, lowering the zipper. Then he moves his hands up my front, palming my chest before he grabs the fabric in both hands and pulls it away with one quick, heavy yank. The buttons of my blouse go scattering across the marble, their metallic clink almost deafening in the quiet of the night.

He pulls the blouse past my shoulders, then leaves it there, the cloth bunched around me. I feel him as he moves behind me, drops in a crouch and starts to lower my jeans, his deft fingers making good work of the denim that's stuck to me like a second skin. I realize the man is skilled in what he needs to do to set a woman's body on fire.

When he lowers the jeans all the way to my feet, he taps my ankle wordlessly and I lift my leg, letting him slip my heels off, then my jeans. One leg, then the other. It's like a merry little dance we're performing. Another tap, and I lift; he slips the heels back on. Four-inch black stilettos that put height on me but still make me shorter than he is.

When I feel his breath on the nape of my neck, I'm wearing nothing but my underwear, my heels, and my blouse draped against my shoulders. The mental image I get of me in this position, in so little yet still in so much, makes me faint with desire.

"Hands above your head," he says, when he notices my hands starting to fall. I lift them back up quickly and listen through the rustling behind me. He's getting undressed. I close my eyes and listen carefully, trying to picture each item that comes off as he strips. I hear the tearing of a wrapper, the tiny grunt he emits before he moves back toward me.

His presence hangs like a dark shroud around me, an extended pause, before he presses his lips to the base of my neck.

12

ROMEO

I feel like taking out my phone and snapping a pic. I want to freeze this image forever in my mind, like a tattoo etched into my memory. Her emerald green top falls past her shoulders, and the top ends barely covering her tight ass. Her toned thighs continue to long legs that are spread apart, like she's waiting for me to pat her down. And those heels...damn! Those sexy heels are every man's wet dream.

I rip open the condom wrapper and roll the latex onto my pulsing dick. I squeeze the base, willing the throbbing to settle down long enough for me to make it the two steps toward her.

I kiss her neck, trail soft kisses against her skin and revel in the tiny shivers that course through her body. My hands go to her waist, hook into her pants, start to roll them down slowly, then let them fall around her ankles. I press into her back, lift my hands to her breasts and cup them over her bra. Just the right size cup to fill my hands. But it's not enough; I snap the clasp and let the bra fall down her chest. I move my head back, watch her in the window. She's watching me, her bottom lip caught between her teeth.

This alone is enough to drive me wild. And not many things drive me crazy, but this girl. This girl...she's doing something to me that's shooting sharp blades of fire straight to my loins.

"I warned you, little one," I whisper close to her ear. She whimpers, and the sound makes my dick lurch in hungry defiance.

"You did," her voice is a sultry caress against the window. "You also made me a promise – are you going to deliver?"

A challenge. I love a good challenge. She looks at me from beneath hooded eyes, daring me to make true on my promise.

"I'm going to fuck you into tomorrow and I'm going to have zero remorse once I'm through with you," I whisper.

"Show me," she urges, pushing her ass back into me.

Damn, this woman.

My arm slides across her chest, almost suffocating her as I hold her to me. I move my other hand to her mouth, tell her to open. I stick two fingers in there and tell her to suck. She watches me in the window as she sucks on my fingers like they're a delicacy she can't get enough of. I can't wait to replace them with my dick. I remove my fingers and slide my hand down to her pussy. She's bare and soft, her skin hot under my fingers as I slide them through her soaked folds. She's already so wet for me, and I see just how ready she is with every whimper she emits as I work my fingers back and forth, rubbing against her clit. I pinch her nub, and she releases a strangled groan, her knees threatening to give way. I hold her up, not missing a beat as I glide against her smooth skin, exploring her most intimate region.

"Fuck!" she hisses. She clenches beneath my fingers, and I know she's on the verge of erupting. I remove my fingers, move both hands down to her waist and press her flat into the glass, until her tits are two soft globes against the panel, looking out at the city below.

"Eyes on me," I command, meeting her gaze in the window. They're full of desperation and longing, a silent plea to let her come. She watches me carefully, her pants filling the room. Her chest rises against the glass, her labored breaths igniting a fire within me.

I move into her, line my dick up with her opening, and slowly slide inside her. There's no give in her tight hole, even though I know she's about to cream all over me. Instead of reversing and pushing back in, I push on, driving into her painfully until I hit her walls. She lets out a small yelp and bites into her lip, but she doesn't take her eyes off me. I start to move. Slowly, slowly, picking up a rhythm, my hands anchored at her waist. With every thrust into her, she pushes up against the glass wall, and even from behind her, I can see the heavy peaks of her nipples as they expand with the icy friction.

She moans into the glass, throws her head back even as she rocks back into me, meeting me thrust for thrust. My fingers dig into her the flesh at her waist as her body erupts like a volcano beneath my ministrations. The walls of her pussy tighten, clenching against me as she explodes and I thrust harder, further, until my own climax finds me, and I rush head long into oblivion.

Her legs are shaking so hard, she can't stand straight. I lift her off her feet and carry her to my bedroom, set her down on the edge of the bed and catch the way she pulls her blouse against her chest before I turn to the bathroom.

"Where can I shower?" she asks, as I step back into the room. I throw her a long, assessing gaze as she averts my eyes. I lean against the vanity and cross my arms. I'm naked as the day I was born with my dick saluting once again; he obviously didn't get the memo that we finished the marathon not more than five minutes ago.

My fake girlfriend, flushed with the afterglow of sex, tries to do everything she can to avoid my gaze.

"Hey," I walk over and lift her chin to meet my eyes. "What's the rush?"

"I should get going."

"Is that so?" I lift an eyebrow. "You a love 'em and leave 'em kind of girl?"

"What? No!" She flusters, embarrassment coating her skin. "It's late," she reminds me.

"You have a curfew?"

She shakes her head and shoots me an irritated look, then pulls the torn blouse tighter.

"I made you a promise," I remind her. "I don't break promises."

For the first time since we fucked, her eyes meet mine of their own volition. There's a trace of fear there, though I'm not sure if it's of me or of what happened between us.

"This about the ex-boyfriend?" I ask her. She drops her eyes. It's definitely about the ex-boyfriend. "Tell me."

"Thank you for saving me tonight," she whispers. But me being here is going to bring trouble to your doorstep."

I frown; I can't help the snicker that escapes my mouth.

"Trouble is my middle name, little one."

She rolls her eyes, shakes her head and fists a hand on the bed.

"He's not a nice person," she tells me. "You've probably been the bravest one to stand up to him so far, but he doesn't take rejection very well."

"Meaning?"

"Meaning every time I've had any sort of contact with a guy other than him, he's managed to make trouble for the guy and create problems for me."

"But your table was surrounded by guys tonight," I remind her.

"And you will have noticed I didn't so much as entertain any one of them. The last guy I danced with. *Danced* with..." she enunciates "ended up with his car on fire."

"Ahhh," and I finally get it. She's not with him, but neither will he let anyone else have her. "You're worried that he's going to hurt me somehow? Because you went home with me?"

She nods, lowers her head in shame. When she's not the one who has anything to be ashamed of.

"Well, let me put it into perspective for you. You're already here, so the damage is already done. Does it really matter to him whether you spend one hour, two, or even six hours here with me? I promised you a ride to remember, and I plan on delivering."

She doesn't argue any further. Instead, I move forward and pull her across the bed until we are both lying on our sides facing each other, covered by a thin blanket. It's something I've never done with anyone else before, the experience alien. Her big brown eyes focus on me, and I can sense her vulnerability. By morning, she'll be gone, and I'll probably have already forgotten what she looks like. But I'll make sure to pay her ex-boyfriend a visit and try to set him straight. He's an asshole who used his ego to instill fear in her for no reason. For now, I let myself get lost in the beauty of her honey gold eyes. They're rich and entrancing in a way that I can't resist.

"You have beautiful, soulful eyes," I tell her, caressing a lock of her hair between my fingers. I push it back over her shoulder and continue to watch her. The blanket rises and falls with every lift of her chest, her breaths rapid and excited. I wipe a hand against my jaw, trying to slow down my thoughts. My desire. My need to be inside her again. I push her onto her back. Her breath catches as I lift to hover over her, my eyes flicking across her face. She licks her lips in anticipation, her bedroom eyes driving me insane. She wants me just as much as I want her.

I slide down her body; her beautiful body that's curvy in all the right places, athletic in others. She's perfectly imperfect but all I can see is her beauty. I stop at her navel, lick around her belly, slow sensual movements before I lower myself to her thighs. She closes her legs self-consciously, and I lift my head to meet her gaze.

"We're going again, little one," I inform her.

"I need to shower."

I shake my head, then lower it to her pussy and inhale the heady scent of her arousal.

"Not before I taste your cum."

13

BAYLIN

This man. This man has got a mouth on him, and he knows what to do with it. He eats me out until I'm panting toward my orgasm. My moans fill the room as I climb and climb and climb, then he pulls away, leaving me hanging off the ledge, wanting more. Over and over again, denying me the rush of an orgasm. Prolonging the moment. It becomes difficult for me to breathe, and I just want to come. But he has other ideas.

He ties my hands to the headboard after I move my hand to my pussy to relieve myself.

"You come when I make you come," he grits from between clenched teeth. His eyes have darkened to a hypnotic denim blue, threatening to sweep me up in their magical trance.

"I want...to come," I hiss back, my lower body lifting off the bed, seeking any sort of friction. He's sitting on his knees between my outstretched legs, moving his hands slowly down my thighs. He bends, bites my thigh, and an intense sensation moves through my body until I arch my back. He licks up the same thigh, back to my pussy, then licks through my folds again, lapping at the liquid pooling on my skin. As soon as my pleasure braces at the edge of orgasm, he pulls away again, and I groan in disappointment.

I watch as he retrieves a condom, rips at the packaging, then rolls it against his long shaft. He yanks on his dick...once, twice, then runs his palm through my folds until his skin is coated with my arousal. He starts to pump his dick, and I watch on in fascination as he strokes his hand up and down deliberately, his eyes never leaving mine.

When his hands fall away, he removes the tie, releases my hands then quickly flips onto his back and takes me with him. He lifts me until I'm on top of him, drives his dick into me like it's a stake, and tells me to ride him.

"Ride me until you come, little one." His hands burn into my flesh where they latch onto my hips, a bruising, vicelike grip that alternates between pleasure and pain. "Ride me hard, baby." He lifts me off his dick, then slams me back down until I'm enveloping him like a second skin. So deep. His thrusts come hard and fast as I grind down, taking every last inch of him.

"Fuck!" I hiss, as my orgasm builds and threatens to explode. And when it comes, it's explosive; with one final thrust, he pushes up into me with a roar, parking inside me as I moan through my orgasm, tidal waves of pleasure washing over me relentlessly.

My THIGHS ache and my arms feel heavy, as though held down by weights. He runs a bath, filling the room with warm steam that drifts over every surface. The bathroom is luxurious, bigger than my dorm room, with a beautiful white tub that stands in the center. I watch him effortlessly pour liquid into the water, turning it a mesmerizing shade of deep blue. The aroma of the sea fills the air, soothing my tired muscles. He guides me to the bath, helping me settle in before joining me, holding me close against his chest. Instantly, I feel tension melting away as I inhale the refreshing scent of the ocean.

"You're exhausted," his husky voice whispers in my ears, as his fingers trail through my hair.

"Feels like I'm floating," I murmur in response, feeling content and at peace in the moment. We sit in comfortable silence, surrounded by the calming scent of the sea.

As the tension continues to seep out of my body, I can't help but marvel at the subtle magic of the bath. The water seems to hum with a gentle energy, as if it holds secrets from ancient times within its cerulean depths. I lean back against him, feeling the steady rhythm of his heartbeat matching the lapping of the imaginary waves. Only the present moment matters as we sit this way for endless minutes; even as the water grows tepid, we're reluctant to move or break this trance we've found ourselves in.

I feel his lips brush against my temple, a feather-light caress that sends shivers down my spine. I let go, surrendering to the embrace of the bath, of his arms, of the unknown. The water cradles me, a liquid cocoon that seems to wash away not just the grime of the day, but the worries and fears that nestled deep within my soul earlier.

Time loses meaning in the tranquil space. We are suspended in a bubble of warmth and serenity, insulated from the chaos of the world outside. The only reality is the here and now, the sensation of water against skin, the gentle rise and fall of our intertwined breaths.

I feel him shift behind me. "We need to eat," he murmurs into my neck. I feel the hard ridge of his dick as it glances against my skin, ready to go again. But he's right. We do need to eat something if we plan to keep going.

"Mmm," I hum, reluctant to move. He cups some water and lifts it to my shoulders, releasing the water like a waterfall to roll over my skin. He kneads my shoulders, his fingers pressing into my flesh and I throw my head back into his chest, pure ecstasy overcoming me. Every sensuous touch, every breath he releases across my skin, ignites a fire within that threatens to consume me.

When he's done, he rises and holds out a hand to me. I rise with him and he moves into me, his erection pressing against my navel. My eyes fix on our connected bodies, mesmerized by the image. He lifts my chin until our eyes meet, pulling me out of my stupor. His pupils are dilated, his gaze intense as he penetrates my focus. Without warning, his mouth is on mine, his tongue lashing at me with violent ferocity. His bites down on my lip, drawing blood, then pulls away and licks his lip, his gaze dark. My chest rises, my breaths coming quick and powerful. He steps out of the bathtub and lifts me out, carrying me across his chest, his mouth sealed on mine once again as he walks us out of the bathroom, trailing water behind us.

"Time to eat," he mumbles, before throwing me on the bed and prowling towards me.

I WAKE WITH A START, my heart pounding in my ears. A thin layer of sweat coats my skin. I look around the room, realize where I am and that I must have fallen asleep after our third round of mind-blowing sex.

A tiny trickle of early morning light filters through the blinds, and a quick look at the clock on the wall tells me it's just shy of five am. Something must have woken me up, because there's a sinking feeling in the pit of my stomach.

I throw my legs over the side of the bed, look back and find my fake boyfriend sleeping with a hand thrown above his head, his lower body covered by the thin blanket. I can't stop the heaviness that settles deep in the marrow of my bones. It's not guilt, it's not self-loathing; it's something else altogether that I can't quite put my finger on.

I rise from the bed and retrieve my bag in the living room. There are eight missed calls on my phone and two voicemails. All from my mother. I call her back without listening to the voicemails.

"Baylin! Where are you?"

The concern in her tone has me on edge and I'm instantly on high alert. She's not one to be easily agitated.

"You know where I am, mama. What's wrong?"

"Your sister. You have to come home. She's...your sister...," her voice cracks, and she pours her heart out in the sob that shoots through the phone line.

"What's wrong with Maggie?" My hackles rise. We're two sisters, and apart from university which has put some distance between us, we're inseparable.

"She's been in an accident, Baylin. You must come, quick."

The bottom falls out of my world as my mother continues to sob through the phone. I don't stop to ask how bad it is. I don't ask her what happened. I just grab my jeans off the ground and tell her I'll be on the first bus out.

I don't bother showering. Even though I smell of sex and sin. I step back into the bedroom, where my savior is still asleep, his shallow breaths filling the room. My blouse is damaged beyond repair, so I leave it and borrow his shirt, slip it on and tuck it in at the waist. The shirt is so big, I'm swimming in it, but I can't help the shiver that runs up and down my spine as his scent is transferred to my skin.

I don't stop to wake him up. I don't even leave my number. Somehow, I don't think he's the sort of guy that does do-overs with one night stands. I stand staring down at him in his peaceful sleep, a smile playing on my lips before I grab my bag and head for the door. I slip quietly out of the apartment and exit the building, and as I walk quickly down the street, I realize I never even got his name.

THE PRESENT - 2023

A sinner's true punishment is the silence of their conscience.

14

ROMEO

Pine needles crunch underfoot, my breaths coming in measured puffs as I dodge between trees, their branches reaching out like hands trying to drag me back away from my prey. Even the forest is working against me, trying to keep me from my little bird. My heart races, thudding against my ribs in a frantic rhythm of determination as adrenaline courses through me.

I had to discard my mask a while back; if anything, it was just hindering my progress, and I didn't want to lose Baylin to any of the numerous ravines here before I carried out my plan. If she was going to die, it would be by my hand and mine alone.

Imagine my surprise when I learnt that Baylin Reyes, the woman who could bring down our carefully constructed house of cards, is the very same woman I met five years ago in my club. The one I spent countless hours trying to discreetly track down after she slipped out of my apartment without so much as a backward glance. No woman's ever done that to me before; it's always been me trying to unclench their fingers from around my soul, but this woman...this woman broke all the rules and she left me. The one woman I would've wanted another round with. The one I wouldn't have minded seeing again. Nothing permanent, just great sex without all the drama that usually comes attached to girls. I knew from the moment I saw her that she was different...in so many ways.

I see her in a break in the trees as she hooks a sharp left in an effort to throw me off her scent. I feel the hollow of my cheeks tighten as I try to suppress a smile. Little bird has made this so much fun for me; it's more entertainment than I've had in a while.

I pump my legs, speeding up, and I can swear I hear her heart shuddering through the woods as her pants reach my ears. She may be fast, but I can guarantee I'm faster and better versed when it comes to the woods. This, after all, is my playground.

Suddenly I see her, barely forty yards ahead of me, her hands on her knees as she takes a moment to catch her breath. This time, I can't prevent the smile that plays on my lips. Just the thought of what I'm going to do to her has me salivating in a way that makes my loins ignite with fire.

She starts to move again, and I gain on her, almost leaping through the air the final stretch until I collide with her body, sending her sprawling to the mossy ground. My body is a cage, pinning her beneath me. She lashes out, bucking her hips to throw me off her, her elbows and knees seeking any possible advantage over my hulking form.

"Good try, Baylin," I growl, straddling her, our heavy breaths mingling in the charged air.

"Get off me!" she spits, her voice a mix of fury and fear.

My muscles tense in response to her defiance, a rod of thrilling excitement coursing through my body. Her eyes pin me, wary and fearful of what's to come. She tries to put on a brave front, but there's no hiding the fact that in this moment, she is absolutely terrified of me.

We are two forces of nature, locked in a battle that is about more than just physical strength. It's about wills clashing, about her desperate need to protect what is left of her fractured world. And me, her enemy, trying to protect the future of what remains of my family. We lay suspended in that one breathless moment, two souls united by blood and violence, divided by drawn lines between good and evil.

"Up!" I command, lifting her to her feet.

She struggles against me as I take out the length of rope from my pocket and start to wind it against her wrists. She argues with me, cursing and kicking at my shins. She almost slips in the process without the use of her hands, and I hold her upright, giving her a stern look.

Her skin chafes against the coarse rope as she tries to loosen the secure knots. I push her up against the rough bark of a nearby tree. My shadow sparks in her eyes as I loom over her, igniting her fear and dimming her world. The rustle of leaves in the slight breeze is a deceptive peace that mocks my captive, making her question if there's someone else out here.

"There's no-one here but you and me," I taunt her. She tilts her head in defiance, narrowing her eyes at me, trying to show me she's not afraid. Brave little thing, my little bird. But she has no idea what's coming her way. "Let's make this interesting," I murmur.

The glint of the gun in my hand is cold, an unforgiving metal that I wield with a lover's touch. I can feel her heart hammer out of her chest as her breaths pick up. I aim the gun, not at her, but at the trees around us. Then I start to spin on my feet. Around and around and around, my eyes closed until I'm a mass of dizzying nerves.

I don't know where I stop, but when I do, I land on the balls of my feet with ultimate precision, not as though I was just whipping myself into a frenzy of dizzying heights. I fire indiscriminately, without opening my eyes. My twist on Russian Roulette. The bullet could so easily have pierced her heart. Or her head. She screams as the shot echoes like a thunderclap, stripping away another shred of her dignity, giving me more control over her.

I open my eyes, find her own are open wide and horrified, tears staining her pink cheeks. A viciously cruel smile touches my lips, her fear caressing my wounds like a balm.

"You're certifiably crazy," she whispers, falling to her knees. I should have tied her to the tree.

"Perhaps." I shoot her a thoughtful look, my eyes gliding down the length of her body. I prop her up, lean my body against hers to hold her upright. I need her standing for this. "Perhaps I'm just a madman. Perhaps I'm crazy. How far do you think my crazy will go?" I move closer, my breath whispering against her face.

She says nothing as she squeezes her eyes shut, her lip quivering. I angle the gun at her chest, tracing the outline of her V-neck. It's cold out, and I can feel the chill biting at her skin. The gun only adds to her torment.

"Are you scared, Baylin?" I taunt her. Her name sounds like butter on my tongue. My hand betrays me, caressing the side of her cheek, my fingers webbing across her face. Her skin buzzes under the touch of my fingers, the sensation leaving her breathless, though I don't think her breathlessness is born of anything but cold, brutal fear.

She doesn't look away from me, even after I lower the gun and lift both hands to her top. With little effort, I rip down the front of her shirt until the fabric hangs limply on either side of her body. She's wearing a black bra – even her underwear is in mourning, the black wrapping against her olive skin. She whimpers, and a torrent of tears scales the valley of her cheeks.

Her tears are beautiful, a torrential downpour as her fearful eyes follow my hands. I pick the gun up, aim again at the trees, and start to spin.

"Stop!" she screams, but I don't.

I turn round and round and round until my adrenaline spikes dangerously and my cruel laugh fills the forest.

I shoot after I come to a stop, then open my eyes, the sound of her pleas like music to my ears. My dick strains against the fabric of my dress pants as I stare at her. She's not beautiful by any measure, but there's something mesmerizing about her. She's absolutely stunning when she cries.

Her knees are weak as she tries to hold herself up but fails, lacking the support of her tied hands. I step up to her shivering body; if she stays out here much longer, she could succumb to hypothermia, and then where would that get me? That would ruin all my fun.

"So lovely when you cry," I murmur, though it's more to myself than anything else. I close in on her, stick my tongue out and lick up her cheek, tasting the saltiness of her tears. The liquid fuels me, making me harder. I lick her other cheek, even as she turns her cheek and tries to avoid my touch, a far cry from the way she molded her body to mine five years ago. She still tastes the same, her body still feels the same against mine.

I move a hand down and unbutton her jeans, then flip the zipper down. When she tries to slink to the ground, resisting my touch, I weave a hand around her neck and watch as her eyes expand in terror. But there's also something there, something so minute, it's barely perceptible.

"Is my little bird turned on?"

She shakes her head vehemently, her eyes a silent plea for me to stop. But I don't. I push her jeans down past her waist, but before I can lower them past her thighs, she lifts a knee and aims it directly at my chest.

I stumble back and she runs. My little bird runs. With her hands tied in front of her. Before she can get far, I grab my gun and fire. She stops running, shrinks into herself but doesn't turn around. Her shoulders quake as I approach.

"I would've liked to take my time and finish our little game on a high, but I'm running out of options here, little bird."

My voice is scathing, blunt. She stands, her head bowed, her small whimpers filling the forest. Even the permanent residents of the woods have disappeared out of fear of what may happen next.

"Don't call me that!" she hisses.

I ignore her. Instead, I push her to her knees, untie her hands and retie them behind her back, rendering her completely helpless. I stand behind her, put the gun to the back of her head and take pleasure in having her at my mercy once again.

"Please. What do you want? I haven't done anything to you," she reminds me.

"It's not what you have done, it's what you may do," I tell her.

"Please, I can't...I can't breathe."

"That's a normal reaction when you have a gun pointed at your head, *Baylin*." I let her name roll over my tongue. I never quite got her name all those years ago, and now her name feels like a melody on my tongue.

I push her forward, until her face hits the dirt, then take great pleasure in turning her over, my tainted little bird with her tear-stained face now filthy with the sins of the earth.

She lays on her back, looking up at me, waiting. I crouch down beside her, continue pushing her jeans down until they're off and I discard them over my shoulder.

She's wearing black cotton panties, her tummy a flat valley that leads down to long, toned legs. She whimpers again, crosses one leg over the other in a feeble attempt to protect her modesty. My nostrils flare, but it's not because she's hiding herself from me. It's because even in her current state, even with fear trickling down her spine, I can't miss the wet patch that stains the front of her panties.

A flush of warmth spreads through her as she sees me looking at her crotch, shame coloring her cheeks.

"Damn you," she whispers, a tremor in her voice. "Damn you to hell and back!"

I straddle her body, then bend down to meet her. My mouth is on hers, my kiss demanding, taking, giving. My tongue teases past the seam of her lips, even as she fights me, while my hands are everywhere, igniting fires I have no right to feel.

"If I'm going to hell, little bird, I'm taking you right along with me."

15

BAYLIN

Five years ago, I spent the most amazing night with a man who I never saw again after that night. He never told me his name and I never asked – it was just a momentary escape from my ex that evolved into a crazy night. But now, five years later, that same man that was once nameless stands in front of me, only now he has a name. Now he has a role. Romeo Riccardi. My own worst nightmare come to life.

I can feel the uncertainty and danger vibrating off him. He's like a wild animal, hungry and untamed, with a gaze that mirrors his desires. But this whole situation is wrong and insane. He abducted me, and he probably killed those men at the supermarket. I am most likely going to die by his hand. No, I'm definitely going to die by his hand. Psychopaths don't kidnap women, take them to secluded cabins in the middle of nowhere, and then let them live to tell the tale. Especially not someone like Romeo Riccardi - handsome face, dirty body, living by his own rules as a crime lord who wields his power without mercy.

The question hangs between us, unspoken but heavy with significance. And foolishly, I answer it with the only truth that matters in that moment - the undeniable need reflected in my own eyes. I know

I'm going to regret this later as the life lays bleeding out of me, but all I can think of is the euphoria, the high I'll feel, no matter how temporary, that may take the edge off as I meet my demise.

He stands, lifts me by the shoulders, and slams my back up against a nearby tree. Rough bark scratches painfully against my skin, and I know I'll pay in pain later after I release from this daze I find myself in.

He stalks towards me, his hands on the hem of his pants before he slides them down. He toes his boots off, his blazer is next to go, followed by his shirt, and my breath catches. There's not an inch of skin along his arms and chest that isn't covered in ink. Colors swirl against his taut body, yet they're still not enough to hide the obvious muscles that he has obviously worked so hard to maintain. I'm mesmerized by the canvas that is his body, a work of art no amount of fear could ignore.

His lips crash against mine, and I can feel the weight of his sins pressing against me, threatening to consume us both in a fiery inferno of desire and destruction. But in this moment, none of that matters. In his arms, I find a dangerous kind of solace, a twisted sense of belonging that both terrifies and excites me. It's as if we are two halves of a fractured whole, drawn together by forces beyond our control. And though I know that this dance on the edge of madness will inevitably lead to my ruin, I cannot bring myself to pull away. In his arms, I am both a captive and a willing participant in this dangerous game of cat and mouse.

Romeo's erection presses into my body, his hard frame pinching at my soul. He takes my mouth with unbridled madness, his hand wound around my neck. Move one inch, and he could snuff me out with one squeeze. Of that, I'm sure. His fingers are like liquid gold around my skin, before they move toward my head and he grabs at my hair, pulling my head back.

I regard him through the slits of my eyes as his mouth leaves me and he looks down at my face, his mouth curling into a cruelly defiant streak on an otherwise beautiful face. His blue eyes darken, stormy waters as he moves toward my neck, kissing then nipping until he breaks skin. Sharp pain shoots down my neck, and I feel the warmth of his tongue as he sucks at my neck, erasing the evidence of his madness.

"Intoxicating," he breathes, licking his way across to my mouth again.

And just as quickly as his mouth clamps against mine, he lets go and moves back. He runs both hands down my sides, then tears my panties off in one swift movement. I gasp at the suddenness of his actions, but my protestations die in my throat as he lifts one of my legs and winds it around his waist, holding me up against the tree.

He removes his boxers, and although too afraid to look, my eyes lower of their own accord. He's hard, his engorged dick throbbing painfully at the tip, screaming for release. There isn't a flicker of emotion as he pushes into me, pushes past my body's natural refusal, inching into me until he's seated all the way inside, violating me in a delicate dance between captor and prey.

He starts to move, thrusting in and out, in and out, a perfect fit inside me. I edge close to my orgasm, my teeth biting down painfully on the insides of my cheek. For just this moment in time, for just this day, in this time and place, I forget the pain of where I am and in whose arms I'm now held captive. I erase all thoughts of my life ending today or tomorrow, and I chase the high of my orgasm. I run after it desperately, my moans filling the air around us, as he rams into me, two animals in the privacy of the woods.

"Want to come, little bird?"

I ignore him and throw my head back, moaning softly into the trees. He pushes into me, rests his body up against mine, two souls intertwined in this merry dance. His hand presses into the back of my head, bringing me into him, and he rests his head on top of mine, squeezing the life out of me with his closeness. And with one last thrust, he angles upwards and touches something deep inside me, wrenching my orgasm from me at the same time that he throws his head back and roars with his own.

～

THE STEAM from the shower clouds the mirror, blurring my reflection as I stand there, stripped bare not just in flesh but in spirit. The water cascades over me, but it can't wash away the chaos of emotions that cling to my skin like a second layer—guilt, desire, confusion. My tears mix with the water until it becomes hard to distinguish one from the other.

I close my eyes and let the hot water envelop me, switching off all emotion as I think of what happened in the woods today. The chase through the woods, then the subsequent madness of Romeo shooting off rounds in the woods, endangering my life. The stupid game that led to me running again, then his unravelling me after he undressed me and gazed upon me like I was an offering in the wild.

Then he fucked me. Hard. Rough. Up against a tree. And I wanted him to. I came. I fucking came harder than I've come before, all the while thinking this is the moment where his hand around my neck will squeeze and he'll be done with me. But he didn't kill me. Instead, he fucked me until we both came – hard – then he carried me back over his shoulder to the cabin and dumped me unceremoniously in the shower.

I can't even start to think of the emotions wreaking havoc on me, getting fucked brutally by a man who may or may not be my future killer. And loving every minute of it. I wanted him to fuck me. I chased that high. I wanted to feel full, and complete, and thoroughly fucked, and I didn't care that the beautiful man standing in front of me is a killer. What sort of a person does that make me?

I dry myself off with the towel Romeo left out for me. He also set down a set of clothes; obviously he's thought of everything. A spark of hope shot through me when he placed the clothes on the bench; perhaps he wasn't going to kill me after all. Why would he have gone to the trouble of bringing clothes, then, if he was only going to kill me? But my hopes were dashed quickly as he looked lazily from the clothes to me and read my emotions well. Obviously, it's a talent of his, reading emotions.

"Don't read too much into it, little bird," he had said. "I'm always prepared for everything." And with that, he had turned and walked out of the bathroom, shutting the door behind him. Which had surprised me, because what sort of a monster gives his captive her privacy?

~

"You haven't killed me yet," I say, as I sit at the small table and he moves a plate in front of me.

After I'd showered, he'd handcuffed me to the bed while he showered. The handcuffs didn't deter sleep from finding me, and I quickly proceeded to fall into a fitful sleep until I stirred sometime later. I was surprised to wake and find him dressed in another impeccable outfit – his signature black dress pants and black shirt, though this time with a tan sports coat and tan boots. He was an oddity out in the woods, dressed more like he was ready to go to a country club.

"We're having too much fun," he scoffs, pointing his chin at my plate.

"Why do you dress like that?"

"Like what?"

"Suitably fashionable, but no-where near prepared for the woods."

"Did you see me struggle in this get up earlier when I mowed you down?"

My lips form a flat line, and I shake my head. No, he did not struggle. If anything, I did. While he just looked like he had stepped out of the pages of a magazine, even after stalking me through the woods.

"How long will I have to stay here?" I ask him. If I can just get him to keep talking.

"As long as it takes."

I perk up in my chair, suddenly interested in everything he has to say.

"As long as what takes?"

He shakes his index finger at me slowly, tells me I'm a naughty girl. But then he surprises me with his next words.

"Long enough for Detective Handler to forget you exist."

16

ROMEO

I haven't seen her in five years, but so much has happened since then. I secretly tried to find her after that night, but she seemed to have disappeared completely. Then the family business demanded all of my attention. And then Sandro died. Just thinking about him makes it hard for me to breathe. He was the only one who truly understood me and acted as both my brother and my best friend. He kept my madness in check until he was gone. After his death, everything changed and I became someone unrecognizable; a beast with a heavy burden to carry.

I gave up on finding Baylin after some time, chalking it up to being "one of those things." Business kept growing and expanding into new areas. Men like us, we can never have enough money if we stay still. So we worked harder, played faster, and rose to the top, competing with the heavyweights in our playground. But there was always a void without our youngest brother. He never got to enjoy the fruits of our labor; instead, he was killed by unknown assailants at a truck stop.

The most thrilling thing that has happened since my depression over Sandro's death was running into Baylin again. Salvatore told me she witnessed the killing of Jacob Arens. And imagine my shock when, as I waited outside her house, she walked out casually and went on her way while I sat in my car unnoticed. What confused me even more was Detective Handler's interest in her. I kept an eye on her from afar until Handler started stalking her; that's when I decided to take matters into my own hands because I couldn't risk losing another brother or getting caught up in a system that would destroy us. So I took her from the street with help from Alphonse and brought her to safety at the cabin.

At the cabin, nestled deep within a dense forest where the light struggles to pierce through the thick canopy above, I watch Baylin with an intensity bred from years of growing darkness within me. The air is thick with the scent of pine and the undercurrent of my looming menace.

She watches me as I pace back and forth on the creaking floorboards, my mind racing with conflicting emotions. Seeing Baylin again has awakened in me a newer, darker sentiment that twists inside me like a viper. In the years following my youngest brother's death—a wound that has never truly healed—I've been transformed. The pain has metastasized into something grotesque, turning me into a creature driven by retribution and sadistic pleasure.

My plans for Baylin are meticulous and cruel. I envision days of psychological torment, weaving in threats and revealing truths at calculated intervals to fracture her composure. I imagine her confusion turning into terror as she realizes the depth of my transformation into depravity.

But even as I laid out my plans with cold precision, a part of me— the human part that hadn't yet succumbed entirely to the abyss— fought against the tide of my darker impulses. It whispered of forgiveness and redemption, words that seemed alien in my current state but flickered in my mind like dying embers.

In this secluded world I've created, where only the sounds of nature's ambivalence can be heard, I stand over Baylin. I watch her stir slightly, her eyelids fluttering as consciousness begins to claw its way back. A twisted anticipation built within me as I prepared to embark on my macabre journey.

As she awakens fully, confusion etches across her lovely features before settling into recognition—and then dread—as she sees my transformed visage: not the man she once knew but a specter intent on destruction.

Our eyes meet—hers wide with fear; mine darkened with purpose—and in that prolonged moment, I feel both damned and divine; an absolute monster reveling in the terror I can invoke yet silently mourning the loss of what could have been if fate had been kinder. The cabin is primed to become our world—a stage set for tragedy or redemption—and I step closer to her to begin this grim performance.

Baylin's voice trembles as she breaks the heavy silence in the dimly lit cabin. "What do you want from me, Romeo?" Her whisper barely makes it through the stillness.

A cold smile curls on my lips, void of any warmth or compassion. "I want you to understand, Baylin," I reply with a chilling edge. "Understand the agony that consumes me at the thought of you exposing what you saw."

Her eyes search mine, begging for mercy that I no longer possess. "I can't believe this," she says softly, her hands quivering against the rough bindings. "This has nothing to do with me."

"You were there," I remind her.

"I was there, but I'm not involved. Please don't drag me into your war."

"You weren't involved until you were. Wrong place, wrong time." My tone hardens with each word. "And now Detective Handler has his eyes on you. You're involved in a world beyond your comprehension."

Tears fill Baylin's eyes and her breath hitches in fear. "You don't know what you're saying, Romeo," she implores. "I swear I didn't see anything. I can't tell what I don't know."

A mocking chuckle escapes my lips as I circle around her, predatory and unyielding. "Oh, Baylin," I murmur mockingly, "it's far too late for that now. Detective Handler doesn't follow the same rules."

I kneel before her, my gaze piercing through her composure. "You will understand my pain, Baylin," I declare with determination. "You will witness the darkness within me, and I'll make sure you never come near that precinct again."

Silence falls between us once more, suffocating in its heaviness. Baylin's eyes brim with tears as she stares into my soulless gaze. In this moment, we stand on the edge of destiny - two souls connected by tragedy and fate, hurtling towards a collision of despair and redemption. There is only one way this ends. There can be no other way; despite the fire she ignites within me, she will eventually become expendable. She's too much of a threat, and I know Detective Handler is waiting for his chance to strike.

"You saved me once," she whispers, recalling that night at the club years ago. When I saved her not once, but twice, from her abusive ex-boyfriend who wouldn't take no for an answer. It's funny how things work out - I would do it all over again. Save her every time. Only for her to die by my own hand.

17

ROMEO

My little bird's hands move of their own accord, sliding across her slick skin, tracing lines of tension and unrest. She thinks she's alone in the sanctuary of the cabin's modest bathroom, but I have eyes everywhere.

My breath hitches as I watch her fingers find a rhythm that promises release from a source other than me. I'm both mad and fascinated in equal measure. Mad that it's not my fingers tantalizing her clit, and fascinated by her movements as she spreads her folds and plunges a finger deep inside her core.

I stand outside, leaning forward against the rough wooden wall of the cabin, my gaze fixed on the small, illicit window into her vulnerability; a crack in the wall so small it's barely noticeable. I watch with predatory stillness, my body responding to the sight of Baylin lost in a moment of stolen privacy as she showers. My lips part slightly, an involuntary reaction to the intimate spectacle, feeling the heat stir within me as if her fire has seeped through the walls and into my veins.

A shiver runs down my spine as her movements grow more frantic, more purposeful. There is shame, yes, but it's overshadowed by the raw need to release, to feel something other than the crushing weight of her own grief and helplessness. For a fleeting second, I'm tempted to show myself, to let her know that my invasive eyes are watching her unravel. The thought licks at the edges of my restraint, as I continue to watch her in rapt fascination. I've already had her once in the forest, yet even that wasn't enough. The more time I spend with her, watching her, tormenting her, the more I find I want to bend her, break her, bury myself deep inside her.

My hand moves to mirror hers, my self-control fraying at the edges as I observe every quiver and sigh that escapes her. The fabric of my pants tightens for the second time today, constricting me as I ache to break through the barrier of my desire.

"Fuck," I whisper, the word both a curse and a prayer—the embodiment of everything forbidden and yet inevitable between us.

I reach into my pants, releasing my jerky dick into the cool night air. The angry head looks back at me in defiance as I start to run my hand along the length, cupping the head and rubbing my palm over it to spread the pre-cum over my skin. My hand moves along my shaft, up and down, as I milk it, moving to the head then back down until my hand hits my balls, tight and full and begging for release. I squeeze, as tight as pleasurably tolerable, before I release again, delaying my own gratification.

I bite down on my lip, suppressing a moan as I teeter on the edge of oblivion. I start to pump harder, throw my head back and see her face in my mind's eye, then open my eyes and look back through the crack in the wall. Her jagged movements are coming faster and more frantic, as she grits her teeth and rubs at her clit, tamping down her impending orgasm. And in that moment, whether by some twist of fate or the ironically hot and intimately private connection we're not sharing, I explode dramatically, ropes of come coating my hand as I squeeze every last drop out of my dick.

As I finally shatter under the relentless pressure of my own strokes, waves of release crashing over me, Baylin mirrors my climax, her silent moans muffled behind a torrent of water as it slides down her body. And though we're divided by walls and secrets, for one brief instant, we share the same breath, the same pulse, the same aching hunger that no amount of distance could diminish.

"YOU HAVE MORE chance of survival if you do as you're told," I warn her, as we get into the car. The gun is strapped to my left side, and I've promised her I'll use it if she steps out of line. Not that I think we'll run into anyone where we're going, but who knows how many other psychos are roaming these here woods. I've been told this area is a favorite hunting ground for serial killers, which is precisely the reason I decided to buy this place. It might be way off the beaten path, but it serves the purpose intended. Not that I'm a serial killer, by any means.

I'm going stir crazy sitting in the cabin all day and decide to go for a drive. But I can't very well leave my little bird alone at the cabin. There's no telling what she'll get up to.

We drive for about forty minutes in relative silence, passing only sparse traffic on the main road. I've engaged the locks on all doors so there's no chance that she'll jump out of the car. Not that she tries anything. I think she understands the danger I pose to her. And I believe she knows she's safer with me than out there in the middle of nothing where there's no chance of escape.

We wind up the steepest hill until we get to a lookout high above the forest and I park the car. It's deserted, just like I thought it would be. Not many people come up this way, especially not after it became a notorious suicide spot. Only two ways to go out in this town; if a serial killer doesn't get you here, the cliffside will. I smirk as I think of this and turn to look at my little bird, who sits looking out at the view.

"Just so you know," I start, and she turns to face me, her curious brown eyes settling on me in interest. "Dolton's Rock – notorious suicide hotspot."

"And?"

"I could so easily throw you off the cliff's edge and no-one would be the wiser." I watch her face blanch, drain of its color. "You witnessed a traumatic event. You're depressed, beside yourself with grief. Disappeared without leaving a note because you didn't want to burden the ones you love. Eventually, they'd find your body...maybe just bones, but they'd still have something to bury."

"Why are you telling me this?" she asks, horrified. Her hand goes to her chest, and she clings to the fabric of her shirt as though clinging to life itself.

"Just to remind you that if you do anything stupid, I will not think twice about throwing you over this mountain."

My eyes are always on my little bird as I call my brother.

Baylin sits on a bench under a tree and looks out over the valley, lost in her thoughts. At times, she flicks her eyes in my direction, but otherwise leaves a welcome distance between us as I dial into my brother's network.

"Brother," he greets me, more pissed off than I've ever heard him.

"Lazaro."

"Why the fuck would you take off and take the girl with you?" he fumes, then launches into a tirade about my reckless behavior and how Detective Handler is breathing down his neck, asking about Baylin Reyes.

"Careful brother, or I'll think you don't trust my judgment."

"Well, right about now, I don't."

I consider his words for a moment. On any other day, they may have hurt me, but not today. I know Baylin Reyes is under control. My control. The moment I realized who she was in relation to the shooting and that she was the same girl I shared a crazy night with five years ago, the plan seemed to come together without much effort.

Lazaro lets out a sigh, and I can just see him pacing his office, his fists clenched and itching to wrap around my neck. I know that Lazaro is at the end of his tether as he tries to reign me in; more than once, he's told me he needs his brother back, not a kid that needs babysitting. But this is the only way I know how to be a brother to him. Saving him is the only recourse now.

Truth be told, I wasn't really thinking when I snatched Baylin Reyes off the side of the road. My plan, the one I had thought out, seemed to morph and expand and take on a life of its own once I saw that Detective Handler was putting on the heat for her to testify against us. I knew there was a danger that she could relent and cave to his demands. I couldn't let her do that. If either one of us went to prison, we'd lose everything we'd ever worked so hard to build, and we'd be left with nothing. Everything would have been in vain. And I sure as hell wasn't going to let my brother or I spend a day in prison, even if it meant I had to put my little bird down.

"Come home, Rome," Lazaro's pleading voice crackles through the line.

"A few more days," I tell him.

I don't know why I need a few more days. I don't know what will change from now till then, but maybe if I work on her hard enough, I can bring my little bird around, and we won't have to worry about her testifying against us. She does, after all, have so much more to lose than she has to gain by giving her evidence to the courts.

18

BAYLIN

The world explodes in a cacophony of gunfire, jolting me from the fragile grasp of sleep. My heart hammers in my chest as I stumble out of the rickety bed and peer through the dust-smeared window. There he is—Romeo Riccardi—unloading round after round into the unsuspecting trees. His broad shoulders tense with each recoil, the set of his jaw a testament to some inner demon I can't begin to comprehend.

"Enjoying the show?" His mocking voice cuts through the crackle of spent bullets like a blade as I emerge on the porch behind him.

I flinch, disturbed that he saw me coming without so much as looking my way. "What are you doing?"

His laugh is dark, sending shivers down my spine. "Target practice." That same shiver multiplies as he turns around to face me. Target practice could only mean one thing. There are two humans here, and one of us is not going to make it. Will today be the day that I forfeit my life?

"This is not a fair fight," I mutter, my hands fisting at my sides.

"Who said anything about playing fair?"

He strolls towards me at a leisurely pace, seemingly in no hurry. His gun dangles casually by his side, as if it weighs nothing at all. He stops and cocks his head to the side, giving me a curious look before flashing a lazy smile. With one smooth motion, he tucks the gun into his waistband and pulls out a piece of fabric from his pocket. He shrugs off his blazer and rolls up his sleeves, each movement deliberate and calculated as he takes the last few steps towards me.

I find myself transfixed by his every action, my lips parting slightly in awe. Despite knowing I should resist, I can't deny the intense fire that he ignites within me. I am both ashamed and aroused as his piercing gaze cuts through my soul, leaving me vulnerable and exposed.

"We're going for a run, little bird."

"Again?" I ask, alarmed. What is it with him making me run?

"Something to pass the time," he tells me, and I suggest a game of poker instead. I don't know what I'm thinking; I have no idea how to play poker. But anything would be better than running through the forest again.

"Turn around," he growls.

"Why would I do that?"

"Turn. Around."

His tone cuts sharply through the silence, telling me there's no room for argument. I turn around, and before I can open my mouth again, there's a blindfold around my eyes, and I feel his ministrations as he ties it at the back of my head.

"What...what are you doing?"

I try to calm my nerves as he guides me down the porch steps, steadying me when I stumble before I can fall. This small gesture of kindness is a stark contrast to his otherwise cruel treatment towards me.

"Where are we going?" I gasp, as he hurries me in the direction of the woods.

"Enough of the questions, little bird."

His rich voice is smooth like syrup, and I can tell by the heat of his breath caressing my skin that he's already turned on.

I swallow the knot in my throat, acutely aware of the darkness that now renders me hopeless, forcing my other senses to heighten.

The scent of pine and earth fill my lungs, the distant call of birds the only sound aside from my erratic breathing.

"The forest is full of ravines," he says. "Walk the wrong way, and you could fall into one and break your neck."

"Why are you doing this?" It's barely more than a whisper, and I don't try to keep the fear out of my voice.

He sighs, bored. "I'm almost out of bullets."

A sharp stab of panic shoots through me as I realize the meaning behind his words. He'd rather kill me naturally than to shoot me. For whatever reason. I don't believe for a minute that he's almost out of bullets – why then would he be shooting aimlessly at invisible enemies amongst the trees?

With each step we take through the dense forest, the looming threat of the ravines becomes more menacing. The rustling of leaves in the wind seems to mock me, as if nature itself is conspiring against my escape. I snatch my arm out of his and stop walking. Before my fingers glance across the fabric covering my eyes, he cocks his gun, and I drop my hands helplessly. My chin falls to my chest in despair, as I realize this is the end of the road for me.

"There is one rule you must obey," he whispers. "Do not take off your blindfold. You have sixty seconds before I come for you. If you're lucky enough to still be alive, you get to live another day."

"You can't be fucking serious! You want me to walk blind in the woods?" I know I won't make it out of the woods today. Knowing my luck, I'll probably break my neck falling over my own shadow.

"Run!" he commands, and I obey.

I TAKE A DEEP BREATH, steady my nerves and forge ahead, slower than I'd like to go, because I'm testing the ground with one foot before I add another. Aside from the few scrapes I know I now have after walking into thick brush, my hands are working in my favor as I press on through the woods. My ears perk as I listen for Romeo on my heels, and I continue to zigzag across the forest floor to lose him.

The tension hangs heavy in the air, a silent reminder that one wrong move could lead to me at the bottom of a hole in the ground. With each careful step, I lead myself deeper into the heart of the forest, praying that I'll find a way out before I fall to my death.

Blind and disoriented, I continue to dart through the forest. Branches snag at my clothes, unseen roots trip me up, and the thrill of the chase mixed with fear pumps through my veins. He is close—I can almost smell him. The predator tracking his prey.

I stumble again, a gasp escaping my lips as I hit the ground hard. That's when I sense him, his presence like a magnetic pull. My heart races, knowing he's watching my every awkward fumble, and I never stood a chance.

His laugh echoes throughout the woods. *"Crawl."* His voice is suddenly close, coming from my right. I start to crawl, but it's not towards him. I crawl in the opposite direction, fumbling along the forest floor in a bid to escape this madman.

"Crawl, little bird, crawl."

His command is more a taunt, and I hurry away on my hands and knees, the blindfold soaking my tears. His voice is advancing on me with every taunt he throws my way.

"Fucker!" I screech, no longer caring how much he hurts me. He's going to kill me anyway. He set me on this path hoping I'd fall into the cruel abyss, and now he's making me crawl to my demise.

"Wrong way, little bird," he singsongs, but I keep going, more ruthless in my attempts to get away from him than ever.

Something snags at my collar, but too soon I realize it's Romeo yanking me up to my feet by the neck. He drags me through the forest, hand firmly on the back of my neck as he guides me. The world spins, even beneath the blindfold, and I can barely keep up with his relentless pace. Then we stop so abruptly that I nearly collide with him.

He yanks the blindfold away. The harsh light is blinding, but even in the fading light, I can see we're back at the cabin. Before I can protest, he lifts me onto the cold wood floor, his hard blue eyes burning into mine.

"What..." My voice is caught between dread and an emotion I refuse to name.

"Shh," he silences me, his lips crashing against mine with a hunger that matches the wildness around us. His desire is a palpable force, and as much as I want to deny it, part of me craves the intensity of his touch. It reminds me that I'm alive, here in this moment, that I'm a living, breathing human thing with emotion and a yearning to live.

"Remember this, little bird," he breathes against my neck. "You can't run from me. Not really."

And then he claims me, fierce and unyielding, as the night wraps around us—an all-encompassing darkness that is both terrifying and exhilarating. This is Romeo—raw and untamed—and this is me, wild with abandon as I bury the pain that is consuming me.

19

BAYLIN

There's no such thing as afterglow post sex with Romeo. He tucks himself away, lowers his sleeves, then turns away without helping me up. The rough wood of the floor wreaked havoc on my back, and I know I'll be suffering tomorrow, my pain a torment I can do without.

Romeo's phone shatters the silence just as he reaches the tree line a few yards away. I watch his strong, muscular back as he moves with the grace of a lion.

"Lazaro," he grunts into the phone, his voice a low rumble that vibrates through the night air. He greets his brother like he would a business associate. I catch the tension in his jaw, the way his free hand clenches into a fist.

I sit up, pulling the edges of my torn shirt around me, a flimsy shield against the chill and his burning gaze. He's developed a habit of tearing my clothes to shreds every time he claims me. My heart hammers, each beat echoing the dread pooling in my stomach.

"Are you sure?" Romeo's tone shifts, the undercurrents of danger suddenly spiking as if laced with venom. His eyes, like shards of thin blue ice, lock onto mine. The phone slips from his fingers, landing in the dirt as if it too recognizes the omen of darkness descending upon us both.

The prospect of asking a question dies on my lips as he takes a menacing step towards me. His silhouette looms large against the moonlit backdrop, a storm about to break.

"Testifying?" The word explodes from him, not a question but a sentence—a verdict passed down from the judge in his own twisted court.

"What—" I begin, shaking my head in confusion, but he is already moving, his hands grabbing me with an iron grip that leaves no room for resistance.

"Shut up!" His bellow echoes through the trees, and I feel myself being pushed to the forest floor, the roughness of the earth scraping against my cheek. The scent of the woods and soil invade my senses as he wrenches my arms behind me, securing them with a harshness that tells me escape is impossible.

"What are you doing?!" My voice is a plea muffled by the ground beneath me. But he is beyond reason, his presence a tempest of fury and betrayal.

"What am I doing?" He spits the words out like poison and presses a knee into my lower back, holding me down. "You're going to take him away from me. My brother—my blood!"

"What the fuck, Romeo!"

I can hear the fabric of my clothes tearing more, the sound mingling with the ragged breaths tearing from my chest. Stripped of defenses, of dignity, I lay at the mercy of the man who holds my fate between his calloused hands.

"Even if I have to kill you myself," Romeo vows, his words searing into me, branding me with a promise that I know he intends to keep. "I will not let you testify against him."

"I wasn't going to testify!" My voice breaks, fractured by fear and a sorrow that runs deeper than the scars we both bear.

"That's not what Detective Handler claims."

"Please, don't. Don't do this."

He won't even let me explain. I don't know why he suddenly

believes I'm going to testify, but that phone call he got changes everything in an instant. And it makes him so flipping mad, he can't see straight.

I gasp for air, my face pressed hard against the damp earth, gagging as gritty soil invades my mouth. "Romeo," I choke out, trying to squirm away, but his hand is unyielding, mashing my cheek into the ground.

He growls at me, a dark, heavy shadow looming over me. "Shut up, Baylin."

I try to spit out the humiliation and dirt, my throat burning with both rage and the dust I can't clear. Tears streak through the grime on my face, mixing with the soil as a bitter reminder of my helplessness.

"Look at me," he demands, his voice thick with fury.

When I don't comply fast enough, he grabs my chin, forcing my gaze up to meet his eyes—a stormy sea that threatens to drown me. Hatred clashes with fear inside me, and it must show on my face, because his lips mock me with a wicked, twisted smile.

"I should have killed you the minute we got here." His words reverberate like thunder.

With a rough shove, he flips me onto my back. I stare up at the canopy above, the leaves blurring into an indistinct green haze as tears well again. Romeo's weight settles on top of me, his body hard and unrelenting. Every part of me wants to fight, to claw and scream, but I'm bound, immobilized by ropes of anger.

The cold metal of his gun presses against my forehead. I close my eyes, my lips quaking. If I die now, I get to join Maggie. But if I die now, I won't get to watch Luca grow up into the man he's meant to be. If I leave, it will kill him.

"Romeo, please..." My plea is barely audible, a broken whisper lost amidst the rustling leaves and my own ragged breaths.

"I will always remember this day," he spits, his hatred seeping through the air between us, infecting my ears. He hates me enough to kill me, won't even think twice before he pulls that trigger. "I will remember the look on your face when I pull this trigger. And I will remember the pain that will tear through your body. I will remember, and I will rejoice in it."

My heart flutters, and my breath hitches. I brace myself, closing my eyes tight as I try to shut out the reality that's bearing down on me.

Through the mist of tears, I can feel his finger tighten around the trigger, the cold metal of the gun digging into my skin. My mind races, thinking of ways to reason with him, but anything I say will only feed the fire of his fury.

"Romeo, no," I whisper, but my voice wavers and fades into the darkness that surrounds us. Maybe it would be easier to just let go and slip into the abyss of no return.

The silence is deafening, and I feel the weight of the gun press harder against my forehead. I gather all my strength, trying to reason with him one last time.

"I wasn't going to testify against you. Or your brother - I swear on my life. Detective Handler will do anything to make you think he has a witness. There is no witness!"

Something flashes in his eyes, but it quickly fades, replaced by the same cold rage that's consumed him since he got the phone call.

"Liar," he growls, his voice low and dangerous, the sound of his fingers tightening around the trigger audible in the stillness.

I close my eyes and shake my head, bracing myself for what's to come.

"Tell me what I can do," I whisper. "What will make you believe me? Detective Handler wouldn't fucking leave me alone, but I never agreed to testify."

"Liar," he repeats.

"Testify against what?" I scream. "I was standing a hundred yards away; I didn't see anything."

"You saw me that night," he corrects. "Driving through that carpark."

"That's what he wants you to believe! Please, Romeo!" I beg him. "You could have been anyone!" I roar. "It was dark. I didn't see anything!"

Romeo pauses, seems to consider my words, trying to validate them. He rises, takes a step back, his gaze fixed on me with a glint of uncertainty. I can see the doubt creeping into his eyes as he grapples with my confession. The tension between us crackles like electricity in the still air beneath the porch light.

After what feels like an eternity, Romeo speaks in a voice laced with bitterness and desperation. "I've already lost one brother. I will kill anyone who tries to take what remains of my family from me." His hands ball into fists at his sides, and I can see the conflict raging within him.

"I need you to believe me. I never had any intention to testify. Handler was like a festering disease. He wouldn't leave me alone. But I never promised him anything."

HE CHAINS me to the bed with a length of thick rope, a clear indication of his lack of trust in me. His anger is palpable; I don't know what his brother said to him on the phone, but for some reason, he's even more convinced than ever that I am going to testify against him and his brother.

I study him with a mix of terror and courage as he paces back and forth before me, his eyes filled with blazing anger. This is the angriest I've seen him. The occasional glimpses he's given me into the real Romeo Riccardi have revealed a man who is capable of feeling, of showing emotion. A man who cares. But this man, this version of Romeo is livid. The chains chafe against my wrists, a cruel reminder of my captivity.

"You think you can betray us, and you get a free pass?" he spits out, his voice dripping with venom. "You know what we do to traitors?"

I meet his gaze steadily, refusing to back down. "I owe you nothing, Romeo. I was never anything to you to make me a traitor," I say calmly, even as my heart pounds in my chest. "And I already told you, I have no intention of testifying."

"You make it sound so easy, little bird. But I know deep down you don't mean that."

My eyes narrow in anger as I struggle against my restraints.

"Did you do it?" I ask sharply. "Did you kill them?"

"Looking for more evidence to give your detective friend?"

"He's the one who approached me, Romeo. Not the other way around."

Without warning, Romeo grabs me by the throat and slams my head onto the mattress, leaving me gasping for air. His grip is unbreakable, and I can feel my vision fading as he squeezes tighter. "You'll regret this," he snarls, his face twisted with anger.

But even as I struggle to breathe, I refuse to show any fear. "Killing me won't change anything," I manage to say through clenched teeth. "Detective Handler will still be there tomorrow."

A flicker of surprise crosses Romeo's face before he releases me, taking a step back. "You're a fool," he says, his voice now icy and calculating. "And I'll have to remove that foolishness from you."

He reaches for a knife on a nearby table and starts cutting the ropes that bind me to the bed with precise movements. I watch in dread as he frees me from my restraints.

As soon as I'm free, the knife falls to the floor and Romeo lunges at me with his hand raised, ready to strike. I dodge his attack with unexpected agility, then duck and run for the door. He grabs me by the back of my shirt, pulls me back, and my leg shoots out, kicking him in the shin. He doesn't let go as we engage in a fierce struggle, our arms locked around each other as he tries to hold me down and I try to extract myself from his grip. He's a large and formidable man, with a body like an expert assassin's. The room spins as we push against one another, and Romeo gains the upper hand. The glint of the knife catches my eye, and I realize he must have grabbed it during our struggle. I can feel its cold edge against my skin as he prepares to strike again.

Despite his fighting skills, Romeo allows his anger to take control and blind him to reason. I use this to my advantage and kick him again, sending him tumbling off me. Taking advantage of the moment, I scramble to my feet and bolt for the door.

He tries to grab me again, but I dodge his grasp and race through the doorway, stumbling down the porch steps. My heart is racing, adrenaline coursing through my body as I sprint into the cool night air.

I can feel his presence behind me as I reach the tree line. For a moment, I feel a sense of triumph before it is quickly replaced with fear. In the dark forest, I know without a doubt that I am running towards my potential death.

With tears streaming down my cheeks, I take a deep breath and push myself forward. My heart is pounding in my chest as I run for my life, ignoring the pain shooting up my legs.

Suddenly, he appears, sneaking up on me from behind until he grabs the back of my shirt and yanks me backwards. I fall hard on my back, screaming and flailing my legs to keep him away from me.

He pins me down with one knee on my stomach and straddles me, his cruel smile crushing any hope of escape. "Here's what you don't understand," he hisses through gritted teeth. "There is nowhere you can run where you will ever be safe from me. There is no place you could hide where I won't find you. I own you, little bird. And I will own you until I put your beautiful little body in its grave."

His eyes are mesmerizingly clear as he hauls me up to my feet and pushes me back toward the cabin. I stumble, then right myself, biting down on my lip as I take slow steps back toward my prison.

"If you even think of running again, little bird, I'll take great pleasure in hunting you down. And just know that next time, I will have no mercy on you."

Back in the cabin, he ties me to a chair. He folds my hands behind the back slats and ties my wrists together, even as I push and struggle against him. He binds my feet together and then wraps the rope around the legs of the chair so that even if I stand, the chair goes with me.

His typically piercing, blue as ice eyes have now become a deep, dark shade of midnight blue. I can't help but stare in awe at the sudden change in his appearance.

"Let's try this again, shall we?" He grunts and paces around the room, running his finger lovingly along the sharp edge of his knife.

"If you're going to kill me, just get it over with," I hiss.

He chuckles, a deep, menacing sound that sends shivers down my spine. There's madness in his eyes as he traces the tip of the blade along the lines of his palm, drawing a thin line of blood. The metallic scent fills the air, thick and cloying. "Oh, I have no intention of killing you just yet," he replies, stepping closer until I can feel his breath ghosting over my skin. "There are...other ways to make you suffer." He takes a step closer to me, his presence overwhelming. I steel myself as he raises his hand, watch in fascination as a thin line of blood trickles down his palm.

"Lick," he says, holding his palm up to my mouth. My vision swims with tears as his bloody scent lingers just a hair's breadth away from my mouth. His pupils dilate, his excitement suffocating the room.

"Just kill me," I whimper.

"No, no, no, no, no." He shakes his head. "Where's the fun in that?"

I drop my eyes to the ground, refusing to lick his palm, an act which only serves to ignite his anger.

"Do it!" he hisses.

My tears come faster. My heart screeches to an electrifying halt. And the world spins on its axis as I shake my head in refusal. It's not enough that he's taken my freedom away from me, now he wants to torture me also. What cruel hand of fate intervened to ensure that I crossed paths with this monster?

"No!" I yell, my voice firm and resolute.

"No?" His voice is calm, deceptively smooth. A cruel glint of malice enters his eyes.

My head snaps back as he tugs on my hair, causing me to cry out in agony. With a tight grip on my cheeks, he forces my mouth open. Dread floods through me as I realize his intentions. I struggle to keep his hand from entering my mouth, screaming incoherently. Tears stream down my face as he relentlessly tries to force his massive hand inside my mouth. I plead and thrash, feeling terror and desperation course through every inch of my body. The skin around my mouth begins to tear under the pressure, the sound of it ripping adding to my torment. As if that wasn't enough, he slowly spreads his fingers inside my mouth, causing unbearable pain. His palm covers my tongue, cutting off any chance of catching a breath. The metallic taste of blood mixes with saliva in my mouth, but I cannot swallow due to his suffocating grip. Suddenly, he removes his hand and pinches my cheeks again, calmly surveying the blood on my tongue as if it were no more than a minor inconvenience.

"Now, *swallow me*, little bird."

20

ROMEO

My little bird is a beautiful sight as she takes a deep breath and I release her, observing as she drinks in large amounts of air. I didn't know how much she could handle, but the images in my mind of my blood filling her stomach have me incredibly rock fucking hard.

A trickle of blood runs down her chin, and I struggle to contain my excitement at the thought of our blood mixing together.

"Such a good little bird," I murmur, watching as the blood stains her mouth. Without hesitation, I lower myself to her level and crush my lips onto hers in a wild kiss. She tries to turn away, but I grip her face firmly with my hands and hold her in place, tasting the blend of our blood.

I lick at her wounds, enjoying the slower flow of blood from her chapped skin. My tongue glides down to her chin, savoring every drop. Unsatisfied, I trace my tongue up her cheek, over one eyelid and then the other. She is the most exquisite creature I have ever held in my grasp, my little bird. The most accommodating to my madness.

Her body trembles against my touch, resisting me, adding fuel to my desire. It is an all-consuming lust that speaks of possession and fixation. I am fixated on my little bird; I want to do everything with her - both good and bad, but mostly bad. I crave to explore every inch of her body, mind, and soul until she shatters under my control. And when I am finished with her, she will be so broken that she will submit and see nothing else but me – nothing that came before me and nothing that could possibly come after.

"You're insane," she spits out, her voice laced with venom, as I pull away from her. My eyes are glazed over with desire, and I can see the vulnerability shining through her brown irises. She's almost broken, and that only makes me want to play with her even more. I crave this game of cat and mouse between us; it's what keeps us alive. Keeps things interesting. As long as I have Baylin by my side, that's all I'll ever need. Regardless of whether she wants to be with me, my little bird makes me come alive, my obsession for her tantalizing. She accuses me of being deranged, but my madness is all for her.

"You've called me every name under the sun," I scoff in response. "But your body doesn't lie. Every time we're together, the liquid pooling between your legs tells a different story."

Baylin's chest heaves with anger, her fists clenched tightly at her sides. "Does is?" she retorts, her voice trembling with barely restrained emotion. "It's not excitement, it's disgust. Disgust for myself, for letting you manipulate me like this." Her words strike a chord within me, awakening a primal urge to dominate and control her even further. As Baylin sits before me, vulnerable yet defiant, I realize that my obsession has only served to push her further away.

I reach out to touch her cheek, my thumb brushing away a stray tear that escapes her defenses. Baylin flinches at my touch, but she doesn't pull away. Instead, she meets my gaze, searching for something undefinable in my eyes. I hold her gaze, letting her see the turmoil within me, the battle between the darkness that consumes me and the light that she throws on my soul.

"I know I've hurt you," I begin, my voice barely above a whisper. "But just know, I intend to hurt you so much more than you can imagine. And I won't stop, not until you fall to your knees before me."

Baylin's eyes glaze over, her tears making them look like twin mirrors as her grief overwhelms her.

"Kill. Me."

I tilt my head in confusion. What could possibly possess my little bird to want to die? And then she says the magic words.

"Kill me and bury me with them."

I ROAR. I'm absolutely mad with rage as her words reverberate in my mind, threatening to tear down the last threads of my sanity. They float on the air in the cabin. They slam my senses and leave me seething with madness. She wants to die. She wants to leave me. She wants to deprive me of her presence, chalk up her own soul as another bloodstain on my hands. She would rather be dead and buried than here with me.

"If death is what you want, it's not what you will get. You won't get the easy way out," I inform her, and her head drops to her chest.

Lifting her chin with a forceful grip, I stare into her eyes, once full of fire but now clouded with fear. She trembles, and the darkness in me feeds on her terror, reveling in the control it has over her. I grab her by the shoulders, forcing her to look at me.

"You are mine," I growl, my grip tightening as she winces in pain. "You will never think of death again. You belong to me now."

Her body trembles under my touch, a mixture of revulsion and terror evident in her every shiver. "I'll never be yours!" she hisses.

I will find a way to break her, make her see that I am the only one she should crave. With a menacing smile, I press a chilling kiss to her quivering lips, relishing the taste of her despair. This cabin will be our sanctuary, our prison, until she understands that there is no escape from me.

She whimpers softly, her tears dripping down her cheeks as she stares back at me, her eyes wide with dread and shock. I can see the fear building in her heart, her resolve beginning to falter. But I won't let her win. I need her to know that I will never let her go, that only death will ever separate us again.

My grip on her chin tightens, forcing her to look into my eyes.

"You will learn to want me, to desire only me," I say, my voice harsh and unyielding. My words hang in the air, heavy and laden with the promise of a new future.

As her body trembles under my touch, I trace my fingers down her cheek, feeling the cold sweat that has formed on her skin. She tries to pull away, but my hand grips her wrist tightly, holding her in place. "You will never escape me," I growl, my eyes burning with an intensity that rivals the flames of hell.

She whimpers again, her sobs growing louder as she crumples into herself, her body shaking uncontrollably. A flicker of emotion, something foreign to me, threatens my resolve, but I know what must be done. I must break her, so that I can save her. I must remake her into what she should have been all along: *mine*.

THE DIMLY LIT room is filled with the warm glow of a flickering candle, casting an eerie light on Baylin as she slumps in her chair. Exhaustion has taken over her body, and her chin rests heavily on her chest. I flick my cigarette to the ground at the same time as I blow out a haze of smoke; it filters around me like a halo, but I have no delusions that I'm an angel. I move back into the cabin quietly, inhaling the metallic tang of blood. Gently, I lift her head and call out her name; she stirs and gazes at me with a mix of fear and hope.

I untie her restraints and guide her to the bed, where she sits on the edge and eagerly accepts the bottle of water I offer her. She drinks it all in one go without saying a word. The scopolamine in the water will quickly incapacitate her – possibly even kill her. But she's already managed to survive multiple close calls before, so I doubt this will be what finishes her off. But giving her the drug is what little mercy I can offer her. Escape from the pain of what I'm about to do.

Once she finishes drinking, she licks her lips as if still parched, a side effect of the drug taking hold. Her pupils dilate and she begins to slump into herself, overcome by drowsiness.

"Easy there, tiger." I catch her before she falls from the bed and carefully lay her onto her side as planned.

I retrieve my knife and heat the tip over the candle flame until it turns a fiery orange color. If Baylin does end up dying, it won't be because of an infection from my negligence.

She watches me with glazed eyes, barely able to move as the drug continues to take effect. Her body is limp like a ragdoll's as I approach her methodically, knife in my hand.

I bend a knee onto the bed, slide a hand down the length of her arm, then tear her shirt off her body. She barely flinches, which tells me she's so far gone that she won't feel a thing. In one swift motion, I press the fiery tip against her delicate skin just above her collarbone. A soft gasp escapes my lips as a thin line of crimson appears on her unblemished flesh.

Without hesitation, I continue to draw the blade across her skin, carving my name into her body with purpose and precision. Each stroke deeper than the last, marking my territory on this unwilling sacrifice. Though she whimpers in pain, her gaze remains locked onto mine, seeking reassurance or perhaps explanation. No matter how hard she tries to fight internally, she can't so much as lift a finger to help herself.

Completing the final incision, I watch in fascination as blood wells up and seeps from her wound. With a final look at my handiwork, I help her to her feet, wiping away the silent tears that have streaked down her dirt-streaked cheeks. She can barely stand as she trembles against me, and I walk her to the bathroom, where I clean the cut and apply an ointment and gauze from the first aid kit. It's the least I can do, if only to stave off possible infection.

I can't take my eyes off the gauze that now covers the reminder of me branded into her skin. She will always carry me around with her, there'll always be that reminder, no matter what happens. And even if she dies...even if fate intervenes and I decide she's outlived her expiry date and I need to change that, she will still be buried with the whisper of me burned into her flesh, scarred but bound to me forever.

21

BAYLIN

I'm alone when I wake.

The dim light filters through the bedroom window as I slowly open my eyes. The room feels foreign and unfamiliar to me, causing my groggy mind to struggle as I try to remember where I am. I try to lift myself up from the bed, but a sharp pain shoots through my shoulder, causing me to wince and fall back onto the mattress.

The throbbing in my back pulses with every heartbeat, a constant reminder of something awful though I can't quite piece together the events leading to this moment. My head spins as I try once again to sit up, clutching the sheets in a tight grip to steady myself. I take deep, labored breaths, each one shuddering through my body like distant thunder.

Gritting my teeth against the pain, I swing my legs over the side of the bed. The room sways around me for a moment, and I pause, closing my eyes until the feeling passes. When I open them again, it's with a steely determination. My body aches, and a heavy weight sits on my shoulders. Slowly, I stand and make my way to the bathroom, holding onto furniture for support.

The cool tiles of the bathroom floor are a stark contrast to the warmth of the bed I just left. I flick on the light switch; the sudden brightness makes me wince with pain. As my eyes adjust, I catch sight of myself in the mirror—my disheveled state stares back at me with wide, frightened eyes.

With trembling hands, I lower my shirt from my shoulders, where the majority of the pain seems to reside. There's a bandage on my left shoulder; I reach for it, but the movement sends a sharp pain shooting through my entire body, causing my breath to hitch. So much pain. I take another deep breath, bracing myself as I slowly peel away the gauze. The air hits my raw skin, irritating it, and I involuntarily gasp at the sight.

Romeo's name is etched into my flesh with cruel precision. The letters are swollen and angry looking, a vivid red against my otherwise unblemished skin. A sick feeling churns in my stomach as tears prick at the corners of my eyes. How could this have happened? Why would he do this to me?

Anger flares up inside me, alongside confusion and hurt at his brutality. I press a hand against the cool surface of the mirror, as if seeking support from my own reflection. My mind races through fragmented memories of last night—but all I see is darkness.

"Romeo," I whisper to myself with a mixture of disbelief and a raging anger that sweeps through me, unhindered.

I find painkillers in the cabinet and empty two pills into the palm of my hands, before swallowing and cupping my hand under the tap to wash them down. For a moment, I consider emptying the contents of the bottle and taking them all. Maybe then this pain would stop. Maybe then I'd be free of this nightmare that landed on my doorstep unannounced.

The thought of leaving Luca behind stops me. It would be so easy for me to lay my head down and leave this world, but what would become of Luca? He's my responsibility, my world. I can't let him down like that.

My steps are unsteady as I make my way through the small, lifeless cabin, my mind racing as fast as my heart. With each step, my resolve strengthens, but so does the gnawing fear in the pit of my stomach. This side of Romeo is so far removed from the Romeo I met five years ago. He's so different from the Romeo of a week ago. True, he kidnapped me and brought me here against my will, but this is a whole other brutal side of him that I haven't seen yet. And now that I know what he's capable of, dare I face him and his wrath once more? I shake my head to dispel the doubts clouding my thoughts. I need answers, and I need them now.

I find him outside, chopping wood with mechanical precision. The sound of the axe splitting wood is sharp in the quiet morning. Romeo doesn't notice me at first, his back turned to me, muscles shifting under his t-shirt as he works. I take a moment to observe him; I've never seen him in anything so casual – he's always either been naked or dressed to the nines, and I find it hard to reconcile this industrious, casually dressed man with the ruthless killer that also happened to scar my skin. Ink runs down both arms, a myriad of patterns and symbols and climbing vines that claim his skin in such a way that it's hard to find anywhere that hasn't been touched by a tattooist's gun.

Finally, I steel myself and call out to him. "Romeo!"

He pauses mid-swing, the axe held aloft, expectantly waiting to see what comes next. Then slowly he turns to face me. His expression is unreadable at first, but as his eyes take me in, a flicker of something —guilt, perhaps—passes over his features.

"Baylin," he says carefully, setting down the axe and wiping his brow with the back of his hand. "You should be resting."

"Should I? Why is that?" I reply firmly, my voice steadier than I feel. "What happened last night?"

Romeo's gaze shifts slightly, and he nods slowly. "You already know why."

"Fuck you, Romeo!" I screech, unable to hold back. There's nothing civil about what he's done, therefore he doesn't deserve my patience. He doesn't deserve my composure. I hurry down the porch steps and march toward him. I shove at his chest, but the mountain is harder than ever, and he refuses to budge. He stares down at me through his hooded gaze, so much control, yet so much turmoil in his roiling blue eyes. A lock of his thick black hair has fallen into his eyes, making him look almost childlike in his innocence. He pushes his hair away and continues watching me.

Finally, Romeo speaks, his voice low. "You were saying something about fucking me?"

I fight back the urge to slap him, even as his rich cadence screams to something primal deep inside me.

"Why would you do that? What gives you the right?"

"Do what exactly, Baylin? You need to be more specific, seeing as we've done a whole lot the past few days."

"You're an insane bastard. Why am I shocked!" My voice drips with bitterness and anger as I glare at him in disgust. And then I strike the final blow. "I shouldn't have expected anything more from a killer."

His expression turns to stone, his jaw clenching as he puts on his façade. He shows no emotion as he looks at me with a quiet disposition.

"Are you quite finished?" His voice is steel, stripped of any warmth it may once have held.

I cross my arms and lean back against a tree, trying to perfect my mask of indifference. "I could go on," I retort, the challenge clear in my eyes.

For a moment, he looks as if he might turn back to his wood chopping, his body turning slightly towards the wood block, but then he pauses, and when he faces me again, there's a flash of something raw and uncertain in his eyes. "And what would that achieve, Baylin? Would it make you feel better? To tear down what little we have left between us?"

I flinch at his use of my name; he's always referred to me as 'little bird', and now he calls me by my name. "What we have left?" I scoff, shaking my head and looking away from him. "Romeo, there is nothing left. *There was never anything there to begin with*," I hiss.

Romeo flinches at my words. He steps forward, sets his hard gaze on me and digs his fingers roughly into my arm. "You can tell yourself that all you want," he responds. "Tell yourself whatever makes you sleep better at night. But *you* belong to *me* now."

22

ROMEO

I push the heavy wood door open, my body radiating a consuming heat despite the chill in the late afternoon air. Sweat glistens on my skin, cascading down my muscled back as I step into the dim light of the cottage. My shirt clings to me, a damp testament to the exertion of splitting logs, each fiber accentuating the strength coiled beneath.

Baylin stands at the far end of the room, her gaze fixed on the dancing flames in the hearth, seemingly lost in their hypnotic flicker. The tension from our earlier argument hangs heavily between us, an unseen but palpably thick barrier. Her arms are crossed defensively over her chest, her posture rigid against the emotions she struggles to contain.

The air shifts as I close the door with a soft thud, my presence filling up the room like a storm cloud ready to burst. I pause for a moment, watching her silhouette framed against the fiery glow. Despite my physical fatigue, my eyes burn with an intensity that belies my calm demeanor, seeking redemption or perhaps a sign of forgiveness.

The lingering tension hums between us like a taut wire, and suddenly, her disregard for me pulls at something deep inside of me.

I'd thought taking her was the worst thing I could do to her, but it turns out, there are worse things I'm capable of when it comes to Baylin Reyes. And what baffles me most is the enjoyment I get from destroying her spirit.

"How long have you been standing there?" I ask her. Anything to break the tension, to get her to turn around and look at me. I could brand her all I want to make her mine, but it means nothing if she refuses to cast her eyes my way.

"Don't," she responds, without turning around. Her voice is brittle yet firm. "Just... don't."

I hesitate, each word now as heavy as the axe I had wielded outside. My hands clench and unclench at my sides as I struggle with myself, with wanting to reach out to force her to turn around and look at me.

"No matter what I say now, nothing is going to change what's happened."

Baylin's shoulders tighten further but then relax marginally, as if she has resigned herself to that fact. Still facing away from me, she sighs—a soft sound muffled by the distance between us.

"I don't want anything to change," she points out after a long pause. "I want to always remember the monster you are; I want this brand to remind me that I need to hate you, that you took my freewill and I will never, ever forgive you for that." She turns slowly to face me then, her face shadowed not just by the diminishing light but by lingering resentment. Her eyes search mine—looking for something I'm not altogether sure she will find. Not in this lifetime.

We stand there like that for what feels like hours but are only seconds—two figures connected by an invisible thread spun from our shared past and uncertain future.

Finally, she steps towards me tentatively, as if crossing over a fragile ice sheet that could crack beneath her feet at any moment. I remain still, allowing her for once to take the reins of the conversation.

When she is close enough to touch me but still doesn't make a move to do so, I gently lift my hand and brush away a stray strand of her hair, tucking it behind her ear.

Her breath hitches slightly at my touch—gentle and laden with words I know I'll never speak. It's then that she reaches up and removes my hand, her sharp eyes a warning. As if anything she says or does could keep me away from her. As if wild horses could drag me away from her. As if anything or anyone could keep me from touching her and laying claim to her. But then she hits me with the words that I know will haunt me for a lifetime to come.

"You can mark me any way you want, Romeo. Claim me and brand my body with your weapons. But you'll never have my heart and soul."

I SECURE her to the bed once again, but this time she doesn't struggle against me. She submits quietly and offers her hands for me to tie. Her expression is blank as she stares through me, seemingly resigned to her fate. As I fasten both of her wrists to the bedposts, she shows no reaction when my hand trails down the center of her chest, teasing her skin. It's almost as if she has shut down completely, which grates on my nerves.

I leave her tied to the bed and step into the shower, washing away the sweat of the day. The wood chopping took a lot out of me, but it always helps clear my mind, especially when the only thing I can think about is Baylin.

As the water cascades down my back, the scorching heat forces me to think of nothing but my present discomfort, a welcome distraction from the turmoil that awaits outside the bathroom door. The steam wraps around me like a cocoon, offering a temporary haven from the gusts of conflict howling through my soul. I don't understand, any more than she does, the irony of the circumstances that brought us together. Five years ago, for one night of madness, and then most recently when she turned up again; wrong place, wrong time. What were the chances that I would run into her after all this time, and under such circumstances?

Stepping out from the shower, I towel off and pause before the foggy mirror, wiping away the condensation to confront my own reflection. There's weariness in my eyes that runs deeper than physical exhaustion. Lazaro wants me to go home. The girl was never meant to be part of the plan. Once I knew there was a witness and that he had eyes on her, I'd taken things into my own hands. Lazaro has always been slow to act. I'm more action focused.

I return to the bedroom, where she lies still as ever, her breathing steady but her eyes closed now. The sight tugs at something vulnerable within me. I move around the small cabin, the towel tied around my waist, and find myself before the fireplace, looking into the flames. There's only so much longer we can stay here. I know this. I have to start making plans to return home. But the girl. The girl. What do I do with Baylin?

When I turn back around, I find that her eyes are open, revealing a glimmer of curiosity amidst the resignation. Something sparks in her eyes as she takes in my semi naked body. My little bird, for all her protestations, is nothing if not turned on by me. I can't help the smirk from rising to my face. I loosen the towel, drop it to the floor, then move toward the bed. Her eyes are firmly planted on my dick as it slaps against my stomach, ready for action.

The silence stretches between us—thick and charged with unspoken thoughts and fears. Her dilated pupils tell me she's turned on, but she's too afraid to want me. She's too afraid to play on that weakness, to display her vulnerability.

I pull up a chair next to the bed and take a seat, sensing an unlikely peace settling between us even though she is restrained by ropes. It's strange how, despite our roles as captor and prisoner, we are inexplicably connected, and I can feel that this connection cannot be severed. Our souls seem to find solace only in the deepest, darkest depths of the depravity that binds us together. And they always will.

23

BAYLIN

The remnants of our argument echo in my mind—a heated exchange that has left me feeling both vulnerable and furious. I had never intended to let him get under my skin, but Romeo has that effect on me, always pushing my buttons, always igniting a fire within me that I both crave and resent.

The sound of the bathroom door creaking open pulls me from my thoughts. Romeo, freshly emerged from the shower, droplets of water glistening on his skin like jewels, walks around the room casually. He is utterly unapologetic, his body a powerful testament to the hours he spends training, every muscle defined and accentuated by the low light. When he turns toward me, his eyebrows rise in surprise when he sees that my eyes are open. He moves with a grace that is both alluring and infuriating, dropping the towel from around his waist as he settles onto the chair in front of me. I think there is nothing as significant as this one moment in time that threatens to stop my breathing.

I can't help but stare, my resentment battling with an undeniable attraction that surges through me. How could he have branded me, marked me in a way that signifies possession, and yet, I'm still so turned on by the very sight of him? The conflict roils inside me, a tumult of emotions that leaves me breathless.

I shift my gaze, trying to shake off the warmth that spreads throughout my body. But each time I look away, my eyes betray me, darting back to the way his damp hair hangs over his forehead, or how the contours of his body seem to invite me closer.

He leans forward, undoes my shackles, and I rub at my wrists, smoothing away the pressure of being bound. He rests his elbows on his knees, the chair creaking beneath him. "You can't keep avoiding this. I know you're angry, but—"

"Angry? Is that what you think I am?" I cut him off, my voice rising. "You think you can just brand me like I'm some kind of possession, and I'm supposed to be okay with it? It's demeaning, Romeo!"

"I didn't mean for it to be," he says, his expression shifting from defiance to something softer, more vulnerable.

My heart skips a beat at his admission, and I feel the walls I had built begin to crack. The heat between us is palpable, a magnetic pull that is impossible to ignore. Despite my anger, I am drawn to him, every nerve ending alive with desire.

"Then why did you do it?" I whisper, the fight leaving my voice as my body betrays my mind.

"Because I couldn't stand the thought of anyone else touching you," he admits, his gaze intense, locking onto mine with a raw edge that makes my pulse quicken.

And just like that, the air shifts. The argument fades into the background, eclipsed by the burgeoning desire that ignites between us. I take a deep breath, my resolve wavering as I close the distance between us. I can feel the heat radiating from his body, the tension mingling with the scent of soap and something distinctly him.

Before I know it, I'm standing in front of him, the world outside this moment fading away. Our eyes lock, and in that instant, everything shifts. The anger is still there, but it is overwhelmed by a wave of longing that surges through me.

Without thinking, I sink to my knees, my hands resting on his thighs, feeling the warmth of his skin beneath my fingertips. The intensity of our connection engulfs me, and I don't want to fight it anymore. I lean in, my lips brushing against his skin, trailing soft kisses along his thigh, feeling him shudder at my touch.

"Baylin..." he breathes, his voice a mixture of warning and desire.

But I am done with warnings. I want to erase the distance between us, to consume him just as he has consumed me. I wrap my hands around him, feeling the weight of him in my grasp, and look up at him, my eyes dark with unspoken hunger.

With that, I take him in my mouth, savoring the taste of him, the way he reacts to my every move. His hands tangle in my hair, pulling painfully, a low growl escaping his lips as I work him. I am lost in the rhythm of our bodies, the way he gasps and groans, the tension between us escalating to a fever pitch.

When he pulls me up to him, our lips finally meet in a heated kiss that ignites every nerve in my body. The taste of him lingers on my lips, and I can feel the desperation in the way he holds me, as if he is afraid that I will slip away again.

"I need to be inside you, Baylin," he murmurs against my mouth, his breath warm and urgent. "Now."

His words send a jolt of electricity through me, and I feel a rush of desire pooling low in my belly. I pull back just enough to search his eyes, wanting to see the raw need reflected in them. What I find is a mix of hunger and vulnerability that makes her heart race even faster.

"Then take me," I breathe, every ounce of my anger dissipating into the air, swallowed by the heat of the moment. I climb onto his lap, straddling him, feeling the hard press of his body against mine. My skin tingles with anticipation as I settle against his dick, my heart racing in sync with the primal beat of our connection.

With a swift, deft motion, he lifts me, and I gasp as he stands up, his strong arms cradling me against him. He carries me to the bed, our lips crashing together in a frenzy of passion, lost in the heat of the moment. As he lays me back on the bed, he hovers over me, his eyes dark with lust and determination.

We're both breathing heavily, the air thick with desire as he gazes down, taking in every inch of me with an intensity that makes my skin flush. I feel exposed and vulnerable, yet utterly powerful under his scrutiny. The battle of emotions we'd just shared only heightens the electricity between us.

"I want you to know," he says, his voice a low growl, "this isn't just about the brand. It's about you. It's always been about you."

His words ignite a fire within me, and with a fierce determination, I wrap my legs around him, pulling him closer. "Show me," I urge, my voice barely a whisper, heavy with need.

Without another word, he captures my mouth again, deepening the kiss as he presses his body against mine. The world around us fades into nothing as our bodies meld together, moving in a rhythm that is both primal and raw. He explores me with a fervor that makes me gasp, every touch igniting my skin, sending waves of pleasure cascading through me.

The tension that had once filled the room is now transformed into a passionate dance, our bodies entwined, every movement a testament to our fiery connection. I surrender to him completely, craving every inch of him, every caress, every whispered promise.

As we lose ourselves in each other, the boundaries of anger and resentment melt away, leaving only the raw, undeniable chemistry that has always existed between us. Our bodies move in perfect harmony, a symphony of pleasure that builds and builds until it reaches a crescendo that leaves us both breathless.

In this moment, nothing else matters. The world outside ceases to exist as we find our release together, a culmination of desire that leaves us panting and entwined, hearts racing in unison.

As we lay together in the aftermath, the reality of our emotions settles in. I feel a mix of vulnerability and exhilaration, knowing that our connection has deepened in ways I had never anticipated. In that moment, I realize that while the brand may have been a mark of possession, it was also a testament to our bond—a bond that is complex, fierce, and undeniably real.

24

LAZARO

The city's heartbeat pounds in my ears, the noise almost drowning out the worry gnawing at my gut. Romeo's voice on the phone – it was off, frayed at the edges like a rope about to snap. The last time I heard that tone, grief had nearly swallowed him whole. I can't let history repeat itself.

Because when Romeo loses control of himself, the world starts to burn.

I slip away from my men unnoticed, the city's chaos cloaking my departure. I have to do this secretly if I'm to get away from the prying eyes of Handler and the Feds. I know they're too preoccupied now, trying to locate their 'star witness', who's not so stellar at the moment, but that's a whole other story. Handler even approached me about the disappearance of Baylin Reyes, to which I just scoffed and raised my eyebrows like he was crazy, then told him as much. He had let it go for a couple of days, but then he came right out and told me she had signed an affidavit to testify; he even went so far as to tell me that she had outright fingered me and my brother. A lie if ever there was one, because I was no-where near the scene of the shooting that night, but I can't take any chances here. There's no telling how far he'll go in his vendetta against us. I'm sick of him trying to indict us on trumped up charges because we won't play ball with him. Nothing like a crooked cop to keep things interesting.

The drive to the cabin flies by in a blur. Each mile that stretches is taut with tension, my thoughts fixated on Romeo. I'm not just the head of the Riccardi family; I am his brother, his keeper. And my sole focus right now is on him not spiraling into crazy. I can't have him go back to that time when we lost Sandro and he went over the edge. His madness had been all consuming without the buffer of two brothers cushioning him.

Pulling up to the secluded cabin, the silence hits me first. His car is parked beside the cabin, but the little structure is empty. No signs of life, no hint of my brother's presence. My instincts scream that something is amiss. I step out onto the porch and listen. Then I hear it – the faintest trace of a voice carried by the wind.

I track the sound into the forest, moving with the same kind of stealth that has kept me alive in this treacherous world. I must be a few hundred yards into the woods when I stop, rooted to the spot at the sight in the distance.

There, amidst the towering pines, Baylin Reyes swings from a tree, her hands bound above her head. What at first looks like a hostage scene quickly becomes anything but as my eyes swing around to my brother. The scene before me is primal, carnal, a dance of flesh and desire. Romeo drives into her, each thrust met with a moan that speaks not of pain but of pleasure, deep and consuming.

I should look away, but I can't. I'm transfixed as I stand watching them, my eyes unable to tear themselves away from the scene. This is more than lust; it's a connection that's raw and undeniable. Baylin Reyes isn't hurt or afraid as I thought she would be. She is alive, alight with a fire I hadn't expected of her, one I haven't seen in anyone for a long time.

I can't tear my gaze away as I watch them from between the trees, far enough away that they don't see me, yet close enough that I hear every titillating detail of their lovemaking.

Because that's precisely what it is between them. For a harsh, vengeful king like my brother, there's no room for anything other than straight up dirty sex. But this, this is something else. This is all the feelings, all the reverence and adoration wrapped up in one neat bow. This is a man standing on the edge of insanity, about to fall into something greater than himself.

Romeo is entranced, completely consumed by her. And perhaps, this isn't a sign of him losing his sanity. Maybe it's a sign that he's gaining something else entirely – something that we all secretly crave deep inside. A connection, a bond that is intense enough to light up even the darkest corners of our world.

And as I stand there, an uninvited voyeur to their passion, I feel an unfamiliar ache in my chest. Not just for Romeo, but for myself. For that balance between who we are and who we want to be, between love and duty, family and freedom.

I watch as Romeo reaches out to her, his hand palming her naked chest, sliding down her skin reverently, mesmerized by the power of their connection. Baylin's eyes meet his with a fierce intensity, mirroring the storm of emotions raging within him. It is as if the entire world has fallen away, and only they exist in this exquisite moment of vulnerability.

THE PORCH WOOD is cool against my palms as I watch the night reclaim its silence, the forest's fevered whispers subsiding. An hour passes, an hour that is filled with primal calls echoing through the trees—a stark reminder of how close we all are to our basest instincts.

And then they break through the forest walls—Romeo, emerging from the dark brush with a naked Baylin in his arms, her slight form curled against his chest. There isn't a flicker of emotion across his face when he sees me. Nothing. Stone-cold Romeo, with his fortress walls built high and impenetrable. But Baylin... she presses into him, her cheeks flushed with a mix of spent passion and embarrassment, hiding from the reality that sits waiting on the front steps.

"Go shower," I hear him murmur after he carries her past me and into the cabin without so much as a glance in my direction, as though only they exist in their own little bubble. The door shuts behind them, leaving a weighted silence hanging in the air.

It's only a minute before he reappears, stepping out into the cool night alone. I straighten, ready for the confrontation I know is coming. It's time to unravel the knot that Romeo is tying himself into.

"Lazaro," he starts, but I cut him right off.

"What are you doing, Rome? What the fuck are you doing?" I heave a sign of exasperation, my voice low, each word laced with an edge.

He leans against the railing, looking everywhere but at me, knowing full well what I'm talking about. "What does it look like I'm doing, brother?" He gives me a warning look.

I scoff, feeling anger build in my gut. "She's going to testify against us, Romeo. Against me. Against you."

"No, she's not." His words are like a sharp slap, but his gaze flickers, just for a second, betraying a hint of doubt. Here I am trying to keep us afloat, and he's cruising down easy street, not a care in the world.

"We committed a crime in front of her!" I hiss, leaning toward him. I don't know why he can't see the many faceted dangers of what he's doing.

"Crimes," he corrects, suitably bored. He gets petulant like this sometimes, and I just want to slap him into tomorrow for his nonchalance.

"Fucking hell, Romeo! Why can't you just fucking leave things alone when I tell you to! Now you've gone and developed feelings for..."

"Feelings?" His laugh is bitter, hollow. "There are no feelings here, brother."

"Keep telling yourself that," I say, shaking my head. "You've complicated the hell out of this situation, Romeo."

"Well then I'll uncomplicate them." He pushes off the railing, digs his hands into his pockets and shrugs. He challenges me with his piercing blue eyes, so much like my own, yet so different. He can't possibly be thinking about killing her, not after what I saw in the woods earlier. There's no way. Rome is many things, but heartless is not a word I would use to describe him after tonight.

"You know where the line is," I remind him. "We don't cross it."

"You said it yourself; she's going to testify against us."

"You really think you'll be okay to sleep at night if you kill a woman, Romeo? You really, truly believe that?"

I don't want her testifying against us, but nor do I want to have more unnecessary blood on my wands. There are some lines even I won't cross, no matter the cost. This is one of them. The situation could just as easily be managed by sequestering the girl, rather than killing her and bringing more suspicion on us.

"We do what we have to do to survive in our world."

His voice is a steel cage that wraps around me. I can't believe what he's saying. Maybe he has descended into the depths of insanity, after all.

"There's no way you're going to kill her, Rome. I think you're falling for her. Whether you want to admit it or not."

"Feelings are a weakness we can't afford," he shoots back, but his voice lacks its usual conviction.

"Maybe," I concede, the soft night air brushing against my skin. "Or maybe they're what keep us human in this messed-up world of ours."

He doesn't answer, and in his silence, I find all the confirmation I need, even if he doesn't yet see what I see.

WE SIT at the small oak table, facing off as our large frames dominate the space. From her place on the bed, where she sits cross-legged, Baylin's eyes dart back and forth between Romeo and me, her expression heavy with unspoken questions as she struggles to decide who is the more intimidating one between us.

Her voice remains steady as she speaks, but I can see the tremor in her hands. She has to ask, even though she doesn't want to. "Which one of you did it?"

I respond with just two words: "Which one?"

Those words will always haunt me, making me wonder if they were the catalyst for everything that followed. They were the first words I ever spoke to her, setting the stage for all the drama that unfolded afterwards.

"Who killed those men?" Baylin asks, her gaze shifting to Rome. His jaw is clenched tightly, a muscle twitching like a time bomb ready to explode. Despite his earlier denials, something has changed in him over the past few days. It's subtle, but I can see it – and I know anyone who knows him as well as I do would see it too.

"Does it matter?" he snaps at her, a stark contrast to how tenderly he touched her when she was pressed against him.

"To me it does...to know why they were killed. Everything about them matters to me," Baylin whispers. "I need to understand why your kind of evil exists."

She keeps her eyes locked on Romeo's, completely under his spell just like he is under hers. But there's also something else there as his eyes slant towards her; his eyes blaze and he's suddenly pissed off. And I think it's not because of the questions she's asking, but the fact that he has to compete with the ghosts of the dead for even a sliver of her emotions.

Even though he may never let his emotions be known, will never let them affect his future, his heart is not dead to all. I know that Baylin Reyes may never truly understand the depths of Romeo because he will never allow himself to show her the real Romeo Riccardi.

"They were at the wrong place at the wrong time," Romeo finally admits, his voice low but still edged with warning. His gaze flickers to mine silently communicating a message between us, before they return to Baylin.

Baylin's breath catches, realization dawning in her eyes.

"For nothing? They were killed for nothing?" Her voice trembles, the weight of this shocking revelation crashing down on her like a heavy cloak. I exchange a knowing glance with Romeo; Baylin is the wild card between us. She's the unexpected element we never saw coming.

"Who was the shooter?" Baylin asks, desperate for answers.

"What difference does it make, little bird?" Romeo's use of this affectionate nickname takes me by surprise. It would almost be endearing if I didn't know my brother's dark past. I am well aware of the kind of man he is – dark, cold, and devoid of any real emotions except where family exists.

I watch them with a detached perspective, feeling almost ashamed to witness the intense chemistry that exists between them. Even the air between them shrivels in embarrassment. It's unsettling to see how she gazes at him so innocently, completely unaware of the hidden darkness beneath his charming exterior.

Baylin continues to stare at Romeo, waiting for an answer.

"It changes nothing," I speak up, surprising even myself with the words that come out of my mouth. They both fall silent as all eyes turn to me. "It doesn't matter who the shooter was," I tell her, explaining that innocent men were caught in the crossfire of something bigger than any of us anticipated. "We had the first teenage overdose in this city in seven years because of two of those men; we weren't going to risk anymore."

Baylin closes her eyes and lets out a tired breath before looking back at either of us.

"I won't testify against either of you."

I think she says this because she just wants answers. It's her reassurance that she won't turn against us if we give her what she wants. But I can only give her what I have.

"It won't change anything," I reiterate. "They died to prevent further carnage; that's all you need to know."

"But Detective Handler seems convinced that it was you or your brother," she says, mentioning the pictures he showed her and pointing us out. "You were at the precinct the day I was there." She points a long, slender finger at me.

Romeo breaks the tense silence by finally addressing the elephant in the room. "It's personal for Detective Handler; he's fixated on sending us to prison," he says sharply, locking eyes with her. "He will stop at nothing to make you testify so he can do just that."

"I don't want to testify," she whispers, and I truly believe she doesn't want to be involved in any part of the investigation into the murders. She's smart enough to know that in these parts, the less involvement a person has in such matters, the safer they'll be.

"Unfortunately, Handler is not going to make that an option for you," I tell her.

"Can we just not..." Baylin hesitates, searching for the right words. "I'll leave. I'll move away."

Romeo lets out a bitter laugh. "There's no escaping from someone like Handler," he reminds her, referencing the detective's relentless pursuit and giving me a pointed look to drive his point home.

"Enough," I say, pushing back from the table. "This isn't getting us anywhere. Handler wants Baylin's testimony, and she can't stay hidden here forever."

"Then what do you suggest?" Baylin asks, her large brown eyes pleading for some kind of mercy, mercy I probably can't offer her.

Romeo's glacial glint meets mine, and I see it then, the realization that grips him as suddenly as the sun grips the light of day. No matter what he's shared with Baylin Reyes, he sees only one way out of this. I see another.

"Run," I say abruptly, standing up so quickly, my chair slides across the floor unceremoniously.

Baylin stands, her slender figure trembling slightly. Her eyes are cemented to Romeo's. "If I go—"

"Go, before I change my mind," I add.

Romeo's eyes darken as he watches her, anticipating her next move. I don't think he really believes that she'll leave. She pauses only for a moment, then her mouth parts, but she quickly shuts it and heads for the door.

25

ROMEO

At the base of the stairs, she hesitates and gazes out at the forest that has been both her prison and her sanctuary for days. When she turns to face us standing on the porch, there is a sense of unease in her expression. The dark forest looms ominously at the edge of the clearing, almost as if it's silently promising her harm. She tries to look away – at the sky bruising into evening, the cabin with its false sense of shelter—but something inexplicably pulls her attention back to me.

She takes a few hesitant steps back towards me before stopping abruptly. I stand alongside my brother, stone-hearted, knowing that she may not survive the night as the sun slowly dips below the horizon.

Guilt lances through me, shredding at my heart. But duty binds me, a nagging voice in my mind reminding me of the consequences of betrayal. She was never meant to escape this place alive. And now, as her eyes search mine for a glimmer of mercy, I harden myself against her silent plea.

"Romeo."

It's one word. One plea. Confusion lights her brown eyes, and my breath catches as I watch her anguished face. Baylin, just as much in the wrong place at the wrong time as those dead men, sentenced to darkness and misery in these woods as we watch on. Her voice is barely a whisper as she implores me.

"Don't Romeo," she pleads, her voice quivering with fear and desperation as she looks between me on the porch and the ominous woods behind her. "I swear I won't breathe a word to anyone. Don't do this."

I feel a pang of guilt clawing at my insides, threatening to unravel the mask of indifference I wear so carefully. But I cannot afford to show weakness now. The consequences of letting her live are too great, a threat looming over not just my own life but the lives of everyone in my inner sanctum.

My body hums, adrenaline coursing through my blood, thick with malice and heavy with intent. I can't let her destroy us, so I'll destroy her first. I need to do what I know my brother will never have the stomach to do.

"Run!" my brother whispers urgently, as though he feels my impending breakdown as it clouds the air all around us.

Baylin gives Lazaro a sorrowful glance before locking eyes with me. When she doesn't get an answer from either of us, she turns and heads for the woods, her pace accelerating as my heart knocks about my chest, adrenaline spiking through me. I want her to run, but I want her to stay. The two conflicting emotions war within me, knocking about the cage in which my soul resides.

Lazaro's voice cuts through the tension, a calm so chilling it could freeze blood. "You're a dumb fuck, you know that?"

"Brother," I warn, the word slipping past my lips like a prayer for sanity in a world gone mad. We stand in that charged silence, watching as my little bird stops walking at the edge of the woods.

"You're not the same with her," he tells me, as I make a move down the stairs, following my little bird slowly. I maintain my distance, keeping my eyes on her at all times, even as Lazaro tries to be a distraction as he comes to stand beside me

My laugh cuts through the fading light sharply. "I'm not anything with her, Lazaro. You need to take off your rose colored glasses and see this for what it is."

"You have feelings for her. How could you hurt her if you care for her?" He looks at me as though seeing me for the first time, as though I am a complication he's trying to untangle.

"Feelings? Is that what we're doing here?" My gaze flickers from my brother to Baylin, and for a moment, her vulnerability walking alone through the forest cracks through my hardened exterior. My arm sweeps toward him, a cruel pantomime of dismissal. "I don't know what you think you see here brother, but you're blind."

"Am I?" There is an undercurrent of steel in Lazaro's voice, a warning that he isn't to be challenged.

"Enough of this," I hiss, turning intense eyes on my brother; now he's really pissed me off. All this talk about feelings and changing and things that he thinks matter. Nothing matters. Nothing has since we lost Sandro.

Baylin walks deeper into the darkness. I can see her timid body visibly shaking even from the distance between us.

I cup my hands around my mouth and yell to her. "Run, little bird! Into the woods."

This has become our sickening ritual since the day I brought her here. She whirls around, facing me, small hands clenched at her sides. She blinks, confused, her heart pounding a frantic rhythm against her ribcage as questions stop her dead in her tracks.

"What are you going to do, Romeo?" she asks. She turns her gaze from me to my brother and back again, searching for an answer. Her voice is filled with emotion, clear and concise even from this distance.

"Let's make this interesting, shall we?" I say, a smirk playing on my lips as I turn to my brother. "If Lazaro shoots and misses, you get to walk away."

"Romeo," Lazaro growls.

The pure terror that appears on her face is satisfying. I know Laz would never harm her; his moral code is too strong to be influenced easily. However, she doesn't know that. Her fear intensifies my thrill and makes me want to fall to my knees before her; it's so overpowering, I can almost taste it.

She hesitates, searching Lazaro's impassive face. He offers her nothing. No hint of his intentions. But behind my brother's piercing blue eyes, I know there's more at stake than Baylin's life—it's loyalty, love, and the fragile balance of power within our family. Baylin might be our wild card, but I'm the dice. Roll me, and you might not like what you get.

"If not..." My voice trails off, but the unspoken threat hangs heavy in the air. I can see her mind racing as she calculates chances and outcomes, knowing that to refuse would mean something far more sinister than she could possibly imagine.

"Fine," she says, forcing a false sense of bravado into her voice. Her legs tremble as she backs away, the darkness of the forest beckoning like a cold embrace.

"Don't forget to dodge the bullet," I call out, almost casually.

I cast one last glance over my shoulder, meeting Lazaro's gaze. There is no comfort there, only the harsh reality of our world—a world where love is a liability, and our bond is woven from barbed wire.

And then I watch as Baylin turns and runs, disappearing into the shadows of the trees, every step an act of defiance, every breath a hope for survival.

THE FOREST IS a blur of green and brown as she sprints between the trees. I can feel Lazaro's gaze like a physical weight on my back, but I don't chance a look over my shoulder. I watch as the damp earth beneath her feet gives way to patches of slick leaves, and Baylin stumbles, nearly losing her balance. It's not as easy to navigate the woods in the dark as it is in the light for someone not accustomed to them.

"Run, little bird, run!" My voice echoes through the trees, taunting her maliciously. My words spur her on, fear propelling her forward even as her mind screams for her to turn back; the forest in the dimming light is not a safe place to be.

I track her methodically, hunter seeking prey, as I continue through the forest, my long strides gaining on her. She's chosen a route we haven't done before, and I know exactly where she's headed.

"Romeo, whatever you're thinking, don't," Lazaro warns as he trails behind me.

"Just want to offer my little bird some support," I tell him, as I move away from him, edging deeper into the forest.

Lazaro wants her to live. He wants her to get away. Under any other circumstances, so do I. But these are not just any circumstances. She holds all the power in her hands. She's the one that can destroy us with the stroke of a pen, the scrape of a chair, the stringing of a few carefully select words. She could destroy us. And I know she will.

I'd already made my mind up what to do with her when Lazaro told her to run. If he doesn't have it in him to do what must be done, I will. And I would do it knowing that I'd be crossing a fine line, but the end would justify the means.

I reach into my waistband, take out my gun and hold it up.

Lazaro sees what I'm doing and yells.

Baylin stops running suddenly and raises her arms out like a bird about to take flight. It's the most beautiful thing I've ever seen. She narrowly misses a drop into the ravine and changes course.

A sharp crack splits the air, so sudden and loud it seems to come from everywhere and nowhere at once. Even from this distance, I see the stain of blood as it spreads across her back, radiating out across her shirt in streaks of pain. Her legs buckle, and the ground rushes up to meet her, before she goes rolling through the woods and disappears into the landscape.

"Baylin!"

Lazaro's shout comes from somewhere far away as darkness closes in, the edges of my vision dimming until there is nothing holding me up but the cold embrace of how badly I've fucked up.

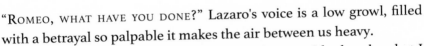

"Romeo, what have you done?" Lazaro's voice is a low growl, filled with a betrayal so palpable it makes the air between us heavy.

My jaw is tense as my brother approaches me. I had to do what I had to do.

"She was a liability, Lazaro. I did what I knew you couldn't. You should be thanking me."

"You don't get to make that call, Romeo," Lazaro spits back, stepping closer to me. The tension between us is electric and dangerous.

I hand the gun to my brother, muzzle down, and walk past him towards the cabin.

"She was a liability, brother."

Lazaro's fists clench at his sides. "You shot an innocent woman in the back!"

"Nothing about her is innocent!" I shout, my composure slipping.

Nothing about her is innocent. She made me want her, I want to tell him. She made me warm and light and full, taking away the cold, the dark, the emptiness of who I've been for so long. She would have destroyed me, in more ways than one. She would have brought me to my knees. She would have destroyed us.

But I don't tell him any of this. Instead, we stand face-to-face now, two titans locked in a silent war that seems to stretch beyond the confines of brotherhood and into something much darker.

"Damn it, Romeo," Lazaro's voice cracks with a pain that mirrors my own physical agony. "I love you more than anyone or anything in this godforsaken world. But this...you've finally crossed that line we swore we'd never cross."

His face shutters as he finishes his sentence and I turn away, continuing towards the cabin. My muscles tense as my brother's words swim around in my head, touching at a distant memory. An agreement. No women, no children, no drugs. The three sins we swore we'd never commit. Three rules we wouldn't break.

I've crossed almost every damn one of our lines since I met Baylin Reyes. Since I brought her to the cabin. I don't tell him that, though;

there's no point in twisting the knife inside him and painting me any uglier than I already am.

"I did the hard part," I tell him. "You bury her."

I can feel my heart pounding against my chest as I change direction and turn towards my car. I stride towards the driver's seat, desperate to escape this wretched place. The engine roars to life, drowning out the overwhelming silence that now pervades my surroundings. With one last glance at the deserted landscape behind me, I push down hard on the accelerator and speed off towards the city. There's nothing left for me here now, not without her by my side.

As I drive away, a gaping void opens up in my chest, gnawing away at my insides with every passing mile. She's gone, and with her goes any hope of finding solace in this desolate world. My brother's figure disappears into the woods behind me, but I refuse to turn back, knowing that it will only intensify the pain of her absence.

26

BAYLIN

I stumble down the slope, each drop sending a sharp jolt of pain through my shoulder. My breaths are shallow gasps against the cool air, and my vision blurs at the edges. I'm dying...I must be. They've left me here to rot and I can't believe this is the way my life ends. The pain is agonizing as I lie somewhere between night and day, resting on my stomach, waiting for the life to drain out of me. I don't know how long I lay there, but I hear the crunch of leaves underfoot, and soon the sound of footfalls in the woods nears me.

"Baylin? Baylin!" His voice is closer now, tinged with an urgency that seems out of place for a man of his calculated demeanor.

My body teeters on the brink of oblivion as I rest at the edge of the ravine. Ironically, surviving because my fall got stuck on a gnarly branch growing out of the earth. Who would have thought?

Strong arms encircle me, pulling me back from the precipice. Through the fading life of my eyes, I see it's Lazaro who pulls me back from the edge of oblivion, his grip both ironclad and gentle as he drags me away from the edge, away from the abyss meant to be my grave.

"I've got you," he mutters. I feel myself being lifted, carried like a child back through the dense forest towards the cabin that has become my gilded cage.

"Romeo," I whisper.

"Shh...Shh...shh." He tells me to save my strength, not to speak or move unnecessarily. But all I want is Romeo, not his older brother who shot me and now carries me through the woods, possibly to finish what he started.

The warmth of the interior hits me in waves as Lazaro walks into the cabin and kicks the door shut with his foot. He lays me down on the couch on my stomach with surprising care, his hands steady despite the chaos that had unfolded moments before.

"Where is it?" Lazaro's fingers track up and down my back through the fabric of my blood-stained shirt, looking for a bullet hole.

I shrink away from his touch. The fucker shot me.

"I need to give you something for the pain."

I don't tell him that I'm going to need a lot more than painkillers. I need a medical kit, or I'm very well going to bleed out here. It's like he reads my mind, though, because he moves swiftly, gathering supplies with an efficiency that speaks of a life lived in perpetual readiness for violence and its aftermath.

I see his face through the haze of my cloudy eyes; I'm on the verge of checking out, but I can't help but take comfort in the similarities between him and Romeo. He's older, his face lined with the burden of responsibilities he shoulders. But he's no less handsome than his younger brother. There's an old scar running across the edge of his lip, which ironically only adds to the beautiful mystery in front of me.

I'm lucky that I've been hit in the back of my shoulder. Nothing that won't heal quick enough. If anything's going to kill me, it will be the horror of being shot, not by the actual bullet lodged between skin and bones.

I direct him through the procedure, my mind clear even as my body screams in protest.

"Cut away the fabric... sterilize the area..." My instructions are concise, every word laced with years of practice; I know I can clean a bullet wound with my eyes closed, but I don't know what this man's angle is. He may just be here to finish the job he started. But in the moment, he's following my every instruction as I walk him through the steps and my mind maps his fingers as they trail against my now damaged skin.

Until he stops, and I feel the air in the cabin change. It's charged with something electric as his fingers glide across my shoulder, fluttering against my skin.

"How..." I turn my face, watch as he shakes his head. His eyes are fixed on my shoulder, confusion lancing through them.

"What is it?" I ask.

He shakes his head, tells me it's nothing, then asks me what he should do next.

Lazaro follows my guidance, his hands surprisingly gentle as he works to remove the bullet lodged in my shoulder. There is a focused intensity in the way his hands move against my skin after he cuts away the fabric and lets it fall away from my shoulder.

"Got it," he says, holding up the bloody piece of metal between the tweezers. A sigh of relief escapes me, and darkness nibbles at the corners of my consciousness.

"Stay awake," Lazaro urges, dousing my shoulder with more alcohol before he wraps it with bandages. "You'll live," he proclaims, as the edge of darkness once again claims me.

I STRUGGLE TO SIT UP, wrapping a thin blanket around my chest as I do so. Lazaro emerges from the bathroom, drying his hands on a small towel. His penetrating gaze meets mine as he approaches.

"Careful, you don't want to tear your stitches," he says.

I doubt his threading a needle and passing it through my skin constitutes stitches, but I say nothing as the pain in my shoulder intensifies.

"Where's Romeo?"

Lazaro clenches his jaw, a tell-tale sign that they must have had a disagreement.

"He went back to the city."

"So now it's your turn to babysit me?" My words sound flat against the silence of the room. Lazaro doesn't respond as he heads to the kitchen and takes out two cans from an overhead cabinet.

"I'm not hungry," I protest as he dumps the contents into a pot.

He turns to me, his stern glare reminding me of his brother. "Did I give you a choice?" It seems Lazaro can be just as imposing as his brother.

"Why would you shoot me, only to save me?" I finally voice the question that has been nagging at me since waking up. My eyes scan the quiet cabin before settling on him once again.

He inhales deeply and avoids eye contact, continues stirring the pot before switching off the stove. He shovels soup into two bowls and sets them on the table, then comes to sit opposite me on the sofa.

"Why did Romeo leave?" I ask him.

"He thought you were dead."

"Did you purposely aim to miss?"

He's silent for the longest time, until I stretch my leg and nudge his.

"I don't understand what you're doing...what's happening. You want me dead, but then you rescue me. You stitch me up and now you're going to feed me. What am I missing here?"

"The only thing you're missing, Baylin Reyes, is a timeline of your future. I don't know what that looks like, and I would highly recommend that you don't ask questions you don't want the answers to."

"You could have shot to kill me. Did you purposely aim to miss?"

"There you go again. Did you not hear anything I just said?"

"I heard you loud and clear. Why did Romeo leave?"

"I told you why."

A bitter laugh bubbles up from deep within me, tinged with disbelief. "Explain that to me," I screech. "Why did he really leave?" My voice wavers, the pain lancing through me undeniable.

"Romeo is...complicated."

The stretch of silence that follows tells me he's not going to elaborate. Do I even want to understand what that means? Do I really want to know why he left me out here in the middle of nowhere with his deranged brother after the way he touched me? I can still feel the touch of his fingers on my skin, even long after he's gone.

Lazaro's eyes meet mine briefly before flitting away, a flicker of guilt clouding his expression. But I refuse to show any sign of weakness, any indication that his or his brother's actions have affected me. Deep down, I know that understanding Romeo is something that probably will not happen in this lifetime. The curiosity gnaws at me, urging me to peel back the layers of his complexity and unearth the truth buried underneath, but even that is not enough to sustain my need to know.

"I can't believe he just left me here for dead," I say, my voice bitter. It feels like a betrayal, what he did, like a fresh wound that's deeper than the one on my shoulder.

THE WAY he moves around the room, it's like watching a storm on the horizon – you know something fierce is coming, but you just can't look away. Lazaro never fumbles with the bandages or the medicines; every motion is precise, deliberate, as if he's done this a thousand times over.

"Keep still," he says softly, his hands gentle as they trace the lines of pain etched into my skin. I wince, not from the touch, but the kindness behind it. It is disarming, coming from a man I know could command an entire room with just a look. The same man who put a bullet in me while I had my back turned.

"Just a couple more minutes." His voice is low, a rumble that seems out of place in the quiet of the room. It isn't just the apology but the weight of it that makes me glance up at him. Those blue eyes, deep and mysterious, are worn with a warmth that is ultimately lacking in his brother.

"Lazaro," I start, my voice barely above a whisper, "why are you doing this?"

"Because I have to," he answers without further explanation. There's a simplicity to his words that makes me believe there's a human side to the man that runs the underworld with an iron fist.

"Even at the expense of your own freedom?"

His hands stop moving against the bandages, his eyes lowering to meet mine, a thoughtful look on his face. He says nothing as he holds up a mirror to the wound, and I check for any signs of infection. He continues to change the bandage, winding it tight against my skin, before I hand him the scissors. He snips the end and tucks it under layers of fabric before he steps away, surveying his work.

"Tell me about the tattoo," he says.

I drop my eyes, shame curling through me. Though I'm not the one who should be ashamed. I didn't inflict that pain on myself; Romeo forced it upon me. The reminder of the scar on my skin makes my insides turn over painfully.

"Your brother branded me."

"Why?"

"He wanted his name to be the last one to pass between my lips. He wanted me to always remember that he owned me."

"That's my brother, complicated as all fuck."

He nods, agreeing with his own words, and I continue to watch him as he paces around the small cabin. He is so much more than the head of a crime family; he is a man who's lost as much as he's fought for, a man who bears the weight of a legacy that is both a shield and a shackle. In the dim light of dawn, with his guard down, I see the cost of that power etched into the lines of his face.

"You and he got close pretty quickly," he says, as though an afterthought. He stops pacing and turns to face me, leaning against the kitchen bench.

I nod, swallow. "Depends on what you constitute as close."

"I saw you together in the forest."

A deep crimson blush moves up my neck, settling sharply against my skin. Invisible flames lick at my body, and I feel the heat of embarrassment as it cascades over me.

"His pain made me feel. Feeling anything, even pain, is better than feeling nothing at all."

I tilt my head up to gaze at Lazaro, hopefulness written all over my face. His expression is hard to read as he stands over me, the weight of a huge dilemma pressing down on him. On one hand, he saved me after he pulled the trigger that almost took my life. On the other hand, my survival could mean the potential downfall of the Riccardis for their crimes. I know that one or the other of the brothers would most likely want to finish what Lazaro started.

I can see the wheels turning in Lazaro's mind as he ponders the gravity of the situation. What would it mean for him if I live and the threat of me testifying hangs over his head like an invisible thread?

"Get some sleep," he finally responds with a heavy sigh. The room falls silent, heavy with tension and unspoken fears, mostly mine.

27

LAZARO

The persistent scratch of a nearby branch against the window soothes me, bringing a sense of peace that has been absent for a very long time. Every hour that passes that I'm away from the city, the tension in my body seems to ease. It's been so long, I'd forgotten the comfort of peace, something we don't see much of in our world.

I'm equal parts angry at Romeo as well as incensed. I've seen the gradual decline of his mental state over the past few years, but I never thought I'd be standing on the edge trying to pull him back from his insanity. Because ultimately, that is what this is.

He kidnapped Baylin Reyes and brought her here to the woods. He somehow focused all his attention on some sort of weird love/hate relationship with her. From what I gather, some sort of cat and mouse game where he made her run through the forest, and he portrayed the hunter. I saw him with my own two eyes, mauling her in the forest, his passion for her insurmountable. And then I watched in horror as he shot that same woman in the back, deliberately missing a vital artery and hitting her shoulder instead.

Never mind the branding. My crazy brother signed his name across her shoulder, giving her something to always remember him by. I know he must have drugged her to do it; she told me she didn't remember it, only that she woke with a stabbing pain in her shoulder - then Romeo took her to the bathroom and held up a mirror to show her his mark. She told me she'd had no words; that was when she'd understood she'd only ever be free of Romeo if she was in a body bag.

No matter how crazy things ever got with Romeo, I can't remember him ever been as reckless, as unforgiving as he was here in these woods with this woman. A woman who, by any standards, could be our downfall. But she's still a woman, and we don't kill women.

"Does he know?"

I break away from my thoughts when I hear Baylin's voice, and I turn to face her. She's up and moving around, which is a positive sign, but she's the nurse, so she would have a better understanding of her condition.

"What's that?" I ask.

"Does your brother know I'm alive?" Her tone turns sharp at the mention of Romeo, and I can't blame her for feeling that way.

"No," I reply honestly.

She nods to herself and then announces that she needs some fresh air. When I offer to join her, she politely declines by raising her hand. A wave of frustration washes over me as she rejects my company. It appears that she now despises me as much as she does my brother.

"I need to clear my head."

I don't even consider the possibility of her trying to escape; there's nowhere for her to go in this secluded location. And not to forget that she was the one begging to be spared just yesterday from being thrown into the woods.

I watch with bated breath as Baylin walks away, disappearing into the edge of the forest. A part of me wants to follow her, to make sure she's safe, but another part knows that she needs space - from me, from Romeo, from everything that has happened. I can't shake the feeling that something is about to change, that our fragile peace is on the verge of shattering.

I watch her through the window as she walks to the edge of the forest and stands at the tree line, her arms crossed over her chest as she looks off into the distance. I turn away from the window, giving her privacy, but as the minutes blend into an hour and beyond, I find myself walking past the window to check on her. She's still there, only she's gravitated to a nearby boulder and sits there, her knees tucked under her chin as she sits with her own thoughts.

I see a glimmer of vulnerability in her usually composed demeanor as she reaches up and quickly wipes away tears. From where I stand, I can't see them, but I know they're there. My mind races with questions, wondering how everything went so wrong and how our one night of madness could have caused so much destruction. I try to push the thoughts aside, not one to dwell on past events, but for some reason, Baylin's situation has gotten under my skin. There is something about her that pulls at me in a way that I don't typically feel towards most people I meet. I chance breaking into her thoughts and leave the cabin, heading to the tree line.

"You okay?" I ask softly, approaching her cautiously. She looks up at me, her eyes reflecting a mixture of pain and uncertainty. So many questions swirling in their depths.

"Why do you care?"

I sigh and look out at the dark forest, hands on my hips when I turn back to face her. "Let's just say I'm invested in not having any more blood on my hands," I tell her.

"A little too late for that."

Her reminder snaps at something inside me and has me swallowing back the lump in my throat.

"I don't know how I got here," she says. "A month ago, my life was near perfect. Now...I'm flailing. I don't know where or what I am."

"Sort of the way I've felt my whole life," I tell her.

She shakes her head shortly, her eyes darting back to the woods.

"You had a choice," she whispers. "You chose this life. I didn't."

I'm quiet as I watch her conflicting eyes dart back and forth against the tree line. I don't know that there's much more that I can say knowing that she's right.

"Why did you save me?" she asks. "It would have been so easy for you to walk away and let me die alone in that ravine. I never would have made it out on my own."

I shrug, although I do know. I know why I saved her. I know that I couldn't let her die; I couldn't let my brother live with that for the rest of his life. One day – if he hasn't, already – he's going to regret killing the only person outside of his family he ever felt anything for. And when he does, he's going to hate himself. Then he's going to self-destruct. Because that's what Romeo does when he realizes he's fucked up. He spirals. He loses control. And it takes a whole lot of steel to drag him back from the depths of his despair.

"Tell me," she urges.

"I couldn't let you die out here alone."

Her eyes are wide and desperate. "Who's going to pull the trigger on me next time – you or your brother?"

She holds her hand up, stops me. She doesn't want to hear it. She doesn't want to know. So my words die on my tongue. I don't tell her that it was never my intention for her to get hurt. I maybe would have kept a watchful eye on her, but to hurt her? Not my style. I also don't tell her that Romeo is the best shooter we have. There's no way, even from that distance, that he would have missed a vital organ, unless he was deliberately trying to miss. He nicked her shoulder only because that's where he was aiming. He never meant to kill her. I have to believe that. I have to believe that there is still some redemption in my brother.

"DOES IT HURT?" The words slip from my lips before I can stop them. My hands pause, hovering over the raw edges of her wound as I wait for her response.

My gaze doesn't waver, but a muscle ticks in my jaw—she clamps down on her pain, shutting me out.

"It's nothing I can't handle," she says, her voice carrying that familiar calm that's now edged with steel.

I nod, recognizing the stoicism for what it is: a shield. "You're good at hiding your pain," I respond, resuming my work with the antiseptic-soaked cloth. I'm changing her dressing for the fourth time in two hours. She got so fired up earlier that she must have torn a stress vessel, because her bandage is soaked in blood even before I have a chance to move away from her.

I stand behind her as she sits on the chair, her shoulder hunched forward, supplies laid out on the table like an offering between us. Her breaths are shallow, her skin paler than the moonlight filtering through the blinds. I reach for a clean cloth, dampening it with antiseptic. "This might sting," I warn, though my touch is as gentle as if I were tending to a child's wound rather than the battered body of a woman who's taken a lead bullet and a tumble through the woods.

Her jaw clenches as I begin to clean the wound, but she doesn't flinch. With each careful swipe, I can feel her body tense.

"Keep still," I murmur, more to remind myself to remain focused. "Almost done," I breathe out, my hands now steady as a surgeon's as I work to erase all traces of the violence that has left her in this state. Violence at the hands of my own brother. A brother who's now gone to ground, probably off in some corner licking his wounds. It's intimate, this act of caring for her, and with it, the line between duty and desire blurs into obscurity. But as I look at every line etched into her back, every violent streak, I know that isn't the only line in danger of disappearing.

I reach for a fresh bandage, my fingers brushing against the raw edges of her wound. Her body tenses under my touch, a sharp intake of breath betraying the pain she's trying to hide.

"Talk to me," she urges softly, and I think she's hoping to distract herself from the sting of antiseptic on torn flesh. "It helps, sometimes."

Baylin's gaze meets mine as she turns to look over her shoulder, and there's a storm brewing in those deep brown depths—a tempest of doubt and fear that she's kept at bay behind a fortress of steely resolve.

"What do you want me to say?"

"Anything. How did you find yourself in this life?"

I'm quiet for the longest time. I wonder how much of my life she could possibly stomach.

"Ever since I was a kid, I've known my life would never be just my own," I begin, my voice a low rumble that fills the silence between us. "Every move I make affects the family, every decision is about balance, power... survival. Sometimes, I wonder what it would be like to just... breathe without the weight of the Riccardi name on my shoulders."

My confession hangs heavy in the air, and I feel the gravity of my world—the relentless pressure, the ceaseless demands—pressing down on me.

She watches me, something flickering behind her eyes—a glint of hope, maybe, or the dawning realization that she is truly in the company of monsters.

"Baylin..." My voice is a whisper, a tentative reaching out across the chasm that our lives have placed between us. And as I resume my task, winding the bandage around her shoulder, I let my fingertips graze her skin once more, a silent promise of solidarity.

In the quiet of the room, with only the sound of our breathing and the soft rustle of cloth, I sense the shift between us. The boundaries we've drawn around ourselves are blurring, and the distance is closing, filled with the warmth of shared vulnerability. It's a dangerous thing, this closeness, a risk that neither of us can afford.

But as I secure the bandage and meet her gaze, it feels like the most natural thing in the world to lean into that growing connection, to acknowledge the attraction that simmers just beneath the surface.

"Better?" My voice barely rises above a whisper, but it feels like it echoes in the space we've created—this tiny sanctuary carved out from the perilous life I lead.

She nods, the softness of her response matching mine.

We stay like that for a moment longer, neither of us moving to break the contact. It's strange, this feeling of peace that wraps around us.

Her eyes lock onto mine, and there's an understanding there that words can't touch. It's the kind of look that says more than a thousand conversations ever could. We're two people, worlds apart in life, yet in this sliver of time, we're just Baylin and Lazaro. Nothing more, nothing less.

"Thank you," she murmurs.

"No need to thank me," I tell her, even though part of me—the guarded part that's seen too much—screams that I should be as far away from her as possible.

She smiles, and it's a rare thing, that smile. It lights up her face, chases away the shadows that usually cling to me like a second skin. My heart stutters at the sight, because I know that smile is for me—and it goes against everything she believes in.

28

BAYLIN

There's only silence around us, save for the occasional crackle of the fire in the hearth. From my spot on the couch, I watch Lazaro, tracing his features in the dim light and feeling the dangerous pull between us as he sits gazing into the fire.

It has been two full days since Lazaro saved me from the edge of the ravine. My wound is healing better than I could have hoped, with frequent changes of dressing and a burning alcohol rub that sears my skin like flames.

I get up and approach him, every instinct warning me to stop, screaming at me to go back. But it's like my feet have grown a mind of their own and my body betrays me, yearning to close the distance between us. As I draw near, he looks at me carefully. A lock of his dark hair falls into his face, so much like Romeo's, and I brush it back and smooth it down. He reaches out, his hand brushing against mine as he steadies my awkward stand, sending a jolt of electricity straight through my heart. I feel like I'm floating, like I'm high on some super drug that threatens to pull me down.

"You're getting better," he says softly, his thumb caressing my wrist where my pulse flutters like a caged bird.

"Lazaro..." His name is a whisper, a question, a plea.

He stands up, towering over me as shadows dance across his face, turning him into both the villain and hero of my story. My gaze flickers to his lips, full and tantalizingly close to mine, and I feel that magnetic attraction again, pulling me closer to the edge of reason.

"Baylin, I can't..." But his words die off as his fingers weave through my hair and tilt my head back. There is a battle raging in his blue eyes, a storm of desire and regret mirroring my own inner turmoil. And all I can hold on to is that he said he "can't", not that he doesn't want to.

Yet when our lips meet, all thoughts of right or wrong vanish. The kiss starts off tenderly, a question to which my body screams yes, before deepening into an insatiable hunger that speaks of dark rooms and even darker secrets. A soft moan escapes me, and I cling to him, my hands gripping the fabric of his shirt.

In that moment, I feel everything - his heart beating against mine, the warmth of his body seeping into my bones, the taste of him promising both destruction and redemption. It's mad, this heat, this need that blurs the boundaries I have so carefully built.

When we finally part, breathless and flushed, the world snaps back into focus, sharp and unforgiving. Confusion floods over me, drowning out the last remnants of bliss. How could I have such feelings for Lazaro when the memory of Romeo, his brother, taints my soul?

"Lazaro," I whisper, my voice shaking.

I kissed Romeo's brother. I liked kissing Romeo's brother. It's confusing as fuck, that little spark of chemistry between us. The same man who shot at me and tried to take my life is now kissing me back, and I can feel a spark of electricity between us that shouldn't exist. Every part of me rebels against this intimacy as I struggle to hold onto my sanity; only a crazy person could find pleasure in such a situation, where men would rather see me dead than standing above ground. Only a crazy woman would have such wanton feelings towards men who personify such evil.

Lazaro's gaze holds concern and something else I can't understand. Is it longing? Or am I just wishing for something more? My mind is filled with questions and uncertainty. How could I have feelings for both brothers?

My lips tingle, and I can't stop thinking about this one careless moment with Lazaro. A forbidden thrill that both excites and scares me runs down my spine. But now, with guilt eating away at me, I know I have to make a choice. Romeo has been the rock I never knew I needed through a distant pain that has never really healed. He helped me heal and erase the pain. Yet, there's something about Lazaro that makes me yearn for passion and comfort. He's the safe choice between the two brothers. And yet, he shot me. He shot me as I turned away and ran.

"What are we doing?" My voice breaks, confusion pervasive in the stale air of the cabin.

His eyes search mine, heavy with pain and longing. In silence, he looks at me, and in the depths of his mesmerizing blue eyes, I see a reflection of all that I am feeling.

And there it is, laid bare - the heart of my dilemma. To fall for one Riccardi is a risk; to be entangled with both is a fate worse than any tragedy I could imagine. Yet despite the chaos, the turmoil, and the guilt, there is something about Lazaro that makes me forget the darkness, even if only for a fleeting moment.

I move away reluctantly and go back to my place on the couch and drape a woolen blanket over my legs as I watch Lazaro move about the room with that silent grace of his. He's a tempest in a tailored suit, but now he is the calm after the storm, collecting the scattered remains of our restraint. His back is to me as he straightens the books on the shelf, a task that seems like it's an excuse to keep his hands busy more than anything else.

"As soon as you're well enough, we'll head back to the city."

He doesn't look at me as he speaks, though his words are heavy with implication. A nauseating wave of fear sweeps over me. The city —with its gray buildings and endless noise—feels like another world compared to this secluded place where secrets whisper through the trees and danger lurks in the shadows. But it isn't just the location that has me hesitating; it is the thought of what awaits us there—the tangled reality of who we are.

I know eventually, the time will come, and we'll have to go back. But the thought of leaving the relative peace of this place and going back home to face an uncertain future tamps at something deep within me. I miss Luca. I miss mama. I miss everything about my life the way it used to be. But that's not the way things are now. And I still have the matter of Detective Handler dogging my every move, testing my patience.

"Back to the city," I echo quietly, pulling the blanket tighter around myself. The fabric is soft, but it does little to shield me from the uncertainty that creeps into my bones. "To what, exactly? More of... this?" I gesture vaguely between us, unable to give voice to the maelstrom of emotions churning inside me.

Lazaro turns to face me, his eyes searching mine for something I'm not sure I can give him.

"Sooner or later, we have to go back." There is resolve in his stance, but I catch the flicker of something else—something softer—in the blue depths of his gaze.

"Lazaro..." I trail off, biting my lip. My heart races at the thought of what I have to face when I go back.

"Things are already complicated enough as it is," he admits, crossing the room to sit before me. His hand brushes against mine, sending jolts of electricity up my arm. "But I assure you, you'll always be safe."

'Complicated' is an understatement. It is a knot so tight; I doubt even his deft fingers could untangle it. And yet, as I look into his eyes, I find myself wanting to believe him. Wanting to believe that we can find our way back.

Conflict rages within me. Love and hate. Trust and betrayal. Hope and despair. They are all there, warring inside my chest, each demanding to be felt, to be chosen.

As I sit here, looking into the eyes of the man who has both broken and healed parts of me, I know one thing for certain: no matter where I stand with the brothers or what the future holds, my heart has already made its choice.

And that realization is as frightening as it is liberating.

29

LAZARO

Baylin moves slowly around the cabin, taking small laps in the tight space between walls to get some exercise. As she walks by me, I put down my phone and fix her with a hard stare.

"You guys were here for a while. How did you pass the time?"

She gives me a crooked grin and I immediately regret asking. It's pretty obvious what they were up to, especially considering how I found them in the forest when I arrived at the cabin.

"I'll pretend you didn't just ask that," Baylin replies with a hint of amusement in her voice.

Heat rises to my cheeks as I remember seeing her naked in the middle of the wilderness. I quickly look away, trying to push back the anxiety that's building up inside me.

"I've never seen my brother act like that with anyone before."

"Like what?" Baylin tilts her head, genuinely curious about my thoughts.

"Like you're his whole world."

She scoffs and loosens her arms from their crossed position, letting them hang at her sides.

"Then you don't really know your brother, Lazaro."

"I know enough to see that he's different with you."

Baylin gives me a hard stare before frowning, dropping all her defenses as her carefully crafted facade starts to unravel. It's clear that she feels the same way about him. That kiss we shared – the one that made me realize I never wanted to kiss anyone else again – it shouldn't have happened. And it can't happen again. I need to make sure we leave this place quickly and return to the city as soon as possible.

She can never find out that Romeo was the one who shot her. He probably regrets his actions already, but if she knows the truth, it will only ruin whatever connection they have. And I can't let that happen. Even if it means she will spend the rest of her life believing I shot her in cold blood, so be it. She can never know the truth about Romeo, or she will end up hating him. And I am not willing to find out what a vengeful Baylin Reyes is capable of. Frankly, I'm not sure anyone wants to find out.

~

Romeo's three calls go unanswered until I decide to call him back.

"Why are you still there?" he asks. I don't bother to ask how he knows I'm still at the cabin we've barely used until now.

"I'll be back soon," I tell him.

There's a pause before he says he didn't ask when I'd be back. I repeat myself, telling him I'll be home soon to avoid any more questions about why I'm still at the cabin.

"Detective Handler is still poking around," Romeo says, and I can tell he's itching to get rid of him. But we don't need more attention right now. Killing Handler would just make things worse and bring more unwanted attention to us.

"I'd expect nothing less," I reply.

"Be careful, brother," he warns. "He's especially interested in where you might be."

"I have nothing to hide."

"Don't you?"

His words hang in the air. I can tell he wants to ask about her, but he doesn't. Romeo's pride might get him into trouble. He switches topics to work and warns me again to be careful before hanging up without saying goodbye.

I end the call, my heart racing. Baylin is on the sofa, looking out at the peaceful woods around the cabin. The afternoon sun shines through the trees, casting pretty patterns of light on her face. She turns to me with a mix of fear and curiosity.

"Was that Romeo?" she asks.

"I need you to get better so we can go back to the city," I say, avoiding her question. "Detective Handler won't stop until he finds you."

"He's like a leech," she says. "He just won't let go."

"Seems like you're not a fan."

She shakes her head and scoffs. "He's not someone I'd help, no matter who he is. The son of a bitch tried to use my nephew against me," she says with anger.

"That's how he got you to testify? By threatening your nephew?"

"No way. He tried, but I was about to leave town with my nephew when Romeo grabbed me. I was never going to testify, Lazaro."

For some reason, I believe her. She knows what we're capable of; even the police can't protect her from us if we really want to get to her. I believe she wasn't going to testify. Detective Handler uses shady tactics to get what he wants, and I trust Baylin decided to run rather than face his harassment.

"He was telling everyone who would listen that you agreed to testify. I think perhaps to force our hand and get us to do something reckless he could nail us with."

"Peachy. Looks like you fell right into his lap."

A sudden thought hits me. Baylin was there the night of the shooting. She could have been a witness, but she might have easily become a victim herself. The idea bothers me more than I expect it to.

"What were you doing there that night?" I ask, curiosity getting the better of me.

Her eyes turn away, glazed with tears as she relives the painful memory.

"I was grabbing groceries for dinner."

I observe her as a smile dances across her features, only to be replaced by a cloud of sadness in her eyes.

"We were planning to spend the night curled up on the sofa with my nephew Luca. I'd just stepped out of the store. That's when it happened."

"You really were in the wrong place at the wrong time," I tell her, musing at the irony of the situation. The what ifs. What if she hadn't stopped for groceries? What if she'd been one or two minutes late? What if she'd never been there in the first place? It wasn't hard to understand why Baylin was struggling with her grief; questions like that could really play on a person's mind, killing their closure.

"Wrong place, wrong time," she whispers, but when she does, she looks at me in a way that tells me she's not referring strictly to the dead men. The same rule could be applied to us. It could be applied to her and my brother. It could be applied to any or all of the factors that had a hand in throwing us together.

She takes a deep breath, the weight of her words settling between us like an unspoken truth.

"I never imagined that my life would intertwine with the ones whose hands are soiled with blood," Baylin says softly, her voice tinged with a mix of sorrow and disbelief. "Yet here I am, I think forever bound by a cruel fate that's determined to knot us together in ways that will only lead to disaster."

Her gaze flickers to my face, searching for understanding, for absolution perhaps. But all she finds is a mirror reflecting her own turmoil and conflict. I'll always be the stranger whose actions shattered her world, a constant reminder of her loss.

For Baylin, it's been one unfortunate event after another since that night. She may have been spared from a bullet the night of the shooting, but her own living waking days have become sullied by nightmares as she's moored in her own horror. Every move she made eventually led her to us. To my brother and I. And now, it's so clear to see her inner turmoil as she tries to reconcile the contradiction of feeling drawn to the men who shattered her world with their own brand of violence.

30

BAYLIN

The old cabin groans under the weight of our whispered silence. Lazaro's eyes, sharp and cold as ice, are narrowed in intense thought. His jaw muscles clench tight, a sign of the storm brewing inside him.

He sets the phone down, his glance barely passing over me before he moves to stand in front of the fire, not quite dressed after his shower. I watch as the tiny rivulets of water staining his skin curl and dry up, as the line of muscles in his back shift and flex with every breath he takes.

His hands clench. Unclench. Anxiety swells all around him and I hear his hiss as it resounds in the room.

"What is it?" I ask.

He's silent for the longest time before he turns around, looks at me as though assessing whether or not to confide his secrets to me.

"Detective Handler is on his way. He seems sure you're here."

"Well, I am," I point out.

He doesn't say what he wants to say, but his eyes give me the whole story. Detective Handler coming here could only mean one thing - that he believes I've been taken against my will and he's planning a rescue mission. One that could end up with disastrous results.

"He's going to make you testify, Baylin."

"He can't make me do anything." I stir from my position across the room and stand, making my way toward the flickering fire. Shadows cross against his face as he looks down at me.

"Even after that?" He points to the bullet wound in my shoulder.

"I can't be that person, Lazaro. You hurt me when you shot me. Romeo eviscerated me by walking away so callously." I watch the flicker of pain that crosses his face, the tightening of his jaw. It gives me little comfort, but it's something. "But this is not about me. I have others to think about, and I don't want to spend my life looking over my shoulder or wondering whether or not my nephew will make it home in one piece."

"You said he threatened you with your nephew," he tells me.

"He did. And you're a threat to Luca also, though not in so many words. I think I'll take my chances on the Riccardis, not the whiny detective that's a pain in my ass."

"He's determined."

I cut him off, a demure sort of panic tightening my chest. "So am I." I run my fingers through my tangled hair, freeing the knots in the ends.

Lazaro reaches out, his touch warm against the cold tension in his eyes. "Mighty brave words for a helpless little girl," he says softly, his own fingers tangling in one of my curls.

Before I can reply, our moment of calm is shattered by a loud, deafening knock on the door that echoes through the room and jolts us apart. My head whips toward the sound, my heart racing. Lazaro doesn't seem in the least bit fazed by the intrusion, as though he was expecting it.

"Police! Open up!" Detective Handler' voice on the other side is unmistakable.

"Already?" I hiss.

Fear flickers across my face, while defiance dances across Lazaro's. Our delicate balance is once again tipping into chaos. I hold my breath, trying to steady the frantic thud of my heart. Each beat seems to scream out in aching pain.

"Do you trust me?" Lazaro asks, his eyes finding mine as his hands skate against my bare arms.

I nod once, my tongue tied. He reaches up to my hair and musses it, then nods toward the bathroom door. "Go put a robe on, cover up your wound, stay there." I move easily toward the bathroom, leave it cracked open and watch with one eye through the shaft where the hinges meet the wall. The view is limited, but I can't help but be the quiet trespasser to this new development.

He moves toward the door, his posture shifting from protective to resolute. He looks back once as I disappear into the bathroom and close the door. My fear is intense, my breath coming in short, quiet gasps. I hear the whoosh of cold air as the door swings open and Lazaro greets Detective Handler with feigned surprise.

"Detective Handler," I imagine he quirks an eyebrow "what brings you here at this hour?"

"Lazaro," Handler says in a gravelly voice. "Thought I'd stop by for a chat."

"Out here in the middle of nowhere? You're a long way from your jurisdiction."

Handler ignores the jab, and I watch his eyes scanning the room in the pause that follows. "You wouldn't happen to know where Baylin Reyes is, would you?"

Lazaro lets out a slow, forced laugh. "I might. What's it to you?"

"She's part of an ongoing investigation into multiple homicides."

He makes a point of emphasizing the s in homicides.

Handler's eyes narrow as they roam around the room, then finally settle on Lazaro's shirtless torso. I press myself closer to the wall, invested in every word that passes between these two men. Lazaro's back is to me, but I can imagine the cold calculation in his gaze.

"And this has what to do with me?" Lazaro's voice is smooth yet laced with danger.

Handler steps further into the room, and Lazaro does nothing to stop him. Each step feels like a countdown, bringing him closer to discovering me. "Because she's officially a missing person. And I know how much you like control; she's a loose end you can't control."

Lazaro's laugh is low and unsettling. "And?"

"And I know you had something to do with her disappearance."

"Knowing and proving are two different things, detective. Your obsession with Ms. Reyes is starting to look unprofessional."

Handler scowls but masks it with a sneer. "My 'obsession' keeps criminals like you in check."

"Allegations, Detective," Lazaro says sharply. "Let's stick to facts."

Handler's eyes skim the room, briefly flickering towards the bathroom but not stopping. For a moment, I dare to breathe.

"You boys seem to have a real hard on for Ms. Reyes," Detective Handler says, as his eyes come back to meet Lazaro's. "I know you abducted her. I will find her body, and I will bring you down. One way or another."

"Make yourself comfortable," Lazaro says, pointing to an armchair. "Looks like we're in for a long night."

"Cut the crap, Lazaro," Handler says, not taking a seat. "Where is she?"

I can hear my own shallow breaths, each one echoing loudly. My heart races as an impending sense of doom sweeps over me.

Outside, Lazaro's voice is calm and collected, a stark contrast to my own turmoil.

"Lazaro," Handler's voice is sharp, making my head snap to attention. "Would you like to add abduction to your long list of offences?"

"Detective, you wound me with your accusations," Lazaro says, sounding almost hurt. The detective moves closer, and the air grows thick with tension. I hold my breath, praying Handler won't hear my pounding heart. "Your concern for Ms. Reyes is touching," Lazaro says with a chilling politeness. "But I assure you..."

My heart beats right out of its cage, its thumping beat jolting me out of my head. I don't let Lazaro finish. Instead, I step out from behind the door and make my presence be known. Lazaro told me to trust him, but now it's he that needs to trust me. He saved my life; when he could have so easily walked away and saved himself, he decided to stay and save me. I won't ever forget that, regardless of what comes to pass, regardless of the bullet wound in my back.

I wrap a towel around my hair and tighten my robe, then emerge from the bathroom.

"Babe, what's taking you..."

I feign surprise as I look up, stopping short as my eyes meet the detective's.

"Detective!" I squeal, frowning. I step up to Lazaro's side and continue to watch the detective as the emotions on his face morph from shock to suspicion to rage.

"What the fuck are you doing here?" he asks. He is downright fuming.

I look up at Lazaro innocently, smile and force a bashful look onto my face. I wind an arm around Lazaro's waist; it doesn't quite cover half of his substantial back.

"Is there a problem?" I ask.

"You're a missing person; I've been looking for you."

"And you found me!" I beam. "Did you need something that couldn't wait until I got back to the city?"

"This man kidnapped you," he seethes. Technically, he didn't, so me lying is not that far a stretch.

"No, he didn't."

"How do you know Riccardi? I thought you said at the precinct you hadn't seen him before?"

He looks like he's caught me in the lie of the century and gives me a satisfied smirk.

"Well, that's true. I hadn't seen him before. He was waiting for me outside the precinct that day when we passed each other in the hall. Call it kismet, call it twin flames. He asked me out and now here we are."

I hug into Lazaro's side and steal his warmth. He's like an inferno about to combust. He's all rigid muscle and strength, and I hum to myself, feeling like I could get used to burying myself in his side.

Detective Handler gives me a skeptical look.

Suddenly, a loud thud from outside freezes everything. Detective Handler's head snaps toward the window, his body tensing.

"Must be some animal," Lazaro says, looking at the window, his jaw tightening. The detective's eyes swing to the window, his hand moving to his gun.

"Wildlife can be a nuisance here," I say, trying to divert Handler's eyes, although I don't even know what I'm diverting them from. I know what I heard, and it's nothing I've heard the past few days I've been here. The detective's eyes remain on the shadows outside the window.

"Will that be all, Detective?"

I swing my eyes up to Lazaro's. The two men are locked in a silent battle of wills that I can't infiltrate.

"Ms. Reyes is coming with me."

"Excuse me?"

I move away from Lazaro and pull my robe tighter.

"I don't for one second believe that you are here of your own voli- tion. I'll be escorting you back to the city."

"Like hell you will," Lazaro says, stepping in front of me and pushing me behind him. "She'll go no-where with you."

"She's wanted for questioning in a crime perpetrated by a member or members of your family, and now she's here with you. You really expect me to believe this is just a coincidence? Admit you took her by force."

"He'll do no such thing," I quip, looking around Lazaro.

"Stay back, Baylin."

"You'll be safe in our custody," Detective Handler explains. "We can protect you."

"I don't need your protection, Detective. I want you to leave."

"Ms. Reyes…"

"You heard the lady. Best you leave now. And if I see you lurking around her again, you'll have only yourself to blame for what happens."

"Is that a threat?"

"No Detective, it's a promise."

"You seem intent on doing this the hard way." Detective Handler takes out his gun, waving it at Lazaro. "Step away from the girl. Ms. Reyes, you're coming with me."

"You've got to be fucking kidding me!" I yell and stamp my feet. "I'm not going *anywhere* with you."

"So, you won't believe she's here because she wants to be," Lazaro starts, "and you'll kidnap her anyway? You'll commit the crime you're accusing me of? To what end?"

"Ms. Reyes," Detective Handler says, ignoring Lazaro. "Step out and come with me, hands up slowly."

"Over my dead body," Lazaro asserts, his anger palpable. I swing concerned eyes towards him, begging him not to do anything stupid. But he's gone. He's lost to me as Detective Handler cocks his gun and aims.

"As you wish," the detective mutters.

Too many things happen all at once. Lazaro pushes me out of the way and rushes the detective. The two men fall onto the ground like dominoes and struggle over the gun. The gun goes off and I scream.

31

ROMEO

It's all I can do not to lose my shit. My entire body trembles with rage as I press my fist to my mouth, trying to contain the guttural scream that threatens to escape. Seeing my innocent little bird pressed against my brother like that fills me with a murderous fury. The love I have for him is overshadowed by the primal urge to protect her from harm. From him. From me. From the world. And yet, she's sunken into him like he's her safety blanket and he's all she needs.

I know Lazaro saw me watching them in disbelief from the window. Before I can even process what I've seen, I stumble back and almost topple over the planter. It's heavy, weighted down with soil and water, but I manage to push it back, creating a diversion outside. My heart races as I quickly retreat down the stairs, gasping for air. The wound of seeing my little bird like that cuts deep, crippling me with a pain that's alien to my own wretched soul.

I don't know what has happened between them, but the way she was looking at my brother, and the way he looked back at her in wonder - I've never seen him look at a woman like that before. It's like a dagger through my heart, twisting and turning until all I feel is an agonizing mix of anger and sorrow. It explains why he's still here, why he hasn't come home yet. The reason he was so evasive every time I called and questioned him on why he was still at the cabin.

The silence is shattered by a gunshot, snapping me out of my daze. Without hesitation, I rush back up the stairs and through the front door of the cabin to find Lazaro locked in a struggle with Detective Handler. Another stray shot rings out as they grapple on the ground.

"Baylin, get down!" I scream, a stark contrast to putting a bullet in her back. Today feels like a day to save her.

My heavy footfalls pound against the floor as I spring into action, tearing them apart from their deadly dance.

I grip Detective Handler by the collar, his blood spattering at my feet. I sneer at him and snap, "Isn't there anywhere we can go to get a little space from you?" He meets my gaze with equal animosity, tightening his grip on his weapon.

"You think you can escape me, punk?" He scoffs. Lazaro appears by my side in an instant, ready to protect me with his own gun.

"Stay back," I warn my brother before turning my attention back to the detective. I tighten my hold on his collar until it's almost choking him.

Detective Handler chuckles, a malicious grin forming on his face. "Look at you!" he taunts. "Both of you fighting over a girl like fools. I never thought I'd see the day when the Riccardis crumbled over a girl. You ruined your own selves." His words send shivers down my spine, like a volcanic quake on the verge of eruption.

With a quick flick of my wrist, I disarm him and secure his gun in my waistband alongside my own.

"You just couldn't let this go, could you?" I roar, pulling back before striking Detective Handler squarely in the face with my fist. Lazaro tries to pull me off him as I continue to pummel him relentlessly until he slides to the floor, lighter than a feather.

Out of the corner of my eye, I catch Baylin huddled in a corner of the room, clutching her chest with one hand and deep frown lines etched on her forehead. I stop and release the detective's limp body as she watches us like a curious but frightened spectator. Tears are pooling in her eyes when she finally meets mine, and it's then that I realize that I'm the one she fears the most. This realization cuts deep within me. While I may have been the one giving her endless orgasms for days on end, it's my brother who balances out my rough edges. He is her comfort, her anchor, her true North. And I am nothing but the devil who took advantage of her and stole what she did not willingly offer.

"Fuck!" Lazaro roars. "Fuck, fuck, fuck, fuck, fuck!" He pushes his hands through his hair, testing his own sanity, and I turn away from Baylin to follow his eyes.

Detective Handler lays on his side, his lifeless body unmoving, his glassy eyes fixed on a spot across the room.

"Oh my God," Baylin whimpers. "Oh God. You didn't even punch him that hard."

Her eyes meet mine as she slides across the floor to check his vitals. She takes longer than required, and I have to believe she's trying to wish a pulse back into the man. Baylin is a fixer; that's what she does. When she finally looks up at us, she rests on her knees and shakes her head, telling us he's gone.

"What the fuck did he come out here for?" Lazaro screams. "And why the hell are you here?" he rages at me.

"He came alone, brother," I remind him. "Which means he could only have had bad intentions."

"Why did you come?" he asks again, his eyes never leaving mine.

My eyes flick from him to Baylin as I watch them with interest. In return, they look at me as though I hold the key to some puzzle they yearn to decipher. It's Baylin who breaks the spell, clears her throat and brings us back to reality with a thud.

"What are you going to do with him?" she asks in a small voice. Baylin angles her head and looks at the detective in fascination. It's almost mesmerizing seeing her reaction to his dead body. Almost as though she's become desensitized to the violence we bring to her world. It's inevitable, when you align yourself with the Riccardis.

"We killed a police officer," Lazaro says, in disbelief. "We fucking killed *a police officer!*"

"*I* killed a police officer," I correct him. "You leave; I'll take care of this."

"No," Baylin says, surprising us both. "We bury him, then we all leave."

"This doesn't involve you, Baylin," Lazaro says.

"The hell it doesn't." She rises from the floor, paces a few steps, then wheels back to us. "I'm not getting done for accessory to murder. Something like this could kill my career, and I'm not ready to lose anything else in my life."

BAYLIN REYES IS the unexpected element in our plan. She stands guard at the top of the cliff where I had previously tried to scare her with the idea of suicide. It was actually her suggestion to use this spot, instead of the ravine on our property.

"It's a steep drop," she says confidently. "If they find his body, they'll never be able to prove anything other than a fall."

Lazaro scans the surrounding forest before giving Baylin a skeptical look. "It's too close to the cabin," he argues.

"Coincidence," Baylin dismisses his concern, her gaze fixed on the edge of the cliff. She looks as if she wants to throw herself over, but something holds her back. "You said it yourself," she reminds me. "It's a well-known spot for suicides."

"Which brings up another question," Lazaro points out, poking holes in every scenario presented. "Why would someone like Detective Handler want to kill himself?"

We are both quiet as we turn to look at Lazaro. He raises a valid point.

"I'll handle that part," I tell him, my mind already racing with a plan.

"Let's get started," Baylin chimes in, kicking at the ground with her shoe.

I can't help but feel amazed by her transformation. Just one week ago, she was a timid mouse screaming and fighting against me. Yet here she is now, a fierce warrior princess helping us dispose of a dead body in the woods. In doing so, she has effectively made herself an accessory to murder, proving her trustworthiness and earning her freedom.

"Look at you," I say, giving her a smirk. "Who knew you had it in you to be a killer?"

32

BAYLIN

We drive back to the city. It's an unspoken agreement that I'll ride with Lazaro, while Romeo drives his own car back. I can't believe everything that's happened in the last four hours, let alone the past two weeks.

Romeo drives off in a huff, kicking up rocks and debris as his car fishtails away from the cabin when I refuse to get into the car with him. Despite his absence and the growing connection I'd felt with his brother, I can't deny the pull to him, even as my head tells me to look away, to understand his destructive nature and turn the other way. Romeo, wild and unpredictable, stirs something reckless within my heart. While Lazaro, with his piercing blue eyes and authoritative presence, has become a force that both terrifies and attracts me to him. How could I feel so drawn to two men who are night and day, bound by blood but divided by their very natures?

Lazaro's calculated calmness, the way he runs his family with an iron fist cloaked in a velvet glove, commands my respect. With him, there is a sense of stability, a promise of protection that goes beyond physical safety. And yet, the fire that Romeo ignites in me is undeniable. His passion, his intensity... it threatens to consume me, to burn away the shadows of my past until all that remains is the raw truth of my desires.

The sturdy fortress around my heart crumbles as I continue to look out the window at the rapidly passing landscape. In less than an hour, we would be back in the city, and I'm not going to lie and say it's where I want to be. It's the last place I want to be, especially with my chest aching and mind racing with thoughts of two brothers who are as much my sanctuary as they are my undoing. And now there's a secret that binds the three of us together like glue; a secret that we all must keep to save ourselves from ruin.

"What happens when we get home?" I whisper into the night, half-laughing at the absurdity of it all. Two brothers, two worlds colliding within me. One offers a love that's a slow burn, a flame carefully nurtured; the other is a raging wildfire, fierce and uncontrollable.

Lazaro's head turns, the blue of his eyes finding me in the dark like twin searchlights. I can feel the power that radiates off him, the authority he wields with such effortless grace. But tonight, I need to see the man behind the mantle.

He knows exactly what I'm talking about, but he changes the direction of the conversation to suit the narrative he wants to give me. Which is more than I've ever gotten from the closed off walls that Romeo has carefully built and safeguarded around himself.

"He wasn't always like this, you know." He turns his head back to the road, but not before I catch a glimpse of the faraway look that caresses his face.

My heart hammers against my ribs, each beat a reminder of the razor's edge I walk upon.

"I met him, you know. Five years ago. In a club one night."

I watch as his expression tightens, the faintest crease forming between his brows. Lazaro isn't a man accustomed to surprises, yet here I am, unravelling before him.

"You're *that* girl?"

"That girl?"

"Sandro told me Romeo met some girl at a club and took her home. Then tried for months to find her but he never did."

"He looked for me?" I'm just as surprised to find this out as he is to know I'm the girl that Romeo had been searching for.

Lazaro scoffs before he continues. "I thought it was his ego, because no-one leaves Romeo, but when he wouldn't stop looking, Sandro understood what I could never." He shakes his head, silently admonishing himself for a blindness I don't understand, one he refuses to elaborate on.

"He's not the same man as he was then," I whisper, almost to myself. Or possibly, my internal voice reminds me, he always was this monster, but you only had him for one night. That's not long enough time to know someone completely. Even the almost two weeks I spent with him at the cabin was still not enough time to give me a whole picture of who Romeo Riccardi is.

"He changed after Sandro died." Clouds formulate in Lazaro's eyes. "Everything changed. But most of all, Romeo did. He hates himself. He blames himself. And I know he believes if he could go back and do things differently, he would be at that truck stop. But I'd still be down a brother."

Silence swirls around us as we continue towards the city, a heavy weight coming down between us.

"What about us?" I ask him.

"There is no us," he tells me, and I swallow the lump that sits heavy in my throat, constricting my breathing.

Unspoken words tangle on my tongue, a knotted mess of fear and longing. I can't formulate the words I want to say. I can't put in words the emotions swirling inside me. For the past two weeks, all I've known is pain and fear and grief. And the Riccardis, for some inexplicable reason, have become my coping mechanism. Would I even know how to function in my own world after I've become so entwined in theirs? There's something undefinable between Lazaro and I, but there's also something with Romeo. I'm not going to lie about that. They've stripped me of more than two decades of being a person that I'm no longer sure I can properly portray.

Lazaro pulls over on the side of the road and lets out a long, labored sigh. For a long moment, he is silent, his gaze never leaving mine. When he finally speaks, his voice is a low rumble that fills the space with a vulnerability I've not heard from him before.

"Baylin, I am not a man who shares. My life, my world, it demands all or nothing. But... Romeo is my blood, my brother." He pauses, the weight of his struggle evident in the clench of his jaw. "I've fought battles, made decisions that would turn a weaker man's stomach. But this..." He gestures between us, a helpless motion that speaks volumes. "I won't do this to my brother."

The confession hangs heavy between us, a truth laid bare. And in that confession, a thread of connection twines tighter around my heart. Lazaro, the unyielding force of the Riccardi family, is showing me the chinks in his armor. And through those cracks, I see the glimmer of something raw and achingly human.

"I'm not trying to cause you pain," I say, reaching out tentatively to rest my hand against his. "Yet your own voice is drowning in it."

He flinches, then looks down at my hand covering his, a lifeline in a sea of uncertainty. His thumb traces circles on my skin. "You say that like you think I'm capable of feeling pain."

"You are," I urge, my own resolve strengthening. "I see you, Lazaro. I see you and I feel your pain, every last thread of it. In the very marrow of my own bones."

He shakes his head, looks away, his jaw ticking back and forth. "What I can't understand," he starts, "Is the cruel hand of fate that brought you back into our world. You dodged a Riccardi bullet five years ago; what the fuck brought you back into our world?"

His question, I realize, is a valid one. I myself don't even understand how Romeo and I, by chance, came to be in one another's lives once again. What are the chances? We shared one night five years ago, then I went my way, and he went his. But in those five years, I lost my sister, and he lost his brother. Our fates somehow seemed destined to collide once again in a different place, at a different time.

"I don't understand it any more than you do," I tell him. "But maybe five years ago, life wasn't ready for us. Maybe it wasn't our time. Or maybe it was never meant to be me and Romeo..." I whisper, my words lingering as the thought strikes me.

"More than anything," he confesses in a hushed tone, "I want you in my life. Despite the dangers, despite the madness. But even more than that...I need to protect you from the chaos that's going to follow you if you remain in my life."

A shiver runs down my spine, the gravity of his words anchoring me to the spot. Here, in the cocoon of night, Lazaro peels back the layers of the crime lord to reveal the heart of a man—a man who wants me by his side. But won't fight for me.

"I WON'T SEE you again, will I?" I ask, as we pull up to my house. The lights are on, although an eerie calm envelopes the whole neighborhood.

I stand by the window, looking at him, memorizing every inch, every crease, every line and wound etched on his face. This may very well be the last time I ever see him; after today, there's nothing to keep us in one another's lives. Contrary, with Detective Handler' death, it's imperative more than ever that we stay away from each other, so we don't bring unwanted attention to us.

Lazaro gives me a hard look but says nothing as he turns his face back to the road in front of him.

"I meant what I said, Lazaro. There isn't a power on earth that could make me testify against you or your brother, regardless of what happens."

"Even after everything we did to you," he scoffs. Maybe he doesn't fully trust me, after all.

"Even after," I whisper.

"I would suggest that you forget about us, Baylin. Erase us from your life. Remove us from your memories. Get on with your life but do so without us."

I shake my head, reluctant to do as he says. I shouldn't be surprised, but I am when I realize how easy it is for he and his brother to simply walk away from me. Like I never existed. Like I meant nothing. One brother robbed me of my freedom and touched my body in ways that could be considered criminal. The other is taking my choices away from me; the choice to be a part of their lives, to have one or the other. To stay safe in their cocoon.

"Stay safe, Baylin."

"Don't do this!" My voice is a hoarse whisper. I can't even begin to contemplate a life without them.

"Goodbye, Baylin."

His voice is firm, resolute, rendering me helpless. He doesn't look at me as he says it, doesn't even try to remember my face. His nonchalance stabs at something deep inside me. Something fragile, something already broken.

ONE YEAR LATER - 2024

Redemption is the ultimate plot twist for the sinner who thought the story was over.

33

BAYLIN

A tight knot of despair clenches in my stomach, the walls whispering secrets I wish I could unhear. In my trembling hand, I grip the crumpled lifeline that might as well be a grenade – Marlon Abruzzi's contact info, scrawled out like a sentence I am still deciding whether to serve.

It was a colleague at work who gave me Marlon Abruzzi's details. She said she'd interviewed for the job but had been so freaked out by the number of guards surrounding his home that she'd left without even taking the interview. At this point in my life, guards are precisely what I need, and desperate for a job, I had called and set the appointment. For me, there is no such luxury as being picky with job opportunities, especially when one presents itself where I know I'll be protected from the likes of Lydia Black.

The weight of my choices bears down on me, each step an echo of the conflict raging inside me. Trusting a man like Marlon is like dancing with the devil, but then again, hadn't my life become a series of lesser evils?

The choice is made before I even realize it, my fingers smoothing out the wrinkles in the paper as if they can iron out the creases in my fate. I've already sent my mother and Luca away; all the way across the country to a little ranch out in the middle of nothing where I know they'll be safe, courtesy of Luca's aunt Jolie, who's always complaining that she doesn't see enough of her deceased brother's son. She's sweet, really, and the invite couldn't have come at a more opportune time for me to get my life in order.

I try to shake off thoughts of the only family I have left to concentrate on the here and now. I haven't seen them in weeks; not since things came to a head and Detective Handler's partner Lydia Black threatened to cause more trouble for me. Like it wasn't enough already that she had interfered in my life to such an extent that I found myself out of a job. The fucking bitch would not leave me alone, persistently dogging my every move, until the heavy police presence wore thin on the Director's patience, and he had to let me go. She deserved to rot for that alone.

I look around the dimly lit room I've walked into; it reeks of danger and old money. Shadows cling to the corners like thieves, just waiting for their moment. The single lamp on the desk flickers with an irregular heartbeat, casting more shadows than light. A heavy desk dominates the space, its dark wood gleaming like a promise or a threat – with Marlon Abruzzi, it's hard to tell which.

The man sits with an air of authority and mystery, his sharp features and confident posture demanding attention, screaming power. He exudes a sense of danger, like a king in his own shadowy kingdom. His eyes are intense and unmoving, as if they can see into the depths of one's soul. They seem to follow every movement and evoke a sense of fear in whoever meets their gaze.

"Miss Reyes," he says, his voice the calm in a storm I've yet to fully comprehend. "Please, sit."

I obey, not because I want to, but because men like Marlon don't really ask – they command with velvet-covered steel. His tailored suit is a second skin, accentuating the authority that radiates from him like heat from a flame. His salt and pepper hair is slicked back casually from his forehead, ending at the nape of his neck.

"Mr. Abruzzi," I start, but my voice falters, betraying the turmoil beneath my skin. The air between us is thick with tension, and I know one misstep could send me tumbling into an abyss with no end. This is the moment, teetering on the edge, where my fate would be sealed by the words of a man who holds lives in his hands like a deck of playing cards.

"Take your time, Miss Reyes," Marlon coaxes, and I wonder how many have fallen for that deceptively gentle tone. How many have trusted and lost everything in rooms just like this? But I don't have the luxury of choice anymore. Desperation drove me here, and now it would drive my tongue.

"Thank you," I manage, my voice steadier than I feel, "for agreeing to meet with me." Sitting across from Marlon Abruzzi, I know I am gambling with more than just my own life – but what choice do I have?

I bite my lip, a vain attempt to steady the quake in my voice. He watches me with an intensity that could slice through like glass. The coldness in his eyes sharply contrasts with the otherwise handsome features of the older man, his face partially obscured by shadows that seem to hold their breath alongside mine.

"Mr. Abruzzi," I begin again, forcing my voice to remain even, but he cuts me off.

"Marlon, please. It's Marlon. Mr. Abruzzi makes me feel older than I am."

"Marlon," I correct myself. "You're in need of a nurse. I'm in need of protection." I sound way more confident than I feel.

A muscle twitches in Marlon's jaw, his expression otherwise unreadable. My heart hammers against my ribs, and I clutch my hands together to keep them from trembling.

"Well, if it's protection you need, you've come to the right place. But I do need to know what – who – you need protection from."

"I'm in a bind—the kind that ends with me six feet under or in a cell for the rest of my life." I let the words hang between us, heavy with truth.

He lifts his eyebrows in surprise that I would be so forthcoming. But I expect his curiosity – a man like Marlon Abruzzi doesn't take on strays for the sake of charity. He needs to know what he's getting into at all times.

"Before you start," he says, moving forward. "For the sake of transparency and nothing else, anything you say in this room stays in this room. But I want it all, the full story."

The condensed version of my recent life up until now flies right out the window. I don't think he's going to appreciate me cutting corners on this one.

So I tell him the whole story. Everything. About the supermarket shooting, Detective Handler pursuing my testimony, Romeo kidnapping me to the cabin, then the subsequent showdown with Detective Handler and the Riccardi brothers.

"You've been busy," he arches a perfectly shaped brow. I don't know whether it's surprise that I actually told him the whole story, or disbelief that this actually happened.

"I've been running, but there's only so far you can go before you run out of road. You have influence, resources. And I'm in need of those now more than ever."

"Why now? You say this happened more than a year ago."

I let out a huge sigh, my restless hands dancing in my lap. "Detective Handler's partner has made my life a living hell; she's searching for her partner and has gone to extreme lengths to get me to talk by any means possible."

"And you haven't?"

I shake my head.

"That's a lot of loyalty right there," he points out, before he leans back in his chair, fingers steepled in contemplation. His silence wraps around us like a vise. Outside, the distant wail of sirens pierces the stillness, a haunting reminder of the chaos I'm trying to escape. The world outside continues to spin while mine stands on the precipice of collapse.

"Miss Reyes," he finally says, his voice devoid of inflection, "It intrigues me—why both sides are so eager to clip your wings." His gaze flickers over me, assessing, calculating. "Why did you not go to the Riccardis for help? Since you have a history?"

I swallow hard, fighting the urge to look away from those probing eyes. His eyebrows shoot up as I pull down one side of my shirt and point my shoulder in his direction, the battle scar of my time with the Riccardis on full display.

"I think I've outstayed my welcome in their world," I tell him, and I don't mean to, but my voice comes out far more bitter than I intend it to be. I lower my eyes in shame, overcome by memories of how Romeo branded me, and how Lazaro shot me.

Marlon's fingers tap a slow, rhythmic beat on the armrest of his chair, the sound unnervingly methodical in the quiet room. Each tap is a second ticking by, each second a thread fraying in the fabric of my fragile hope.

The room feels colder, as if the shadows themselves are leaning in, hungry for Marlon to say something. The weight of his stare is almost unbearable, filled with a chilling promise that he can either be my savior or my end.

"They shot you?"

My response is one quick nod of my head.

"And yet, they didn't kill you. The Riccardis don't miss, Miss Reyes. They didn't want to kill you."

His words wrap around me like a rich balm. I'd always wondered why Lazaro had shot me only to save me, but once we'd come back to the city and it looked like I wouldn't get my answers, I'd let it go. There was only so much bandwidth I could assign to the Riccardis after the way they disrupted my life.

"Baylin Reyes," Marlon muses, his tone carrying the ghost of a challenge. "Desperate enough to seek refuge with the devil himself." He pauses, and for a fleeting moment, I think I see the faintest glimmer of intrigue in his eyes.

Marlon leans back in his chair, the leather creaking under the shift of his weight as he studies me, his gaze penetrating enough to scour the darkest recesses of my soul. I know he sees the vulnerability in my eyes. And that he'll probably take advantage of it. Outside, his world thrives—criminal empires built on fear and obedience—but inside this room, it's just him, me, and a dangerous proposition hanging precariously in the air.

"Why should I protect you, Ms. Reyes?" he finally asks, his voice low and deliberate. His fingers continue to tap a slow, rhythmic beat on the mahogany desk—a telltale sign of his contemplation. "The police are like hounds sniffing for a scent. Why bring them to my door?"

My heart pounds fiercely in my chest as I lay my last card on the table. My next words could very well get me killed, but I have nothing left to lose. "They're already at your door," I remind him.

"So you understand the nature of what I do?"

"I don't care what it is you do, Mr. Abruzzi. I just want somewhere safe where the police can't reach me until this blows over. And I will work my ass off to prove my loyalty to you."

"Any chance that detective Handler will ever be found?"

I shake my head, vehement in the knowledge that the detective's final resting place isn't accessible except by extraordinary means. No-one would come across his body unless they were specifically looking for him in that place.

"I never meet with anyone before doing the relevant checks. I know you have an unblemished record at the hospital you worked at for years. It must have been like a punch to the gut to get fired because of Detective Black."

I say nothing, sitting silently as my gaze flickers over Marlon. I know I didn't mention Lydia Black's name, which tells me he definitely did his homework before this meeting. As did I. If there's one person that can get me out of this mess I'm in, it's Marlon Abruzzi, king of kings in the underworld.

Marlon steeples his fingers and regards me with a look that chills me to my bones yet gives me a sliver of hope. The silence stretches between us like a taut wire.

"You understand what this means, Baylin?" His voice is almost a whisper now but thick with unspoken threats. "You come under my wing; you play by my rules. Absolute loyalty—anything less is betrayal, and I do not take kindly to traitors."

And then, the room falls silent once more, save for the distant sirens that sing a lament for the damned.

34

MARLON

S he finally calls.

After waiting for what feels like forever, she finally calls. As soon as she walks into my office and sits in the chair across from me, I know without a shadow of a doubt that Baylin Reyes is exactly where she belongs. It's taken me a long time to find her, but now that I've seen her in the flesh, I'm certain that I'm on the right track. I know exactly whose child she is, and exactly what must be done to assuage this guilt I've carried around all my life. Baylin Reyes has been almost thirty years in the making.

However, it wasn't easy to set up this meeting. The trail of bread-crumbs I left for her never seemed to lead anywhere, and it was only Detective Black's hounding of Ms. Reyes that eventually got her fired from her job at the hospital. Detective Black had unwittingly done me a favor. Ms. Reyes' termination made it difficult for her to find work at any other hospital, making it easier for me to lure her in with an enticing job offer from one of her former colleagues who was paid off to assist my plan.

Everything has started to fall into place, and now I have Baylin Reyes right where I want her. Right where she is meant to be. By my side.

It's a crazy kind of relationship that develops between us. We're not friends, and we're not lovers. We're in that unfathomable place between the two, where we are neither this nor that, but we're something in between. Her role goes way past being my nurse. I insist she take her meals with me, although she remains tight lipped about anything to do with her personally. Other than what she told me about her ordeal with the Riccardi brothers and the drive by shooting that started it all, I'm finding it hard to get anything else out of her.

In the evenings, I request that she read a little to me while I sit in my den, smoke from my cigar swirling around us. Truth be told, I don't mind the company, and she doesn't dare venture outside for fear of running into Detective Black. It's a strange ritual we've developed, but there's comfort in knowing there's safety inside these walls.

As the weeks blend into months, our routine solidifies into something resembling a life. My health, with Baylin's help, is steady, and her guardianship over me becomes more than just a job—it morphs into an unspoken commitment. In Baylin, I've found the sort of dedication I've never seen in others over the years.

We discuss books, art, and occasionally, when I'm in a reminiscent mood, my days as a young entrepreneur braving the wilds of both Wall Street and obscure foreign markets. She listens more than she speaks, entranced by my voice as it fills the room with echoes of a past rich with both triumphs and regrets.

She never speaks of the guards or why it's necessary for me to have so many, quiet sentinels standing over my empire. I never mention the connections that surely thread through my past and present, weaving a tapestry too complex for an outsider like her to understand. I respect her boundaries, as she respects mine, focusing instead on what I need most from her—companionship, care, and a willingness to exist in this bubble alongside me.

I rarely leave the house, but on the occasions that I do, Baylin accompanies me always, and there are no less than half a dozen cars that travel with us. 'Safety in numbers', I tell her, and she smiles at that and tells me she's not one to argue when protection is what she's needed all along.

One evening, as autumn bleeds into winter and the nights grow longer, I hand her an old leather-bound book with delicate care. It's time to up the ante – there's so much I want to know about her that she won't share, and I devise a way that could possibly bring her out of the comfort of her own shell.

"This was my wife's favorite," I tell her softly, my eyes fixed on the spine of the book. "Would you mind reading it tonight?" The request takes her by surprise, as we haven't finished the book we started a week ago. We never deviate from a book unless it's finished, and I know she feels the nostalgia in the room as she cracks the book open. It's a first edition of Crime and Punishment, bound and worn, brown leather with gold lettering on the spine. The pages have yellowed with age and are slightly frayed at the edges. The smell of musty old paper and ink wafts from within the book's pages, evoking a sense of history and wonder.

"Crime and Punishment." It's merely a whisper that escapes her lips as she traces the lettering on the cover of the book. When she lifts her eyes, she looks at me the oddest look on her face, her brows creased in confusion. She shakes her head slightly, as though shaking off her imagination, and starts to read.

I close my eyes and travel back to a time when another voice filled this room. It is during these moments that I feel closest to my past.

When I hold my hand up and signal for her to stop, she closes the book and sets it down. I don't open my eyes, yet I can feel hers on me, studying my face carefully as she waits for me to come out of my trance.

"You never speak of her," she says, as my eyes flutter open.

"You never speak of your family," I counter.

She shrugs, her shoulders falling helplessly, and tells me there's not much to tell. I know she exiled her mother and nephew and the reasons why. They're the only family she has left. But I need more. I think the only way she's going to open up about herself is if I give her the same.

"Tania killed herself," I offer, after a long silence.

My confession catches her off guard, and I watch as her hand trembles, her eyes unfocused on the tangled undergrowth outside the window, unsure how to react despite her shock.

"She was beautiful," I begin, voice hoarse but steady. "Her spirit was like sunlight dancing on water. But inside, she was fighting demons I could never tame."

I stop, take a deep breath before continuing with strained words. "She had grace in everything she did, even when she was in unbearable pain...I didn't know until it was too late to save her."

The space between us becomes charged with an unspoken understanding, as if the room has shrunk and we are now confined in this prison together.

"What was she fighting?" Her whisper is barely audible, as if speaking the words might shatter me into pieces.

I study her closely, noticing how her usually composed facade falters. Her soft eyes now resemble the soft hues of a dewy morning - distant and full of ache. The emptiness behind her gaze speaks of long nights filled with echoes of grief that I could never truly comprehend; she is naturally a healer, but she has no idea how to stop my pain.

I shrug in response. "There was too much darkness in her days," I continue, each word taking a piece of me with it. "She was prone to mood swings; had everything at her disposal, yet still she couldn't calm her demons. One day, I came home to find her...she had hung herself from the old oak tree overlooking the valley. It was her favorite spot at our country estate; she said it brought her some semblance of peace."

And that was where my wife found her peace. Under a tree overlooking a valley brimming with assorted florals. There's a bittersweet irony to her dying amidst a canvas of color when she owned so much darkness.

"That must have been heartbreaking for you."

"Beyond. I let everyone know it was a heart attack." My confession hangs heavy between us, undeniable. "I couldn't bear for her pain to be exposed for all to see, for them to whisper about her every step I took. This was better...she deserved much better than that. And anything otherwise would have reflected badly on me."

She lets me speak, lets me spill all my secrets, as though for the first time. It could very well be the first time. I don't remember ever sharing this story with anyone.

"As if losing her, failing her, wasn't enough, the stigma of a man like me losing my wife in such a way would have made me seem weak. Like I was losing control. If I can't control the residents of my own home..."

"What would that have meant?" she asks me, her brows creasing.

"War. Every hoodlum and wannabe gangster would have been lining the pavement outside ready to jump." I look away then, out the window where the first stars are starting to twinkle in the dusky sky. "I buried my heart with her under that oak tree. No children to fill our halls with laughter, no second love to mend the void she left behind. I've lived with the ghost of her ever since."

A profound grief clings to me, like the ivy climbing the walls outside. I don't tell her that my story didn't start with my wife, nor did it end with her. I don't tell her any more than that, any of the other burdens I've been holding close to my chest. In so little time, she has become my greatest confidant, yet still I am aware that there are some stories not yet ready to be told.

We sit in silence for what feels like an eternity, until my next words, barely audible, carry on a breath too weary to leave my lips.

"I told you because...you remind me of how important it is to confront our demons rather than let them consume us from within."

And though she has distanced herself from her own family out of necessity rather than tragedy, in this moment, as I watch Baylin's mournful silhouette against the encroaching night, I understand her pain deeply. In my own tale of loss lies a universal truth about human fragility and the facades we wear to hide all our broken pieces from the world.

With a deliberate nod, acknowledging the gravity of what I've shared, she reaches across the space between us - not just physical but emotional - offering her hand as both comfort and solidarity. I grasp it with a thankful squeeze, a silent expression of gratitude etched in that one simple gesture.

35

MARLON - 1995

T he sun had already begun its slow descent behind the verdant hills when we arrived at our sacred spot, the old wooden dock creaking a familiar greeting under our feet. The lake, a vast expanse of shimmering blues and greens, lay tranquil, disturbed only by the occasional leap of a fish or the gentle paddle of a duck's feet. The air was thick with the scent of pine and wildflowers, a perfume that seemed to capture all our summers spent here since we were teenagers.

We unloaded our gear, setting up old, trusty fishing rods that had seen better days but still promised the thrill of a catch, then slipped effortlessly into the comfortable rhythm that years of friendship had honed. Stevie baited his hook with practiced ease, casting his line into the reflective water with a soft splash. Beside him, I followed suit, my movements slightly clumsier, always the less experienced fisherman between us.

For eight years, Stevie and I had made an annual tradition of coming to the lake, a pact we had formed on our very first trip when my parents gave us permission to use their lake house for a weekend of fishing. Even now, well into our mid-twenties, there was nothing that could keep us from our annual pilgrimage as we closed the distance between us and crammed the weight of a whole year passed into a week. That first summer when we'd been seventeen had been a summer of magic, and every summer after that *served to remind us that no matter the miles between us, nothing could destroy the bond that had formed between us during our formative high school years.*

Stevie's curls fell into his eyes as he threw his line. We stood knee deep in the water, looking out at the tranquil shimmer reflected against the sun. Two men, bonded since childhood, enjoying detached moments from the rat race of the cities we'd escaped. Once neighbors, now we resided on opposite sides of the country. This was our meeting point. This was our sanctuary. Our days in the sun for a moment in time - a week — which inevitably would fly like the blink of a shuttered eye.

That summer, what would come to be our last summer at the lake house, the conversation started as it always did—with small talk about the drive over and comments on the weather. Some banter back and forth about who was the more expert fisherman. Light conversation that reminded us that even though we existed hundreds of miles apart, in two different worlds, we could pick up as though no time at all had lapsed since our last trip to the lake house. But as the evening light turned golden and painted the lake in hues of orange and pink, our words meandered to deeper waters.

I kept my eyes fixed on the bobbing cork of my fishing line as I spoke. "I got myself tangled up with these guys downtown last month; thought they were legit businessmen, but it turns out they were nothing but trouble wrapped up in expensive suits."

Stevie turned, eyebrow arched in interest but not surprise. I'd always had a knack for finding trouble without so much as looking for it.

"What kind of trouble are we talking about?" he asked, casting his line out with a smooth flick of his wrist.

"The kind that makes you wish you'd taken up an office job selling insurance," I replied as I released a heavy breath. "Not the kind of people I'd bring home to dinner." I watched my line as something tugged at it. "Made some choices I'm not proud of."

Stevie continued to look at me, his oldest friend, his expression tight with concern underlined by years of unconditional loyalty. "You gonna be alright?" he asked quietly.

"Yeah," I nodded slowly, "I'm steering clear now. I've got myself a new

job—honest work. I'll work my ass off until I repay the debt." My eyes met Stevie's, grateful for the lack of judgment I found there.

"What about your parents?" Stevie asked. "Do they know?" My parents had always been comfortable, but not comfortable enough that they would clean up this mess for me. No, they were all for responsibility, and I would only go to them if the situation became untenable. Not a second sooner.

"I'd rather keep them out of this one," I admit. "I'd rather not bring this sort of trouble to their door."

Stevie nods once, offering his understanding, then tells me if there's anything he can do, he's ready and waiting. I give him a tight smile, my heart fluttering anxiously; I think I'm bound to always be the failure between us. No matter how hard I tried to measure up, to emulate myself based on Stevie's beautiful soul, I knew I could never, because Stevie was well and truly one of a kind.

As the sky deepened into twilight and stars began to prick at the darkening canvas above us, Stevie breathed in deeply and shook off the worry clinging to him after my confession. Stevie was loyal to a fault, and when he cared, he did so without exaggeration. He smiled suddenly, his face lighting up with a different kind of seriousness.

"I met someone," he announced, unable to keep the joy from his voice.

"Yeah?" My interest piqued instantly; I turned to face Stevie and waited for him to tell me more.

"Yeah," Stevie reaffirmed. "Her name's Jenna. She's...she's wonderful, man." His hand unconsciously reached for something in his pocket before he withdrew it empty but not without a secretive smile. "I'm going to marry her."

I couldn't help but laugh softly at the sheer certainty in Stevie's tone—the kind that spoke of love that was deep and sure. "That's great, Stevie," I clapped him on the back warmly. "Really great. When do I get to meet the lucky girl?"

"I think I'm the lucky one," he told me, his voice laced with conviction.

"What is she like?"

"She's great, man." He speaks to me, but his eyes have settled on something far off in the distance, as though he has transported himself to her side. "She has this laugh that sounds like music. And she's smart, really smart; teaches special ed kids at a local school." Stevie's face lit up as he talked about Jenna, each detail painted with affection and admiration.

"I'm happy for you, man," I say, as I swallow back the lump in my throat. Neither of us had ever come close to even thinking about marriage. Through all the disastrous relationships we'd had over the years, we'd never missed a beat, never skipped a summer at the lake house. But how would that change after we got married and had families? The question spears through my heart, its sharp point leaving behind a deep, painful wound.

"Stop that, Marlon. I know what you're thinking. And you're wrong. One day, it won't be just you and me. One day it will be us and our wives and our kids. We'll all congregate here at the lake house; our wives will sit around and bitch about us, and our kids will splash in the lake and become best friends while we fish."

That day, we spent hours under the starlit sky until we were surrounded by nothing but the sounds of nocturnal creatures and whispering trees around us. We talked about everything; our dreams for future trips to this very lake and bits from our daily lives—until our voices grew tired and our hearts lighter.

We made our way back to the shore, dragging our equipment with us, then set up the campfire, preparing to cook our dinner. I had caught one fish —a small bass—which we released back into its watery home after admiring its slippery strength briefly. Then I looked over at Stevie's bucket, brimming with a dozen or so fish as he started to scale and gut them. He did it with such precise movements, it was as though he had been born with a fillet knife in his hand. The fire crackled, throwing light on his concentrated face, highlighting the smooth yet deliberate strokes as he prepared each fish. I gathered twigs and branches to keep the fire robust and steady, watching the flames dance in the deepening darkness.

As the heat from the fire curled around us, I couldn't help but think how strange it was—this ancient, almost primal rhythm of life we had somehow stepped into. We were no longer just a pair of friends cooking dinner; we were participants in a cycle far older than ourselves, drawn into a communion with the earth and its creatures. There was something intimate in the way we caught and released, caught and consumed, a quiet acknowledgment of the fragile balance between us and the wild world that made us *who we were. Stevie worked silently, the fish in his hands almost reverent, as if each one held some secret it was offering only to him. Meanwhile, I fed the fire, watching the smoke rise into the cold night air, feeling the weight of the moment settle over me. In a world that seemed to be speeding toward some distant, unknowable future, this small, fleeting ritual of fire, fish, and companionship felt like an anchor—grounding us, if only for a night, to a place where things still made sense.*

36

BAYLIN

"Tell me about your family."

"There's not much to tell. It's just me, my mum and my nephew." I'm distracted as I remove the cuff from around Marlon's arm and pack it away. I can't stand the thought of his condition worsening, but his blood pressure seems to be spiking more lately, and that has me worried.

"I find that hard to believe. You need to give me something before I meet them."

I pause my movements and look down at him as he sits in his wingchair. "You want to meet them?"

"Of course I do." He says it like it's the most absurd question he's ever heard. True, we've become more comfortable with each other over the past few weeks, but I haven't spoken with Marlon about my family – there really isn't that much to tell, and what there is ignites old memories that reopen old wounds.

I blink back the moisture that pools in my eyes. It's touching that he would want to meet what's left of my family, especially after only knowing me such a short time. At that moment, I realize the depth of the bond Marlon and I have unwittingly woven around ourselves. His insistence on meeting my family, sparse and fractured as they are, feels like a stitch in the fabric of our relationship, drawing the weave tighter, more intimate.

"My mother... she's strong. Stronger than anyone else I know. But she's had to be, you know? Life never really gave her a choice." I pause, lost for a moment in the rush of memories—some bitter, some sweet.

Marlon watches me intently, his eyes reflecting a sea of understanding. "You love her very much. Are you close?"

"We are," I confirm, feeling a solid weight settle in my chest—a mixture of responsibility and utter devotion. "Does that answer your question?"

Marlon's eyes are locked on mine. "It's not about how much you tell me about your life that matters. It's about understanding that part of your life that interests me."

I feel a lump form in my throat as his words wash over me-so straightforward yet so profound. It's strange how his words unravel me, loosening knots of resistance I've built over the years. I start to pack the medical equipment away as he waits for me to reveal more. When I finish, I sit down on the ottoman across from him and take a deep breath.

"Why do you never leave the house?" I ask him. His home is built like a fortress, locked down tighter than Fort Knox. He rarely, if ever leaves. Even his guards are kept at arm's length.

"I see what you're doing here, Baylin," he smirks. "Subtly trying to change the subject."

I shrug my shoulders and tell him I'm interested in an answer. He shakes his head at my insistence on changing the subject.

"A part of me died when Tania died. The part that had any will to be out in the world. I found myself lost in the memories of her. I somehow feel closer to her when I'm alone."

"That's not healthy," I tell him. "You still have a lot of living to do."

"Losing her was the hardest thing I've ever had to deal with," he whispers.

"I lost my sister in my last year of university. The single worst moment of my life, I think. So I know what it's like."

He asks me how she died, and I tell him. All about my beautiful older sister Maggie and her wonderful husband Daniel. The amazing life they were building together, along with their son. He smiles at some of the more poignant memories I share, like the fact that Maggie had wanted to have ten children.

"Was it an accident?"

"Drunk driver. I lost my sister and her husband, and that pain was compounded by the driver's negligence. He had two young children in the car with him. For the longest time, I couldn't comprehend how someone that drunk could get behind the wheel of a car and drive his own children to their deaths. It was devastating."

"People like that don't usually see past their own selfishness," Marlon tells me. Don't I know it.

"And your father?" he probes with cautious curiosity.

I shrug slightly. "I never knew him. It was always just us girls and then Luca came along and filled our lives with sunshine."

"What happened to him?"

I shrug. "I don't know. As far as I'm aware, he's dead." He quirks an inquisitive eyebrow and I go on to explain. "My mother's story has changed so many times, I don't think she even knows what happened to him."

"That's got to play with your mind."

"It does. It did. Not anymore. I got to a point where I realized I have to look past what I can't change and just go on with my life, I guess."

"It must have been hard," Marlon says softly. "Taking on your nephew at such a young age."

"It was... is sometimes. But we manage."

He leans forward slightly, resting his elbows on his knees as he regards me seriously. At times, he stares at me with the most curious look on his face, as though viewing things through a looking glass, and I can't help but wonder what he's thinking.

"You're an extraordinary young woman, Baylin. I hope you know that." My face goes red at the compliment. "If I'd had a daughter, I would've wanted her to be just like you."

"You don't have any children?" I ask, and he shakes his head. How sad that must be for him, I think, to be without a wife and without any offspring to continue his legacy.

"We lost a child," he tells me, averting my gaze. "That damn near broke us. My wife was never the same after that."

Sadness swells and overcomes me. His story is heartbreaking, the pains he's endured unfathomable. Working in the ER for so long, I've been in contact with all sorts of heartaches and traumas, but for some reason, Marlon's sadness scrapes at something at the very depths of me.

"The one regret I have is not having children," he says. "Not for lack of trying, but after we lost the first, Tania couldn't carry a baby to term. She kept miscarrying; I think that played on her mind a lot, another demon to carry."

I consider my own current circumstances, and I hear the ticking of my own clock. Tick tock, tick tock, tick tock, my biology mocks me. I don't know how much time I have to play with, considering the difficulties I would face trying to find a life partner here between these four walls.

"You're thinking about your own biological clock," he surmises, noting the look on my face. He's not wrong. It's all I can think about. I nod, unable to hide my concern any longer.

"Yes," I admit, the word heavy in the air between us. "And being here won't slow down that clock."

He leans back, folding his arms as he contemplates the sterile walls that confine us. "No, it won't." His voice trails off, and for a moment, we both lose ourselves in our separate but similarly constrained worlds. "But eventually, you'll leave here, and you'll find your own way. You'll build a life with someone, away from here. Have the kids you always planned to."

"Nothing in my life has turned out the way I planned it," I tell him. Not a complaint, but an observation, driving home the reality that one could plan to their heart's desire, but sometimes greater forces dictate a person's true fate.

He looks at me, his eyes reflecting a well of sadness. "Look around you Baylin." He holds out his arms, encompassing all the grandeur of his home, his lavish lifestyle. "This was never what I planned for myself, either," he says softly. "But somehow, this is where I ended up. Where I was always meant to be."

His words stir something deep within me. Fear and empathy intermingle painfully in my chest. "How did you deal with an outcome other than what you'd constructed?" I wonder aloud, not just about his past struggles but also seeking guidance for my own uncertainties.

"Sometimes you just have to trust the process, Baylin. Believe that there's a greater purpose for the way things turn out," he responds after a thoughtful pause. "Like the way you somehow found your way to my front door. This is probably never where you imagined life to take you, but this is most likely what you need right here, right now."

The raw honesty in his voice resonates with me more than I expect. I think about my own situation; how isolation already feels like a small death of possibilities, each day another reminder of what can't be.

"But you keep going," he says suddenly, as if reading my thoughts. "You have to believe that there's more to your life than the losses and the what ifs."

I nod again, feeling a small spark of resolve flicker inside me. His story is not mine, yet our fears and our losses connect us in profound ways. Maybe sharing this burden is the first step toward believing that time hasn't run out for me just yet.

37

MARLON

"So, tell me more about this girl of yours." I flicked my eyes over to Stevie. The goofiest grin formed on his face as he turned my way, and I couldn't help but think how that smile suited him. There was something so befitting of my best childhood friend being the first one between us to fall flat on his face in love.

"She's amazing, Marlon," Stevie started, his voice thick with infatuation as he shuffled the oars and steadied the boat. "I can't wait for you to meet her. That smile... her smile makes me feel like the world stops spinning for a moment just to watch her."

Stevie chuckled, shaking his head in disbelief at his own words. "She has a daughter...just the cutest little thing, still an infant."

I listened, genuinely caught up in his description as we continued to maneuver our small boat towards the shore. The bottom of the vessel scraped gently against the sand, bringing us to a steady stop.

"And you think she's the one?" I asked.

"I don't think anything, brother. I know she's the one for me." He threw his head back briefly before catching himself and focusing back on me. "I'm telling you, Marlon, she's one of a kind. I'm really going to marry her."

"You set a date yet?"

He grinned from ear to ear, smiled at me, then told me the sooner the better. His girl Jenna was pregnant, and he couldn't wait to be a father.

"That's a lot of change for you all at once," I frowned. "Are you sure you're ready to take the leap?"

"Brother, I've never been more certain of anything in my life."

"I'm really happy for you, Stevie."

He looked at me pensively, gave me a small, wistful smile, then delivered more good news.

"Jenna's open to moving," he told me. "I was thinking, once we're married, I wouldn't mind moving closer to you so the kids can be around uncle Marlon."

I wasn't blessed with a brother. But I could imagine that if I had been, I would have wanted him to be exactly like Stevie. He was the calm to my storm, the balance to my troubled heart whenever I found myself lost. Even at the same age, Stevie was wise beyond his years.

I smiled at him, clapping him on the shoulder with brotherly affection mixed with a touch of envy for his certainty in life. As much as he was certain about the possibilities of his life, I was confounded about the direction of my own life.

We both hopped out of the boat, dragging it further onto the shore to secure it from drifting back into the lake's embrace. Stevie took the lead, while I brought up the rear, wading through the water as we pushed the boat further into the shore. There was a quiet calm all around us, the usual peace we'd become accustomed to.

Suddenly a sharp crack tore through the air – an unwelcome sound that broke through the tranquility surrounding us. Instinctively my head snapped towards the direction of the disturbance as another shot rang out.

"Get down!" I shouted, though too late because Stevie had already started crumpling before me, struck in the chest by a bullet aimed for me. He was standing at that point where the water meets the shore, and his body hit the sand hard; his weight interrupting the lapping ripples as his eyes snapped wide with shock.

"Stevie!" My voice was hoarse with desperation as I crawled over to him amidst another flurry of gunfire that chipped wood from our stranded boat

and sent splinters into the air. I fell on top of him, covering him with my own body, a blistering pain searing through my arm.

When the shooting stopped, I scrambled back and looked down at my friend as the life started to drain out of him. He clamped a hand over his wound with a shaky breath; his other hand gripped mine tightly, as if holding on could keep him anchored to this life.

I pressed my hand against his in response, tears mingling with grit on my face as I tried to apply pressure to his wound. I did everything I could, pressing down on the wound where the blood was spreading across his chest. His heart. The fucker got him in the heart.

"She...would've loved to meet you," Stevie gasped out painfully as he attempted that goofy grin one last time.

His grip loosened; his deep, dark eyes faded as they fixed on something beyond me or this beach or even this world until they glazed over completely, and his breathing became shallow.

"No, Stevie! No, no, no, no, no," I gasped, begging him to stay awake.

I dropped my head against his still warm chest for just a moment before urgency snapped me back to reality; the reality that these bullets were meant for me. My heart shattered and my mind reeled with grief and anger at the realization that my best friend was dead because of me.

～

I BURIED Stevie behind the lake house. I didn't know what else to do as I dug that hole and lowered his body into it, dirt caked to my face along with the tears that refused to stop. I drunk myself into a stupor, the pain too great and vivid, like a nightmare I couldn't escape. Every time I closed my eyes, all I could see was the life draining out of Stevie's eyes, a life taken due to my own selfish entanglements with the wrong people. There was no doubt in my mind that Stevie's death was a direct consequence of my involvement with the loan shark whose money I'd lost. Whether they'd killed Stevie as a warning that I had to cough up and pay, or they killed the wrong man instead, I couldn't be sure. But what I was undeniably and unequivocally certain about was the fact that Stevie had taken his last breath prematurely because of my own stupid negligence.

When morning came with its pale light filtering through the trees around the lake house, the hangover was brutal, but not as brutal as the emptiness that gnawed at my insides. Stevie had been more than a friend; he had been my brother for life, and now, without him, I felt adrift in an ocean of uncertainty.

I knew I couldn't just wallow in my own self-pity; Stevie's sacrifice had to mean something. It was clear what had to be done; the only way forward was through retribution and justice. And they would only be exacted by my hand.

I sat there on the porch of the lake house for the longest time, loading my gun with a grim determination, each bullet carrying a piece of my broken heart. I shot at a can I balanced on the lip of the boat, practicing over and over again, honing the skills that Stevie and I had perfected over the years when we gave ourselves up to the wilderness. Franco Two-pence, the damned loan shark who'd been muscling me, would pay for what he'd done, and I made a pact with myself that I wouldn't back down until I had exacted my vengeance and destroyed him. I set my own path with a terrifying clarity that scared me but was fraught with inevitability.

The sound of the gunshots echoed across the water, splitting the quiet of the evening like cracks in a fragile dam. Each shot felt like a reaffirmation of something deep and hollow inside me—something raw and unforgiving. There was no going back from this. I'd crossed the line long ago, and now I was hurtling toward something darker, a place where the only thing left to lose was my soul. But then, a strange thought struck me as the last bullet left the chamber, its whistle lost in the wind; what if this path I was so sure of wasn't mine at all?

I paused, the gun still warm in my hand. It was as if the forest around me—silent and watchful—had started to murmur, its ancient wisdom reaching me through the rustling of the leaves. The vengeance I was so consumed by, the one I believed would fix everything, might only push me further from the person I once was. The person Stevie and I had been before the world turned hard and unforgiving.

I could almost hear his voice, soft and steady, the advice he would give me if he were here; "You're not just fighting him, man. You're fighting yourself." I shook my head, trying to push the thought away, but it lingered like smoke in my lungs. What had started as a debt I needed to pay back had become something more—a war within me that I wasn't sure I could win. Maybe I wasn't just after Franco after all. Maybe I was after the pieces of myself that I had already lost in this pursuit of vengeance.

The night seemed to stretch longer, the weight of the gun heavier in my hand. For the first time in a long time, I felt the full weight of my choice. And suddenly, the shooting no longer felt like practice—it felt like the first step into a darkness I couldn't outrun.

38

BAYLIN

"You'll be safe," Marlon assures me.

Marlon's words are meant to soothe, but they only add to my anxiety as I straighten his bowtie with trembling hands. His dark blue eyes seem to hold me captive, piercing through me with their intensity. As I attempt to pull away, he grabs my wrist firmly and gazes at me with a thoughtful look. Then, unexpectedly, he brings my hand to his lips and grazes the skin of my knuckles. But there is nothing romantic about his touch; it feels possessive, almost paternal. Like a father admiring his daughter, proud of her very existence. The unfamiliar sensation floods over me, foreign and intoxicating like a distant land I've always dreamed of visiting but never had the chance to explore.

"I don't know that this is the best idea," I tell him.

"Nonsense," he scoffs and lets go of my wrist. "Above all else, the one indisputable rule that no-one will break at the Manor is that there will be no bloodshed. The door is closed to anyone who crosses that line, and they are banished immediately for the term of their natural life."

"Has anyone ever been banished?" I ask, my lip trembling.

The thought of being around that many people is causing chaos to erupt inside me. Marlon shakes his head slowly in response, and I think the movement is meant to set my mind at ease, but it unfortunately has the opposite effect, because I'm suddenly more nervous than I was before, and my wayward mind remembers that there's always a first time for everything.

"You must come," he insists, even as his eyes glide up and down the length of my body. I'm wearing a floor length black ballgown that was delivered to the house this morning, perfectly tailored to fit my frame. "I won't force you to, but I'd love to have you by my side. Shall we?"

He turns, offers his arm, and with a heavy sigh, I slide my own in the crook of his arm and lean into him. I reach out my other hand to swipe a side table and collect my clutch.

"I'll stay by your side all night," he assures me.

"It's the Annual Misters Gala," I remind him. "The most important meeting of the year. You're supposed to be networking, not babysitting your nurse."

He lifts his lips in a lop-sided grin, looking much younger than his mid-50's. I can't help but smile back at him; in another time and another place, Marlon Abruzzi would have been the very embodiment of the perfect gentleman.

THE MANOR which holds the Annual Misters Gala is swarming with armed guards; it seems every businessman that turned up for this event has brought his own personal army with him. It's more like a palace from a bygone area that sits quietly empty and erupts from time to time with life.

"It's like nobody here trusts anyone else," I whisper to Marlon as I take note of the overwhelming amount of security.

There's so much money and power in this room, it's inevitable that trust would be amiss. A necessary precaution in our line of work," he reminds me.

Our eyes meet and I can sense the question on the tip of my tongue, but I hold back. I may have told him that I don't care about what he does, and maybe part of me still doesn't, but I can't deny being curious. He may be one of the biggest players in the underworld, but I have no idea how far his reach travels or the true nature of his work. Possibly, I don't even care; he's kept me safe all this time and that was the deal we made.

"Look around," Marlon gestures subtly with his chin. "Every person here is tied to something bigger than they appear. Deals made in shadows, promises bound by more than mere words."

"And you?" I ask quietly. "What binds you?"

Marlon's gaze lingers, serious and unreadable, as if he's debating what to tell me and what to withhold. Ultimately, he offers a rueful half-smile. "This world—our world—it's built on fragile alliances and trust that's paper thin. Tonight, everyone is playing their part in a carefully choreographed dance."

I nod, understanding yet not entirely understanding at the same time. There is so much about this world that remains cloaked in mystery to me.

We continue moving through the crowd, weaving between clusters of sharply dressed individuals whose eyes flicker with knowledge and secrets. Every now and then, someone nods at Marlon, their expressions guarded but respectful.

"Everybody's staring at you," I say, keeping my voice low, almost lost amidst the murmur of conversations and the soft classical music floating in from unseen speakers.

"They respect strength," Marlon replies without looking at me. "And they fear it too."

As we approach a secluded balcony overlooking the city, Marlon pauses and gestures for me to follow him outside. The cool night air is a sharp contrast to the warmth of the bustling room we leave behind. Out here, standing above the cityscape with its twinkling lights and distant sounds of traffic, the air feels clearer somehow.

"You weren't wrong inside," he starts, his voice serious. "Nobody trusts anybody in this game. But tonight, I need you to trust me."

His earnest tone strikes a chord in me. I nod slowly, not fully understanding my own agreement. "I do trust you," I admit, though I'm not sure when that conviction had solidified within me.

Marlon looks out towards the city, his profile etched against the backdrop of skyscrapers. "I need you to really trust me, Baylin."

I shiver slightly, not from the cold but from the gravity of his words. "What's going on, Marlon?"

Before he can answer, a man approaches him and whispers something in his ear. "I need you to stay here," he instructs, when he looks back at me.

"What? No—"

"It's not negotiable." His voice brooks no argument; it's the tone of someone used to being obeyed. "You'll be safe, Baylin. I have eyes on you."

As he disappears back into the fray, I'm left alone with a rising panic and myriad questions swirling through my mind. He said he wouldn't leave me, and now he has. With so many people around. I hadn't understood, until this very moment, how the mere thought of being around such a large crowd of people could affect me; it had never been a problem before, but now I feel a thin rod of heat trickling down my spine as anxiety overwhelms me.

Coming here with Marlon had been a mistake. Even the hospital I'd worked at for years, always bustling with thousands of people, the stench of death and destruction rampant through its corridors, never caused me this much anxiety.

"Baylin?"

The sound of my name cuts through the hum of the party, sharp and unexpected. My breath catches in my throat as I hunch over, trying to steady myself. I would know that voice anywhere—the deep, rich timbre that still haunts the corners of my memories. The air around me shifts, thickens. I don't need to look up to know he's standing there. I can feel him.

When I finally do glance over, I see him—Romeo, framed in the dim light of the balcony door, his tall figure cutting through the crowd like a ghost. His icy blue eyes lock onto mine, unyielding, unreadable. The absence between us might as well be nothing at all; the silence is so thick, I almost suffocate in it.

"Romeo," I breathe, the name feeling foreign on my tongue but undeniable. I try to steady my voice, though it trembles. "What are you doing here?"

He approaches slowly, a predator with the precision of someone who knows exactly what he's after. His hands are casually stuffed in his pockets, his presence overwhelming and at ease all at once.

"A better question," he says, his voice edged with that familiar sarcasm, "is what are *you* doing here? You look like you've seen a ghost."

I force a laugh, but it's hollow. A façade so thin it barely holds together. "You're the last person I expected to see here."

He doesn't laugh. Doesn't even smile. He simply looks at me, his eyes flicking around the space, taking in the luxury of the ballroom, the expensive guests, the opulence of it all. "Where have you been, Bay?" he asks, his tone sharper now, searching for something in my face he doesn't trust. I know he's seeing through me, seeing how out of place I feel in this gilded cage of a room. We don't run in the same circles, so I'm as out of place here as he is at home.

"I'm leaving now," I whisper, my heart thundering in my chest.

His steps falter, halting just short of where I stand. For a moment, we're so close I can feel the weight of his gaze, the electricity between us crackling and threatening to burn. He watches me, studying me as if I'm a riddle he needs to solve. His eyes narrow, an unspoken question hanging in the air.

"Baylin."

His voice softens—just a little. Barely audible, but it slices through me, stripping away the walls I've spent over a year building. That vulnerability, so rare in him, catches me off guard, disarming me before I can brace myself. Romeo is different now, bigger somehow, harder—yet beneath it all, there's something unmistakable: he still has the power to break me.

"Where are you going?" he asks, his tone quieter now, edged with something I can't place. I want to answer, to explain, but the words stick in my throat. There's only one thing I know for certain: I can't stay.

"Please," I whisper, taking a step back. "I can't...do this."

His jaw tightens, but he doesn't push. He simply nods, his hands slowly pulling out of his pockets, the movement deliberate. He watches me, and I feel the weight of his gaze anchor me to a moment I can't escape.

I turn away, nodding silently, unable to look at him any longer. The conflict within me is so violent, it threatens to tear me apart. Romeo Riccardi was always a dangerous temptation, a dark pull I couldn't resist, but I've learned the cost of giving in. And yet, in the quiet of this moment, I can't deny that part of me still longs for him— still aches for the connection we once shared.

The space between us feels unbearable, suffocating, like a shrinking cage I no longer fit into. My mind is a tangle of guilt, longing, and fear. Before I can leave, his voice cuts through the silence, harder now.

"What's going on here?" He indicates the space between us, and when he steps closer, I feel the pull of him like gravity—dangerous, inevitable. Even after everything, there's no denying the way we still ignite each other.

"Nothing," I lie, but the tremor in my voice betrays me. I wasn't prepared for this—wasn't prepared for him, not like this. His presence has shattered whatever fragile control I had left.

"Don't reduce us to nothing, Baylin."

His words hit like a physical blow. He's daring me to deny us, to erase everything that ever was, and it's a challenge I'm not sure I can survive.

I move past him, muttering an excuse, my heart hammering in my chest. I don't want to fight this. I don't want to face the storm he brings, but I can't seem to outrun it. Marlon's eyes are supposed to be on me, supposed to keep me safe, but right now, all I want is to escape —to breathe. To think.

I rush through the room, dodging partygoers, the chaos of my thoughts louder than the music or laughter. My breath is quick, uneven, and when I finally stumble outside, the cool night air feels like a balm against my burning skin. I make my way through the manicured garden, the moonlight casting shadows on the stone paths, long and haunting. I find a bench beneath a weeping willow and collapse, my back pressed to the rough bark as I let the night wash over me.

Here, beneath the stars, I let myself unravel.

And then, from behind me, that voice.

"Baylin."

His voice is a mantra on his lips. It's a whisper at first, low and dangerous, a storm on the horizon. I don't turn, but I know he's there —looming, inexorable. He moves closer, his presence as heavy as the moonlight that illuminates him, sharpening every line of his face.

I finally look up, and the intensity of his gaze knocks the breath from my lungs. His eyes, those cold blue eyes, are searching me— seeing right through the walls I've built around myself.

He steps closer, his hand reaching out like a promise or a threat, and the closer he gets, the more my resolve cracks, piece by piece.

"Romeo," I whisper, the name barely escaping me. The tremor in my voice betrays everything I've fought to bury. "Please."

He doesn't pull away.

"It's been more than a year," he says, voice steady but edged with something I can't read. "You're still holding grudges?"

"A lot can happen in a year," I reply, but the words taste like ash, bitter and heavy. The space between us isn't just measured in time— it's the weight of everything we've lost. Everything we've failed to fix. "Time didn't stand still for us the last time we met."

"Time?" He scoffs, a harsh laugh slipping from his lips. It's not a laugh at all, just a jagged edge of disbelief. "Is that what the world has told you? That time heals, that it smooths the edges? Baylin, you of all people should know... we don't always get the luxury of time."

His words pierce deeper than any knife. He's right. Time hasn't healed anything. It's only made the wounds worse, sharper. The year between us hasn't been about healing; it's been about forgetting—

and now remembering, with the weight of everything between us coming crashing down.

I want to tell him how much I've missed him. How much I wish I could turn back time. How much I would've given to undo the silence, to undo the time that has passed. But I can't. The words catch in my throat, swallowed by the void that's always existed between us.

"Do you regret us?" he asks, and there's something raw in his voice, something vulnerable. The question hangs in the air, too heavy to avoid.

"Regret?" I whisper, shaking my head. "No. But I wonder if we were meant to be two different stories all along."

I rise from the bench, my legs unsteady beneath me. The words are so much more than just a question—they're a truth, one I don't want to admit.

"Whatever we were..." I begin, my voice breaking on the edge of the finality I feel in my bones. "It was over before it started."

39

ROMEO

The dimly lit ballroom is a swirl of silk and shadow, where whispers of power float like smoke in the air. The annual Misters Gala is known for its exclusivity, drawing the elite of the underworld—men and women who hold sway over fortunes and fates. Chandeliers drip with crystal, casting a soft glow on the polished marble floor, where figures clad in tailored suits and extravagant gowns mingle, their laughter tinged with a hint of menace.

I stand near the entrance, sipping my drink as I cast my eyes across the crowd. My tailored black suit hugs my athletic frame, a stark contrast to the casual attire I've become accustomed to. I follow their eyes as everyone's attention turns toward a new arrival. And then I see her – Baylin Reyes, a vision in a long flowing gown that hugs her svelte curves, accentuating her every move. Her hair cascades down her back in soft waves, and her smile is radiant and, dare I say, the most genuine in the room.

Her hand is tucked into the arm of an older man, a man whose presence gnaws at me. Marlon Abruzzi. I know who Marlon Abruzzi is. Every damn person in this room does. The notorious arms dealer is known for his ruthless dealings and cold demeanor. My jaw tightens as I watch them engage in conversation, their laughter echoing like a sinister melody. What is Baylin doing with him? The thought twists in my gut, igniting a flame of jealousy I thought I had long buried.

Marlon Abruzzi leans in closer, his hand brushing against Baylin's arm, a gesture that makes my fists clench involuntarily. I take a deep breath, forcing myself to remain composed. The last thing I want is to stir the pot in a room full of the most important men in my life. This is neither the time nor the place. But I can't stay across the room, a mere spectator to her presence.

Her long black dress flatters the hell out of her beautiful body. She's radiant with her minimal makeup, her silky brown waves loose against her shoulders. There are changes; she's shortened her hair, she's developed some curves, yet even I don't miss the glow of her skin as she remains by Abruzzi's side and smiles quietly as she's introduced to people whose names I know she won't remember tomorrow.

I hear the whispers as they walk through the throng of people, greeting others as they move along. People are generally surprised that Marlon Abruzzi has a woman on his arm. It's the first time they can recall such a thing since his wife passed some twenty years ago, I hear one woman say. I don't know what the story is with his wife, and I don't need to know. But I'm more than curious to know what Baylin is doing hanging off his arm like she belongs there.

I watch in morbid curiosity from my corner of the room as they circulate, forgetting my resentment that I had to attend tonight in Lazaro's place. My asshole brother couldn't even do me this one favor and let me be a no-show instead of stepping into his shoes because he didn't want to be here. And now I'm suddenly glad that I came, because I've finally found Baylin.

I had eyes on her when we came back to the city, my own eyes. I watched her sometimes as she sat in the café at the hospital. From across the road when she walked home. She rarely left her home, but when she did, I would follow her as she ran her errands and avoided – at all costs – the supermarket where the tragedy that brought us together again happened. But then I lost her. One day, when I hadn't been to the hospital to see her for a few days, I realized she was gone. So were her mother and nephew.

I don't know what I had hoped to achieve by following her around, but it somehow brought me some comfort knowing that she was nearby and she was okay. Safe. Although I don't know how safe she would've been with Detective Knight being a proverbial pain in the ass. It looked like Detective Handler had rubbed off on Knight, because the woman just would not let up. She harassed Baylin day and night, so in a way, I could understand why Baylin would want to disappear. There was only so much she could handle before she cracked.

As Marlon steps out of the room to attend to some business, I seize the moment. I stride across the room with purpose, my heart pounding in my chest. The chatter around me fades, and all I can focus on is the woman who has held my thoughts captive since that first night in the club all those many years ago.

SHE'S LYING. When I follow her out to the garden and she relegates us to the past, like she's neatly packed us away in a box, I know she's lying when she tries to act like this is not hurting her. Instead, she pretends like what happened between us was a moment in time, a lapse in judgement that she's already discarded and moved on from.

"You seem to be enjoying the company of a rather dangerous man."

Her smile falters slightly, and her gaze falls to the ground before she speaks again.

"Marlon's been a good friend to me."

We were once friends, I want to tell her. But then I remember, we weren't, really. I raise an eyebrow, intrigued. "Is that all?" I ask, the edge in my tone betraying my skepticism.

"I appreciate your concern, but I can handle myself," she hisses, trying but failing to keep her voice steady. "I know what I'm doing."

I study her, the fire in her eyes igniting something deep within me. "I know you're capable, but Marlon Abruzzi's world is not one you want to play in. It's a dangerous place, Baylin."

She steps closer, lowering her voice so only I can hear her, even as her voice turns venomous. "And what about your world, Romeo? You want to criticize Marlon, yet you forget what you did to me. It's no more dangerous with him than it was with you and your brother."

I hesitate, torn between the desire to protect her and the undeniable attraction I feel for her. I've tried to dull my senses with others over the years, but my mind always comes back to Baylin Reyes. "True, but I'd rather not see you get hurt."

She scoffs, disbelief coating her features. "that's rich coming from you," she hisses. "You branded me like I was a piece of cattle. Your brother shot me in the back. Hurt is..."

"What?" I interrupt her.

Baylin's words swim in my head. You branded me...your brother shot me. You branded me...yes, I did. Your brother shot me...no, he did not. Does she not know that I'm the one that shot her? Why would Lazaro keep that secret? Why wouldn't he tell her that I shot her?

"What happened at that cabin?" I ask her, and suddenly I'm more curious than ever as to what happened between her and my brother while I was gone. What else are they hiding from me?

"Nothing happened, Rome! Nothing! Your brother shot me, then he brought me back to life, and..."

She trails off, her eyes glazing over as she looks off into the distance, as though remembering something. I see the moment it clicks in her mind, when she lifts her head and looks at me with shuttered eyes.

Our eyes lock, an unspoken understanding passing between us. I feel the tension rise, electrifying the air. I want to reach for her, to pull her closer, but the weight of the truth she's just unveiled pushes me back away from her. She knows. She suddenly understands. She may have forgiven many things, but this she would never forgive.

"I couldn't understand why he would shoot me, only to nurse me back to health," she whispers. And suddenly, her tears are coming. The revelation is too much for her to bear. And it's too much for me to live with, knowing that I almost killed her. I put a bullet in her, and it's the single biggest regret of my life, but I can't undo it. I can beg for her forgiveness, ask her to understand that I was in a bad place, but she will always look at me as the man who tried to end her life.

40

MARLON

I find Baylin in the garden; distressed and almost incoherent, and I hate that I left her alone when I told her that I wouldn't. I let her down, and my arm around her shoulder is little comfort as we leave the gala without ever returning into the manor.

We walk from the garden and straight to our waiting cars, with Baylin looking at me a little perplexed. I realize for the first time that she's somewhat afraid of me. I hate the tears that stream down her face, the liquid that pools in her brown eyes even as she dabs at them.

"You can't leave," she says, pulling my arm as we walk down the path. "This happens once in a year – you can't leave."

"I can do whatever the hell I like," I tell her, and she recoils at my tone. It's unfortunate, because I'm not angry at her. I'm angry at her tears. I don't want to see her upset. And I don't want to stay here if that's only going to torment her. She means so much more to me than that.

"Stay," she whispers. "I'll be fine to go home with the guards."

I shake my head vehemently. There's no way I'm staying without her. There'll be other years, and we did what I needed to do anyway, which was basically to put in an appearance. And that other thing she can't ever know about.

"I've had enough for the night," I tell her. "Let's go."

Baylin goes to her room as soon as we're back home, and I let her. She needs to decompress. She's told me all about her time with the Riccardi brothers, but there's obviously so much more she left out of the original story. So much more that I guess I got tonight. The way that her eyes met Romeo Riccardi's across the balcony tells me there was so much more to them than she told me. It didn't matter either way, as long as it didn't pose a threat to anything in my own organization. But I knew...I just knew there was something about her time with them that was unresolved, and tonight was the perfect opportunity for me to find out what that was. Although, I'd been expecting Lazaro Riccardi to attend, not his younger brother Romeo. I still feel like I got what I needed, which is a start.

She surprises me when she knocks on the door of the den a little while later, wearing sweats. Her comfort clothes. She never wears sweats unless she's depressed or just needs to flat out sit around and do nothing but feel sorry for herself. She does that a lot, and I find myself inventing ways to make her a stronger woman. She needs to be strong for the inevitable storm that's coming. I need her to be able to take care of herself if she needs to.

"Are you okay?" I ask her.

She looks at me like I've gone mad. Like she's the one that should be asking me that. She nods timidly, slips into the chair by the fireplace and picks up the leather-bound book, asking me without words if I want her to read to me.

"I'll ask this just once," I tell her. "Then we never bring it up again."

She looks at me with wide, fearful eyes. Baylin hates losing control, and I won't do that to her. I won't take her control from her.

"Ask," she prompts.

"Whatever happened between you and the Riccardis – should I be worried?"

"What? No!" She looks at me in confusion, slips from the chair and comes to stand before me. She reaches out and palms my cheek, tears filling her eyes again. "I swear to you, I haven't had contact with either of them since I came back to the city. And whatever it was between us – it's dead. They made their choice very clear, and I chose to honor it. I still choose to honor it."

I nod, confident that she's being honest with me. Whatever there was between Baylin and the Riccardi brothers is long gone, and she's not entertaining re-opening old wounds. I can't protect her otherwise. I can't protect her if she insists on walking in the shadows of their violence. Not when our world hangs precariously on the edge of war.

I MAKE it my business to know everything there is to know about everyone in the underworld. All my friends. All my enemies. The same rule applies to all. I know the stories I've heard whispered about the Riccardis, but I get my best man onto digging up everything there is to know about them, in case I've missed anything. Baylin Reye's safety has now become my number one priority, and there's no way I can protect her if I don't know what I'm up against. It's to my advantage to know these things about any and all in our world. I read through the file in front of me, my eyes scanning each and every line, careful not to miss anything.

Lazaro Riccardi has always been the levelheaded son in that family. That's why, undoubtedly, he's the leader. I remember hearing, a few years ago, about the youngest brother, and the tragedy that struck the family when he was gunned down by an unknown assailant at a truck stop. His murder was as much a surprise to the underworld as it was to the family, and to this day, his killer had not yet been found. The middle son, Romeo Riccardi, had apparently gone a little loopy after his brother's death. And by loopy, I don't mean loco. He had literally turned into a beast. Of the murdering kind.

We all heard the stories. Romeo's transformation was not just an emotional or psychological shift; it was as if he had shed his humanity like a snake sheds its skin. Where once there had been a charming, albeit reckless young man, there now lurked a creature driven by rage and an insatiable thirst for vengeance. A creature called upon by many to do their bidding.

Lazaro watched his brother's descent with a heavy heart but knew better than to confront him directly. Instead, he tightened his control over their operations, hoping to shield Romeo from further self-destruction. All the while, he marshaled the family's considerable resources to hunt down the killer of their youngest sibling — a task that proved daunting as leads either vanished into thin air or led down rabbit holes that spiraled into dangerous territories.

I put the file down, look out the window at the passing landscape as I travel toward my destination. I'm on my way to see Lazaro Riccardi, and I don't want Baylin involved, so I set up the meeting first thing in the morning, hoping to be back before she even knows I've stepped out.

Lazaro Riccardi sits behind a solid wood desk, wearing a grey suit that sets off his blue eyes. He rises to greet me, his warm eyes flicking over me briefly, the result of many years of shared mutual respect. We haven't had occasion to come into contact often, but when we have, it's always been a cordial transaction. His reputation as a wise and savvy businessman in our ruthless world has garnered him the respect and admiration of all those who reside in the shadows.

"It was regrettable that you could not make the gala at the Manor," I tell him, gauging his reaction. And by the way he looks at me, he already knows.

"Ahhh...that," he says pointedly. He invites me to take a seat, then sits back in his own chair. "Romeo did mention something about running into you there."

"It would go without saying that I would be there," I remind him. I'm one of the main stakeholders of the event; everyone in our world knows that. He nods his apology, puts a hand to his chest, quietly asking for forgiveness. There's nothing like the respect between one leader to another; it can't be bought; it can't be traded; it's earned. And he gives it in spades, which is precisely the reason I don't bring out the boxing gloves as I sit opposite the head of the Riccardi family.

"To what do I owe the pleasure of your visit, Don Abruzzi?"

"Baylin Reyes."

There's the slightest flicker in his eyes before he recovers and asks me how he can help.

"She was apparently with you last night at the Manor." He's seeking clarification. Clarification I'm only too happy to give him.

"She was," I admit.

"That was quite the surprise to my brother, I have no doubt. In what capacity?"

"Baylin Reyes is now under my protection," I tell him. "She works for me, and as long as she is in my care, she is untouchable."

Lazaro shifts in his seat, trying to get comfortable. He fidgets with the chair, debating whether to ask a question that he knows he'll likely keep to himself. Finally, he speaks.

"She's in need of protection?" This is obviously news to him.

"Let's say a certain detective has developed a crush on her," I muse. "Baylin took up a position with me; we have a mutual agreement, and I want to ensure that nothing gets in the way of that."

Lazaro nods once, seemingly impressed by my explanation, even through his own confusion. It's obvious they haven't had contact with Baylin, otherwise they'd know she was working for me.

"This concerns me how?"

"Not sure that it does. I just wanted you to know, since it appears there's some history between her and your brother. He's not exactly the type to let go of things easily."

Lazaro swallows back his fury, and he does it well. I hadn't intended it to, but it seems my words have hit a nerve.

"I've dragged my brother back from the edge of madness...too many times to count," he tells me, as he sits back in his chair, a far away look on his face. "He won't hurt her again."

He flicks his eyes toward me, and I can't ignore the sincerity in his eyes. His very admittance that Romeo hurt Baylin tells me he wouldn't lie about it never happening again. Whatever happened between them was probably more than any of them expected, but I have to believe that they don't have any ongoing animosity towards Baylin.

"I know there's history between you, and I just wanted you to know that I will not allow anything to hurt her."

"That is not our intention," Lazaro tells me, his jaw ticking back and forth.

"Then what *is* your intention?"

"When it comes to Baylin Reyes? Absolutely nothing."

41

BAYLIN

Seeing Romeo Riccardi at the Annual Misters Gala dredged up old feelings which I'd believed were long dead. If it were at all possible, he's more devilishly handsome than he was before. He's harder than before, his jaw sharper, and I know that I didn't imagine it, but he was larger than life. Taller, bigger, a mountain of muscle and strength threatening to blow me off like the stale wind surrounding us. His icy blue eyes were scorching, burning through me like lines of fire, reminding me of the power they once wielded over me.

I haven't seen nor heard from the brothers since we came back to the city – that much is true, but that doesn't mean that they don't sometimes cross my mind. Despite everything, despite every single little thing that came to pass between us, I can't help but think of them at times. You don't spend two weeks with someone at a cabin, with no connection to the outside world, and not form some sort of rapport with them. Regardless of what they did to me. Despite the pain and suffering they caused me. In lieu of the massive secret we are keeping. That time is time that I'll never get back, but it's also time that I wouldn't erase, no matter what comes to pass.

Except maybe the biggest bombshell of all. Romeo didn't deny it when I realized that he was the one who shot me at the cabin. I don't know why I didn't put the pieces together earlier, nor why Lazaro was seemingly so willing to take the blame for the bullet lodged in my shoulder, and the reason why. Why, after everything, had Romeo raised his gun and aimed it at me? To what end? And do I even want to know?

I replay the scene over and over in my mind; it's hopeless, I know, but I somehow think I'm going to get a different outcome each time I relive the torment of that moment at the Gala with Romeo, but no matter which way I look at it, the outcome is the same...

There was something he didn't want to share with me, some secret or truth he wanted to keep hidden. After watching regret flicker across his face for a few moments, something clicked in my mind and I realized the truth.

"You shot me," I whispered, disbelief caressing my words. I said it aloud, but I had a hard time believing it. Even to my own ears, it seemed preposterous that Romeo would have shot me. Would he? Could he? The bastard.

Romeo's shoulders tensed at my accusation, but he didn't deny it. The silence between us grew heavy, suffocating me as I tried to process the revelation. Romeo was the one who put a bullet in me. Anger simmered beneath the shock, a fierce heat that threatened to consume me whole.

"Why?" The word escaped my lips before I could stop it, filled with a mix of hurt and betrayal. Romeo didn't owe me anything, but he shot me!

He finally met my gaze, his eyes holding a storm of emotions that mirrored my own.

"I did what I thought had to be done," he began slowly, each word heavy with regret.

Nothing about my time with the brothers was normal, and I can't expect it to be even now. All I know is that they both hurt me, both kept secrets from me, but one brother hurt me more than the other. He destroyed me.

Yet still, seeing him was like coming home after a long, extended hiatus in which there didn't seem to be any end. Seeing Romeo Riccardi felt like I had come full circle, even though I know the danger. I know the pitfalls of being in the same world as the Riccardis. I've tasted their life firsthand. I've lived it. And I don't want to go back to that dark and empty place ever again.

I can still feel Romeo's hands on my body, late at night when I'm sleeping and wake with a start, having just seen a dream in which the vision of him is so vivid, I could almost swear he's in the room with me. I can still smell his heady, woodsy scent in the air, the whiff of it destroying my composure; it's a scent that lingers on and on, refusing to leave me, and I welcome it. I welcome the memory of him to assault my senses, to remind me that he was a living, breathing titan that slept beside me, touched me, loved me in his own tortured way.

And the way that Lazaro nursed me back to health, even after his own brother shot me. Romeo shot me down, then Lazaro carried me through the forest, laid me down and patched me up. He could've just left me there to die. No-one would have known. I may not have been found until many years later, if ever.

Instead, Lazaro went looking for me in the forest and rescued me from the tip of the ravine. He put all my broken pieces back together. They killed me, but they also healed me. And Lazaro healed the cracked pieces of my heart that Romeo left behind when he left me in that forest.

LYDIA BLACK FINALLY FINDS ME. By some stroke of luck (or misfortune, as I prefer to look at it) she finds out where I am and she's standing at my door barely two days after the party at the Manor, insisting that she speak with me. I only know this because of all the noise she makes, because the maid refuses to let her enter, and the guards are standing by, ready to evict her from the front stairs. Marlon, too, comes out of his study and approaches the front door as I stand hidden in the shadows of the doorway, watching the commotion.

"I thought I made it clear that you aren't welcome here." Marlon's voice is laced with intimidation, a coiling tension that makes it hard for anyone to see past his anger.

"You can tell me all you want," Lydia bites back. "The fact is, Baylin Reyes is part of an ongoing investigation, and we won't stop until we get her testimony."

"We?" I can almost imagine Marlon's brows as he quirks one in response. "The only person I see on my doorstep is you, Detective Black. Tell me, do you make it a habit of conducting your own investigations?"

There's silence on the other side of the door, before Lydia shifts and comes into view. I step back into the shadow of the room before she can see me. I've managed to avoid her all these months, and I hope to go on avoiding her. No good will come of a conversation between her and I, no matter the subject.

"I need to speak with Baylin Reyes." Her voice is tight, and she doesn't seem to be in a hurry to go anywhere.

"That's not going to happen." Marlon, always the voice of reason and certainty in my sea of unrest. I exhale a breath I didn't realize I was holding. "Not without a warrant." I suck in another anxious breath.

"It will just be a friendly chat." She's grasping at straws, but that's what the detective does best.

"Take your friendliness elsewhere; Baylin Reyes is not in the market for more friends."

I hear the click of the front door as it closes suddenly and step out of the shadows, staring at Marlon as he walks back down the long hallway.

"You needn't worry yourself about her, Baylin," he reassures me. Although I'm nothing but worried. It's been several months of relative calm, with Lydia Black leaving me alone. But now she's back, and so is that damn bone of hers.

"How did she find me?" I gasp.

"It could've been any one of a number of ways," he tells me. He takes me by the elbow and steers me toward his office. "Don't worry about Detective Black; she'll tire eventually, and she'll move on to other things."

I shake my head, not entirely convinced. "You seem so sure, but I wish I had your confidence."

"She's just fishing, Baylin. Don't give her a second thought."

He manages to convince me that Lydia Black is not worth my energy and promises me that things will blow over. When I tell him that I'm worried she'll cause problems for him, he just scoffs then laughs.

"Oh, I'm counting on her trouble," he says. "And I can't say I'm not looking forward to the challenge."

Lydia Black comes back the next day, then the next, holding on to her bone for dear life. On the third day, Marlon threatens her with a restraining order.

"Unless you have a warrant for her arrest, Baylin Reyes is exorcising her right not to be questioned. If you insist on meeting with her, you can do so at the precinct, in the presence of her lawyer."

Later, Marlon tells me that Lydia Black visibly blanched when he made her the offer. I couldn't understand why, until he explained it to me.

"For some reason, she wants to meet you away from the precinct. She's doing this off the books. Which means, this whole mess goes way beyond Detective Handler. It's bigger than me or you. Bigger even than the Riccardis. Lydia Black is either trying to bury or uncover something, and she needs your help to do it."

"How could I possibly help her?" I shriek. Marlon shrugs his shoulder, a faraway look entering his eyes before he breaks the silence once again.

"My guess is she wants to know where Handler is because she needs something from him."

"Well, he's dead," I remind him.

"And that is what she's afraid of."

42

MARLON

I lean back in my leather chair, the flicker of the dim lamp casting long shadows across my cluttered desk. I stroke my chin thoughtfully, my mind whirling with scenes of carnage. Turning the folder over in my hands, I consider the weight of the information it contains, information powerful enough to sway public opinion and twist the arm of law enforcement.

"Lydia Black," I mutter under my breath, a hint of disdain lacing my words. The detective has been a thorn in Baylin's side for months, doggedly pursuing her with an intensity that suggests a personal vendetta rather than mere professional duty. It was time to redirect her focus to other things.

My plan is simple yet risky. Leaking a series of documents, photos, and audio recordings that hint at Detective Handler's corrupt dealings before his untimely demise. The evidence is explosive, suggesting Handler had accepted bribes from various criminal elements in exchange for protection and other favors. Among these were several incriminating photos and a voice recording of Handler negotiating a significant payout between rival gangs, even as he double-crossed both sides. His corruption was so wide reaching, it encompassed even others within his own department.

The cornerstone of my strategy lays in how this information will be disclosed. I need to ensure it appears as though the leak is not only from an anonymous but also an unimpeachable source, lending credibility to the allegations and causing maximum disruption within the ranks of the police department.

I tap into my network of contacts and find what I need—a disgruntled former journalist with deep ties to law enforcement and a grudge against the system that had unceremoniously spit him out. Ellis Monroe has the skills and contacts necessary to give the story legs.

"Ellis," I speak into my encrypted phone later that evening, "I think it's time we chat about mutual interests."

Ellis, intrigued by the prospect of exposing corruption within law enforcement, agrees to meet me under strict confidentiality at one of my safe houses—a nondescript apartment downtown.

At the meeting, I lay out the files before Ellis. "This is explosive stuff," I begin, watching Ellis' eyes flick over the material with rising interest. "It paints a pretty damning picture of Handler, and by extension, those who were close to him."

Ellis picks up one of the photos, examining it closely. "This could do it," he says thoughtfully. "This could get Black off your back."

"That's the plan," Marlon confirms. "We drip-feed this to the press. Start small—ambiguous hints at corruption—then escalate to the hard evidence. It'll create doubt around Handler's integrity and shift focus away from an investigation. No-one will give a damn where the man is.

Ellis nods slowly, mapping out potential headlines in his head. "With my contacts in media," he says slowly, "I can get these into some investigative pieces. Frame it as a piece on corruption ravaging Handler's reputation."

"They won't care where he is, as long as he stays gone."

"And what about after?" Ellis asks pointedly.

"After," I reply smoothly, "we watch as they scramble. Detective Black will have to direct her energy towards cleaning up their internal mess instead of harassing an innocent nurse."

After Ellis leaves, I sit back, a smirk pulling at the corners of my mouth. The game is set, the pieces are moving, and soon the entire board would change. I feel a cold satisfaction knowing that Detective Black will be consumed by this new chaos, her vendetta temporarily forgotten.

~

THE SUN IS BARELY PEEKING through the horizon a few days later when Baylin comes rushing into my office, waving her iPad around.

"Oh my God, Marlon!" she squeals, excitement lancing through her movements. "Have you seen this morning's news?"

I try for nonchalance as I look up from my work, my eyes going to the iPad as she turns it my way. I get only a brief look at the story before she turns it back toward her and starts explaining what she's looking at.

My plan had begun to unfold. The first article hit the news with just enough ambiguity to cause whispers and rumors to start swirling through the city.

"*Unknown Sources Question Integrity of one of the PD's finest,*" she reads, then lifts her eyes to meet mine. "They're saying there's undisputed proof that detective Handler was in the pocket of several criminal enterprises and fled to avoid a bounty that had been placed on his head."

The bounty was a nice touch, not something that Ellis and I discussed. But it does the job, nonetheless. I don't tell her that I've already seen the news; it's always the first thing I do in the morning before I leave my room.

The response to the story breaking has been immediate and exactly what I had anticipated. The police department is put on the defensive, statements have been made about internal investigations, and media vans are now camped around the precinct where Detective Handler worked. The police commissioner has appeared on several news segments, his face drawn, insisting on the department's integrity but confirming that they are taking all allegations seriously. Which is precisely what I want and need to happen.

Baylin's eyes don't leave mine as she continues to stare at me with a newfound curiosity.

"How much of this did you have a hand in?" Baylin whispers across the desk, her eyes scanning mine for any sign of deception.

I shake my head and scoff, look at her like she's lost her mind. "This is beyond even my reach," I tell her. What she doesn't know won't hurt her.

Baylin sighs, her mind racing with possible scenarios. "This means... this could mean my life would go back to normal."

I nod in agreement as her expression becomes tinged with a sense of sadness. I wonder if normal means she'd want to leave this place, leave me.

Baylin's hands tremble slightly as she clasps them together, resting them on the cold, dark wood of the desk that separates us. The room feels claustrophobic suddenly, filled with unspoken words and hidden desires.

"Normal," she murmurs, almost to herself, her gaze drifting towards the window where the city sprawls indifferently beyond. "I haven't thought about what normal feels like in... a long time."

I watch her closely, taking in every crease of worry that has formed on her brow over the months and every flicker of longing in her eyes. It pains me to think she might leave, disappear back into a world where I can't reach her. The selfishness of my desire to keep her near wrestles with my wish for her happiness. But self-preservation urges me to hold back the words clawing at my throat.

When I finally speak again, my voice is rough with restrained emotion. "You could see your family more often, live without looking over your shoulder."

She nods slowly, turning back to look at me. Her eyes are glistening slightly, and it strikes me then how much of a facade our professional relationship has been. Beneath the surface exchanges and the practical dealings, there's something deeper, a bond forged in adversity—a silent acknowledgment that neither of us is quite as tough as we pretend to be.

A small smile tugs at the corner of her mouth. "I'd like that," she admits. "But..." Her voice trails off as she avoids my gaze again, focusing instead on a loose thread on her sleeve.

"But?" I prompt gently, leaning forward. The distance between us feels both infinite and negligible.

Baylin pulls at the thread nervously before letting go and meeting my eyes once more. There's a vulnerability there that she rarely shows.

I watch her closely, seeing the conflict play across her features. Baylin is a master at hiding her feelings well, but now they simmer just beneath the surface, impossible for me to ignore. "You know," I start, leaning back in my chair and folding my hands together. "Sometimes we think we want to go back to the way things were, only to realize that 'normal' wasn't as great as we remembered."

Baylin turns back to face me, her expression unreadable. "Maybe," she concedes. "But it's stable. Predictable. Safe." Her eyes drop to the ground, a stark contrast to the restless energy that often charges through her.

I nod slowly. "Safe," I echo thoughtfully. "But since when have you ever played it safe, Baylin?" There's challenge in my tone, a probing test of her spirit I've come to admire since our paths first crossed under less than conventional circumstances.

She smiles faintly at that, the ghost of her old life lighting up her eyes before fading just as quickly. It's clear she yearns for more than just predictability; yet fear of the unknown holds her tethered to this time and place.

The silence stretches between us, filled with all the things unsaid: truths neither of us are brave enough to voice. We both know there's something deeper, more meaningful, between us than mere necessity or convenience. But admitting that would mean confronting emotions neither of us are prepared to handle.

It strikes me then that maybe 'normal' isn't what she needs.

Maybe our definition of normal is flawed. Maybe what she truly needs is something beyond our narrow definition of normalcy...something wild and untamed.

43

BAYLIN

After the story broke about Detective Handler's corrupt dealings, Detective Lydia Black seemingly dropped off the face of the earth. Literally. She took a leave of absence and disappeared as quickly as she had appeared, for which I was never more grateful.

The sigh of relief I let out could be heard all the way across the country as I spoke on the phone to my mother and shared the good news with her that she and Luca could come home soon.

Marlon, after much convincing, agrees to let me out on my own to do some shopping. It has been so long since I've been alone that I've almost forgotten how to function as one single unit. He'd agreed, and I'd jumped at the chance to be out in the open without any threats hanging over me.

I know that right about now, Marlon's thanking his lucky stars he's a cunning bastard and had his guards follow me at a distance, so nondescript that even I didn't know they were there. Not until I needed them, anyhow.

Two masked men pull up beside me as I stroll leisurely down the strip, breathing in the scent of freedom. Their car brakes harshly beside me, and they jump out of the vehicle and approach me, one muffling my screams with a hand to my mouth. Shoppers, stunned into submission, stand by awkwardly watching the drama unfold as the men brandish guns in their direction and threaten to use them if they don't stand back. I watch as my bags go flying through the air and land in various places on the ground, shoe boxes and clothes strewn everywhere. My eyes land on the book I had purchased for Marlon, a scream forming in my throat as my heart gallops rapidly and I realize that I may never see him again.

This is it; I think to myself. This could be the one defining moment in my life where I lose my voice, my struggle, my will to survive. There is no way I would make it out of this one; no one is coming to save me, and I am finally, inevitably, going to meet my maker and pay for my sins. I stomp on one of the men's feet, struggling against him. He lifts me off my feet, and a hand lands on my jaw, winding me. The heat from the slap radiates across my face. I hear screams to my right, but I can't see anything, and just as easily as I'm off my feet, I hear a pop, and I am floating to the ground. I hit the pavement with a heavy thud, just as I hear another pop, and the world around me goes dark.

WHEN MY EYES FLUTTER OPEN, Marlon sits by my side, the dim light flickering above casting shadows on his handsome face. I look around, my eyes finding their focus, and find myself laying on the sofa in the den. The walls of shelves, filled with books that I've spent hours devouring and reading to him, make the room feel more like a fortress than a sanctuary. My eyes land on his, the tension between us thick with unspoken emotions.

"What happened?" I whisper, as I lift a hand to my temple.

"The nurse needed a nurse," he tells me, and although he's trying to inject some semblance of humor into his words, his voice falls flat, and I can see that he's fuming. "It was premature to let you out of the house on your own." He's angry at himself for allowing me to convince him I would be fine on my own.

"Marlon, don't," I squeeze my eyes shut, trying to block out the pain, then fold over the side of the sofa, trying to sit up.

"Stay where you are, Baylin," he orders, pushing me back onto the sofa with one finger. There's an edge to his voice.

"Want to get up..."

"For fuck's sake, Baylin! You have a concussion. You could cause more damage."

I lay back down, looking up at the ceiling, letting out a sigh. Shards of what happened start to hit me, and I groan as I remember that I'm supposed to be dead. Technically. I was literally in the clutches of two unknown men, and now somehow, I'm home with Marlon.

"How did I get here?" I ask.

"You were lucky enough that I don't take your safety lightly. I had someone follow you. And it's a good thing I did, too."

"I thought we discussed this, Marlon, and we agreed the threat of Detective Black was contained enough for me to step out of my comfort zone."

"I was wrong. I was wrong to think you'd be safe. Obviously."

"I don't understand why you're so angry. I'm here and I'm safe, aren't I?" I shift on the sofa, nervously fidgeting with my sweater.

Marlon's determined gaze meets mine. "I can't help but worry for your safety. If someone is trying to harm you, I won't just stand by and do nothing."

"No-one could have known that would happen," I remind him.

"No. But we can plan for possible outcomes."

I shake my head; it hurts like a bitch and I'm sure I need more painkillers. I'm going to be sporting the hangover from hell in a few hours.

"I won't go out on my own again."

It's Marlon's turn to shake his head. He looks away, biting the corner of his lip, as though trying to hold his tongue. He curses, his voice low, but it's loud enough for me to hear him.

"I already promised not to go anywhere alone again, Marlon. What more do you want?"

I make a solemn vow to myself never to leave the house without security again. Detective Lydia Black may be off the grid, and the Abruzzi family's power and influence may have protected me from her efforts, but there's no way of knowing if she'll just pop up again and cause more problems. Although Marlon suspects she may have been the one who attempted to kidnap me, I struggle to believe she would go to such extreme lengths.

Marlon slams his hand down on a side table, causing a small quake that sends a pen rolling off the edge. His eyes are ablaze, burning with a protective fury that frightens yet comforts me. "It's not about what I want, Baylin. It's about ensuring your safety. I almost lost you today!"

"But you didn't," I bite back, angry at myself more than anything else. I don't like to see Marlon upset.

"You don't seem to grasp the gravity of the situation. Detective Black is like a fucking leech when it comes to you. And she may be gone now, but maybe she's just biding her time."

I sigh, trying to temper his rising anger with a calmness that I'm far from feeling. "Maybe we have another player on the field," I retort, and he rears back, as though I've punched him. I know the thought has probably already crossed his mind.

Marlon stands abruptly, his chair scraping back against the old wooden floor like a scream in the night. He begins pacing; each step he takes seems measured, deliberate. "You came to me for protection, Baylin. You promised me your loyalty and you've given it. It's time for me to uphold my end of the bargain."

I watch him pace, his movements echoing my pounding heart—fast and unyielding. The room feels as if it has shrunk, walls inching closer under the weight of our fears and conflicts.

"Marlon," I start, my voice steadier than I feel, "I appreciate your concern—I do." My hands clench into fists by my side, nails digging into my palms. "But we can't let this consume us. I won't leave the house unaccompanied again. I promise you."

He stops pacing and looks at me, his expression softening slightly. "Baylin," he says quietly, regret threading through his words like silver wisps of smoke. "I can't stand the thought of something happening to you because I failed to protect you."

The vulnerability in his voice pulls at me; it's a stark contrast to his usual confidence and control. It reminds me how deeply intertwined our lives have become since I walked through his door months ago.

I rise slowly and hold my arms out to him, and he surges forward until he's sitting in front of me again. I take his face between my hands gently but firmly, compelling him to meet my gaze directly. "Marlon, look at me," I command softly. "Nothing happened—I'm safe because of you. And nothing will happen because we're taking extra measures now. I need you to not get so worked up that your blood pressure will rise again."

He breathes out slowly, nodding slightly as he places his hands over mine on his cheeks. There's nothing untoward about the move, but the echo of a childless man who feels like he's come home. A heavy silence lingers between us, before he sighs and moves away, his face ravaged, appearing more his age than ever before.

"Nothing happens in my city without me knowing about it, Baylin. *Nothing.* And the one who dares to touch you will pay with his or her life."

44

LAZARO

Marlon Abruzzi is back. He's not the sort of man you deny an audience, so I decide this time to meet him over breakfast in the restaurant; an informal meeting that might loosen him up a little. While I have immense respect for the man, he made it clear during our last encounter that he is fiercely protective of Baylin.

"I appreciate you making time for me," Marlon greets me as he joins me at the booth.

I'm not sure what brings him back to my doorstep, but I greet him with a warm smile as he unbuttons his coat and takes a seat across from me. The waitress comes by to take our order, and we make small talk until she returns with our meals. I notice that Marlon doesn't touch his food, but instead takes a sip of his coffee which seems to perk him up.

"I was surprised when I received your call," I admit. He holds my gaze for a few moments before looking down at his cup and then back up at me. I glance towards the door where his security team stands watchfully, their eyes following my every move.

"When we last met, you mentioned that you hold no grudges against Baylin Reyes," he begins, flicking his eyes towards a point behind me. I turn to see Romeo emerging from the office and slowly making his way towards us. He knows about my meeting with Abruzzi today but understands not to interfere. His curiosity must have gotten the best of him. I nod towards the door, sending him away, and my brother continues toward the door before I turn back to meet Marlon's glacial stare. Something's made him mad.

"That's still the case," I tell him.

He sighs, seems to consider his words one last time before he lets them spring forward.

"And yet you shot her in the back so she wouldn't testify against you."

My eyes flicker in surprise that Baylin shared this with him, and I have to wonder how close they are for her to have disclosed that to him. He seems to know exactly what I'm thinking, because he leans forward and answers the question that sits idly on my lips.

"She and I agreed when she came to work for me that we keep no secrets from each other. You know who I am, therefore, you know I wouldn't have hired her without knowing everything there is to know about her."

I don't disclose the fact that I wasn't the one that shot her. It changes nothing. "Our business with Baylin Reyes is in the past," I remind him, and he seems to believe me, because he sits back in his chair then drops a bombshell on me.

"Baylin was mugged a few days ago."

I feel the tight muscle that ticks in my temple as I swallow the meaning of his words.

"And?"

"And...my security was thankfully there," he tells me, although I feel like he's watching me carefully for a reaction.

"You think we had something to do with that?"

He shakes his head.

"I haven't come here to make an accusation against you," Abruzzi says, and it's a sign of his respect for me that his mind didn't dare think that I would be responsible.

"Then what?"

"I think whoever tried to take her did so to get to me."

"She's your nurse," I remind him, downplaying her importance to him. It's not like she's a senior member of his organization.

"She is. But she's in my constant company. Anyone with two eyes can see she means a lot to me."

I recline in my seat with a knowing look, and the pieces start to fall into place on their own. Marlon Abruzzi left the Annual Misters Gala early. Too early. It's unheard of that a major stakeholder would do so, a kind of slap in the face to everyone at that gala. Anyone there that night could have misconstrued their relationship as a weakness when he left before a decent amount of time lapsed with a young woman by his side.

"What exactly is the relationship between you two, if you don't mind me asking?" Clarity, I seek clarity.

"Baylin has become a constant companion, a loyal one. She's like a daughter to me."

"Hence your willingness to protect her."

He agrees silently, nodding his head. "I would do anything to protect her."

"You've come to me because there's obviously something on your mind."

"I don't for one instance believe that Baylin is the direct target here. Someone's trying to get to me through her."

I tend to agree with him but say nothing, waiting for him to go on.

"I have no doubt they'll try again, and I fear that one day, they may be successful."

"You have no direct heir, which makes you an easy target."

"I wouldn't say easy, but I'd say whoever's muscling in on my territory wants to earn his keep the easy way. He won't last."

"You don't seem too concerned for your safety," I muse.

"I'm a realist, Lazaro. I plan based on probabilities, and in all likelihood, someone will make an attempt on my life. I need to be prepared for that when it comes."

"We can organize protection."

Protection is our middle name. Blood and revenge thrum in our veins, and the Riccardis are more than willing and capable of step-ping up to the plate. And, truth be told, I may not tell him this, but Baylin's safety is still important to me. I've been nothing but grateful that she's been in Marlon's capable and safe hands up till now, although now it seems alternative arrangements will need to be made.

"I have a strong protection detail," he tells me. "But you know, as well as I do, that if something's going to happen, there's no stopping it."

"How can I help?" And I mean that with every sincere bone in my body.

"I need to know that Baylin Reyes is protected after I'm gone. That's all I'm concerned about."

"And you want me to offer her that protection?"

"We more or less have the same values, Mr. Riccardi. You could have killed Baylin when you had her and knew she was a witness to a crime perpetrated by your men. And yet, you let her live. Despite the challenges that presented to you."

I still don't tell him that I never even entertained the idea of killing her. I wonder how much he knows about our time at the cabin, her relationship with Romeo and the fact that I nursed her back to health. I'm not sure he knows everything, but he knows enough to trust us to protect what he now considers his most valu-able asset.

"Let me protect you," I offer. "Let's avoid another attempt on your life and let us protect you."

Abruzzi shakes his head, gives me half a smile and looks toward the window for a few seconds, obviously experiencing a moment of reflection.

"She's the sincerest person I've ever met," he says, sliding his eyes back to meet mine. "I hope you know how loyal she is. Do I have your word that you will protect her?"

I give him one short nod. I don't even have to think about it, although I'd like to think it won't come to that. If the need arises, I will protect Baylin with my life.

"You'll be rewarded for your efforts," he says, as he rises, once again buttons his coat and stands by the table. He cuts me off before I can reply, then thrusts his hand towards mine for a handshake. His other hand moves to my shoulder, where he curls his fingers against the fabric of my suit and squeezes.

"My services are available to you at any time," I assure him.

"I'll be in touch, Lazaro. My lawyer will reach out should the need arise."

I watch as Abruzzi turns to leave, noticing for the first time how frail he looks. Even in his mid-fifties, the man can still hold his own, but I can see that the situation with the attempted attack on Baylin has taken its toll on him. There's a flurry of movement at the door as his security surrounds him, flanking him on all sides to ensure his safety.

"Stay safe, Don Abruzzi," I hiss through gritted teeth. The mere thought of Baylin ignites a fire within me, but the thought of any harm befalling the Don sends a jolt of icy fear coursing through my body. Every nerve ending tingles with anxious energy as beads of cold sweat trickle down my spine, a constant reminder of the danger that's landed on my doorstep.

45

MARLON

I sit in the quiet of my room, staring out the window at the garden below. The day hums with life, a sharp contrast to the storm brewing inside me. I am alone, not just in the physical sense, but in a deeper, more visceral way. My thoughts drift back, as they so often do, to a day long ago—a day that changed everything.

Years have passed, but the weight of that loss hasn't diminished; if anything, it has only grown heavier with time. I rub my eyes, trying to focus, but the memories are always there, just beneath the surface, waiting for a moment of weakness to resurface. The images of Stevie's face, pale and bloody, the sound of his ragged breaths, the feel of his fading pulse in my hands—these things never leave me. They are as vivid as the day they happened.

I can't shake the feeling that the world, as it moves on, has left me behind in some irreparable way. No amount of time or distance can fix it. The pain has calcified inside me, and yet, for all its agony, it is all I have left of my brother. A brother that was too good for this world.

That night at the lake is a wound that has never healed, and I'm not entirely sure it ever would.

I close my eyes, letting the memory of Stevie take over, and for a moment, the years seem to fall away, leaving only the two of us, the brotherhood we shared, and the terrible price we had to pay.

It's been years, but that night, I dream of my old friend Stevie. In my dream, I relive the scene at the lake, the bullet embedded in his body, and the life draining out of him as I tried desperately to keep him alive. Not a day goes by that I don't think of him, don't miss him. Even the absence of my wife wasn't as painful as the absence of my brother. The brother who took a bullet for me. The brother who lost his life in my place. That bullet had been meant for me, and it was never more evident than when I caught up with Franco Two-pence four months after I buried Stevie.

In the end, it all came out. Every damning little piece of evidence that he had shot my best friend. He had killed him. Whilst at the lake house that last Summer, I had practiced my shooting skills. I had honed the skill and was ready for anything that was thrown my way. But that Summer, I made two decisions.

The first was that I would never go back to that lake house. It carried with it the memory of the darkest point of my life, a memory I wanted so desperately to remain buried in the shadows of the forest. The second decision I made was that I wouldn't shoot Franco Two-pence. No, a bullet was too good for him. Instead, in a bid to pay tribute to my dear departed friend, I decided to scale and gut him like the fish we'd been catching that last fateful summer.

And so, I did.

As soon as I caught up with him, I strung him upside down by the legs from the rafters of an old warehouse. Above the piercing sound of his screams, I cut his clothes away from his body.

With his clothes in tatters on the cold cement floor, Franco hung there, exposed and vulnerable. His body twisted and writhed like a fish on a line, eyes wild with primal fear. I leaned close, baring my teeth, scaring him into submission.

I took out my knife—a sharp, serrated blade that gleamed under the dull flicker of the warehouse lights. I turned the blade, held it up to his face, showed him the name engraved on the handle.

"Stevie," I whispered. "It's ironic, don't you think, that I would use the knife of the man you so callously shot to gut you."

Franco whimpered; the sound was music to my ears. I started at the ankles, making shallow cuts, just enough to break the skin. Franco's screams escalated into a crescendo of agony as I calmly explained what each incision was for.

For Stevie. For the life he never got to live. For the love that was cut short. For the child he would never hold. For the move he would never make. For the brother that would never walk him down the aisle. It went on and on and on, with me using the knife to cut methodically across his skin, a sharp line for every loss I'd feel in the absence of my best friend.

His blood dripped down onto the dirty floor, pooling beneath him. The scent of iron filled the air, metallic and thick. With precision, I continued to cut, peeling back skin with an almost surgical care, each movement charged with a dark satisfaction. The sight of muscle and sinew exposed to the chill air sent shivers through me—not of disgust, but of a profound sense of purpose.

Vengeance. There was something so deliciously cathartic about it as it nestled around my empty heart.

When it came time to silence his weakening screams once and for all, I hesitated only for a moment—then I severed what dignity he had left with a final brutal act and stuffed it into his mouth. A parting gift for his family.

Using clamps from an old toolbox, I pinned back the sections of skin to expose his innards fully. They glistened wetly in the dim light as Franco's gurgles and moans became muffled by his own blood filling his throat.

Reaching inside, I drew out organs slowly, placing them in metal buckets with an eerie detachment. I'd always been a little queasy around blood, but this was like second nature to me, the heart, kidneys, liver set aside like grotesque trophies.

Too quickly, it was over. He was nothing more than an empty shell dangling in the gloomy space of that forsaken warehouse, unrecognizable and stripped of all that made him human. As I turned away from his lifeless body, my mind replayed every scream and plea—not with regret but with an echoing affirmation that justice, in its most primal form, had been *served. Dimly aware of my own transformation during those hours, I stepped outside into the night air feeling not relief but an overwhelming numbness as the weight of my actions settled heavily upon my shoulders, putting a smile on my face for the first time in months. Franco Two-pence was now as empty as I felt.*

46

BAYLIN

Marlon has taken to waking early and leaving the house even before I'm up. The past few days, he's changed the rules and broken with routine, and I can't help but wonder if change is coming. Almost always, I travel with him no matter where he goes, but he's taken to going out on his own, 'running errands' that don't require my presence, he tells me.

Today, I wake before he does, and I'm standing in the hallway, my arms folded against my chest, waiting for him to make an appearance on his way out of the house. He lifts his eyebrows in question as he sees me, then the side of his mouth lifts in a smirk.

"Couldn't sleep?" he asks, as he approaches me. His coat is shrugged onto his shoulders without his arms sitting in the sleeves, and he carries the cane that is synonymous with Marlon Abruzzi, even though I know very well that he has no need for it.

"The cane tells me you're going out, looking for trouble."

"Careful, Baylin, you sound like a possessive housewife."

He's amused more than anything else, and I think he knows, without me saying anything, that I'm only looking out for him.

"I'm worried about you," I tell him.

He moves toward me until we're merely a foot apart, then leans in and gives me a quick peck on the forehead. It's as unexpected as it is welcome.

"It's unfortunate that I never had a daughter, Baylin. I'd like to think she would have been just like you."

"Then let me worry about you like a daughter would," I let out. "Let me do my job and ensure your health and safety."

"My health, yes. My safety – that's what security is for. Now, don't you worry about me. I'll be back shortly. Maybe we can have lunch together today."

We usually have breakfast and dinner together. Today, Marlon has opted for us to have lunch together. Everything about his schedule is changing, and I find I'm humming with nervous anticipation as I wonder what other changes are in the wind.

"What's going on with you?" I ask, as we settle into our places at the dining table later that day.

He lifts an eyebrow in question.

"We never have lunch together," I point out. Actually, he's never home around lunch time. He's generally out at meetings but always makes it home for dinner. Some days, he catches breakfast with me before he leaves, although he doesn't eat much; he's not a breakfast sort of person, and instead opts for coffee and fresh fruit.

"Change is good," he tells me. "Where's the enjoyment in doing the same thing, day in and day out?"

"You know what I mean, Marlon. Now tell me, what gives?"

Instead of answering my question, he changes the subject, reminding me that the holidays are coming up, and asking what my plans are. I can't even begin to think about plans with everything that's been happening lately.

"I'm sure you'd like to see your family," he says. "If they don't want to come up just yet, what say I fly you down there?"

I am taken aback by his suggestion. Spending the holidays with my family would be wonderful, but I can't leave Marlon alone. The thought of him being by himself tugs at my heart and won't let go.

"Will you come with me?" I ask, hopeful.

"But it's a time for family," he replies.

I stare at him in disbelief, my jaw dropping slightly.

"You are part of my family," I assure him. Yet, a wave of confusion washes over me as I wonder if I have crossed a line. Maybe he doesn't see our relationship in the same way that I do. Perhaps he wants some time away from me during the holiday? My mind races with different scenarios, and I shake my head to clear them out.

Marlon notices my distress and quickly reaches for my hand, his touch warm and reassuring. "I didn't mean it like that," he says gently, his eyes searching mine for understanding. "I just meant that I wouldn't want to impose."

I squeeze his hand, feeling a mixture of relief and lingering anxiety. "You'd never be imposing, Marlon. They know how good you've been to me, and they can't wait to meet you."

His eyes soften, the corners crinkling with a hesitant smile. "Really? You talk about me?"

"All the time," I assure him earnestly. "They're as much your family as they are mine if you let them be."

Marlon looks away for a moment, considering this. The silence hangs between us like a delicate curtain, fluttering with possibilities. Finally, he meets my gaze again, his decision reflected in his eyes before he even speaks.

"I'll try to clear my schedule," he says hesitantly, and it's not a commitment, but nor is he flat out refusing to go with me, so I believe that's a step in the right direction. A surge of relief and joy washes over me, and I reach out to squeeze his hand.

"They really can't wait to meet you," I whisper, and he smiles as he picks up his fork and starts to eat.

"Tell me more about Luca – what sort of a kid is he?"

Before I can respond, the room trembles with the fury of an explosion. The contents of the table rattle as they dance across the aged wood, and there's a dangerous cacophony of thunder clapping through the air. I sit rigid in my chair, but all too soon, going by the way his expression shifts from calm to alert in an instant, I can see that this is more than a thunderstorm. The sharp crack of gunfire shatters the quiet atmosphere, echoing through the room like madness, causing my heart to leap into my throat.

"Get down!" Marlon shouts, launching himself across the table at m. He reaches out and pushes me to the ground, the force of his movement sending me sprawling.

As I hit the floor, I barely register the chaos around me, my mind racing. More shots ring out, louder and more jarring than the first, followed by the sound of shattering glass as bullets tear through the window behind Marlon.

"Stay low!" he yells, trying to shield me with his body as he reaches for his gun. His voice is steady, but I can hear the tension coiling in it.

My breath comes in short gasps as I press myself against the cool floor, my heart pounding in my ears. The air feels heavy and thick with fear. I can see Marlon's broad shoulders tense as he positions himself between me and the source of the gunfire, instinctively becoming my protector.

"Marlon, we need to get out of here!" I plead, glancing at the window, now fragmented by bullets.

He opens his mouth to respond, but before he can utter a word, a third round of shots rings out—a deafening crack that echoes off the walls. Marlon stiffens, his eyes widening in shock.

"Marlon!" I scream, instinctively reaching for him.

He tumbles backward, hitting the leg of the table, and I feel the breath catch in my throat as I realize what's happened. The blood blossoms on his shirt, a dark red against the fabric, spreading rapidly. Time slows, and the world around us fades into a blur of noise and chaos.

"Stay down!" he gasps, his voice strained. But even as he speaks, I can see the pain etched across his face, a stark contrast to the fierce protector he had been just moments before.

"No! No, no, no!" My panic surges through me as I crawl toward him. I can feel my heart racing, each beat echoing in my ears like a countdown. "Marlon! Talk to me!"

His eyes meet mine, fierce determination still shining through the pain. "Go—" he coughs, blood splattering onto the floor. "Go-run."

"Don't you dare!" I shout, tears welling in my eyes. "You're not leaving me!"

But he can barely manage a smile, the corners of his mouth twitching in an effort to reassure me. "Told you... you're a survivor, Baylin. You'll survive this, too."

"Marlon!" I cry out, scrambling to pull him closer, desperate to keep him alive.

But the fight is leaving him, and I know we have to move. I have to get him to safety. As sirens blare in the distance, I grab his arm, my voice trembling. "We have to leave, now!"

With a last surge of adrenaline, I help him to his feet, my heart racing as I feel the warmth of his blood on my hands. Together, we stumble toward the door, the world outside spinning into mayhem.

As we reach the threshold, Marlon falls against me, his weight almost too much to bear. I steel myself, determined not to let him go.

"Leave me. Keep going," he urges, his voice a strained whisper, the fight in him flickering like a dying flame.

"Never. I'll never leave you."

With one final push, I pull him into the hallway, where the sounds of chaos mingle with the wail of approaching sirens. I stumble backwards, struggling for air as panic rises within me, and we go tumbling to the floor. The smell of gunpowder fills my nostrils, a grim reminder that death is an unwanted guest in this home today.

Marlon's eyes flicker with a faltering light as he looks up at me, his lips parting to muster a whisper that drowns under the continuous gunshots that erupt outside.

His hand trembles as it reaches out, his fingertips stained with his own lifeblood, and brushes against my cheek in a touch so fragile it threatens to shatter my heart into pieces. His grip tightens, not with the strength that once fought off danger at every turn, but with the desperation of a fleeting goodbye.

"Baylin," he breathes out, each syllable a visible struggle against the dark tide rising within him. His eyes, once a piercing blue reminiscent of clear skies, now mirror the stormy gray of encroaching shadows. "My angel," he manages to choke out, his voice a broken whisper that fractures the very air between us.

The floor around us is strewn with shards of glass and splinters of wood — remnants of our shattered sanctuary. Blood pools beneath him, a stark contrast to the pale severity of his skin. I press my hands against the wound, the warmth seeping through my fingers doing nothing to stem the tide.

My heart screams in silent agony, echoing through the hollow chambers left behind by his dwindling presence. "Don't leave me," I beg, voice cracking under the weight of impending loss. "Please." Tears blur my vision and carve hot trails down my cheeks as I cling to his weakening form.

Marlon's smile is a ghostly imprint of its former reassurance. His hand lifts with an almost imperceptible effort to brush a lock of hair from my face—a final act so tender it feels like a punch to my soul.

With one last labored breath that seems to pull the light from the room and darken the world outside, Marlon's eyes close gently. A final pulse of blood escapes him and seeps further into the floorboards beneath him. His hand falls limp by his side.

A guttural roar erupts from me, an outpouring of grief and rage and crippling loss that shakes the very walls around us. It is a sound that marks the end of everything he had meant to me; it is raw, it is fierce, and it changes me forever.

Marlon is gone; protector and friend lost in one unforeseen moment destined to redefine my path. The silence that follows is deafening—the empty space where his voice should be is vast and untenable. But amidst this desolate quiet, fueled by memories and carved in sorrow, I vow an unspoken promise to carry forward the unyielding spirit of Marlon who guarded me until his last breath.

47

LAZARO

Baylin staggers down the corridor, her clothes drenched in blood, her grief obvious in her eyes. There's so much blood, one could believe it's hers, but I know better.

I came as soon as I heard; an attack on Marlon Abruzzi's home, not two days after our last meeting. In all honesty, I had put feelers out to try to find out who had tried to kidnap Baylin, or anyone that was looking to attack Abruzzi, but I'd come up with nothing and had started to think it had been a random attack on Baylin and nothing more. I'd believed that Abruzzi was merely taking extra precautions, but now this latest incident proved otherwise.

The hospital is bustling with doctors and nurses and patients, a melee of noise that seems to fade into the background as she reaches me. She's in shock, her mind a frail tsunami about to crash against the hospital walls. I rush to grab her before she goes sliding to the ground, lift her by the waist and heave her against my chest. I steer her into a nearby chair, her legs no longer able to support her. A nurse rushes down the corridor, handing me a blanket, which I wrap around Baylin's shivering shoulders.

"We'll find out who did this," I whisper to her, grabbing a clean cloth from a nearby cart and gently wiping some of the blood from her face.

Baylin nods slowly, her eyes distant, burning through me with an unspoken promise of retribution. "They knew," she murmurs almost inaudibly. "They knew exactly when Marlon would be there. He's never home for lunch."

The implication hangs heavy between us; this was no random act of violence but a calculated strike at the heart of Abruzzi's empire. Whoever was behind this not only wanted to weaken Abruzzi but also intended to ignite fear among his allies and enemies alike. If they knew he'd broken his routine and would be home, that means he was being followed. And the level of activity during that attack could only mean one thing – this was a sophisticated attack on a man that no-one dared to cross.

"Let's get you cleaned up," I say, keeping my voice steady despite the anger simmering within me. Baylin was at the house when it was attacked. She could have been hurt. She could have been killed. It was a brazen daylight attack on a man believed to be untouchable.

"I won't leave him," she whispers, her glazed eyes tearing up again.

"I just need you to go to the restroom and wash up, change into some clean clothes."

I hand her the bag of clothes I had my assistant deliver, then sit by her side as she starts to cry again, shaking her head in refusal.

"I won't make you leave, Baylin. Just get changed-you can't sit here in your bloody clothes while they operate on him."

Baylin looks down at her shirt and smooths it down, like she's stroking the arm of an old lover. More tears come. Marlon Abruzzi was lucky to get out by the skin of his teeth, and only because the police and ambulance services were efficient enough to get to his home in time, their wailing sirens enough to drive away the attackers.

An aerial attack, the likes of which we've never seen. Drones fitted with laser targeting systems and machine guns, the new weapon of choice. I'd wondered how the attackers had been able to breach the premises, until one of Abruzzi's surviving soldiers told me the shooting had seemingly come from the sky. We'd already accessed the cameras and found at least four drones had been hovering in the sky above the Abruzzi home. The attack was meticulously planned and funded by someone with deep pockets and an unrelenting determination, someone who was hellbent on toppling the capable walls of the Abruzzi empire.

I help Baylin up, her knees almost giving out beneath her as I walk her towards the rest room and hand her the bag of clothes.

"I'll be in the waiting room when you're done," I tell her, my eyes flicking up and down her bloodied clothes.

She looks up at me with sad, red rimmed eyes, her tears not subsiding.

"Why are you even here, Lazaro?" she asks, her voice cracking under the weight of her own confusion and fear.

I hesitate for a moment, feeling the weight of her gaze as I search for an answer that would make sense to both of us. Marlon Abruzzi extracted a promise from me. A promise to keep Baylin safe, to protect her. He came to me because he knew I would. He could've gone to any one of a number of people, yet he trusted me enough to know that I would do everything I possibly could to keep her safe.

"Where else would I be, Baylin?"

The truth is, I have many reasons to walk away, but none strong enough to actually make me do it. A war is the last thing any of us needs or wants, but my conscience dictates that I not leave Baylin alone unprotected. She's caught in a conflict much larger than herself, one that will undoubtedly consume everything and everyone it touches.

I walk to the small waiting room and sit down, my mind racing as I consider possible suspects behind the attack. The Abruzzi family has enemies, plenty of them, as all men in our business do. He also doesn't have any heirs, which makes it doubly hard for one man alone to maintain control of an empire. But this kind of military precision indicates someone else—someone who not only wants Abruzzi gone but also wants to do it succinctly, making as much noise as possible.

"It's confirmed, drones only. No ground warfare." I look up as Romeo appears around the corner with half a dozen of our men. I'd sent him out to the Abruzzi home to see what he could find. Heavy police presence meant he couldn't get anywhere near the house, but he could at least get some intel from some good friends who owed us some favors. "Where's Baylin?"

I point in the direction of the restroom, then sigh and run a hand through my tangle of hair.

"Any idea who?"

My brother purses his lips and shakes his head. Absolutely no indication who launched the attack, although with the caliber of weapons they used, I'm leaning towards the Russians. As if he's thinking the same thing, he nods his head in quiet agreement and takes a seat beside me.

"You should've told me Marlon Abruzzi asked you to look after Baylin."

I shrug. "What difference would it have made? I didn't think it would come to that. I thought it was the insecurities of an old man questioning his mortality."

"We could've organized more security for Baylin."

"*Now* you care?" I scoff.

"You know why I did what I did. And you know I've regretted it every minute since."

"We have a job to do, Romeo. Don't let me regret asking for your help with this."

48

BAYLIN

I lift the lid and stuff my bloody clothes in the trashcan. No matter how much I scrub, I can't shake the stench of blood that seeps through my skin and travels through my blood. The metallic scent is everywhere, and it makes me queasy as I look at my pale face in the mirror above the washbasin. I wash my hands for what seems to be the tenth time, paying extra attention to the skin under my fingernails, then rinse and repeat. I'm grateful for the change of clothes Lazaro handed me – jeans and a shirt; it covers the condition I was in barely a few minutes ago, but nothing can erase the pallor of my face, or the grey lines that streak beneath my eyes.

I can't even begin to think of the havoc on my emotions if Marlon doesn't make it through this. For a while there, it was touch and go, even as he lay dying and my arms grew heavy with exhaustion from the CPR I administered on him. The ambulance got to him just in time, and now it's a matter of waiting as the surgeons try to stitch him up as best they can.

No guarantees. We'll try our best to save him. It's touch and go. Chances are slim...

The doctors' words are a never-ending revolving door in my head as I try to still my beating heart and calm my anxieties. I've worked in hospitals long enough to know what those words mean. They were prepping me for the worst-case scenario. While I was silently begging them to save him, willing to give up my soul to have him stay with me. In the past eight months I've known him, Marlon has become to me more or less what I would've imagined my own father to be. He's been a father figure, a guiding hand, a protector. All the things I've never really experienced from a male in my circle. No man has ever stuck around long enough to be a father to me, and I hadn't realized how deprived I'd been of the feeling until I met and became close with Marlon Abruzzi.

I look up over my shoulder in the mirror as the door opens then swings shut. My eyes just barely register the tall redhead in heels as she walks toward the basin next to me. She stands beside me, flicks me a tight smile, and I turn to move away and leave the restroom. The door opens again just as the woman's hand shoots out and lands on my arm, and before I know it, I'm falling. I'm weak and nauseous, and there's a smell...a smell that's stronger still than the blood I tried so hard to wash off me, and a cloth comes down against my mouth and nose and darkness embraces me.

WHEN I WAKE, I'm in what looks like a prison cell. I'm sitting on a metal bench, and the room comes into focus slowly but surely as I take in my surroundings.

The air is stale, thick with a dampness that clings to my skin. The walls are a cold gray concrete, rough and unyielding, and there's a single flickering light overhead that casts a sickly pallor across the room. My heart starts to race as I take in the heavy iron bars of a door, the only exit, locked tight and unyielding.

I shift my weight on the metal bench, the sound echoing in the silence, and I bring my hands to my temples, trying to piece together how I ended up here. The last thing I remember is being in the hospital. Then... nothing. Just darkness.

A faint sound catches my attention, and I turn my head toward the corner of the cell. There's a small window, barred and grimy, allowing only slivers of light to filter through. I squint, trying to make out the shapes outside, but the glass is caked with dirt, giving no indication of what's on the other side. My mind races. Where am I and what am I doing here?

I rise from the bench, my legs a little shaky beneath me. I take a tentative step forward, the cold concrete hard against the soles of my shoes. I approach the door, pressing my ear against its metal surface, straining to hear anything from the other side. Silence.

I turn back to the room; the only other feature besides the bench is a tiny, filthy toilet in the corner. I approach it, half-expecting it to hold some hidden message or key, but it's just as bleak as the rest of the cell. I sink back onto the bench, a wave of despair washing over me.

I pull my knees to my chest, trying to think. There has to be a reason I'm here. Maybe someone has mistaken me for someone else. Maybe this is connected to the attack on Marlon's home. Or perhaps I witnessed something I shouldn't have. Again. Lady luck sure has lousy timing, I think to myself, as my mind races with possibilities, each more terrifying than the last.

Just then, a sound breaks the silence—a key turning in a lock. My heart leaps into my throat as the door creaks open, revealing a silhouette against the harsh light from the corridor outside. I squint, trying to make out who it is.

I get to my feet instinctively, my mind racing with questions. Who are you? What do you want from me? But I hold my tongue; I can't afford to show weakness. The figure steps into the cell, and I can finally see him clearly. A tall man, dressed in black, his face obscured by shadows.

"You're awake." His heavily accented voice states the obvious as his eyes bore into mine. Russian, if I had to guess. "Get up."

"Why am I here?" I manage to stammer, my throat dry as I fight to keep my voice steady.

He lets out a low chuckle that sends a chill down my spine but doesn't explain who he is or why I'm in a cell. My mind races, trying to recall any details that could explain this situation. So much has happened in the past couple of years, but I wouldn't have any idea where to start if I had to hazard a guess as to why I'm here. The Riccardis, Detective Handler, Marlon, Detective Knight, the attack on Marlon's home...are they all connected? Or am I simply a victim of being at the wrong place at the wrong time *all the fucking time?*

"Why am I here?"

I repeat the question in a hushed voice, my eyes locked on the stranger standing in front of me. He tilts his head to the side, studying me intently, and I can only imagine what he sees in my expression. After a moment of contemplation, he takes a step closer into the small cell. His smirk grows wider as he speaks, taunting me with his words.

"Let's see if we can jog that memory of yours," he says, a smirk creeping onto his lips.

Fear grips me tightly as I take a step backwards, unsure what's about to happen. It becomes clear that I am not a mere victim of circumstance when he reveals a syringe, indicating that my abduction was carefully planned and executed. And in that moment, it dawns on me that I am well and truly on my way to being fucked.

49

LAZARO

The fluorescent lights above flicker intermittently as Romeo and I huddle in front of the grainy images displayed on the hospital's surveillance monitor. The tension in the small room is palpable, amplified by the low hum of the machines around us.

The security guards shifts uncomfortably as he switches to another screen. It had been a hard sell trying to get him to show us the footage without getting the police involved, but he finally relented and refused the hefty payout we offered him. I need more of this man on my payroll.

I watch the footage on repeat, searching for the exact moment when everything changes. And then I see it; a man and a woman exiting the washroom, the man holding Baylin in his arms as she appears to be unconscious. To anyone else, they could have been a loving couple seeking help in a hospital. The redhead next to them looks like a concerned friend or sister. But I know the truth. As I replay the scene in slow motion, Baylin's hair whips against the man's waist, causing me to seethe with anger. The guard turns the screen to show us another angle, confirming that they left the hospital together. They're gone, and my frustration only grows stronger.

"Damn it!" Romeo spits out, slamming his fist against the wall. The sound echoes, a sharp reminder of his desperation. "How could this happen? She was right here, Lazaro! You were supposed to be watching her!"

My jaw tightens as I watch the footage replay again, my heart sinking further with each loop. Romeo's right. I was supposed to be watching her, and I dropped the ball. I should've watched her closer. I never should have let her go to the washroom on her own. I should have stayed closer to her.

"Losing our heads won't help us find her," I tell him. "We need to think this through."

"Think? *Think?* That's all you ever do!" Romeo shoots back, his voice raw with anger and fear. "She's out there, in the hands of those people, and we're just sitting here! What if they hurt her? What if—"

"What ifs won't bring her back!" I interrupt him, my calm demeanor a stark contrast to my brother's ferocity. "We need information. We need to know who those people are, and why they took her."

Romeo turns away from the screen, running a hand through his disheveled hair.

"I can't lose her again," he says, his eyes wide. "I fucked up last time, but I swore I wouldn't if I ever got another chance. I need that chance to prove to her that I'm worthy." His voice cracks, revealing the vulnerability beneath his bravado. "She was supposed to be safe."

Ever since we came back to the city and Baylin went her own way, Romeo has been a different man. I could say he's broken. I could say he's steadier, calmer, the only craziness coming out whenever he had the opportunity to unleash on one of our enemies. Baylin did that; she's the one that tamed the beast within him, and she's the one who can bring the beast back. I'm not sure which version of Romeo she needs right now. I'm not sure which version will be most effective in finding Baylin and keeping her safe, but I, like my brother, am willing to do anything to find her and bring her back safely.

"She shouldn't have been in that washroom alone," Romeo says, anguish etched across his face. "We should have stayed with her. We should have been there to protect her. And now... now we've failed her."

I step closer to my brother, placing a hand on his shoulder. "Listen to me. We're going to find her. I need you to believe that."

Romeo looks at me, the fire in his eyes flickering as doubt begins to creep in. "We don't even know who we're dealing with here," he reminds me.

I turn to the security guard, ask him a quick question as Romeo's eyes glaze over, and he gives me a short nod. He doesn't like that he's breaking the law, but obviously something in the exchange between my brother and I has him tapping away at the computer quickly as he opens more pages and zooms in on specific details.

"You know there's nothing and no-one our own IT team can't find," I remind him. "We'll know who has her very soon. Then we'll get her back." I stop short of promising him. I'll do everything in my power to get Baylin back, but I won't make a promise to him I'm not 100% sure I can keep.

A silence settles between us, the weight of our shared loss hanging heavy in the air. Baylin had become more than just a friend or an ally to us, despite her absence in our lives most recently. She had woven herself into the fabric of our lives, a vibrant thread that brought color to our otherwise dark existence, and even though time had kept us apart most recently, that didn't mean we wouldn't do everything in our power to get her back. The thought of losing her again was unbearable, especially when I had promised Marlon Abruzzi to watch over her.

"Do you think she knows we're coming for her?" Romeo whispers, a hint of vulnerability slipping through his tough exterior. For all his monstrous urges, I realize that Baylin is the one person that can bring my brother to his knees.

My heart aches for him. "She's a fighter, Romeo. She somehow managed to survive us, she'll survive this too."

"I...I can't stand the thought of her being out there, scared and alone. She deserves so much better than this."

"Then let's give her that better," I say, my voice steady as I turn back to the monitor. "Let's find out who that man and woman are. We'll track them down. We'll get her back, brother. I just need you to focus."

~

"GABRIEL VLAKOV," True says through the line. Every time I speak with my IT wizard, I find I'm still stumped as to why his mother gave him a name like 'Truant'.

"You sure?"

"Torpedo - or muscle man - for the Tarasov family."

"You've got to be fucking kidding me." Romeo grits his teeth and punches a nearby wall. I'm not even thinking about the generous donation I'll have to make to the hospital for the damage; the security guard who showed us the footage is standing quietly by assisting with anything I need, and I know he understands to take care of the damage until we can sort ourselves off. He tips his head in my direction, a quiet agreement, and continues to stand by, waiting for further instruction. The man has taken it upon himself to be indispensable to us, and I couldn't be more thankful if I tried.

"The Tarasov's are a long way from home, I'd say." I frown at True as he continues to feed us information through the screen. "What's their beef with Marlon Abruzzi?"

"Nothing, absolutely nothing," he reports.

"You sure?"

"I couldn't find anything, boss."

"Tell me about the Tarasovs. I want to know everything there is to know about them."

True types away on his keyboard until he is but a single little square in the bottom right hand of the screen. The monitor bursts to life with an array of pictures taken at various angles, then he uses his cursor and starts moving it across the screen, stopping at each individual photo.

"Andrei Tarasov - Pakhan. The boss of all bosses. Deeply entrenched in the banking system and has ties to various political leaders. Currently residing in Russia." He moves the cursor to the next picture. "Boris "the Bulldog" Tarasov. His only remaining brother; the name speaks for itself."

He continues through the pictures as we sit in rapt attention, until six pictures in, he pauses at a picture and Romeo grabs the shirt of my arm and pulls at it until I look up.

"Aleksander Tarasov - eldest son of Andrei and..."

"I know that man," Romeo spits out. "Give me another angle."

True slides another picture onto the screen and Romeo roars. He roars as his hands go to his hair and he clasps at the strands in distress.

"Romeo?"

"It can't be," he whispers, as he staggers forward, looking closer at the screen. "It can't be. If it is, brother, then we're fucked."

50

BAYLIN

My eyelids flutter open, heavy with the remnants of whatever drug they gave me to knock me out. I'm in a tiny cell, the walls closing in around me, and the only light is a dim flicker that makes the shadows dance ominously. I try to sit up, but my head spins like crazy, and the smell of mold is almost unbearable.

"God..." I breathe, as I lift a hand to my throbbing head. My voice sounds strange—cracked and weak, like a rusty door hinge. It is my only company in the oppressive silence that seems to press against my ears.

The door clanks open, the sound cutting through the stillness like a knife. Two men walk in, their footsteps echoing on the concrete floor, each clack like a countdown to my resolve breaking. They wear serious, unfeeling faces to match the air floating through the dank cell. They're dressed in black, their thick European accents causing my stomach to turn over.

"Miss Reyes," one says, his voice smooth but chilling. "You don't look so good."

I don't reply. Instead, I pull my knees up to my chest, trying to shrink away, to be as small as possible. I want to disappear, to make it harder for them to see me and to tear me apart.

"You've been running in some pretty impressive circles," the taller man starts. "The Riccardi brothers. Marlon Abruzzi. You must have all sorts of connections. Where is your protection now?"

"What do you want?" I ask, looking at them from beneath half-closed eyes as I try to stay awake. I'm fading quickly.

"We can protect you," one tells me.

A bitter laugh escapes my lips, sour and empty. Protect me? The idea is laughable. The men's promises feel like ash in my mouth.

"Your loyalty is admirable," the first man continues, "but misplaced. How long before Lazaro sees you as expendable? Before Romeo's temper lands on you? Before Marlon expires and you're left on your own?"

"Stop talking," I say, biting back a whimper. Their words are like fingers digging into my mind, probing for doubts and weaknesses.

"Think about it," the taller man presses, leaning closer, squinting as he looks at my eyes, as though searching for something. "What can they offer you that we can't?"

"Nothing I would want from you," I shoot back without hesitation. Because what they offer isn't safety—it's just a different kind of cage.

"Very well," the first man sighs, stepping back. "We'll give you time to think."

The door slams shut behind them with a finality that feels like a death sentence. I am alone again, but not really. Lazaro's icy blue gaze and Romeo's fiery intensity burn behind my closed eyelids. Why is the world hellbent on destroying these brothers? I have to stay strong, if only to warn them of the impending storm. I have to get myself out of here – wherever here is – and I have to get back to Marlon. Oh, God, Marlon. I don't even know if his surgery was successful, if he'll be around when I make it back home. And the Riccardis, they were there at the hospital the last time I saw them. Would they come for me, even with Marlon out of commission?

I wrap my arms around myself, trying to stave off the cold that seeps through my clothes. Inside, deep down, a small flame of warmth kindles. It's not much, but it is enough to keep the darkness at bay and to keep me from breaking apart. Hope, it's my only salvation right now.

MORE FOOTSTEPS APPROACH, their rhythmic pounding a harsh reminder of my captivity. The door creaks open and the two men in black stroll in, their smirks wide and mocking. I brace myself for whatever is coming next.

"Didn't sleep well?" The first man prods, his voice slick with false concern.

"Like a baby," I hiss back, my voice steady despite the fear creeping inside. Each word is a piece of armor, shielding me from their taunts.

"Still clinging to your precious loyalty?" he sneers, his eyes scanning me like I'm some kind of trophy to be conquered.

"More than ever," I shoot back, my voice hard and defiant.

They circle me like vultures, each taunt and jab meant to break me down. "You think they care about you? You're just a pawn to them." The taller man's words are intended to dig deep, to create doubt.

"Shut your mouth," I hiss, the burn of anger fueling me. I can't be sure, but I think I slur my words; I don't know if they even understand a word of what I'm saying.

I clench my jaw, refusing to show weakness. Lazaro's honor, his strength, is my shield. Romeo's fierce loyalty and protectiveness are my fortifications. They wouldn't want me to crack under this pressure. And I vow not to, no matter the cost.

"Touchy, aren't we?" The man smirks, clearly relishing the anger in my eyes.

"Is that all you've got?" I challenge, even though my weariness is starting to show.

"Sweetheart, we're just getting started." The first man's laughter is twisted, a cruel melody derived from my suffering.

My heart pounds, but it is anger, not fear, driving me. I won't give them the satisfaction of seeing me break. A fiery resolve seems to pulse within me, a source of strength that keeps me from falling apart.

"Go ahead," I say, my voice dripping with defiance; I sound more confident than I feel. "Do your worst."

I push myself up, ignoring the ache in my bones and the cold seeping into my skin. They want me rattled, on the brink of breaking. But I refuse to give them that victory.

They laugh, their voices echoing off the walls, burrowing into my skull. I close my eyes for a moment, retreating into the sanctuary of my thoughts. I don't know if this is real or an illusion. I can't discern day from night, nor can I collect my thoughts long enough to know if I'm hallucinating.

"No-one is coming for you," the man's voice echoes in my mind, his eyes gleaming with the thrill of the hunt. "We're your only way out."

They don't understand me, not really. They see a woman trapped by circumstance, vulnerable to their manipulation. But each vile promise of freedom in exchange for betrayal only makes my resolve stronger.

"Fuck you," I whisper into the stale air, my heart pounding fiercely.

"Oh, we intend to," the tall man snickers. "And believe me, when we do, there's not going to be a single piece of you left that's not battered and broken."

51

BAYLIN

The corridor outside the cell is dimly lit, shadows stretching across the walls like sinister fingers. My heart pounds in my chest as I'm led by the tall man, his grip firm and unyielding on my arm.

"Where are you taking me?" I ask, my voice trembling despite my efforts to sound brave.

"You'll know soon enough," the man replies, a cruel smile playing on his lips.

We walk in silence, the walls closing in around me with each step. I try to remember the layout, in case I need it should the chance for escape present itself, but my mind is a blur of fear and confusion. Eventually, we reach a door at the end of the hallway. The man knocks twice, then opens it, pushing me inside roughly before I hear the click behind me.

I stagger and almost fall into the small, bare room, a makeshift office illuminated by a single desk lamp. A desk stands empty, and the air smells of stale cigarettes and despair. A chair sits behind the desk, turned so I can only see the top of a man's head. Without even knowing my captor, dread settles in the pit of my stomach.

The chair turns slowly, as if wanting to greet me with a surprise, and the air escapes my stricken lungs. In the chair sits a face that hasn't crossed my mind in years, a face that I never thought I'd see ever again.

Alex.

His once-handsome face is now twisted into a mask of bitterness and madness. His eyes gleam with a dangerous light as he looks up at me from beneath hooded eyes, a slow grin spreading across his face.

"Baylin," he breathes, his voice dripping with malice. "It's been a minute."

My breath catches in my throat. "Alex... what are you doing here? Why am I here?"

Alex rises from his chair, his movements deliberate and predatory. "You've got a lot of nerve asking questions, considering the situation you're in. Do you have any idea how long I've waited for this moment?"

"I don't understand." I try to keep my voice steady as I take a step back. "What do you want?"

"Why?" Alex echoes, his laughter cold and hollow. "Because you owe me, Baylin. You owe me for what you did. For leaving me, for running into another man's arms. You didn't even give us a chance!" His roar fills the small chamber that serves as an office.

My mind flashes back to the last time I saw him. That night seven years ago, when Alex's true nature had revealed itself. He had tried to force himself on me, his eyes wild and his grip bruising. I had fought him off, and it was Romeo who had saved me in that alley behind the club, Romeo who had dragged me away from that nightmare.

"You tried to rape me," I remind him, my voice breaking. "We'd already broken up, and you tried to violate me."

"And look where that got you," Alex sneers, taking a step closer. "You disappeared from my life. Do you have any idea what that did to me? How that made me feel?"

"You're insane," I whisper, horror dawning on me. "This is all because I left you?"

"Oh, it's much more than that," Alex says, his eyes narrowing.

"You see, Baylin, you broke me. You shattered my world. And now, I'm going to return the favor."

He moves so quickly, I barely have time to react. One moment he's sitting behind his desk, the next his hand is around my throat, squeezing just enough to make me gasp for breath.

"You'll pay for what you did," Alex hisses, his face inches from mine. "You and Riccardi both. I can't imagine that he's paid enough with his brother's blood. I need more, so much more. But first, I'm going to make you suffer. I'm going to make you regret ever leaving me."

Tears spring to my eyes as I struggle against his grip, my fear turning to desperation. "You killed his brother." The realization dawns on me and spurts forth from my mouth even before I can hold my tongue. It all makes sense now – why they could never find the killer, because they were looking in the wrong place. Who is this man?

"You catch on quick," he says. "Although, I can't say I wasn't disappointed that I killed the wrong brother." He shrugs casually, as if to indicate there's nothing wrong with killing a man he never intended to kill. Like the younger Riccardi was just collateral damage.

"You have no idea what you've done," I gasp.

"Is this where you tell me your white knight is going to come galloping in to rescue you and skin me alive? Well, he can certainly try."

"Please, Alex... don't do this. Let me go."

"Let you go?" Alex laughs again, a sound devoid of any sanity. "Oh, Baylin, you're not going anywhere. Not until we're finished."

He releases me suddenly, and I stumble back, gasping for air. My mind races, searching for some way out, some way to survive this nightmare. A weapon of some sort. Something to save myself.

"Sit down," Alex commands, pointing to a chair opposite his desk. "We have a lot to discuss."

I hesitate, but the look in Alex's eyes tells me I have no choice. I sit, my hands trembling as I clutch the edge of the chair.

"Good," Alex says, sitting back down and steepling his fingers.

"Now, let's talk about how you're going to make this up to me. How you're going to repay your debt."

My fear deepens, a cold dread settling in my bones. I'm trapped, at the mercy of a man who has lost his grip on reality. And I know, with a sickening certainty, that he won't stop until he has broken me completely.

Alex's eyes glint with a maniacal light as he sits down and leans back in his chair, savoring the fear that radiates from me.

"You see, Baylin," Alex begins, his tone almost conversational, "I've had a lot of time to think about you. About us. About how things could have been different if you hadn't run out on me. But now, I have the chance to show you how good we can be together. To make you understand what you did to me."

He opens a drawer in his desk and pulls out a small vial filled with a clear liquid and a syringe. My heart pounds in my chest as I watch him draw the liquid into the syringe, my mind racing with terror.

"Please, Alex," I beg, my voice shaking. "Don't do this. You don't have to do this."

"Oh, but I do," Alex replies, his grin widening. "You see, this little concoction will help you relax. Help you see things my way."

He approaches me with the syringe, and I rise and try to back away, but I only find myself backed into a corner. Alex grabs me by the throat and tilts my head to the side, exposing my neck, and without further delay, he plunges the needle into my skin. The drug takes effect almost immediately, a heavy fog descending over my mind, dulling my senses as I start to go numb.

"That's better," Alex says, stepping back to admire his handiwork. "Now, we can begin."

THE WORLD around me swirls in a haze, colors bleeding together like a poorly painted canvas. I lay there, trapped in this cocoon of half-awareness, neither fully awake nor completely asleep. My body feels heavy, strapped down by some invisible force, and yet I am painfully aware of everything happening around me. The weight of my own flesh is a prison, and I can feel the hands. There are hands moving along my body—these insidious, unwanted hands—tracing paths across my skin, their touch both foreign and disturbing.

I want to scream, to fight back, but my voice is swallowed by the thick fog that envelopes me. I'm stuck in this liminal space, and the more I struggle, the more I realize how powerless I truly am. They're violating me, and the sheer horror of it claws at the edges of my mind. I hate the thought of being trapped within my own body, a silent witness to this atrocity.

~

JUST AS DESPAIR threatens to pull me under, the scene shifts. My surroundings melt away, and suddenly I am in a forest—a vibrant, surreal forest that pulses with life. The trees tower above me, their leaves shimmering with hues I have never seen before. Birds sing melodies that twist and turn like ribbons in the air, and flowers bloom in colors too bright to truly exist in our world.

And then I see him. He stands there, radiant and ethereal, his presence a balm against the darkness that violates me. His smile is warm, it's real and it's rare. It ignites a flicker of hope within me. I reach out, fingers brushing against the soft fabric of his shirt, grounding myself in the moment.

"Where are we?" I ask, my voice echoing oddly, as if the forest itself is listening.

"In a place where time stands still," he replies, his voice smooth like honey. "Where the heart can speak without fear."

Together we wander through the surreal landscape, the forest alive with hope. I can feel the earth beneath my feet, solid and reassuring, and for a moment, the hands that are tormenting me fade into nothingness. We dance among the trees, twirling and spinning, laughter spilling from our lips like a forgotten song. But in the back of my mind, the shadows lurk, whispering reminders of my reality, twisting the joy into a cruel taunt.

"Why can't I stay here?" I ask, feeling the weight of the world pressing down on my chest. "I don't want to go back."

He turns to me, eyes sparkling with mischief. "But you have to. The forest is a dream, and dreams can't hold you forever."

Just then, the air shifts, thickening as if the very forest is aware of my plight. The laughter of the birds turns into distant echoes and the trees began to warp and twist, as though in pain. I feel the hands return, their touch invasive, and I panic.

He fades into the forest, one minute there, then the next as though he never was.

"Romeo. Don't go," I whisper, my soul crushed as I extend a hand, trying to bring him back to me.

"You were never meant for this world, Baylin."

He leaves me, a departing apparition, clinging to the hope of peace. Of life. Escape from the nightmare I've found myself in, as the forest closes in on me, an ominous darkness spreading across my eyes.

52

ROMEO

All the air is sucked out of the dimly lit room as we stare at the monitor. The revelation of Baylin's captor casts a dark shadow over our hearts. The image of Alex, the man I'd saved her from seven years ago, burns into my mind. Lazaro's jaw tightens as he considers the implications after I explain to him who Alex Tarasov is to Baylin, while a quiet rage threatens to consume me.

It was one night of madness. A night where I annihilated the man, not knowing who he was or anything about him beyond the fact that he was Baylin's ex and he was throwing unwanted attention at her. Hell, I didn't even know her. All I knew was that she was a girl in trouble who needed saving, and when she sat in my car and bit into that burger, I knew she was also a girl I wanted to have a taste of. When I think about that night, I know with all certainty that I did what had to be done stepping in to help her. And I knew, taking her to my home, that one night was all we would be. The usual spiel. She was but one in a long line of girls I'd slept with. But she was the first I ever took to my home. And she was the first to ever leave me before I had the chance to open an eye and thank her for a nice night before I dropped her off and went my own way. I don't know how much either point played a part in me wanting to see her again, but I did wake up the next morning after I met her with the urge to see her again. I even looked for her. But she was gone. And I moved on.

The fact that we somehow came full circle and ended up in each other's lives five years later is beyond even my own comprehension. It was as much a surprise as it was a challenge to see her again, albeit under such unusual circumstances. But there was a reason why we met again at some point. There was a power much greater than she or I that was intent on throwing us together again. And I welcomed that power with open arms, until I lost my mind and tried to kill her.

I carried myself away from the mountain house and mourned her all the way back to the city. I mourned my cowardice, and I mourned a future without her. Then I let self-loathing consume me as I finally understood the consequence of my actions and regret embraced me like a long-lost friend.

I look up at the screen before me, and I can barely hold it together as the image of Baylin's ex fills the room. I feel like I could reach into the screen and pull him out, tearing his heart out in the process. It's an impossibility, but it's one of those things that's high up on my to-do list once I catch up with him.

"That bastard," I growl, my fists clenching at my sides. "I should have killed him when I had the chance. Now he's got Baylin, and God knows what he's doing to her."

Lazaro places a hand on my shoulder, trying to steady me. "Calm down, Romeo. We need to think this through. We can't afford to make any mistakes."

"Calm down?" I snap, shrugging off Lazaro's hand. "How can you be so calm? You know what he's capable of. You know what he did to her before! And now... now he's got her again. I can't—"

"We're going to get her back," Lazaro interrupts firmly. "But we need a plan. Charging out there without a strategy will only get us all killed. And that won't help Baylin."

I take a deep breath, my eyes burning with determination. "We have to get to her, Lazaro. Quick."

I know that Lazaro's mind is already working through the logistics. We'll need every resource we can muster to take down Alex and his men. He's Russian mafia, and he's backed by a powerful family. We run through all our allies, we summon Marlon's men, who know that he'd want Baylin protected at all costs, and we round up our men and make plans to meet in the war room to talk strategy. True is working on a location by tapping into resources connected to Alex Tarasov, and it's only a matter of time before he gives us a location.

I nod as I turn away from the monitor, my anger channeled into a fierce resolve as my mind races with images of Baylin, memories of the night I saved her from Alex's clutches. The fear in her eyes, the relief when she saw me, the way she had clung to my protection that night. I had promised her then that I would protect her, and the thought of failing her now after all that was unbearable.

HOURS LATER, we stand in a warehouse on the outskirts of the city, the air buzzing with the tension of men preparing for battle. Doc Samuel, a grizzled navy seal with a network of connections that spans the criminal underworld, stands at the center of the room, his eyes scanning the assembled fighters. He's always been a man we could count on in times of war; the man is like a lion climbing a mountain backwards without so much as a stumble. He's in his signature fatigues, his mane of long brown hair tied back at the nape of his neck, a beard covering the majority of his lower face.

"Alright, listen up!" Doc barks, his voice commanding attention. "Anyone who is not willing to engage death in this war needs to step down now, because this is going to get bloody. It's going to be brutal. And it's not going to be easy. This will be a fight to the death."

No one backs away. The men he's recruited for this mission are just like him - ruthless and eager for bloodshed. They are all skilled in combat and war, and many see it as a privilege to work alongside the renowned Doc Samuels. His nickname, "Doc", is a more polite way of addressing him than his official army designation: "the butcher", a title given to him due to his precision with a knife, especially when decapitating enemies.

He steps up to a monitor and clicks it on, and all eyes turn to the screen that holds several shots of Alex Tarasov.

"Aleksander Tarasov," he starts. "Russian mafia royalty, but the kid's gone rogue and his father can't get a leash on him fast enough. Which is the only thing we have going for us; the kid's so rotten, Andrei Tarasov would arrange a hit on his own son if he could find him. Kid's ruffled a few of our friends' feathers, and it's time we put him down."

Doc goes on to tell us that Tarasov is holed up in a stronghold which we're going to infiltrate. This comes after two false starts, where our team, along with Marlon's, failed to locate Baylin at two locations which led us no-where. Doc is a master at locating and extracting missing persons, which is what he did for years and years before he realized he could make so much more going private. He's a character, that Doc Samuels. But he's a character for hire, and he's got the backing of several dozen of the best navy seals who ever walked the earth. They're gruesome, and they're exactly what we need.

The men murmur amongst themselves, their voices a rumble of determination and solidarity as they prepare for war. I feel a surge of hope, but it's extinguished quickly as I wonder if we'll be too late. I turn to Lazaro, my eyes filled with a desperation I know he feels just as deeply as I do. We never spoke about what happened at the cabin. He never entertained me broaching the subject, and I knew. I just knew, from the way he would clench his jaw any time I mentioned Baylin that the words would be better left unsaid.

Lazaro nods in my direction, before turning toward Doc Samuel as the men mill about the warehouse, working themselves up in the prelude to our attack.

"What about blowback?" he asks. "It's all good and well that his father's angry with him, but I don't for one minute believe that he would appreciate us killing his son. And I don't want that to fall back on these men."

"What are you saying?" I frown. I'm going to kill the bastard with my own two hands once I find him.

Doc Samuel fixes Lazaro with a long, thoughtful look, then flicks his assessing eyes towards me, no doubt wondering why we're risking so many lives for the return of one girl. But his MO is that he never asks the questions that stem from information that's not being offered. So he'll never ask. Instead, he'll do as he's told, and he'll do a damn good job too, pushing his curiosity to the back of his mind.

Doc clicks two fingers, and immediately, his right-hand man steps up and waits for instructions.

"Get me Andrei Tarasov on video."

Lazaro and I look at each other in surprise, then follow Doc to a little side office, where a screen comes to life and we wait for the call to connect.

"Just so we're all clear; we're not hiding what we're doing. The father has no intention of stepping in to save his own son. But I'll let you hear it for yourselves."

The screen flickers until a living room comes into view and Andrei Tarasov appears, sitting alone on a sofa in front of a laptop. His reputation precedes him, the man a veritable lion in our circles, but he's looking gaunt even as he tries to address us by name.

"We have not had the chance to meet in person," he starts, after introductions are made. "But we shall meet not too far in the future."

His heavily accented voice clips through the room, and I wonder what could possibly drive a meeting between us, especially as we operate on opposite sides of the globe. I stand, transfixed by the man who wields so much power, yet can't seem to control his own son, taking in every word as though it's a lifeline.

"Our introduction shouldn't have been under such circumstances," Lazaro says.

Andrei shakes his head sadly, purses his lips, then shifts forward on the sofa, steepling his fingers in front of him.

"No. Tell me how I can fix this," he says, surprising us.

"I'm sure you're aware Aleksander has custody of one of our assets," Lazaro speaks up. Andrei nods and informs us that Doc Samuel has informed him, before Lazaro continues again.

"We need to retrieve that asset, at any cost. This could result in injury – or worse – to your son."

Andrei Tarasov lifts his eyes to the ceiling, masking his emotions, before he drops them again and looks at each one of us in turn.

"I know you are calling only as a courtesy. If I were in your place, I would want to kill him, too. God knows I have wanted to many times. But I could never..."

"When I find him, I *will* kill him," I hiss at the screen. Before our eyes, Andrei Tarasov seems to shrink and age ten years with that one declaration, as a wave of resignation washes over him.

"You do what you need to do," he says after an endless silence. "If you are lucky to find your asset before he kills her, I would expect nothing less."

Andrei Tarasov reaches out a hand and the screen goes black.

"I take it we have his blessing." Lazaro looks at Doc Samuel, and I'm not convinced, but he sighs and addresses us with something he had obviously been reluctant to share.

"You're doing the man a favor," Doc says. "Aleksander Tarasov is not his biological son. He inherited him when he married his second wife, then proceeded to have a daughter with her. He understood very early on that something was clinically wrong with Aleksander and tried to get him the help he needed. Whilst also trying to keep his daughter away from him. Aleksander ultimately ended up violently raping and killing Andrei's daughter a few years ago."

"You can't be fucking serious," Lazaro fumes.

I'm too numb to say or do anything. If the man is capable of doing something so horrific to his own sister, what is he capable of doing to my little bird?

"Gentlemen, I do believe you'd be doing Andrei Tarasov a favor by ridding him of the man who killed his only biological child, even though that man may be his own son."

53

BAYLIN

I don't know if hours or days or weeks pass, but I live in a constant nightmarish haze. The drugs keep me in a state of semi-consciousness, my body limp and unresponsive, my mind a foggy mess. I'm aware, on some level, of what's happening to me, but my trauma response is to shut down, to retreat into a dark corner of my mind where the horror can't reach me.

My dreams have become my only solace, even when I am awake. I am transported back to that forest, but in my mind, it is transformed into a beautiful landscape. It's the same place where Romeo Riccardi played his twisted game of cat and mouse with me. The forest where Romeo shot me in the shoulder, only for Lazaro to heal me again. The two brothers are constantly shifting between the worlds in my mind; they are all I can focus on. One brother created the woman I am now, then killed me, before the other brother brought me back to life again. They have both saved me countless times, despite the torture they put me through. And as I lie on this bench, caught between reality and my dream world, I realize that their actions were meant to prepare me for this moment, for this torture at the hands of a madman. Compared to the sickening man standing before me now, their torture seems like a mere stroll in the park.

Alex's touch is cold and clinical, devoid of any humanity. I can't believe I once found him handsome, charming. He is nothing but the devil incarnate, and if I had a stake, I would drive it right through his heart myself. He violates me repeatedly, his actions driven by a twisted sense of vengeance that exists only in his mind. I feel hands on me that aren't his, rough and callous, as some of the guards take their turns, their laughter echoing in the small room. But the drug keeps me mercifully numb, my body a distant vessel that no longer feels pain as I close my eyes and dull my senses to the merciless onslaught.

I'm grateful for the fog that envelops me, for the barrier that keeps me from fully experiencing the atrocities being committed against my body. My mind dissociates, floating above my body, a silent witness to the nightmare. I can hear Alex's voice, a constant, maddening whisper in my ear, but the words are lost in the haze. Over and over again, he whispers the same mantra, killing any semblance of humanity left inside me, hardening my heart and crushing my tainted soul.

"You're nothing without me," he whispers, his breath hot against my skin. "You deserve this. You deserve everything that's happening to you."

"Never...be yours," I taunt back, and I can't be sure if I said the words or just thought them, until he backhands me and rises, tucking himself into his trousers. My head lolls to the side, my eyes glazed, as my vision splits into two.

~

TIME LOSES ALL MEANING. I drift in and out of consciousness, my sense of self eroding with each violation. I cling to the fragments of my identity, the memories of who I was before all this. I think of Marlon, of Romeo and Lazaro, of the life I had before Alex's madness consumed me. I hold on to the hope that Marlon is alive, that the brothers are looking for me, that they will find me and rescue me from this living hell.

I wake to find myself alone in the room. The drug has worn off slightly, enough for me to feel the cold, hard floor beneath me and the ache in my limbs. I curl into a ball, tears streaming down my face as the reality of my situation crashes over me. No-one is coming for me, and in all likelihood, I will die down here with the rats that occasionally scurry across the floor. Sometimes they stop, fix their beady eyes on me, then hurry away; even the vermin are too afraid of what's left of me.

I don't know how long I lay there, but eventually, the door creaks open, and Alex steps inside. My eyes feel too heavy for me to lift in his direction, but I can just make out his shadow in the flutter of my eyelids against my glazed vision. He crouches beside me, his fingers trailing down my cheek in a mockery of tenderness.

"Are you ready to beg for forgiveness, Baylin?" he asks, his voice soft and coaxing.

I don't respond, my eyes glazed and unseeing as I retreat so far into myself that his words barely register.

"That's alright," he says, standing up. "We'll get there. We have all the time in the world."

My head falls back and forth as I fight to keep my eyes open. I fight against the tide that pulls me down, threatening to sever me from the reality of this world. I push against the madness, but it's useless; I'm so drugged up, I think my body may even have succumbed to paralysis.

"You never should have left me," I hear him say, as he wanders around the cell. I'm losing consciousness quickly, and I don't think that's such a bad idea. I don't know why I'm fighting so hard to hold on, to stay alert for the fury he's unleashing on me. His voice taunts me as he throws accusations and insults at me, and I rapidly lose control of my consciousness until only random words filter through the air.

"...*Riccardi whore...*

"*Kill you...*"

"*Always mine...kill...*"

"*Went there...*"

My mind shuts down. My heart stops. Suddenly, I'm flying. High, high, high above the world.

~

I'M SITTING ON A CUSHION. No, it's a pillowy cloud. I float on a soft, billowing cloud, the world below me a distant memory wrapped in a shroud of mist and color. I feel weightless, unburdened by the heaviness of my body. It is a strange sensation, drifting aimlessly, yet within this dreamlike state, I feel a flicker of clarity.

I gaze into the ethereal expanse, and from the depths of the clouds emerges a figure bathed in light. He is young, mid-twenties, with wild curls that dance like sunlight and eyes that sparkle with an innocence that makes my heart ache. There is something so innocent about the figure, so familiar, and I sit in awkward silence as he moves towards me. Instinctively, I know who he is. With looks like that, it could only be one person.

"Sandro?" I whisper, the name escaping my lips before I can think. The man grins, a bright, childlike smile that lights up the cloudy confines around us.

"Baylin!" he exclaims, his voice ringing with joy, untainted by the dark-ness that has seeped into my life. "Isn't it so amazing that we get to meet again?" He twirls in the air, a flurry of laughter echoing around us.

I blink, feeling a rush of warmth wash over me. "But... how are you here? I thought you were..." My voice falters: I know the Riccardis lost their brother, but why is he here? Or is it possible that I am there?

"I'm not staying," he says with a hint of mischief, floating closer. "There's no room for you where I am, not yet. You have to go back."

"Back?" I echo, confusion mingling with the fleeting joy of his presence. "But I don't want to go back. It's dark and scary... and there's so much pain."

Sandro's expression softens, a flicker of understanding crossing his youthful face. "I know, Baylin. But there's still so much light waiting for you. Lazaro and Romeo... they still need you. They're fighting for you, just like you should fight for yourself."

A lump forms in my throat, and I look away, the weight of my tormen-

tors pressing down on me like a heavy blanket. "*But what if I can't? I'm so tired, Sandro.*"

"*It's not your time yet. You have so much love waiting for you.*"

The words wrap around me, a lifeline in the swirling chaos. "*Love?*" I whisper, the notion igniting a flicker of hope within me.

"*Yes! Marlon is waiting for you.*"

"*Marlon?*"

He nods as the air around us shifts, and I feel the warmth of his spirit enveloping me. "*But... what about you? How did you—*"

His expression turns solemn, but the childlike spark never dims. "*The one who hurt you is the one who hurt me. He took me away, but I won't let him take you too. You deserve to live, to love and be loved, Baylin.*"

A tear slips down my cheek, and he reaches out, brushing it away with a gentle touch. "*You must believe, Baylin. Believe in your strength, in your heart. You can find your way back. Promise me you will try.*"

"*I promise you,*" I murmur, the weight of his words settling in my chest like a warm ember.

He beams, his joy infectious. "*Now go! Fight for your light!*"

As he speaks, I feel myself being pulled away, the cloud dissolving around me like mist in the sunlight. I want to reach out, to hold onto him, but his laughter fills the air, buoyant and free as he starts to fade away.

~

AND JUST LIKE THAT, the cloud fades, and I am left with the warmth of his spirit—an echo of hope in the darkness, guiding me back home.

54

LAZARO

All I can think about is Baylin at the crest of that ravine before she goes over the edge. If I hadn't been there that day to drag her up, she may very well have gone over the side and down the slippery side of that ravine and straight into her grave. She may have fallen into oblivion. She may have become nothing. She may have been a minor blip in our history, erased before our futures could take shape. That's what may have become of Baylin Reyes, whether she would have gone over the edge by accident, or by her own hand, preferring to die on her own terms than by the laws and rules as dictated by the Riccardis.

The very thought of having lost her that day does things to me I can't explain. I was meant to save her that day, and I know I'm meant to save her today. Both Romeo and I, in different ways, have played a part in saving her – and ultimately destroying her. But now, the game has changed, and it's a race against time as we mobilize to find Baylin and launch our attack against Aleksander Tarasov.

When True finally calls with a location, we're beyond ready. Aleksander Tarasov has amassed for himself a little army of loyalists who have actually fallen for his spiel about being heir apparent to the

Tarasov family. He's bought their service and silence with the promise of high-level positions once he's head of the family, something we all know is never going to happen. And that's how we finally find them; by tapping into one of their phones and following the link until it leads us to an abandoned building that used to serve as a layover for prisoners on their way to Federal prisons. Now deserted, the structure is the perfect example of how to hide a prisoner and get away with it.

I strap my vest on and slide in my guns. Two at either side, and one in a holster against my leg under my fatigues.

I look up at the screen – we managed to get a photograph of Baylin from the hospital she used to work at and blew it up so everyone knows what she looks like and to make sure she doesn't become a victim of friendly fire. Her big brown eyes stare back at me, as though daring me to breathe life into them. I don't know what sort of condition she's going to be in when we find her, but I like to remember her this way. The way she was when I last saw her almost two years ago.

As we prepare for the assault, I exchange a silent look with Romeo, who's teetering on the edge of insanity as his knee jerks up and down anxiously. I've never seen him this way. Not even after we came back from the cabin and he understood that Baylin was lost to us. There was no place for her in our world, not after everything that had happened between us, and not after the devastation we caused her. She especially didn't need to be entrenched in a world where she would constantly be looking over her shoulder.

We understand that this is the moment, our one and only chance to rescue Baylin and put an end to the nightmare that has made a home for itself in our lives. We would storm Alex's stronghold, tear it apart brick by brick if we had to, and bring her home.

The night is dark as we move out, the moon hidden behind a blanket of clouds. The convoy of vehicles cuts through the city like a knife, only one destination in mind. The tension mounts as we approach the stronghold, every man acutely aware of the danger we're about to face. We have the strength of dozens of soldiers, the best of the best, who would fight to the death for a successful outcome to this operation. Loyalty...there's nothing like it.

My heart pounds in my chest, my mind filled with thoughts of Baylin. I can't let myself think of what she might be enduring, can't let the fear take hold, otherwise it would suffocate me. I have to stay focused, stay strong. For her. For Romeo.

The convoy comes to a halt, and the men disembark, weapons at the ready. We're all ready, dressed in dark fatigues and army boots, our gas masks in place. It's been decided that we will infiltrate with as little gun power as possible so we don't risk Baylin's safety. Romeo also insisted we take as many prisoners as possible; whatever they had done to Baylin, someone would need to pay...slowly. Someone would need to answer to her abduction and Marlon Abruzzi's near death. Retribution. I can almost taste it on my tongue.

Romeo and Doc Samuel lead the charge, their eyes fixed on the imposing structure before us. This is it. This is the moment that we get Baylin back and put an end to Alex Tarasov, once and for all.

"Remember," Doc Samuel says, his voice low but firm in my comms unit. "Our goal is to get the girl out of there alive. Stay focused, stay sharp, and watch each other's backs."

I hate that he refers to Baylin as the girl, a nameless entity that means the world to us. But I understand all too clearly his need to work without emotion; he can't assign feelings to an asset, otherwise he loses focus. And that's what I need to be doing now, focusing on our target without letting my emotions get in the way of what needs to be done.

I take a deep breath, steeling myself for the fight ahead. This is for Baylin. For the promise we had made to protect her.

"Let's do this," Romeo says, his voice a growl of resolve.

We've laid out the plan well. We hit them hard and fast. Take out the perimeter guards first by kneecapping them, then breach the main entrance. We move in teams and sweep the building. Me, Romeo and Doc Samuel will head for the underground chambers where we imagine they're keeping Baylin.

The first shots ring out, silenced weapons taking down the

perimeter guards with deadly precision. The guards fall silently, their bodies crumpling to the ground without warning. The teams move in quickly and quietly, dragging the bodies into the shadows to avoid detection.

"Perimeter secure," comes a whispered confirmation over the comms. For someone vying for the position of head of the Russian mafia, Alex Tarasov doesn't seem to be big on security.

"Move in," Doc Samuel commands.

The teams converge on the main entrance, a heavy steel door flanked by two guards, who we take out seamlessly before they know what hits them. We take our positions, our weapons trained on the doors. Doc Samuel and his team move forward, planting charges on the door.

"Fire in the hole," Doc mutters, stepping back as the charges detonate with a muted thud. The door buckles inward, and the teams surge forward, weapons at the ready.

With synchronized precision, we throw the tear gas and the guards start dropping instantly, even before they can mobilize to fight back.

The interior of the stronghold is a maze of corridors and rooms, each one a potential deathtrap. The men move methodically, sweeping each room with practiced efficiency. The sounds of gunfire and shouting echo through the halls as we press on, our resolve unshaken as we throw more tear gas.

We lead the way to the underground chambers we marked on the plans we were able to get our hands on. Everyone studied those plans and should know these tunnels like the back of their hand. Our path is lit by the harsh fluorescent lights overhead. We encounter pockets of resistance, Alex's men putting up a fierce fight, but we bring a ferocious desperation to the fray. A desperation that is fueled by rage and the fear of failure. Failure isn't an option here. Not today.

"Down here," Doc says, his voice tight with urgency as we reach a heavy steel door at the end of a dimly lit corridor. "This is the entry to the cells-if I had to guess, I'd say she's down here."

Doc nods to his assistant, his eyes scanning the door for any signs of traps or alarms. "Breach it," he says, and his assistant pulls out a small device and attaches it to the door's electronic lock. He works quickly, his fingers moving with practiced precision as he hacks the lock.

The door clicks open, and Romeo and Doc push inside, their weapons raised as they take the left corridor and I shoot down the right. The chamber is a stark contrast to the rest of the stronghold. It's cold and sterile, the air heavy with the scent of despair and disinfectant.

A row of cells sits empty as I make my way further down the chamber, two men on my heels. There's another door when I'm almost at the end of the corridor, but I freeze when I arrive at the second last cell and see someone within its walls. At the center of the room is a single metal bed, and on it lies Baylin, her body limp, hand falling over the side.

"Baylin! Doc!" My voice is a high-pitched screech within the chamber as I rattle the metal bars, trying to get to Baylin. Her lifeless body lays before me, a sacrifice without a soul, as the night explodes with the sound of bullets and hand grenades.

Doc's assistant pushes past me and activates the lock. Romeo comes up behind me as I drop to my knees even before I get to her, my hands trembling as I check for a pulse.

"She's alive." Relief floods my voice as I lift her from the threadbare bench and heave her over my back. "I don't know how bad it is. We need to get her out of here."

Romeo moves to the door, clearing the corridor for us to move. He speaks into his comms. "We have her. Secure our exit and get ready to burn the place down."

Baylin's head lolls against my shoulder. "I've got you," I whisper, my voice choked with emotion.

As we move back through the corridors, the sounds of the battle grow louder. Alex's men are regrouping, their resistance intensifying. We fight our way through, our determination unyielding as the men cover me on all sides. Yet it seems Tarasov's determination is greater as he tries to hold on to his crumbling fledgling empire.

The teams converge at the main entrance, their faces grim but resolute as they form a defensive perimeter, holding off Alex's men as I carry Baylin to the waiting vehicles.

"Get her out of here. Now!" I order, as Romeo helps me put Baylin into the car. Her head rests on his lap as I look back up at my brother, reluctant to get into the car.

"Lazaro..."

"Don't," I warn him. "Go. Get her to safety. This is not over until I say it is."

"Lazaro!"

My brother's voice echoes through the night, even as I thump on the car's hood for the driver to move away and I turn back toward the warehouse, intent on ending Tarasov.

55

ROMEO

Even as we drive away, I can't ignore the deafening noise as the warehouse erupts into chaos, gunfire and explosions echoing through the night as we speed away. We've succeeded in saving Baylin, but at what cost? What of my brother, who rushed into the fire, determined to extinguish the vermin that held Baylin prisoner? Had I just saved one loved one only to forsake another?

I hold Baylin close, my heart aching with relief and sorrow. She stirs slightly, her eyes fluttering open for a moment before closing again as she falls back into nothingness. Her body is a small, weightless thing leaning into me as I hold her close. Even I can see that her condition is bad as sweat breaks out on her forehead and her head thrashes back and forth against the tidal wave of emotions that radiate off her. She is restless, murmuring in her sleep as we edge closer to the hospital.

Once the car skids to a stop, I carry her out in my arms and rush through the emergency ward, barely registering the men that flow out of a second vehicle that must have followed us to provide extra protection.

Inside the sterile, fluorescent-lit emergency room, the chaos of beeping machines and hurried footsteps surrounds me as I cradle Baylin's frail body in my arms. Her skin is pale, marred by the scars of her suffering, and I can feel the warmth of her fever radiating through the thin fabric of her tattered clothes. The nurses rush to meet us, quickly assessing her condition, but all I can focus on is the haunted look in her eyes—a mix of fear and confusion as the drugs fight for dominance in her system.

I watch helplessly as they place Baylin on a stretcher, attaching monitors that beep rhythmically, a stark reminder of a once beautiful life now slipping away.

My heart races as they work to stabilize her, and I feel a simmering rage bubbling beneath the surface. How could anyone do this to her? How could anyone have it in them to reduce her to this state?

The medical team pushes me out of the way as they wheel her away, but now before I catch a glimpse of her arms—crisscrossed with angry red lines and bruises. Each wound is a dagger to my heart, a silent testament to the pain she's endured. I want to scream, to hunt Alex down and make him pay for this, but all I can do is stand here, fists clenched, watching Baylin fight for her life.

Hours pass like a blur, and the longer I sit and wait, the angrier I get. Eventually, I'm allowed to see her again, even after the doctors declare her condition had been "touch and go." I lean over her listless body, brushing a strand of hair from her forehead, my heart breaking at the sight of her fragile state.

I watch as her eyes flutter open for a moment, recognition flickering in her gaze, but the drugs pull her back down, deeper into darkness. I feel tears prick at my eyes, an emotion as foreign to me as it is painful. Fury mixes with despair as I think of Alex Tarasov—how he terrorized her, how he has stolen her light.

When she falls into a fitful sleep, I make my way to Marlon's room, where the comatose man lays, another heavy weight on my heart. He's sleeping peacefully, unaware of everything going on around him. Lazaro had promised him we'd do everything humanly possible to protect Baylin, and we had failed. One little ask, and we managed to fuck that up, too. But I take comfort in the fact that we have her back, and she's now safely ensconced in a heavily guarded hospital room.

With a heavy heart, I step back, casting one last look at Marlon before I leave the room, determination hardening within me. I would make sure that Baylin is safe and would stay safe. I would ensure the end of Alex Tarasov, if it were the last thing I ever did. And I wouldn't let the ugliness of our world touch her again, not after everything she's been through.

I REMAIN at her bedside for many hours, until Baylin's hand brushes against mine. The nurses offered me a sleeper chair, which I positioned as close as possible to the bed so I could be there when she woke up. I must have drifted off to sleep in the process, half sitting and half laying down. I rub my eyes and sit up, swinging my legs over the side of the chair as I move closer to her.

She tries to talk, but there's only fear in her eyes as she looks around the room and tears threaten to fall.

"Don't speak," I warn her, lifting a cup to her lips. She takes small sips of ice water before she pushes the cup away and drops her head back on the pillow, already exhausted.

I watch as she fights the darkness; her eyes droop and she is pulled down once again, back into the abyss and all it holds. A fine film of sweat forms on her forehead; I place the wet cloth against her skin the way I'd seen the nurse do it before, then lift it a few minutes later to rinse in a nearby basin. The heat emanating from the cloth is enough to scorch my fingers before I run it under cold water.

A sudden sense of loss overcomes me. Something in my heart died today. Or maybe it was a sort of rebirth. Under any under circumstance, I would have stayed at that warehouse, and I would have torn every last man there to shreds...and enjoyed doing it. I never would have walked away from the chance, the satisfaction, of destruction. Ruin is, after all, in my blood.

But I walked away from it. I held Baylin as she clung to me in the back of that speeding car as we rushed to the hospital, and all I could think was "she's alive. She's breathing and she's alive, and because you let her live, I'll leash my beast. As long as Baylin is alive and well, my monster will remain dormant."

56

BAYLIN

The world feels heavy and distant as I slowly claw my way back from the murky depths of unconsciousness. My eyelids feel like lead, and every attempt to force them open is met with a pull from the shadows that have held me captive for so long. But slowly, I start to feel warmth enveloping me, a familiar presence anchoring me to reality.

With a final effort, I pry my eyes open, blinking against the harsh glare of fluorescent lights. The sterile smell of the hospital, mixed with antiseptic, invades my senses, and I try to sit up but I'm met with a wave of dizziness that sends me back against the pillows.

"Easy, Baylin," a soothing voice murmurs beside me.

I turn my head, and there he is—Romeo, his stormy blue eyes searching mine. Relief floods through me, mingling with confusion, fear, and the sort of aching pain that a body should never physically go through.

"Romeo?" I croak, my voice barely a whisper.

"I'm here," he replies, his voice thick with a concentrated certainty. He's here and he's not going to leave me. He can't leave me. He leans closer, brushing his fingers gently over my hair. The act is as foreign as it is surprising. "You're safe now. You're safe."

Memories surge through my mind—fragments of terror, the darkness of the cellar where I was held captive, the torment I endured that resulted in a despair that threatened to swallow me whole. I flinch when I remember Alex's face, his cold eyes filled with malice. He was going to kill me. I know he was going to kill me.

"What... happened?" I manage to ask, my throat dry and scratchy.

Romeo's expression darkens as he hesitates, searching for the right words. "You were... you were in a bad place, Baylin. Alex—he hurt you. But you're safe now. He can't touch you anymore."

"Do you know... what he did to me?" I whisper, rolling my eyes toward the ceiling. I can't bear to look him in the eyes if he knows what I was subjected to. What I went through. I'm both humiliated and degraded as my thoughts start to collect themselves and paint a not so pretty picture of what I endured.

There are too many visions flashing before my eyes, and I'm finding it hard to distinguish between what was real and what was an illusion.

Romeo shakes his head, but he looks at me sadly, a man conflicted. "The nurse will come in to talk to you if you have any questions."

I close my eyes, a wave of emotions crashing over me. "I thought... I thought I was going to die," I tell him, my voice trembling as tears well up in my eyes.

"No." His voice is fierce as he grabs my hand and directs my eyes towards him again. "You're not going anywhere, Baylin. You're a fighter, and you will get through this, too."

I look at him, seeing the sincerity in his gaze, but doubt gnaws at my insides. "I don't feel like a fighter. I feel... broken."

"You're not broken," he insists, his voice firm yet gentle. "You're going to heal. It's going to take time, but you're going to heal and live the life you always wanted."

I swallow hard, trying to absorb his words. "Marlon... is he...Is he...?" The word gets stuck in my throat. I can't even begin to think of a world where Marlon does not exist. In so little time, he's become the most pivotal guiding hand in my life, and I can't imagine a life without him.

His expression softens, and for a moment, I see a flicker of something vague cross his face, causing my heart to clench. "He's still in a coma, but the doctors are hopeful. He'll wake up, Baylin."

A tear slips down my cheek, and I brush it away with the back of my hand. "I don't know if I can face this nightmare, Romeo. Why Alex came back..." A sudden thought rips through my mind as a clawing sensation tugs at my chest. "Where is he? Where's Alex?" I can't keep the fear out of my voice, nor can I stop myself from almost ripping the IV out of my arm in a bid to get up and make my escape. The very thought that he's still out there and I'll always have to look over my shoulder sends threads of anxiety shooting through me.

"Stay still, Baylin." Romeo's voice is unwavering as he pushes me gently back toward the pillow. "He can't hurt you anymore, I promise you."

I take a shaky breath, feeling the weight of his words settle within me. "How do you know? How do you really know?"

"Lazaro's out taking care of it. I just need you to concentrate on getting better."

"What if I can't go back to who I was? What if I'm... different now?"

"Maybe you will be," he concedes, leaning closer. "But that doesn't mean you're not still you. You'll get past this, Baylin. I promise you." I feel a flicker of hope, a tiny ember igniting in the depths of my despair. "I don't want to be a burden," I whisper, the vulnerability in my voice raw and unguarded.

"You could never be a burden," Romeo says, his eyes fierce.

I nod slowly, the warmth of his presence wrapping around me like a lifeline. When I close my eyes, the darkness doesn't seem so suffocating anymore. With Romeo by my side, offering me safety and security, I feel the first stirrings of hope, a fragile but powerful reminder that even in the depths of despair, there is still a chance for healing. And for the first time in a long while, I allow myself to believe that maybe, just maybe, I can find my way back from the edge of darkness.

ROMEO SITS on the edge of the bed, his presence a steady warmth next to me. I look at him, taking in the way his dark hair falls just above his brow, framing a face that is both handsome and intense. There is a ruggedness to him that wasn't there two years ago, a strength that radiates from his broad shoulders and tapered waist, and I can tell that in the years that have passed, he has taken to building himself like a tank. His fitted black shirt clings to his torso, hinting at the lean muscle beneath, and the way he carries himself—confident yet guarded—adds to his mysterious allure.

The door swings open and a nurse interrupts us just as Romeo sets the ice chips down. She's in her mid-thirties, with kind eyes and a professional demeanor, but I don't miss the way her eyes flicker with interest as she glances at Romeo. He stands up, instinctively straightening, his imposing figure casting a shadow that seems to command the room.

"Good morning! I'm Nurse Lisa." Her voice is bright yet slightly breathless as she sizes him up. "I'm here to check on Baylin and discuss her recovery."

"Of course," Romeo says, taking a step back, pointing at the door before he slips out of the room. He has always had a surreal effect on others, his presence able to shift the atmosphere in a room.

Nurse Lisa turns her attention to me, her professional façade slipping in place as she flashes an encouraging smile. "You're doing remarkably well, considering the condition you were in when you were brought in. I know it must be challenging, but I want to talk to you about some important aspects of your recovery."

I nod, feeling a flutter of anxiety in my stomach. "Okay."

She starts by telling me everything I really don't want to know. That I'd consumed a heavy dose of drugs and they'd had to counter that with another drug to get the narcotics out of my system; any longer and I may have developed an addiction. Then she informs me that they ran bloodwork, but didn't do swabs, although it did look like I had bruising on my thighs as they cleaned me up, so she's relatively sure that I've been assaulted. She's only voicing what I already know to be true. There's no two ways about it.

My heart sinks, and I bite my lip, glancing at the door. How much of this does Romeo know?

Nurse Lisa's expression softens. "Given the circumstances of your ordeal, we didn't want to add to your trauma. We will only run further tests at your request. However, we do highly recommend the morning after pill if that is of concern to you."

"I understand." My voice is barely above a whisper. The thought of being pregnant fills me with dread, a reminder of the trauma I want to escape. The thought of being pregnant and not knowing who the father is adds doubly to the nausea clawing its way up my chest.

"Once we assess your situation further, we can discuss options for contraception or other measures to ensure your health and welfare moving forward."

"Thank you," I reply, trying to mask the tremors of fear that course through me. I can feel the nurse's gaze lingering on me before she turns toward the door.

"Is there anything else you need? Any questions?" Nurse Lisa asks.

"Just... I want to know how long I'll be here," I manage, my focus shifting back to the nurse as Romeo walks back into the room.

"That depends on your recovery," Nurse Lisa replies, her voice steady. "But we'll keep you here as long as needed to ensure you're physically and emotionally stable."

The nurse smiles and writes something on her clipboard before she tells us she'll let the doctor know I'm ready for further evaluation. Her gaze flickers back to me one last time before she turns to leave. "And remember, if you need anything, don't hesitate to call."

As the door closes behind her, I let out a shaky breath, feeling the tension ease just a little bit. Romeo returns to my side, his eyes asking me if I'm okay.

"I will be," I tell him. "In time, I will be."

57

LAZARO

I step into the dimly lit corridor, my heart racing as adrenaline courses through my veins. Romeo and Baylin are safely out of the cellar where she had been held captive, but the war is far from over. The air is thick with smoke, the echoes of gunfire and shouts resonating through the underground lair where Alex had terrorized her.

I move deeper into the labyrinth of rooms, the distant sounds of the conflict growing louder. My focus is sharpened; this is not just about rescuing Baylin anymore. It's personal. Alex crossed a line that can never be uncrossed, and I'm more than ready to deliver his justice.

Suddenly, a figure bursts into view at the end of the corridor, and my heart gallops. It's Alex, standing confidently, a sadistic smirk plastered on his face. The sight of him ignites a firestorm of rage within me that surges through my entire being.

"Lazaro Riccardi," Alex taunts, his voice dripping with contempt. "I didn't think you'd come to save your little girlfriend. I expected the other wayward brother, Romeo."

"Shut your mouth," I snarl, stepping forward, fists clenched at my sides. I see the glint of a weapon in Alex's hand, but it doesn't matter.

I feel the heat of my fury consuming me, drowning out any fear. I know it's stronger than anything that can come out of that gun.

I keep moving toward him, holding my hands up for my men to fall back; I'm doing this on my own, and I'll claim this victory, no matter how small, as my own, if only to quench my bloodthirst for this psycho.

Without warning, I lunge at Alex, tackling him to the ground. His gun goes flying across the corridor as we crash onto the cold concrete floor, fists flying. My fury propels me forward, and I land a series of brutal punches against Alex's face, each one fueled by the pain and suffering he inflicted on Baylin.

"You get enjoyment out of attacking a woman?" I growl, my knuckles connecting with Alex's jaw. "Come on, tough man. Show a real man what you're made of."

My words set Alex off, and he fights back with a venomous ferocity I didn't expect, landing a right hook on my jaw. I shake off the pain as rage surges through me. I seize Alex by the collar of his shirt, dragging him across the floor like a dog, the rough surface ripping his pants and scraping against Alex's skin.

"You're going to pay for every tear you made her shed," I spit at him, the venom in my voice cutting through the chaos around us. With every ounce of strength, I pull Alex to the far end of the corridor, where the cell that was Baylin's home for the past few days stands open. My anger heightens; I want nothing more than to tear him to shreds.

"Lazaro!" Doc Samuel shouts from somewhere behind me, but I'm single-minded, my focus locked on Alex. This man almost destroyed Baylin, and now it's time for retribution.

There would be no mercy, even though I'd promised Romeo I'd keep him alive long enough for Romeo to take a crack at him. I'd silenced all of Romeo's incoming calls as he'd tried to contact me. I'd told the team not to entertain his calls, and I'd told the driver who whisked him away from the crumbling stronghold not to turn around under any circumstances.

I know once he's at the hospital with Baylin, he won't leave her.

Even though it's been hours, and I still haven't contacted him, I know he won't leave her unguarded once again. That was the one thing we promised each other-that whoever the lucky bastard was that got to see her when she first opened her eyes would stay by her side until any and all threats were contained. I know he'd never go back on that promise. I know he takes Baylin's safety seriously. And for that, I'm going to make sure that the job is finished so we never have to concern ourselves with Alex Tarasov ever again.

With one swift motion, I open the cell door and shove Alex inside, then slam it shut behind him. Alex stumbles, regaining his footing and scrambling to his feet, panic flashing in his eyes as he realizes his predicament.

"Let me out, you bastard!" Alex yells, pounding on the door. "You think you can keep me in here? You don't know who you're messing with! Do you have *any idea* who my father is?!?"

My face twists into a grim smile, a dark satisfaction coursing through me. I pace casually at the front of the cell, staring Alex down through the bars, even as the sporadic sound of explosions penetrates through the walls.

"Oh, I know exactly who you are," I tell him. "And now it's time for you to face the consequences of your actions."

As I speak, I produce a small whiskey flask from a pouch on my belt. Alex's eyes follow my fingers as I unscrew the flask and toss the liquid haphazardly into the cell. Some of the liquid stains his clothes, and I take immense pleasure in the horrified look on his face when he realizes that it's gasoline. With deliberate movements, I pour the flammable liquid around the cell, the pungent scent filling the air.

"You dumb fuckwit! You won't get away with this!"

I shoot him a thoughtful look that disarms him. "Won't I? You mean the way you got away with your own sister's death?"

"No! No, you can't do this!" Alex shouts, panic now evident in his voice as he realizes the gravity of my intentions. The fact that I know who he is and what he's done is validation enough that no-one will be coming to save him. His own father has turned his back on the monster. He rushes to the door, gripping the bars with desperation. "You'll regret this! You can't just leave me here!"

I step back, my expression cold and unyielding. "You messed with the wrong people, Tarasov. You messed with the wrong girl, and now you're going to pay for your sins with your life."

"You. Fucking. Demented. Bastard!"

A vein throbs at his temple, and I consider how disappointed I'll be if he suffers a heart attack before I'm able to reach a point of satisfaction watching him burn.

"You won't get away with this!" he screeches. "I'll put a bullet in you and your brother just like I did your other brother!"

Something inside me seizes. I try to rewind what I just herd, but I know what I heard.

"What did you just say?"

He ignores me and continues wailing like a banshee. "I will eviscerate every last one of you! After you watch me rape and torture your precious whore."

"What?"

"Did."

"You."

"*Say*?!!?"

My voice is a roar in the chamber as the whole building shudders with the weight of the onslaught. This building could collapse at any moment.

There's complete silence from within the cell as Aleksander Tarasov stares me down, the darkness in his eyes unyielding.

"I shot him at that truck stop, and I watched him as he flailed about like a fish, bleeding out. Then I walked up to him and put a bullet between his eyes," he hisses. "Granted, it was the wrong brother, but I killed a Riccardi, nonetheless."

My eyes look through him, my mind blank as my body goes numb with rage. A blinding veil overcomes me, and I shut down mentally, until I'm reduced to nothing but robotic tendons.

Alex Tarasov continues to scream and yell, but I don't hear a thing. He sounds like he's in some faraway tunnel, fading into the distance, mere background noise that I have a strong compulsion to drown out.

I strike a match, the flame flickering momentarily in the dim light. With a swift motion, I toss it inside and watch as the fire ignites, flames licking hungrily at the gasoline-soaked floor.

"Lazaro!" Doc Samuel shouts again, concern lacing his voice, but I remain focused on Alex, whose face has gone pale, panic turning to sheer terror as he realizes that he's trapped.

The fire spreads quickly, consuming the small space, the heat radiating toward me as I stand guard, watching the flames as they lick toward the monster in the cell. I don't flinch as I watch Alex scramble back, the flames dancing around him, casting flickering shadows across the walls.

"You think you're invincible? You think you're untouchable?" I shout, my voice steady. "Look at you now, you coward. I will watch you *burn*, Alex Tarasov."

The flames roar, smoke billowing through the cell as Alex's screams grow louder, the sound echoing in the confined space. I feel a strange sense of catharsis wash over me, a release of all the pent-up rage and pain I have carried for Baylin and for Sandro. We finally have closure for my brother. I hadn't understood how important that was until this moment as a feeling of calm washes over me.

I step back from the cell as the heat intensifies, allowing the fire to consume the space completely. I witness the final moments before flames engulf the man who had brought so much suffering, then turn my gaze away, even as his screams echo through the chamber. Instead, I focus on the door leading out of the cellar, moving toward it, where a world with one less monster in it awaits.

58

ROMEO

My brother deprives me of the satisfaction of cutting Alex Tarasov's throat. He steals from me the right to eviscerate the man who killed my brother and violated Baylin. He robs me of my vengeance.

But in place of that retribution, he gives me closure.

All the pieces of the puzzle fall into place. We now know what happened to Sandro. And we can take comfort in the knowledge that Aleksander Tarasov will never hurt Baylin again. She won't have to spend the rest of her life worried that he is one step behind her, preparing to attack again.

In place of my vengeance, he gives me twelve soldiers that belonged to Tarasov. Twelve defectors from Andrei Tarasov's camp. The man didn't want them back alive, so I sent him their ears and noses. Trophies; I hear the man is especially fond of collecting body parts.

In that way, I got my little piece of revenge. I don't think it will ever be enough for what was done to Baylin, but the small mercy is that she was so doped up, she doesn't remember most of what happened to her. In time, she will come alive again.

I don't know what this new connection between us means. I hurt her in so many ways that I almost destroyed her. But I know I'm most happiest now that she's right in front of me where I can see her and my heart feels at peace. The past few years have been a whirlwind, with me hanging onto my grief, allowing the darkness to overcome me. Anger. So much anger. I was angry at the world. Angry at her. Angry at Sandro for leaving me, and angry at myself. So I became the monster I had to, in order to satiate the thirst inside me. That cloying, unbearable thirst to demolish everything in my path. To self-destruct in such a way that I was uncontrollable. Now when I look back on my life, I don't remember anything past it being a recycling of the same day and same anger over and over again. I should've been happy when I found Baylin again. Or rather, when she found me. Because that's what it was, really. She found me. By accident. By stumbling onto the scene of a crime as it was carried out. A fantastic stroke of fate, but one that brought her back into my life. I should have been happy, but instead, I self-destructed even more, even as I slipped further and further into the depths of madness.

She still has the tattoo I branded her with. I saw it when I helped her get dressed so she could be discharged from the hospital. She put her arm through the sleeve and I moved the fabric up against her shoulder. My eyes settled right there on the brand, still there, untouched. She hadn't even gotten in removed, or drawn over, my name still burnt into her flesh.

Our eyes caught when she turned her neck to me after I paused, before she looked away quickly, blushing as she lowered her head and started to button up her shirt.

"You never got rid of it," I say, my voice a low murmur.

"I never got rid of the bullet hole, either," she replies, without looking up.

I've somehow managed to mark her on both shoulders. Twice. Branded. Shot. I'm a demon to her soul.

It's my turn to look away as I swallow back my regret. Baylin didn't deserve what I did to her. And saving her now, as I did all those years ago, doesn't make us even. I could spend a lifetime apologizing to her, and still it wouldn't be enough.

"I don't want to talk about the past, Romeo."

She shifts and I look up until we're facing each other again. She tells me she wants to check in on Marlon before we leave the hospital, and then she wants to go home. She has been insistent on going back to the house she shared with her mother and nephew, even against my better judgement, so I've ramped up security and put our best men on her security detail. I know that I'll protect her to my dying breath; even if I have to sit in my car outside her house and watch her every move.

DESPITE ALL THREATS now being contained, I check her house once, twice, three times, to make sure that it's safe for her to be there. There are soldiers at every entry point to the house, and lines against the small perimeter. It's only a small cottage, so it's manageable, but I feel better knowing that we've covered all bases.

"This is a little overkill, don't you think?" she asks, as she sets a cup of coffee in front of me and takes the seat opposite me. She reminds me that the danger is gone now that Tarasov is dead, but I just shake my head and tell her we have to make sure there are no further threats.

"What are your plans now?" I ask her. We've been tiptoeing around the topic of us and neither one will broach the subject. I don't know what we are, what we were and what we could possibly be, but more than anything, I want to try to build something with her.

She shrugs and tells me she'll probably wait until Marlon's better so she can take care of him. I don't know how I feel about that and how it will affect 'us', but I guess that too is me getting a little ahead of myself.

"He'll need the help, for sure," she tells me. "You heard what the doctors said."

"I did."

"You don't want to go back to the hospital? Now that Detective Knight isn't a problem?"

"No. That hospital chewed me up and spat me back out again, especially when I needed them most. I'm more content working as a personal nurse."

"So, you like working for Abruzzi?"

She nods, tells me he's treated her well, and for that I'm truly grateful. I just don't know what the man's angle is, and that's truly perplexing to me. Baylin is possibly the greatest thing to have ever happened to me, and this was never more evident than when I ran into her at the Annual Misters Gala. Just seeing her made my heart soar in a way that was unprecedented, and I hadn't understood how much I missed until that moment. I hadn't understood that the chip I'd been carrying around on my shoulder was precisely that – not having her in my life.

I watch her as her eyes move across the room, taking in an environment she hasn't seen in so long, and I would give anything to know what's running through her head at this very moment. She's still as beautiful as I remember her. Not beautiful in the traditional sense, but beautiful in my eyes. She's warmth and laughter and light. She's everything I cling to in this life – all the good I can't seem to find.

Before her, I existed in shades of night, commanding shadows that obeyed but never lived. My thumb brushes over a knuckle as I lose myself in thought, and it's then that I realize that Baylin is the greatest reward I could have received from this whole situation. With her, I've found daylight. She is the dawn breaking across my darkest sky.

59

BAYLIN

The tarmac is barely visible beneath the shadow of the massive jet, its sleek body a silent promise of escape and new beginnings. My heart hammers against my ribcage as I stand beside Lazaro and Romeo, the cool evening breeze doing nothing to ease the inferno of emotions inside me. The Riccardis had orchestrated my freedom. They had found me and helped me when I was at my worst, and they had continued to protect both me and Marlon until we were better and able to leave the hospital within days of each other.

"It's time," Lazaro says, his voice a gentle nudge against the storm of my thoughts.

I nod, every cell in my body rebelling against the idea of separation. These two men, stern in their resolve yet tender in their protection, have become my anchor in a world that has shown me nothing but chaos. Leaving them feels like tearing a part of myself away—a part I'm not sure I can afford to lose.

"Come back to me, Baylin," Romeo murmurs, his eyes locking onto mine with an intensity that threatens to crumble my last defenses. It's the closest he's come to verbalizing a future for us. Everything until now has been veiled in stolen glances across the room and subtle hints at a future. He has never said the words I've wanted to hear, no matter how much fear they may cause me.

"Always," I manage to choke out, the word tasting like a vow.

With a deep breath, I turn and climb the steps of the jet, not trusting myself to look back. Once inside, I sink into the plush leather seat beside Marlon, the softness at odds with the turmoil inside me. Through the window, I watch Lazaro and Romeo retreat to the safety of their car—two sentinels watching over me until the very end.

As the engines roar to life, the ground crew signals their final clearance, and the jet begins to taxi down the runway. I press my palm against the cool glass, a silent goodbye I can't voice.

"Dammit," I whisper, my pulse skyrocketing. I have doubts about leaving. I have doubts about so many things. Marlon reaches over and takes my hand in his after I buckle up, giving me a gentle squeeze as he forces his way past his own pain. His recovery has been hard, every day a slow slog without direction; not knowing whether or not he would make it. He's never needed me as a nurse more than he does now. He shoots me a steady, reassuring smile as we settle in for the flight.

"We don't have to leave if you don't want to," he whispers.

"I have to."

I know more than anything that I have to step away for a while. It's been a rollercoaster of a ride the past few years, and all I want to do is go far away from this place and remember that there is a life outside of my own trauma. I'm sad to leave the brothers; I know this is not goodbye, it's just farewell. One day, we will meet again, and hopefully by then, I will be in a better place, with a tighter grip on my life and my future. But for now, I'm exhausted from living through the Lydia Knights and the Alex Tarasovs of the world. It's time for me to step away and find myself.

The jet picks up speed, racing towards takeoff as if chased by the very demons of my past. With a lurch, we are airborne, leaving the Riccardi brothers far behind. I close my eyes, letting the hum of the engines drown out everything else as we soar towards the sky.

BRAZIL IS A DIFFERENT WORLD ENTIRELY. The oppressive walls and cold steel bars of my prison cell are now replaced by an expanse of vibrant colors that stretch across the horizon. I step off the jet, the warmth of the sun enveloping me like a long-lost embrace. It is freedom in its purest form—tangible, overwhelming, and intoxicating.

"WELCOME TO PARADISE," a familiar voice coaxes my senses.

"Luca?" I call out, disbelief coloring my voice.

"Who else?" he replies, the corner of his mouth lifting in a half-smile.

My mother appears beside him, sunglasses perched on her nose, looking every bit like she belongs to this lush landscape. After hugging and squeezing them close to me, I turn to Marlon, my brows lifted in surprise.

He shrugs his shoulders, tells me with his eyes that he couldn't help himself.

"We never did get to make that trip out to meet your family, so I thought it would be nice to meet them here," he explains. This man. This man and his generosity; even though he has never met my family and wouldn't know what to expect, he's found it in his heart to bring my family to meet me in Brazil.

"How long have you been here?" I ask, as I ruffle Luca's hair.

"Only a few days," my mother tells me, overcome with shyness as I notice the look that passes between her and Marlon.

"Didn't think we'd let you have all the fun, did you?" Luca teases, drawing my attention away from them.

Together, we walk down the tarmac, the vivid blues of the sky clashing with the deep greens of distant mountains. A flowery scent fills the air, painting a picture of life untouched by the shadows of my former existence.

"Feels like a different universe," I murmur.

When the Riccardi brothers had suggested we leave the country for a while until everything blows over, I had taken that as another slap in the face. Another chance for them to be rid of me. It was only when I found out who Aleksander's father is that I understood the magnitude of what killing someone like Aleksander Tarasov meant. Even I, in my limited knowledge of such things, understood very well that messing with the Russian Bratva would have repercussions.

"It's just a precaution," Lazaro had said, and Marlon, bound by a wheelchair, his strength still diminished, had agreed. We had to take time away until things blew over, and would be called back when the time was right. The Riccardis would smooth things over with the Russians, whilst they would oversee, to some extent, the rebuilding of Marlon's empire.

At least one good thing had come out of this whole ordeal. Lazaro and Romeo had agreed to act as proxies for Marlon while he was away; they would assist in any way they could, as well as appointing a unit which could run things for Marlon, giving him a chance to step back from his day-to-day business dealings. A mini semi-retirement, he liked to call it. I myself think it's just time for the man to smell the roses; he's spent decades building up his kingdom, and with no-one to leave it to, he's started reflecting on all the things he's missed out on in life to build a one-man empire.

"Let's go home," my mother says, her voice steady, filled with a quiet determination.

We reach the car that will carry us away to a new beginning, the final page turned and sealed with the promise of a fresh start. And in that moment, cocooned by the presence of my family, I realize that healing isn't just about overcoming—it's about moving forward, hand in hand, heart with heart, into whatever tomorrow holds.

60

BAYLIN

The sand is warm beneath my feet, a fine golden carpet unrolling with each step I take along the shoreline. Luca's hand is small in mine, yet it acts as an anchor in the fluid world of salt and sun where I've found myself adrift. The market beckons us with its vibrant chaos, stalls brimming with local crafts and fruits so ripe they perfume the air, sweet and tangy.

"Look at these," I say, my fingers grazing a display of hand-woven baskets, their patterns a dance of color and texture. I can picture them in our home, little reminders of this place and time.

Luca leans into me, his presence a silent promise against the hum of the market. Ever since we were reunited a month ago, he won't leave my side, afraid that I'll disappear on him again. It's sad to think that he had come to see me as the replacement for his own parents and yet somehow, I still managed to let him down.

"I wish we never had to leave this place," he murmurs, and I squeeze his hand. Although I can't agree with him more, I know that eventually, we'll have to go home and return to the real world. All we can do is enjoy our time together now and make the most of the freedoms we've been afforded here, away from the mayhem that had found us back home.

We continue to walk through the markets, the vibrant colors of stalls draped in fabrics fluttering like captured fragments of the sky. It's a short distance from the beach house we're staying at, and we make the trek by foot almost daily just to experience the culture of our surroundings. Although Marlon has staff at the beach house, I still insist on buying the produce myself; it's quiet time I can spend with Luca as I try to make up for the time spent away from him.

"It's beautiful, isn't it?" My voice is a low rumble against the ocean's chorus as we head back in the direction of the beach house.

"Mmm," he hums in agreement.

The beach sprawls endlessly before us, a canvas of blues and greens melding into the horizon. It is almost enough to forget the world beyond this moment, beyond this haven that's become our sanctuary.

"Will you leave me again?"

Luca's voice is small as it reaches me, another onslaught of guilt weighing me down.

"I wouldn't have left you if I didn't have to, Luca," I explain, for what feels like the hundredth time. I crouch down until we meet at eye level, my eyes seeking his. "You know everything I did was to protect you. You know that, right?"

He nods slowly, although sadness still resides in his eyes. I know that sending him and my mother away was the right thing to do. Especially after Alex Tarasov appeared on the scene again – there's no telling how far he would have gone. There's no way of knowing how my story would have unfolded had my mother and nephew still been in the picture, and I hate that my mind conjures up all sorts of scenarios of the danger they could have been in had they stayed with me.

As we approach the house, my eyes are drawn to the line of cars parked outside the compound wall. We rarely have visitors, so this is an unusual sight that has my heart beating out of my chest as I hold onto Luca's hand and we cross the street.

My mother greets us at the door with a nervous smile. She and Marlon have become fast friends, as if they've known each other for years. This has been a great help when I need to spend time alone with Luca without leaving either of them on their own. My mother has been keeping Marlon company, and I'm grateful to see how well they get along.

"What is it?" I ask, as fear grips me.

"We have guests," she tells me. Somehow, I feel like she seems afraid of my reaction.

Luca squeezes my hand reassuringly as my mother steps aside and we step further into the house, his curiosity mirroring mine.

My heart skips a beat when I see them—Romeo and Lazaro Riccardi, standing by the window overlooking the garden. Lazaro is gesturing animatedly about something outside, but Romeo's gaze is fixed on us as we enter. There's an unmistakable spark of joy—or is it relief? —in his eyes when our gazes meet.

Lazaro turns and greets us with his characteristically cool, level-headed smile. They stand awkwardly watching me, gauging my reaction at their appearance. My eyes skim the room, landing on Marlon, who sits in his chair, watching me.

"I invited them," he tells me, explaining their visit. "They wouldn't come with us when we came out, but they promised to come as soon as things had cooled down at home. I never got to thank them for everything they did to get you back to me."

My mother, standing beside me, visibly bristles. We'd had to tell her what happened, although she doesn't like to fixate on that event. Instead, she tells us her anger stems from the fact that she didn't know what was going on the whole time I was missing.

Romeo's approach is reserved as he comes toward me and steps forward. His smile is gentle, warm, a stark contrast to his usual dark demeanor.

"Hello, Baylin," he says softly, his eyes searching mine for a moment longer than necessary before he embraces me briefly.

"Come on Luca," my mother starts, from somewhere behind me. "Let's get you washed up before dinner."

"But, Nona..." he starts to complain, until my voice reaches his ears.

"Luca, listen to your grandmother. Go now."

My heart pounds against my chest so hard I'm certain everyone can hear it, even over Luca's voice as he protests while being led away from the room.

"Lazaro and I have a few things to discuss." Marlon rises from his chair, his thin frame reminding me that he hasn't completely recovered from his ordeal. His healing has been slow coming, as has mine, but at least my physical scars have closed. I watch them leave the room, then turn back to Romeo.

"Why are you here?" The moment the words are out of my mouth, I realize how harsh they sound and I damn near kick myself.

"I deserve that," he says, giving me a small smile. "I deserve everything you throw at me and I don't deserve your forgiveness. But I can't imagine a future without you in it."

The weight of his words fills the space between us with a multitude of possibilities. The idea both terrifies and excites me; Romeo shifts in front of me, his presence a force that seems to bend the very light around him. Our eyes meet, and the intensity in his gaze anchors me, like he can see straight through to the chaos of my thoughts. I half-expect the usual shiver to crawl down my spine—the one that always dances along my nerves whenever he's nearby. I've come to understand that the reaction I get when I'm in his proximity is less about fear and more about the anticipation of the unknown.

He reaches out, taking my hand. His grip is firm but gentle, a quiet promise in the way he holds me. My heart skips, clumsy and erratic. This man, wrapped in tailored suits and sharp words, displays a softness that still confuses me.

His thumb traces small circles on the back of my hand. It's a simple touch, but it sends ripples through my resolve. I've spent the past few years building walls, layer by layer, each brick a testament to my determination to survive. And yet, here stood Romeo, dismantling me, brick by bloody brick.

61

ROMEO

I feel her eyes on me, those deep brown pools where strength and vulnerability swim in an enigmatic dance. Baylin's gaze is a force unto itself, and as we walk along the sea's edge, the unspoken words between us grow heavy with promise.

It had been Lazaro's idea to come to Brazil. His idea that we deserved a break, his insistence that Salvatore and Vincenzo could manage without us for a few days. I didn't doubt that they'd be up to the task, but we've never just taken off on a whim, not even for a weekend.

"You need to see her, set things right," he'd told me.

"She'll come back eventually," I reminded him.

But when one week turned into two, then we were edging past a month and there didn't seem like there was any respite in view, he hit me upside the head and told me to get my head out of my ass and do something.

"If you can't see she's the best thing that ever happened to you, I'm not too ashamed to tell you. Marry her before someone else does, Romeo."

Coming from my older brother's mouth, it had sounded more like a command. But one I grabbed hold of and ran with. Hearing him say it put everything into perspective. I'm not a man that can make life altering decisions. Lazaro made it easy for me. He pointed out the obvious, then he put me on a plane and strapped himself right next to me so I wouldn't jump out.

And now I'm standing here beside Baylin, pleading my case to her, though I'm not using so many words. I'm hoping that the longing in my eyes will do all the talking.

In so little time, she's become the axis on which my world turns. My breath hitches when I think of waking beside her every day for the rest of my life. Joy surges, tentative and sweet, like the first drop of rain kissing parched earth. My heart races, each beat spelling out her name, a testament to the incredible woman who sees past the scars and the walls I've erected.

The sun is a molten ball dipping into the sea, casting an amber glow on Baylin's face as she grabs my hand with a tight grip. I look up, surprised, find her eyes then give her a slow smile as we continue to move across the tranquil shore of the beach.

"It's cleansing, don't you think?" Baylin's voice rumbles through the sound of the ocean.

"Mmm," I agree, though the roar of the Atlantic swallows my response. The beach stretches out before us, a vast sea of blues and greens merging with the horizon. It is almost enough to make me forget the world beyond this place, the shadow of what we endured the past few months now a distant memory.

"So, you planned this whole thing with Lazaro and Marlon?"

"I did no such thing," I tell her. "They planned, I executed."

Her laughter settles on the breeze, a melodious remedy to my slowly unburdening heart. Baylin didn't turn me away. She didn't shoot me down. She's as receptive to me as I could wish her to be, and she may be willing to give us a go. She hasn't shut the door in my face yet, so I'm hoping she's curious about seeing where this may lead. I know I'll probably fuck it up somehow, but I know I've got Lazaro's guiding light helping me along if I mess up again.

"So...what is this exactly?" she asks, indicating the space between us.

"It's whatever you want it to be, Baylin."

She nods her head slowly, then looks out toward the sea, her eyes fixed on the far distance, lost in her thoughts.

"You hurt me," she says, after a long silence. Even knowing that I hurt her stabs at something deep inside of me. I can't undo the pain I caused her, but I could die trying to make it up to her.

"I did," I admit. "I hurt you and I did some despicable things to you. But you're the author of our story moving forward, Baylin. You hold the pen."

"That's a lot of power you're suddenly giving me."

"The alternative doesn't even compute," I tell her. "I'd rather cede control to you and have you forever than to go a day without you."

THE SHADOWS of my past are faithful companions, clinging to me like a second skin. As I watch Baylin finish her phone call, I feel the weight of who I was and what I've done haunting the space between us.

For years, I thrived on control and fear, letting the chaos within me take the lead. But those rare moments when vulnerability breaks through? Those are the ones that truly haunt me. Redemption... the word feels bitter on my tongue, a dream I'm not sure someone like me deserves. Yet here I am, daring to grasp it, battling against the tides of my own nature.

Baylin is the unexpected calm in my stormy life, the one who sees through the lies I tell myself.

"Where did you go just now?" she asks, her voice cutting through my thoughts as I stare out at the tranquil blue-green water.

"Same old ghosts," I admit, my gaze fixed on the ocean. "They don't rest easy."

"Let them haunt the night, Romeo. Remember, we're not just erasing your past; we're rewriting our future."

Her confidence acts like a beacon, pulling me away from the edge of my fears. I turn to face her, the resolve hardening in my chest.

"Fear," I finally say, the word heavy on my tongue. "I fear that one day, I'll wake up and all of this—" I gesture vaguely, encompassing everything from the Riccardi legacy to our fragile hopes for the future — "will have been for nothing. That I'll be forgotten, a ghost in my own life."

Baylin turns fully to me, cupping my cheek with her hand. Her touch grounds me. "You are many things, Romeo Riccardi, but forgettable is not one of them. You carve your name into the world with every step you take. And I—" She pauses, her voice trembling with emotion. "I will remember you for eternity."

"An eternity is a long time to be stuck with someone like me," I try to joke, but the quiver in my voice reveals the depth of my gratitude for her belief in me.

"Good thing I'm not going anywhere then," she replies, her smile brightening her eyes, igniting that fierce determination I've come to adore.

Piece by piece, we dismantle the lives we once knew, salvaging what we can for this new existence we dare to dream of. It's a painstaking process, filled with setbacks and doubt. Yet in each other, we find an unlikely sanctuary—a place where growth isn't just possible; *it's inevitable.*

62

MARLON

There's a certain type of madness that attaches itself to grief. For the longest time, even after I annihilated Franco Two-pence, the guilt over Stevie's death consumed me.

It controlled me.

It bled through me until I became a shadow of what I once was.

Every move I made thereafter was with intention.

I knocked down Franco-Two-pence's organization, then building it back up with more strength, more power. I was a man on a mission, reinvesting every single dollar I made, until I became untouchable.

Yet in the background of my mind, the guilt still gnawed. It festered. There was still unfinished business.

It was three years before I started my search. The only weapons in my arsenal were a name and the city he was living in when he met her. Stevie didn't have family, but he left behind the woman he was going to marry and an unborn child. These were the people Stevie loved; his unborn child the only thread to him I would ever have tethering me to this world until I could meet him in the next.

Three months passed before I was able to finally get a lead on the girl he was going to marry. *Jenna Falks.* Special Ed teacher. Whose heart was broken after her boyfriend went away for the weekend and never came back.

My heart shattered all over again at the thought that she believed Stevie had left her in the lurch after he learnt of her pregnancy. I wanted to find her and shake her and scream at her that *Stevie was not that kind of guy!*

But she was already gone. The librarian at the school where she had worked was the only one willing to talk to me, the only one willing to share that a devastated Jenna had packed her bags and moved, and no-one had heard from her again. No forwarding address. A disconnected number. She seemingly dropped off the face of the earth.

It was many years later, after the death of my own wife, that I resumed my search, enlisting the help of a private investigator. My hope was that Jenna had been kind enough to give her unborn child Stevie's name, and we would somehow find her. We did. But with the worst timing possible.

They had just lost the eldest daughter and son in law in an accident and were devastated. I couldn't add to their turmoil. I couldn't be the final nail in their coffin with the weight of what I was carrying.

Maybe I can never be that nail.

I watch Baylin as she moves around the room easily, and I see how Romeo and Lazaro's eyes follow her. Lazaro with wonder, Romeo with a hunger that cannot be easily extinguished. Both brothers are a little in awe of her, but I know that Lazaro will never cross that line. He's loyal to a fault, and that's why I feel comfortable handing the reigns over to him while I take a step back, because only someone like Lazaro Riccardi can take my business where it needs to go.

Romeo and Baylin will be married next week in a small, intimate ceremony with close family and friends. That's what they both want, so that's what I'll give them. I'll walk Baylin down the aisle in place of the father she never knew, and I'll put her hand in Romeo's and give them my blessing, knowing that he will take care of her. Romeo has finally found the closure he needs, and the change in him has been remarkable - I know the only time we will ever see his beast unleashed again is if anyone tries to hurt Baylin, who has now become his epicenter; his whole world, the focus of the rest of his life.

Jenna stands across the room, discussing the night's menu with the chef. She never mentions my old friend Stevie, but she seems to have come to terms with the sum of her life without him in it. She understood her heartbreak, she tasted it, touched it, and then she turned the page and moved on. She moved far away from her memories of the past. She started a new life and she settled down and raised two beautiful girls on her own. Then she lost a daughter and gained a son. She made it work. She worked hard, she gave selflessly, and she became the woman she is today.

She's beautiful and she's strong and she's determined. She is everything I've never had in my life, everything I never want to let go of. I should control my heart, but how can I fault it when it falls a little more in love with her day by day?

I may never tell them about Stevie; what good would it do to resurrect a past that resides in a place more than a quarter of a century old? What good would it do other than to raise the memories of the dead and the recriminations that follow? And I realize, in a final moment of clarity, that sometimes it isn't about the journey, and it isn't about how we got here, but it's all about the fact that *we are here.*

Jenna fusses over Luca, who's wise beyond his years, but is a cheeky little devil when he wants to be. He fills the home with an energy that can't be contained, and more importantly, he's an extension of Baylin. He's an extension of Jenna, the woman who's become like a constant companion to me. She looks up, seeking my eyes across the room, and she smiles. A wide, dimpled smile, as though she hasn't seen me in years and she's just now coming home.

This is what its means to be home.

This is what it means to be complete.

I can't go back and change the past, but I can damn well try to make the future a better one for all of us.

THE END

Thank you for reading THREE SINS. If you enjoyed the journey, it would mean the world to me if you could rate and review the book.

～

WANT MORE OF LAZARO & Romeo Riccardi? Read Lazaro's story in THREE SCARS: https://a.co/d/4kac2ES

～

WANT to know more about Lazaro Riccardi? Sign up to my newsletter and enjoy a FREE reader interview with him:

https://dl.bookfunnel.com/jz1he05cwo

～

I LOVE HEARING FROM READERS! Contact me:
    Email: jazlynsparrow@outlook.com
    TikTok: @jazlyn.sparrow
    Facebook: https://www.facebook.com/share/167H6qq3dW/?mibex tid=wwXlfr